"*The Blackout Book Club* is a fabulous novel that will warm the hearts of readers everywhere. Amy Lynn Green gives us a poignant look at life on the home front during WWII and how comfort and camaraderie can be found in the shared love of books. This will be a wonderful book club read!"

—Madeline Martin, *New York Times* bestselling author of *The Last Bookshop in London*

"*The Blackout Book Club* is an ode to books and libraries, but it's also an ode to human connection. Amy Lynn Green's entire cast of characters comes vividly to life, each woman with a distinct voice that makes the reader feel as much like her friend as her fellow book club members are. I couldn't put this book down!"

—Addison Armstrong, author of *The Light of Luna Park* and *The War Librarian*

"*The Blackout Book Club* is an engaging story that illustrates the power of books to unite and encourage us in trying times. The wonderfully diverse cast of quirky characters brings to life the shared worries and hopes of people on the WWII home front. A wonderful read."

—Lynn Austin, author, *Long Way Home*

"A salute to the power of books and of friendship! Not only does the writing sparkle with Green's trademark wit, but the characters become your dear friends, slowly exposing the hurts and secrets that have shaped them. Come to *The Blackout Book Club* for the fun—stay for the depth."

—Sarah Sundin, bestselling and award-winning author of *Until Leaves Fall in Paris*

"A heartwarming tribute to the power of reading and the friendships it forges during the darkest of times. Green weaves together the struggle of war, the resilience of the home front, and the love that can bind a community together in her novel *The Blackout Book Club*, reminding readers that hope can often be found where least expected."

—J'nell Ciesielski, bestselling author of *The Socialite*

"Fans of Madeline Martin and Katherine Reay will relish this tender, intimate look at the resilience of words and the power they wield in forging the strongest of bonds in the darkest of times. *The Blackout Book Club* is a delicious peek behind the curtain of nostalgia and a stunning portrait of the men and women whose lives are threaded through the poignant tapestry of storytelling: in letters and documents and in books. A book lover's dream, *The Blackout Book Club* solidifies Green as an inimitable chronicler of the American home-front experience."

—Rachel McMillan, author of *The London Restoration* and *The Mozart Code*

THE
Blackout
BOOK CLUB

Books by Amy Lynn Green

Things We Didn't Say
The Lines Between Us
The Blackout Book Club

THE
Blackout
BOOK CLUB

a novel

AMY LYNN GREEN

BETHANYHOUSE
a division of Baker Publishing Group
Minneapolis, Minnesota

Published by Bethany House Publishers
Minneapolis, Minnesota 55438
www.bethanyhouse.com

Bethany House Publishers is a division of
Baker Publishing Group, Grand Rapids, Michigan

Printed in the United States of America

Library of Congress Cataloging-in-Publication Data
Names: Green, Amy Lynn, author.
Title: The Blackout Book Club / Amy Lynn Green.
Description: Minneapolis, Minnesota : Bethany House Publishers, a division of
    Baker Publishing Group, [2022]
Identifiers: LCCN 2022010481 | ISBN 9780764239564 (paperback) | ISBN
    9780764240836 (casebound) | ISBN 9781493439058 (ebook)
Subjects: LCSH: World War, 1939-1945—United States—Fiction. | LCGFT:
    Historical fiction. | Christian fiction.
Classification: LCC PS3607.R4299 B57 2022 | DDC 813/.6—dc23/eng/20220307
LC record available at https://lccn.loc.gov/2022010481

Scripture quotations are from the King James Version of the Bible.

This is a work of historical reconstruction; the appearances of certain historical figures are therefore inevitable. All other characters, however, are products of the author's imagination, and any resemblance to actual persons, living or dead, is coincidental.

Cover design by Jennifer Parker
Cover image of woman by Elisabeth Ansley / Trevillion Images

Baker Publishing Group publications use paper produced from sustainable forestry practices and post-consumer waste whenever possible.

22 23 24 25 26 27 28   7 6 5 4 3 2 1

To all the teachers and librarians
who encourage a love of reading . . .
but especially the ones who had
an impact on my young life.

one

AVIS MONTGOMERY
JANUARY 31, 1942
DERBY, MAINE

Avis gripped the ladder as her husband climbed, a thick swath of black bunting draped over his shoulder. "Be careful, please, Russ."

He looked down at her from under that dashing swoop of dark hair and grinned. "Careful as I always am." Which did very little to reassure her.

Across from them, her brother Anthony climbed another rung, staring critically at the windows of the library's east wall. "Are you sure the curtain's going to be wide enough?"

Avis nodded to her notebook splayed on the floor, the numbers arranged in neat columns like soldiers at attention. "Of course. I measured it."

"Three times, I bet," Russell chimed in, giving her a teasing wink.

"Four," she admitted.

"See? I told you." Russell bunched a corner of the blackout cloth in his fist. "All right, old man, catch!"

"Don't even think—" Avis began, but it was too late. Russell wound up like a pitcher on the mound and tossed the edge of the fabric, causing Anthony to wobble dangerously as he reached to snatch the hem.

If she dared to take one of her hands off the ladder, she'd be rubbing away a headache. "You're going to fall and break your neck."

Anthony slid the eyelet holes along the curtain rod he'd rigged up, and Russell did the same on his end. "If you'd held my ladder instead of your husband's, you wouldn't have to worry about me."

"I'm fairly certain ladders were covered under my vow to have and to hold." She smiled in satisfaction when both of them laughed, Russell's deep and rumbling, Anthony's breaking off in a snort at the end. Two of her favorite sounds in the world, as different as the men they belonged to. Her husband, stocky and confident, more comfortable on a fishing dock than he was at his job at the bank; her brother, gangly and warmhearted, with a quip on hand for any occasion.

At least there was no one else about to hear their nonsense. This close to closing, the library's patrons had gone home to eat dinner and tune in to radio broadcasts about MacArthur and his boys trying to take back the Pacific.

Her hand trembled slightly as Russell climbed down. *Focus on what you can control.* For now, that meant measurements, regulations, and crisp right angles that matched the edges of the window frame, just as she'd planned. "A perfect fit."

"Well done." Russell kissed her forehead. "Miss Cavendish and the air raid warden won't be able to find even a sliver of light."

The periodical reading tables behind them, arrayed in two rows of three, now looked stiff and subdued in the sudden shadow.

When Anthony returned from stowing the ladders in the storage closet, a frown clouded his usually cheery face. "Grim as a funeral in here."

"It's wartime chic, pal," Russell said, slapping him on the back. "Better get used to it."

"Home décor magazines across the country will soon be touting these colors," Avis chimed in. Already, *LIFE* magazine had featured Joan Fontaine in a smart cap from a movie where she played a recruit for the British Women's Auxiliary Air Force.

That prompted a snort from her brother. "You and your silly magazines. When will you read a real book?"

"When 'real books' give me tips for altering last season's styles and a recipe for blueberry cobbler," she fired back, a variation of her usual reply. Just because her librarian brother was a snob about books didn't mean she had to be.

"She has a point," Russell interjected. "Last night's cobbler was excellent."

Anthony shot his childhood friend a look of profound betrayal. "There's more to reading than information, you know."

"I've yet to see any proof of that." Why, she probably learned more in a week's worth of her reading than Anthony did in a year of paging through novels. Still, it was no good trying to persuade him. Only twenty-nine years old, but thoroughly set in his ways.

Instead of rising to her taunt, Anthony breathed in deeply. "I'm going to miss this place."

It crept into the quiet after his words: that familiar fear that tingled through her body. For weeks, she'd pushed off the thought of Anthony's leaving, but now, with the trip to Fort Devens only a few days away, there was nothing to be done.

Russell leaned against the shelves, strong arms folded over his chest. "What'll Miss Cavendish do without you around here?"

"Not sure. Though I did give her a suggestion for a replacement."

Something about the way Anthony said it, heavy with implication, made Avis look up. Even in the shadows created by the newly darkened windows, she could see a smirk spreading on her brother's face, and all thoughts of enlistment faded. "Anthony, you don't mean *me*?"

"Come on, sis." He directed his most charming grin at her. "You do half of our cataloguing when I get behind anyway."

"An exaggeration."

"And you have most of the Dewey decimal system memorized."

Not an exaggeration, which unfortunately meant his idea had some legitimacy. "I couldn't possibly. Not as a married woman." She twisted her wedding band, a lovely solitaire, around her finger. Jobs, her mother had impressed on her, were for women who didn't have a husband's suit to iron and dinner to put on the table each night.

"Thousands of women are taking up war work," Russell reasoned, shrugging.

He always took Anthony's side. She gritted her teeth against a prickle of resentment. It was the price she paid for marrying her brother's best friend, she supposed.

She was about to reply that that was quite a different matter when Anthony's grin softened. "Anyway, I thought you'd be glad for something to do when Russ and I ship out."

Despite herself, Avis's jaw tightened, and behind her, Russell coughed. Anthony looked from one to the other, confusion on his face.

At the same time Russell began with "We haven't actually—" she tripped over him with "Russell isn't—"

Russell filled the awkward pause with a vague "We're still discussing it, that's all. Enlistment, I mean."

Even that was only halfway true. It had been weeks since Russell had brought it up after their last argument.

Unlike the enthusiastic flag-waving masses who'd turned out when the United States declared war, Avis looked ahead to the long separations, half-empty beds, and casualty notices printed in the newspapers.

And, try as she might to ignore it, her mother's warning, the night before the wedding and after too much champagne, whispered back into her mind, *"Keep your man nearby as long as you can, or he might be tempted to wander in other ways."*

Anthony blinked behind his narrow eyeglasses, face reddening. "Sorry. I thought . . . anyway, I didn't realize." He cleared his throat, moving the discussion into safer territory. "Still, it would be good for you to get out of the house, Avis."

"But I don't have a college degree," she said, "and, in case you've forgotten in the five minutes since it was brought up, I don't even read books."

"You could learn." Anthony scooped up the library keys from the empty sugar bowl where she'd insisted he keep them after misplacing them one too many times. "Seriously, Avis, we need someone to keep the doors open."

"It's not as if Miss Cavendish will shut the place down."

At that, Anthony hesitated, looking back toward the oil painting of the somber man overlooking the shelves, the only piece of artwork allowed on the walls. "I wouldn't be too sure about that. It was her father's pet project, not hers. Something about this place . . . well, she pays the bills, but she doesn't seem to like it."

"Why's that?" Russell asked.

"Beats me. With Miss C, you learn not to pry." He tossed the keys in the air and headed to the entryway with his usual jaunty step. "I love this place, sis."

As if he needed to tell her. He'd spent at least half his childhood either here or buried in one of the adventure novels he'd checked out from the shelves.

When he'd left for college, everyone, Mother included, expected he would "make something of himself" and never return. But he'd come back to Derby four years ago, degree in hand, content to spend the rest of his life in the small coastal town working at the association library that had once been his refuge.

"Come on, Avis. Promise me you'll keep it up for me while

I'm gone. Please?" He looked down at her with those big, earnest brown eyes that had worn her down since childhood.

"I promise," she found herself saying.

The whoop he let out while tackling her with a hug was probably the loudest noise the staid old building had heard in ages, and Avis couldn't help smiling.

Really, this place might benefit from a woman's touch. Besides, Anthony wouldn't be gone long, and if she could get through the war cataloging books without actually having to read them, why, no one would be the wiser.

GINNY ATKINS
JANUARY 31, 1942
LONG ISLAND, MAINE

The way Mack Conway swaggered toward the harbor, Ginny Atkins would have guessed he'd hit the bottle a mite too hard, except it was only afternoon. Besides that, a Sunday suit poked out of his coat, his tousled head topped with a spiffy-looking fedora.

She waved at him with her scrub brush. Now that the busy season for lobstering had passed, it was time for three months of repairing traps and painting buoys for next year. Today, Pa had stayed home—"business to take care of," he had said, and she'd been told to take advantage of the sunny day to work away at the grime and bait that scummed up the *Lady Luck*'s deck.

Instead of sauntering past to the bustle of lobstermen and boys tending their equipment, Mack stopped right in front of her. "Fine day, Ginny," he boomed, his voice deeper than normal, aging him past his nineteen years.

Ginny wiped her cold, wet hands on her trousers, suddenly feeling grimy in her scuffed rubber boots and brother's overcoat. Who'd have thought ol' Mack would outdress her? "Where you been, Mack?"

His grin spread even wider, like he'd been waiting on her to ask. "Took a ferry to the recruiting center."

"Already?" And she tried, really she did, to keep the dismay out of her voice.

It had all happened so fast. One day, Roosevelt was saying they were likely to stay out of the whole mess in Europe; next thing you knew, Japan had sunk those ships in Hawaii and all the young fellows on the island were lining up to stuff themselves in uniforms.

"Can't wait to lick those Japs." Mack rapped his knuckles just under his shoulder. "Once we show 'em who's boss, I'll come back with so many medals pinned to my chest there'll barely be room for buttons."

Ginny watched him for a moment, her breath coming out in white puffs as seagulls filled the silence with unearthly screeches. There was a spark she'd never seen before on Mack's face, a pride in the way he squared his shoulders in the hand-me-down coat.

With the lobster boat, traps, and know-how Pa had gotten from his father, Ginny's family was one of the wealthiest on the island, on account of having steady work. The Depression had knocked other folks, like the Conways, down often enough that they stopped trying to get up. Mr. Conway was snow-in-the-woodbox poor, and she'd heard Mack mumble a dozen shamefaced excuses when her brother invited him to go to the movies or grab a soda.

"I bet you will," Ginny said, rewarding Mack with a smile. If he hadn't been weighed down with spit-shined shoes, he might have floated up to join the planes that were always zooming past from the Godfrey Army Airfield.

Then his smile faltered. "Say, Ginny?"

"Say what?" She jammed her hands deeper into her coat pockets as a sudden breeze rammed against her.

"Want to be my girl?"

She nearly toppled into the ice-cold ocean from sheer surprise, but Mack hadn't noticed, studying the ground like he was. "Aw, Mack, you're like one of my brothers."

"No, I ain't," he insisted, jutting his chin up. "Anyway, nobody but you loves this island like I do."

He had a point there. All that most young fellows on Long Island talked about was how determined they were to get away someday. Ginny hated that, hated it when folks took in the rocky coast with its snow-dusted firs and the scent of the sharp sea air and tossed it all aside like a ball of trash.

Mack was different, always had been. Maybe it was on account of his gran's old tales, somewhere between history and lore, wrapping around his legs like seaweed and making him want to stay. Ginny had to admire that, and he wasn't *exactly* like one of her younger brothers. Hadn't she been thinking about how spiffed-up he looked, golden hair glinting in the sun?

"Fred said before I leave I'd better have a girl to wait for me," Mack went on. "Plus, there's gonna be a dance in town, and I need someone to take."

Ginny's shoulders relaxed. If that's all this was, it was nothing serious. "You know I'd dance with you, Mack. And I'll write you too."

His eyes—she'd never noticed, but they were a nice bold blue, like the sky on a cloudless day—crinkled up with a smile. "This Friday, then?"

"Sure." She was probably one of the only girls on the island with a store-bought dress. Pa had gotten it from a shop in Portland for her twentieth birthday the month before. Nice to have someplace to use it.

"All right, then." Instead of saying something sweet or asking her what time he could pick her up, Mack mumbled a goodbye and charged away like he was getting a leg up on his basic training a few weeks early.

Well. Was she really Mack Conway's girl now? Just like that?

She'd probably have to call him by his real name, Marvin, instead of the childhood nickname after the Atlantic mackerel his family fished.

Nah. No matter what, Mack would always be Mack to her.

Couldn't be any harm in it, from what she could see. Mack was a decent sort, and it would do him good to have someone writing to him. His ma couldn't read much, and his pa—well, it wasn't right to speak ill of a neighbor, but he might not notice his son was gone.

Wasn't very romantic, though. On the walk home, after the *Lady Luck* was scrubbed up proper, she compared Mack's asking to all the declarations of love she'd seen in movies. He hadn't even tried to steal a kiss.

'Course, she would have slapped him if he had.

Maybe that's how it had been with her ma and pa. Just two people who found themselves in the same place wanting to stay there, getting hitched and scrapping out a life. They'd gone through their share of trouble—most of it caused by Ma—but they stuck together.

By now, Ginny had reached the gate of the house. Everything was so . . . quiet. Funny. Right before supper, her younger brothers usually tussled in the yard like gulls after the same fish.

Inside, Pa sat at the kitchen table, head clutched in work-worn hands, and her heart nearly stopped beating. "Pa? What's going on?"

Was something wrong with Ma? Had she been taken to jail again? She'd been better these past few years, once Pa cut her off from the family's money to guard her from herself.

Barely lifting his head, Pa thrust a notice at her. Printed in tall, neat letters that she struggled to read were phrases including *coastal fortifications* and *vacate immediately.*

She scowled at the paper. "What does *eminent domain* mean?"

"It means they can do whatever they want, and folks like us haven't got a chance." Pa's voice was cold as the wind battering the door as he took the paper back, crumpling it. "The government's buying our home, Ginny. Making the whole place into a navy base."

No. They couldn't. Her family could fight this.

But her pa went on, voice as helpless and hopeless as she'd ever heard it. "We've got to leave the island."

MARTINA BIANCHINI
JANUARY 31, 1942
BOSTON, MASSACHUSETTS

Martina ran her thumb over the worn spines of her books, swiping at the tears that threatened to pock the covers with wet blotches.

"*Affogare in un bicchier d'acqua.*" She scolded herself using one of Mamma's tried-and-true phrases from the old country. "Do not drown in a glass of water." After all she'd gone through, was she going to cry over a few dusty books?

She took a deep breath. Rosa's collection of fairy tales, tattered and threadbare like Cinderella's rags, would need to come. *Swiss Family Robinson* for Gio, with a hope that he wouldn't outgrow that too, as he had with two pairs of shoes this year. *Emma*, of course, her most reread of Jane Austen.

A glance over her shoulder revealed that the faux-snakeskin suitcase she'd allotted herself for personal items was mostly full already.

So *Jane Eyre* would stay behind. It was easier to abandon the biographies and history books she'd used to study for her citizenship test, but *Oliver Twist* was a loss.

Still, it had to be done. The hiring manager at the foundry had given her the dimensions of the one-bedroom trailer home. She'd marked it out with chalk and her sewing tape. So small. With two growing children and all of their possessions, she would have a single shelf at best for her own nonessentials.

"I *will* come back for you," she whispered to the forlorn books. Better not to wonder when.

"No!" Past the thin door, the floorboards of the apartment creaked with hurried footsteps and her son's voice. "I won't give it to you! I *won't*."

She closed her eyes, longing to kneel by the books a little longer and let the latest trouble run its course. But only for a moment, because deeper than the weariness was the knowledge that she was a mother, so all trouble in the family was her trouble.

When Martina stepped into the hallway, Gio rammed into her, wiry arms wrapped around his prized possession: a portable Motorola radio.

At the end of the hallway, Martina's mother stood with arms folded and dark brows set in a look of *Well? He's your son. Do something.*

What could Mamma want with Gio's radio? She hated the noisy thing.

"Gio! Show respect to your *nonna*." At times like this, Martina couldn't bear to call him George, the name she insisted he use for school.

"It's not *her* I'm disrespecting," Gio shot back, "it's the officer."

Officer? A glance at her mother—who, for all the wrinkles gently scoring her face, looked like a girl caught sneaking cookies before dinner—told Martina there was some truth to Gio's words.

"To your room, Gio." Martina used the tone she heard from matriarchs on every stoop and street corner in Boston's North End, whether the words were in English or Italian. "Finish packing. *Without* the radio."

He reluctantly surrendered it with one last pleading look

before she shooed him away and turned her attention to her mother. "What haven't you told me, Mamma?"

"*Calmati.*" Mamma bustled down the hall, and Martina followed her into the kitchen, where miracles were produced under Angela Bianchini's wooden spoon. "A nice young man came by yesterday to tell me where to get a registration card. He also said I should not travel far from home, and I must turn in any cameras and radios. That is all."

With each addition, Martina clenched the radio more tightly. "You see? Didn't I tell you? This is what I was afraid of."

"You are afraid of all things, *figlia mia.*" Mamma paused to pat Martina's shoulder, as if to soften the criticism. "It is only right they would make sure I am not a spy. I am not an American citizen like you."

"And what's next? Once you've registered, they might put you in prison."

"You—what is the word?" She snapped her fingers, smiling proudly. "*Exaggerate.* This is not the Red Summer."

Martina's shudder was quick enough to cut off the memories from her girlhood that threatened to fill her mind. "Don't tell me it can't happen, Mamma. The newspapers are all shouting for the government to take the Japanese away—even some who are citizens. They might come for us next."

Mamma made a scoffing noise deep in her throat. "There are too many Italians in America. Hundreds of thousands."

"But, Mamma . . ." Martina switched to her mother tongue in case the children were listening. Rosa and Gio could speak some Italian, but school made English drop first from their lips, saints be praised. "I can't leave you now. We'll stay another month or two, to make sure things are all right."

Mamma's hand stilled on the counter, where it had been tapping out an impatient pattern. Then she looked up, eyes steady and sure. "My door will always be open to you, daughter. But you need your own life, away from here. There, you'll have a job with good pay and a home of your own. Somewhere safe, where . . ."

She shrugged, refusing to finish the sentence, but Martina knew what the downward look meant.

Where he *can't find you.* That's why she'd looked for work in Maine instead of one of the many war industries springing up in Boston. A fresh start.

"This is what I want for you, daughter. There will not be trouble."

She had to ask. "But if there is?"

Mamma hesitated only a moment. "If there is, I want you and the children to be far from it."

Martina surrendered to her mamma's fierce embrace, letting it soothe the ache, the fear, the knowledge that, however many books she left behind to travel to Maine, the heroine she would miss most was her mother.

LOUISE CAVENDISH
FEBRUARY 1, 1942
DERBY, MAINE

Fierce barking woke Louise Cavendish in the thin hours of the morning, when the tide ebbed its lowest, leaving behind the smell of rot.

All sleep-induced haze flew from Louise as she sat to attention. Jeeves, her German shepherd, might warn off an errant squirrel during the day, but he hadn't made a fuss at night since his puppy days.

On went her quilted housecoat and slippers, and she hurried down the stairs. Jeeves was a shadow by the front door, his muscled form tense, growling a warning at whoever was beyond the door.

Louise's fingers hesitated before turning on the light switch at the base of the stairs, illuminating the candelabra in the entryway. Father's old hunting rifle was still mounted over the fireplace in the dayroom, and Delphie always kept the kitchen knives razor sharp. Should she . . . ?

No, if there was an intruder, Jeeves had likely scared them off already. And if he hadn't, a woman in her fifties struggling to wield a meat cleaver certainly wouldn't.

He whined and pawed at the door, looking back at her with pleading eyes. "Steady, boy," she soothed, peering out the front window to the grounds of her family's summer home—a flat lawn looming with heavy shadows from shrubbery and the three outbuildings.

And then she heard it: a distant concussive boom, soon drowned out by a renewed burst of barking.

German bombs? Had Hitler's troops really dared attack America's shores so soon after declaring war?

But no, the sound came distinctly from the east, and the only thing east of the cliffs of Windward Hall was the ocean.

"It's only depth charges." She bent down, trying to calm her disconsolate dog. "They've found a German submarine, and planes are shooting it down."

Though there was always a chance they'd gotten there too late, and the U-boat had dived under the surface for another chance at destroying American tankers and freighters.

How Delphie, even with her hearing loss, could sleep through the ruckus of a German shepherd on full alert was beyond Louise, but the older woman didn't venture out to join her. Slowly, with no new explosions to set him off, Jeeves relaxed onto his haunches.

"Good boy," she whispered, running her hands over Jeeves's neck. As usual, he concurred with this assessment, basking in the attention. In the sudden calm, he clearly decided he had single-handedly dealt with and removed the threat.

Maybe the American planes had seen the telltale oil rising to the surface, prompting another boastful newspaper account flashing across the front page with the subtlety of a bad dime novel: *UNCLE SAM SINKS ANOTHER!* and *U-BOAT DISAS-TER AVERTED.*

But Louise also knew that the U-boats were sinking American ships by the dozens, consigning valuable cargo—and the merchant mariners who crewed them—to the cold depths.

All the more reason average citizens needed to rise up and be useful. The Red Cross motto sprang to her mind: In War, Charity.

It had been years since she'd thought of that, ever since that fateful telegram from Father that kept her from joining the forces of nurses serving in the first world war. And now here she was, too old by a decade to be of use in this one either.

Don't mope, she scolded herself, as she always did at the first tug of self-pity. *If anything, this should be a reminder that there's work to be done here too.*

Louise had had nearly a quarter century to get used to the unease of being a spinster living alone in a large house—well, alone besides Delphie, her cook. Never before had Louise felt herself in danger at Windward Hall.

That was a consequence of war, she supposed. One couldn't feel safe in one's home, even if the major campaigns were an ocean away. And now war had come to even the shores of peaceful Derby.

two

AVIS
APRIL 2

When the wall clock by the history section ticked all the way to three, Avis sighed, staring ruefully at the plain black notebook lurking underneath the counter.

Only three entries today. That was something, at least. Ever since she'd instructed patrons to give their requests and come back the next day, the list had sometimes stretched to a half dozen or more.

How had Anthony kept up with it all?

Because he had a degree in library science and two staff members, she thought sourly. *Not to mention me.*

Thank the heavens for the Dewey decimal system. Without the card catalog to thumb through, she'd have been exposed for incompetence her first week on the job, lacking her brother's near-magical gift of being able to select the right book for any obscure request.

She scanned her neat entries, always dutifully jotted down after the patron had left.

Mr. Watson wants a biography to find out how much of
They Died with Their Boots On *is based on true events.*
Proceeded to detail the entire plot of the film.
Mrs. Bell needs to find a book she read as a schoolgirl.

24

Title and author unknown, but it was "about fifty pages long with that famous George Washington painting on the cover."

Carole Stevenson would like a book for a young girl that teaches the folly of laziness. Didn't mention if this was prompted by the child slouched against the back wall, popping a bubble right next to the "No Chewing Gum Allowed" sign.

Begin with the easiest. A quick perusal of the catalog showed they had several volumes on George A. Custer and the Battle of Little Bighorn, and Avis drew out the ones with worn spines, indicating that several people had read them in the past.

She flipped through a few pages, comparing the text to the film's poster. It seemed Mr. Watson would be disappointed to find out that Errol Flynn's portrayal had not, in fact, been strictly accurate.

"It must be a slow day when the librarian has time for pleasure reading."

The blunt assertion made Avis spin around, sending the top book on her stack sliding to the floor.

Miss Cavendish stood at the head of the shelves, holding a basket, her graying brown hair pinned tightly beneath a black hat a decade out of style.

"I wasn't . . . I mean . . . W-what are you doing here?" Avis stammered.

"This is, I believe, the *Cavendish* Association Library." The stern look she gave Avis was a near replica of the portrait looming over the biography section, her father and the library's donor and founder, Luther Cavendish.

"I'm sorry. I only meant . . ." Well, she couldn't exactly say what she'd meant: Miss Cavendish never bothered to darken the library's door outside of monthly inspections.

Breathe. Smile. Take control of the conversation. After all, she'd wanted to speak to Miss Cavendish for weeks now.

"Miss Cavendish," she began, "as you may have noticed, I've been getting behind in my work. With the shortened hours—"

"Those are the times the Committee on Public Safety suggested businesses remain illuminated," Miss Cavendish stated. "We must all do our part to protect our shores. It simply can't be helped."

It was the answer Avis had anticipated, though precious few other establishments were actually following the guidelines. "If I could at least have another staff member. Someone to help with the shelving and cataloguing."

The older woman frowned. "Don't you already have an assistant?"

Could she really have forgotten? "Arlo joined the navy six weeks ago." Which Avis had told Miss Cavendish twice now.

The flicker on Miss Cavendish's face might be hopeful. Or she might have been suppressing a sneeze. Who could say with a woman as much made of stone as the bust of Caesar by the history section?

"I will consider it," Miss Cavendish said at last. "Now, if you would help me arrange chairs for the meeting?"

"What meeting?" Avis kept a precise record of library events—which were rare, these days—and there certainly hadn't been any this afternoon.

"Perhaps I neglected to tell you. The Women's Committee knits for the Red Cross every other Thursday, and our usual location, city hall, is having its plumbing redone."

"I see." She glanced ruefully at old Mr. Hanson hunched over at the reference section tables, who required strict silence for his perusal of texts on the cataloguing of Maine flora and fauna. The Women's Committee would drive all actual library patrons away, but it seemed that, as usual, Miss Cavendish didn't care.

"There will be extra supplies," Miss Cavendish said, removing skeins of serviceable, decidedly dull-colored yarn from her basket. "Perhaps you'd like to join us?"

It was technically a question. One she could say no to.

Except of course that it really wasn't, so Avis gave the correct answer. "I'd be delighted."

If this meeting made her late to come home and fix dinner . . . It's not that Russell would be upset, exactly. It's just that he was in such a mood these days. The least she could do was have a potpie steaming on the table when he got home from the bank.

Still, there was nothing for it but to play hostess to the half-dozen women who trickled into the library bearing yarn and gossip. Their knitting and chatting both took on a pace Avis could barely keep up with: what could possibly be made for dessert with the impending sugar rations, news that Louise had recently hired a wounded veteran to serve as her gardener, whether there would be a Fire Muster this summer. War updates, gossip, and domestic tips all mingled together as their hands worked to knit scarves and socks to send overseas.

One of them might be able to help, you know.

The thought made Avis pause the tortured scarf emerging from her needles. Maybe. After all, between them, the Women's Committee volunteers had more than a century of marriage to her one and a half years.

She'd searched home and family magazines for weeks, hoping to find some tidbit of use, but there were no articles on "How to Cheer Up Your 4-F Husband" or "Tips for Nonmilitary Wives." Still, it was up to her to make Russell smile again. If only someone could tell her how.

He'd come home in a fury from the recruiting office shortly after Anthony left for basic training. "As if a little trouble breathing makes a fellow 'unfit,'" he'd growled.

She'd done everything a good wife ought to: soothed and placated and pointed out that his asthma was a serious condition.

No comfort or logic had helped. Just this morning, holding up the newspaper like a shield, he had muttered, "My country needs me, Avis. And they don't even realize it."

"I need you too, Russ," she'd replied. But there had been no answer from behind the newspaper.

Avis pretended to pick out a knot from her ball of yarn, using the chance to survey the others gathered. Most, she'd known since she was a child, though a few were only passing acquaintances.

Really, what would she say to them? Find a way to change the subject from the current topic, the prevention of aphids in flowerbeds, to say, *"My husband's awfully depressed about not making the cut into the military. What should I do?"*

It simply wasn't done. She would manage just fine on her own.

three

LOUISE
APRIL 7

Louise Cavendish had fought valiantly to maintain her good manners for nearly fifteen minutes, but even the greatest will-power must eventually succumb to the inevitable. She yawned.

The man seated across from her didn't seem to notice. ". . . and with the increase in wartime demand, our casting production has nearly doubled." Milton Hanover adjusted his tailored suit and looked around his office with the same self-satisfaction she'd seen lingering there when she'd been introduced to him at age twenty-two. "Castings, of course, being—"

"The raw metal materials to be sent to the machine shop for finishing. Yes, I'm aware." She surveyed Mr. Hanover's glassy, fishlike expression in response to her interruption, his eyes blinking over a bulbous nose. No need for him to know she'd skimmed a book on foundries and the cast-iron process before their meeting.

"While hearing about Bristol-Banks's process is . . . fascinating, might I suggest a visit to the core room itself?"

Mr. Hanover cleared his throat, as if that might dredge up an excuse for staying in his oak-paneled office. "I appreciate your interest in our foundry, Miss Cavendish, but I'm afraid we don't have the proper safety equipment."

"I had thought the industry standard for foundry workers

was to have hair pinned up, wear closed-toed boots, and avoid trailing sleeves." Louise crooked her elbows with a flourish. "Which, you can see, I have done."

Mr. Hanover's eyes drifted downward to confirm her appropriate choice of footwear, then lifted his head with a look of resignation.

"In that case, I suppose a quick look wouldn't overly disrupt the workers."

Once they crossed the street and passed through the foundry's doors, it became apparent why Mr. Hanover hadn't suggested a tour. Though it was hardly a sweatshop like the ones Louise had fought against in her younger years, the foundry was hot, loud, and ugly. Exposed brick walls, the masonry grimy in patches, were lined with metal shelves, haphazard crates with metal bars poking out leaning against them.

Louise could feel the grit of sand under her feet. They must sweep between shifts, but for the moment, the foundry floor resembled nearby Pemaquid Point—though stripped of the peaceful ocean, lighthouse, and any natural beauty and charm.

The center of the core room was a maze of rough workstations on either side of a conveyor belt. Each station was divided in half with a bin, with tools and what she recognized as metal molds stacked within reach. Two workers manned each station—or perhaps *womanned* would be the term, given the gender of most of the bustling forms. They reached into the boxes, drawing out handfuls of dark sand and packing it into the molds, every motion precise and practiced.

"That, you see, is sand," Mr. Hanover singsonged, as if she might not recognize the substance due to the discoloration.

"Yes, mixed with oil and cereal flour to make it moldable and inflexible."

Another sputter. "Uh, yes." He cleared his throat. "These cores will be inserted into molds to create cavities and interior recesses before molten metal is poured inside." This last line was delivered with less certainty, as if Mr. Hanover was waiting to be told she already knew that too.

Which she did. But since he'd abandoned his condescending tone, she let the lecture pass without comment. "What are they making now?"

"Aluminum castings for bombers."

Lieutenant Frederick Keats, her new gardener, would be pleased to hear that. He'd only been in her employ for ten days now, and already most conversations had some mark of his past as an army pilot, every task made analogous to some aircraft process or tool.

"We've been nothing but pleased with even our new female employees." Mr. Hanover began walking toward the door. "The outlook was quite grim when we lost a third of our work force immediately following Pearl Harbor. But we've found that women's delicate fingers are well suited for many tasks. . . ."

While he went on, clearly hoping his monologue would create a leash to yank her away, Louise lingered, mesmerized by the pattern of metal clanks as workers rapped on the molds, opening them to reveal cores of various sizes, made of solid sand, setting them on metal trays on the conveyors behind them to be baked. Here the overwhelming grinding of machinery from elsewhere in the cavernous building was muted, like the sounds of a distant battle.

And in a way, it was. The battle to produce, to harness American industry and make up for lost time.

Finally, she turned away, through the shovel-scraped room where sand was mixed and carted away, through the thick metal doors, and out into daylight again. Mr. Hanover babbled all the way to his office, ushering her inside. She was sure she detected a sigh as the door clicked closed.

Louise sat back in the leather chair, a deep breath picking up traces of wood polish and cigar smoke instead of oil and molten pig iron. Across from her, Mr. Hanover dabbed at his temples with a handkerchief.

She reached into her purse and withdrew her checkbook. "I'm glad to hear all is going well with production, government contracts, et cetera. But I am not one of your board members. I'm here to contribute a charitable donation to your factory. Don't tell me what you've accomplished. Tell me what you *need*."

It was impolite, she knew. People never liked to be seen as needy, but no number of subtle hints or decorously phrased inquiries could get to the heart of the matter.

Sure enough, Mr. Hanover squirmed uncomfortably, as if anything he said might be relayed to his competitors the moment Louise returned to Windward Hall. "As I mentioned, most of our open positions have been filled. The cafeteria is fully stocked. And we're in the midst of solving the housing and transportation shortage for our workers."

She sighed and closed her checkbook, the leather cover slapping quietly over the scripted paper inside.

Mr. Hanover tensed, as she'd known he would. "Actually, there is one thing. The children."

She arched a brow. "I'm not particularly fond of children, Mr. Hanover."

"And yet you spent a good part of your younger years campaigning for more stringent child-labor laws."

Of course he would remember. She'd probably bored him to tears about that campaign decades ago when her father had invited him to call at their summer home. Activism, she had discovered, was an excellent method for chasing off potential suitors, for it reeked of independence, determination, and other less demure qualities. "That's quite different. Charity is a duty, while fondness is an emotion."

"I'm not sure you understand how true that is."

She frowned at the change in tone, but whatever the meaning of that cryptic phrase, he hurried past it, explaining his idea. Many of the foundry's female employees had children too young to be left alone, and some had no extended family to take on the burden. "Widows, you see, or women whose husbands are fighting in the war," he added quickly, as if to reassure her of their respectability. No divorced or unwed mothers laboring in the core room—that wouldn't do.

Nursery schools and daycare centers, he went on, were provided by the larger factories, like Bath Iron Works, but Bristol-Banks hadn't the finances for it.

"Shouldn't the government be providing childcare, then?" she asked.

"Oh, I'm sure they intend to eventually. After they work out proper sewage, fire prevention, law enforcement, and a thousand other problems for every surging factory town." Mr. Hanover steepled his fingers over a stack of documents, smiling once more now that he was cozily ensconced in another monologue. "It will be years before government agencies have time to consider working mothers. And how many of their young children will be neglected in the meantime?"

It seemed melodramatic, yet if half of the rumors she'd heard of the crowded trailer camp built on the edge of town were true, there might be a genuine need.

"Very well." She opened her checkbook again, along with her best fountain pen, the one with the scrimshaw inset. "How much would suffice?"

He raised a finger, as if in warning. "Ah, but there's the trouble. It's not funds we need, or not only funds. The only local charities are full to the brim and can't take in another child. What they need is a nursery school to open, and for that, they'd need a building, staff, organization—in short, someone to manage the whole project. Ideally by the first of the new year."

Her hands froze on the check. This was something else

entirely. "That is a lot to ask of a childless spinster." At fifty-three years old, what did she know about starting a childcare center?

This time, to his credit, Mr. Hanover didn't dissolve into apologetic stammering but instead raised a mild brow of challenge. "I thought, perhaps, with your connections . . ."

Being of the business set, of course he'd think an heiress like her could drum up a building and staff for a nursery school in an afternoon, or at least after hosting a soiree or gala.

But she was quite literally in a class of her own in Derby, the tiny seaside town where her family had vacationed over summers, and her connections outside of it were scant. Oh, there was her brother in New York who dropped by twice a decade or so, and a few old acquaintances, but it's not as though she lived in a glittering metropolis full of wealthy philanthropists.

No, if this was going to be done, she must do it herself. As usual.

"Thank you, Mr. Hanover," she said, standing. "This has been most enlightening. I'll consider your proposal and be in contact with you as I decide."

As she nodded along to the usual stifling farewell pleasantries, an idea began to form.

A foolish one, naturally. Most ventures worth embarking on were.

four

MARTINA
APRIL 7

The rapping on Martina Bianchini's trailer door twined in her half-asleep mind with the shouts of the riots of the summer of '19.

Her eyes flew open, heart pounding.

She'd fallen asleep on the divan while making dinner. That was all. The afternoon sunlight, warm as a wool blanket, falling on her through the three windows on each side of the trailer promised it was not the middle of the night, when looting and violence could be acted out by men with no justification but power. This was America, the country she and her family had fled to for asylum all those years ago, far away from the mob that had killed her father.

Still, the knocking intensified, and for a fleeting moment, Martina wondered if Patrick had found them again.

"Coming!" She stood, making a useless attempt to smooth her apron's wrinkles. *You're not a refugee, not anymore. You're an American citizen, a war worker. You have nothing to be afraid of.*

Sure enough, when she opened the door, she was not faced with a black-uniformed *squadrista*, an anarchist neighbor, or even her long-absent husband. Just a little boy hopping from foot to foot like he needed to use the privy.

"It's George, missus," the boy said urgently. Eyes wide and fearful.

Have mercy.

Before the child could say anything more, she was out the door, bare feet pounding the dead, matted grass in strips between the bite of gravel and dirt.

George. Gio. Her son needed her.

The government had told them the trailer camp was safe, efficient housing for the workers at defense factories, but most worked irregular hours, leaving the children to play in the open area close to the road.

Martina prayed as she ran, but it had been months since she'd attended Mass. What if no one was listening?

Her young guide pointed a dirty finger at a clump of shouting children on the lawn where the bus dropped them off, schoolbooks and bags scattered on the ground. A quick survey showed no sign of an automobile accident or a wild animal or even a spill from a bicycle.

No, she knew from the tone of those voices what must be happening.

Gio was fighting.

Again.

"*Basta!*" she shouted, barreling toward them, the word coming out in her native Italian. One of her mother's favorite expressions, versatile enough to be spoken in fear, exasperation, anger . . . and right now Martina felt all three. *Enough.*

The knot of children—some jeering encouragement, others crying for them to stop—parted, giving her a clear view of Gio as he heaved his fist into another child's stomach. The boy tottered and fell, and in a moment, Gio was down too, wrestling him in the dirt like a mutt in a back-alley dogfight.

"George!"

At the sound of his American name spoken in that tone, Gio faltered, breaking his hold to turn.

"Get him off me!" the towheaded child pinned underneath him hollered. She recognized him as Lenny Higgins, whose mother worked the night shift at Bristol-Banks. Blood dripped from his nose onto his collar.

It wasn't hard to yank her son up. Gio, his fighting spirit gone with her unexpected appearance, didn't resist, his breathing coming in hard, sharp bursts. From the swelling on his face, it looked like Lenny had gotten in at least one good blow.

Good, she thought, her anger surpassing even maternal protectiveness.

Martina felt a hand slip into hers. Rosa looked up at her with brown eyes, fringed with long lashes. Silent and sweet at age seven, she'd watched her brother attack another child from the sidelines.

"It will be all right, piccola,*"* she wanted to say. But now was not the time for empty promises.

The two boys separated, she drew herself up to every inch of her five feet, only a little taller than Gio. "What happened? Tell me the truth."

"He—" Gio began, but Lenny's voice, pitched shriller, cut through his. "We got off the bus, and he started whaling on me."

Over Gio's protests, Martina heard a deeper sound: a car approaching. Instinctively, she looked over, making sure none of the children were standing close to the road.

The sleek tan roadster, probably worth more than she made in a year, slowed as it passed the trailer camp, and the sight made Martina's temper flare. She turned, instinctively, to shield her son from the sight of the driver. *"You don't know,"* she wanted to shout at the rich person behind the tinted windows gawking at the new government housing. *"You have no idea what it's like to be—"*

What? Hunched over yet another munitions mold at midnight, trying not to let your eyes flutter shut? Falsely cheerful when telling people about your enlisted seaman husband?

Cramped into an eight-by-twenty-two–foot living space that passed as a home?

Or maybe just . . . *tired.*

Yes, that was what she was. So, so tired.

Lenny's whining voice drew her attention back. "He'd have killed me if you hadn't come."

With Gio still scowling silently, it was up to her to see if the boy was badly injured, promise that Gio would be punished, and tell the other children to go home.

"Mamma," Rosa whispered as she tugged them both away. "That boy—"

"Not now, Rosa." Of course there was more to the story. There always was. Some excuse Gio would use to justify hurting someone—usually, given his larger size for his twelve years, someone smaller and weaker.

Her head throbbed as she shut the trailer door and stepped into the galley kitchen. Rosa made for the lone bedroom, a cozy compartment far from the conflict she knew was coming.

Pushing past her, Gio reached for the icebox, but she nudged him away. "No. We don't have the money to waste meat on that eye of yours."

The first fight, Martina had fussed over him, asked what happened, assumed the best. The time for that was over.

"You promised me you'd do better."

"I was defending the family."

Look at me, son. If he could only see her disappointment, maybe it would move him. But Gio's eyes wandered anywhere else: the linoleum, the dollhouse-sized stove, those pictures of his, pinned in the space between two of the windows.

Without thinking, Martina edged past her son, grabbed a corner of one of the pages, and yanked. Down went two images torn from *The Knockout* magazine, Nick Peters and Joe Louis, with a satisfying tear of tape. Then a headline from the *Boston*

Herald's sports page about the 1940 heavyweight championship. Next, a two-color trading card of Max Baer ready to strike.

This, finally, was an outlet for her anger. Something she could do. Remove those glowering men, their bare skin glistening with sweat, their fists raised in violence, from her home.

"No! You can't!" Gio pulled at her arm, and until he shrank back under her glare, Martina wondered if he meant to hit her too.

"These pictures, they aren't going on the wall." She waved the stack of them in his face. "You can keep them in the drawer."

Now he looked at her, now that she was threatening something he loved. His eyes, a lighter whiskey brown like his father's, narrowed. "I didn't punch Lenny because I listen to boxing matches on the radio. I punched him because he called me and Rosa dirty dagos."

Despite herself, Martina flinched, glancing at the bedroom door where Rosa had likely buried herself in a pillow. That word again. Spaniards, Portuguese, and especially Italians, all tarred with the same slur. Marked as something different, distasteful, un-American.

She'd heard it growing up in Boston, and now at the foundry— whispered behind her back and shouted after her, hoping to get a reaction more dramatic than the blush of heat that burned from her cheeks all the way to her core.

But she never gave it to them. Just kept walking, holding her head high. Praying in the name of the Blessed Mother that her son and daughter would live in a different, gentler world when the fighting stopped.

"It doesn't matter what the boy said. You shouldn't have hit him."

Gio opened his mouth to protest, but she would not be interrupted, not again. "You will apologize to him. And there will be no radio for the rest of the month."

"But, Mamma, Da said I have to protect the family while he's gone."

Though she didn't remember that exchange, it was like something Patrick would say, in one of the rare moments when he'd made an attempt at being a father. She clucked her tongue. "You want to listen to the fights? Then stop fighting. It's your choice."

Soon, Ginny Atkins would come to pick her up, and she'd be gone, headed to Bristol-Banks for another swing shift. Gio would be free to take out his radio and tune the dial to anything he wanted.

"Do you promise?" she pressed.

He met her stern eyes with his swollen one. "Yes, Mamma."

That was good. Gio hated liars too, proof that she'd done at least one thing right as a mother.

That must be why, when she urged him not to fight anymore, he said only, "I'll try."

five

AVIS
APRIL 8

By the time Russell came home, the mashed potatoes were cold and crusty, the meatloaf pocked with milky-white pools of hardened fat. Still, Avis left the platter on the dining room table centered atop a pinwheel doily.

The moment she heard a car door shut, she stood and peeked out the window.

Sure enough, Russell was waving to Herb, grinning from the driver's seat. Her nose wrinkled involuntarily. She was all for saving gas for the war effort, but whyever her husband had decided to carpool with Herb Beale was beyond her. The man talked too loudly and couldn't tell when the person across from him had lost interest in his monologue on electric wiring or the intricacies of fishing lures. Which, for her, was always almost instantly.

Avis checked herself in the mirror that hung in the living room before opening the door. "Hello, Russell."

"Hello, dear."

She accepted his peck on the cheek, which he doled out like a *fine* that followed a *How are you?*

No need to be petty and say, *"You're late,"* with hands on her hips. He had to know it was quarter past seven, when Derby Central Bank and Loan closed at five.

41

She watched his eyes roam over her shoulder and land on the dining room table, set neatly for two, all in the hour between the end of her shift at the library and the time he was supposed to arrive home.

In the silence, waiting for his apology, she heard the grandfather clock ticking away the seconds.

"You should have eaten without me."

What he really meant was *"You shouldn't make me feel guilty."*

"I hadn't realized how late you'd be."

He'd already earned three demerits on the marriage evaluation scale created by Dr. George W. Crane, assuming he hadn't been drinking or flirting with other women, which would add an additional six.

One point for not calling to let her know he would be late from work. One point for missing dinner. One point for . . .

Well. She wasn't sure he'd lost that one yet. Better to wait and see.

"Time got away from me, that's all."

The Domestic Helper taught that whenever a husband said "That's all," it was almost certainly not all.

"The least you could have done was let me know, Russ." He'd always liked it when she called him that, but now there was no smile on his face, flecked with a hint of whiskers.

"Look, I tried to call, but you didn't answer."

It might be true. She *had* thought she'd heard the telephone while she was tending the flower boxes, pruning the dead annuals to get ready for spring. "I suppose you've already eaten."

He nodded. "Beale wanted to go out to Sherman's. They've got dollar shrimp on Wednesdays. Couldn't turn him down, since he was the driver."

"That's all?" Despite herself, she'd half expected a story of some important report he'd needed to file or a meeting with the bank president, who, according to Russell, had been hinting at a promotion for weeks now.

"What, do I need to beg for leave to have dinner with a friend?"

Maybe she should let it go. After all, he'd seemed happier than usual, getting out of the car with Herb. She hadn't heard him laugh since he got his 4-F classification.

But even as she thought it, she heard words slip out from her mouth, as if by habit. "No friend should come before your spouse."

Russell's eyes narrowed. "How would you know? You have no friends, Avis. Just your library job, nothing to do in the evenings except wait around for me."

"I am your *wife*, Russell Montgomery." All traces of long-suffering patience were gone, and there was no getting them back. "I know you'd rather be on a troop ship with Anthony, traveling the world, thousands of miles away from me. This isn't the life you dreamed of, but it's the one you have."

She'd gone too far, bringing up the incident with the recruitment office. That same old darkness appeared in his eyes. "You don't know anything about my dreams."

"I would if you'd tell me."

"It's not as if I don't try!"

Crying made a woman's face blotchy and, according to an advice column in *Woman's Day*, was considered theatrical and manipulative.

"I would prefer," she said, fighting to keep a tremble out of her voice, "if you went away."

Russell threw his hands up in frustration. "First you nag at me for not being home, then you tell me to scram. Which is it?"

"Not out of the house, just . . . away from me."

After a pause, she heard his footsteps creaking away as she turned to dismantle the table setting.

Somehow, she'd done it wrong. Again. They made it seem easy to please your husband in books and magazines, full of images of demurely smiling women in sparkling homes.

Well. Even after a long day of work, she'd managed to clean the kitchen, mash the potatoes, put on her favorite dress—the floral one with the ruching around the neckline. And Russell hadn't even noticed.

She missed the old Russell, the one before the 4-F label, who would have lightened the mood by taking a bite of cold meatloaf and declaring it not so bad after all, who never raised his voice or stayed out late, or . . .

Riiing!

The carefully balanced stack of china nearly clattered to the floor as she swiveled to face the telephone on the hallway's end table.

Riiing!

Avis abandoned the table settings on the counter and stormed over. If it was one of Russell's buddies asking him to come smoke or play billiards or . . . whatever it was men did on evenings when they wanted to escape their wives, why, she'd . . .

"Good evening, Avis. It's Louise Cavendish."

"Oh. Hello." It probably sounded too surprised to be polite, but how long had it been since Miss Cavendish had called her at home? "Is this about hiring an assistant?"

"In a way, yes. I'm afraid we'll have no need for additional staff, now or in the future."

Avis blinked. "I don't understand."

"I'm closing the library."

The words—the terrible death-toll words—were spoken in a dispassionate tone, so it took Avis a moment to process them. She'd always known it was a private library, not owned by the city, but in her mind, the Cavendish Association Library was as much a permanent part of Derby as the Cliff Walk or city hall.

"When?" she asked, her mind in a flurry.

"That depends on how soon a contractor can begin renovations." She explained something about a nursery school and

44

war workers, but Avis only half listened, leaning helplessly against the wall.

The shelves. The books. The library—her library. *Anthony's library.*

A pause in the conversation indicated she should say something, but all that came out was "Miss Cavendish . . . you can't close the library. Not now."

"I certainly can." There wasn't the slightest tinge of apology in her voice. "My father was the one who established it and left it to me in his will. That gives me the authority to do as I please."

"But the trouble is," Avis stammered, "I've just announced a community book club."

A book club?

The announcement didn't produce outrage from the other side of the line, just a long pause, during which Avis scrambled to think of what to say next, her heart thudding in her chest.

"Don't you think that I ought to approve decisions like that?"

As if you've ever shown a scrap of interest in library programs before. But of course she couldn't say that, and instead delivered the only line she could think of that might provide a stay of execution. "It's for the war effort."

Miss Cavendish's voice lost none of its cutting edge at the insertion of the magic words. "I'm at a loss as to how a bunch of housewives sighing over chapbook subscription chaff could possibly help the war effort."

"The Office of War Information recommended book clubs as a way to boost morale and encourage people to develop indoor pursuits to assist with blackout compliance." Hadn't Avis seen reading in a list of recommended blackout activities in *TIME* magazine? That counted, surely.

"Hmm." Miss Cavendish seemed to consider this, or at least she didn't launch into another protest.

Keep pushing, before she has time to think. "And we won't be reading trash, only quality literature."

"Fiction." It was more statement than question and tinged with disapproval.

"Well, yes." The association library had a fair number of intellectuals who paid membership dues, including two of the local preachers and a retired professor from Bowdoin College, but no one wanted to dissect *The Rise and Fall of the Roman Empire*, surely.

It might have been wishful thinking on Avis's part, but the harumph Miss Cavendish dispensed sounded less piqued than her first. "And how long is this blackout book club supposed to run?"

"Until autumn. When the cold weather keeps people inside for other reasons, you see." Would that be enough time to convince Miss Cavendish to change her mind?

That got a swift snort. "Preposterous. I can't delay this project for five months. Besides, citizens ought to comply with blackout regulations out of duty."

"Yet only a few will."

"Well, that's true enough," Miss Cavendish admitted, sounding surprised that she agreed with Avis on something. "I can't imagine the trouble the air raid wardens will face when the summer people and tourists arrive."

"A delay in renovating the library will allow you to be thorough in planning the project. And there's a shortage of materials and builders, what with all the new industries springing up."

Avis took in a breath and held it, waiting for a response from the telephone handset. With just enough truth in what she said, maybe . . .

"All right," Miss Cavendish said at last, just as crisply as she'd pronounced the library's demise. "It's settled. You will be allowed to have your community book club, provided the community shows interest, until the end of September, at which point I will turn over the building to be renovated for childcare for war workers. Subject to reconsideration, of course."

"Of course," Avis repeated, hardly daring to believe it. Had her impulsive scheme actually worked?

"When is the first meeting? I would like to be there."

She had begun celebrating far too early. "A week from Saturday at ten o'clock."

No, that was too soon.

But she'd already blurted it out, and as Avis stammered out a good-bye, there was no chance to change it.

"A book club?" she whispered to the empty hallway. What had she been *thinking*? Yes, she shelved books, catalogued them, accepted donations of them, but she didn't *read* them and certainly never discussed them.

Besides, who on earth would she invite?

Russell's words came back to her: *"You have no friends."*

It wasn't true. It *wasn't*. And yet, try as she might, Avis couldn't think of anyone who might want to come. Even the thought of asking made her feel ill.

The sliver of light under their bedroom door told her where Russell had barricaded himself for the evening. She raised a hand to knock—then turned away. Better not to disturb him. Why should he care about her petty troubles when he was busy feeling sorry for himself?

Trying not to think about the harsh words they'd exchanged, she tucked dinner away in the refrigerator. That done, she pulled out the cake stand, hidden in the shadow of the breadbox, and lifted the lid to reveal a chocolate cake with lemon-zest frosting. It looked almost like the one in the recipe from the *Royal Baking Powder Cookbook*, the one she'd paid six cents plus shipping for weeks ago to be ready for today.

And after plunging her fork into it, Avis decided it tasted as good as it looked, a light sponge with just enough sour to cut the sweet. She'd risen early to bake it before work and even had time to fashion a decorative sugar rose over her noon break since Mother had called, saying she'd mistakenly planned a hair salon appointment for today, and might they reschedule their lunch plans? They'd hung up without setting a date.

When the phone rang tonight, she'd had a false hope that her in-laws had remembered. But it was only awful Miss Cavendish with her grim news.

Avis replaced the cake stand cover, climbing the stool to set it on the top shelf of the cabinet, hidden alongside the punch glasses they never used. If Russell had forgotten, he didn't deserve a single slice.

She was perfectly content to eat her entire birthday cake by herself.

Six

GINNY
APRIL 10
DERBY, MAINE

Ginny took a look at the haul she'd bought off the Boy Scout down at the scrapyard for a nickel. One old bugle, a copper jewelry box, a paperweight of the Lincoln memorial, and six chocolate molds shaped like lobsters.

Wasn't any good, letting a treasure trove like this get melted down for a scrap drive. Anyway, as she'd explained to the kid, it was barely enough for the hubcap on a Sherman tank. He'd found her logic—given outside of the troop leader's hearing—persuasive. Or at least he pictured the box of Milk Duds he could buy on the way home with the nickel she gave him in trade and figured it was worth it. Not a bad day's work.

Her arms heaped full, Ginny nudged open the door of Maloney Pawn Dealership with her foot, the art deco–lettered sign in the window unchanged since the early days of flappers and speakeasies.

Unchanged also described Danny Maloney's hairstyle, come to think of it.

"Anyone home?" she called, instead of ringing the bell on the counter.

She heard a muttered curse from behind the moth-gnawed curtain that separated the back room from the rest of the shop,

49

but when Mr. Maloney emerged, adjusting his suit over a pro-
truding belly, he was all professionalism—until he spotted her.

"You again."

Ginny made a tsking sound. "Is that any way to greet your
favorite customer?"

"Favorite cutthroat is more like it," he grumbled. Slow week,
probably. Most weeks likely were in a town as small as Derby.
She could almost feel the dust collecting on his wares—antique
bookcases holding pipes and leather goods, a glass case for
a collection of jewelry and thumbprints, and shelves of mismatched china.

"All right, what've you got?"

She laid out the items on the counter, turning them so their
best sides were up, but Mr. Maloney was already shaking his
head before she could start the pitch. "You know I can't sell
stuff like this, missy. No money in it. Now, jewelry and watches,
that's the ticket. Maybe a fine luggage set or musical instru-
ment."

She hefted the bugle aloft. "What d'ya think this is, a hearing trumpet?"

"Might as well be, dinged up like that." Still, he ran his thick
fingers over the bell of the horn like he could feel the story in
every dent. "Civil War?"

She nodded. "My great-grandfather won it in glorious combat, at the Battle of . . ."

That was the trick with details. You actually had to know
some. "Well, it was somewhere in Virginia. But out with it.
What can you give me for this lot?"

"Other than the bugle, it's mostly worthless, and I doubt I
could get more than two dollars for that."

Two dollars wasn't nothing, but it wasn't enough either.
"Listen, Mr. Maloney. If you could find some way to offer a
little more, it'd really help."

Maybe it was her change in tone, but Mr. Maloney squinted

at her. "None of my business, but you're not in some kind of trouble, are you, missy?"

That was the thing about Mr. Maloney. He didn't push—anyone who buys old wedding and engagement rings for a living knows to be careful. But he was ware she was new to town, living alone, and he cared enough to ask.

"Just saving up for a long-shot dream. You know, the kind you don't want to talk about in case putting it into words makes it go . . ." She made a puff of air.

Mr. Maloney nodded slowly, and Ginny knew she'd won.

Funny. That's what it had taken to soften him up. Maybe he had dreams too, ones that were always out of reach. She gave the tired shop another once-over. Apparently, he'd given up looking for a ladder.

"Five dollars even," he finally said, and she beamed.

"It's a real pleasure doing business with you." Another line borrowed from Pa, the best lobsterman she'd ever seen, who could make deals directly with the fanciest restaurateur, without a supplier go-between.

Mr. Maloney opened the register and fluttered a five-dollar bill in her direction, which she snatched up before he could change his mind.

Yes siree, Danny Maloney was one of a kind, she decided as she flounced out the door. "Don't let me down, Abraham," she said sternly to the five-dollar bill before tucking it safely into her purse. After all, with a weight of responsibility on their shoulders to unite a house divided, she and Honest Abe were just about the same person.

Except, maybe, for the honest part. And the beard.

It wasn't much, but each cent she tucked away in her tin bank shaped like an organ grinder's monkey—another cast-off—would help her family buy back a bit of Long Island at the end of this awful war.

Sure, she'd pretended to believe Pa when he swore he'd take a job in Portland and save every penny of the money the government gave them for their property. But deep down, she knew if they ever wanted to get their home back, it would be up to her.

Ginny whistled her way down the street to the library. Time for a reward for a good day's work. It wasn't the same satisfaction as bringing in a haul on Pa's lobster boat, but living in Derby wasn't so bad, she decided, taking in the lone stoplight, the sunlight glinting off of shop windows with propped-up *Out for Lunch* signs, and the owners of those shops ducking into the corner café. Better than Portland, anyway. *"Too crowded,"* she'd told Ma, explaining why she hadn't moved in with the rest of the family, along with an excuse about it being time to live on her own. It was enough of the truth that it didn't count as a lie, not really.

Libraries smelled funny, like something halfway to molding. Then again, Ginny had met folks who thought the docks were the same way. To them, fish and bait and the leftovers of the tide were less a fragrance and more a stench. Matter of perspective, really.

So Ginny just breathed through her mouth as she approached the librarian, scribbling away in her ever-present notebook behind the registration desk.

"Morning, Avis," she said in what she'd quickly learned was the right tone, quiet enough that the grumpy men in dark suits who came in over their lunch breaks wouldn't glare at her.

"It's afternoon," Avis corrected without looking up, as if the five ticks past twelve were enough to matter. She couldn't have been more than a few years older than Ginny, but the poor thing was aging a decade every month she spent in that dark, musty place, all stooped over with her head full of numbers and such.

Ginny leaned over to see what she was writing, but each line was crossed off in uneven swipes of pencil. "You know, you really ought to get out of this crypt more. You're pale as paste."

"Mmm," Avis replied, ramming a pencil into her complicated upswept hairdo—where two other pencils already poked out.

Only when Ginny hefted herself to sit on the desk did Avis finally look up and, sighing, put on her professional librarian manner. "Can I help you?"

"I hope so." She waggled her eyebrows, hoping for a smile. It didn't work. "Got anything new?"

"You know I can't answer that."

Sure, Ginny knew. But usually Avis made a show of warning her against getting all kinds of ridiculous romantic notions. Today, her shoulders sagged, and her usually perfect hair was mussed.

"Thought I'd at least try." It was silly anyway, having to sneak into the storage closet for a book.

Ginny had never met the Cavendish lady who owned this place, but she imagined her to be like an irritable dragon. The romances stashed in the storage room because they met her disapproval weren't even the steamy sort . . . though that Georgette Heyer sure could write a good kiss. Ginny had whipped through a dozen in a few months—shop girls who married millionaires, ladies who escaped arranged marriages to dash away with their true love, spies with secret identities who revealed themselves just in time.

It wasn't so much the endings, which were more or less the same, that were the ticket. It was the getting there that mattered. Why, after only a dozen storage-room novels, Ginny had learned more about romance than her mother had ever bothered to tell her. Sometimes, she wrote down a line or two to use in a letter to Mack—maybe. If she got up the nerve.

Mack's sure not a brooding duke or noble Southern gentleman.

But who was, really? If a girl waited for some fellow who quoted poetry, spread his coat over a puddle, or stomped moodily around the misty moors, whatever those were, why, she'd be waiting forever.

"One of these days you'll get me fired."

The accusing finger stretched toward her was tipped with nails raggedy to the quick.

Ginny slid off the desk and faced Avis. "Okay, something's wrong. Don't argue," she added, when it looked like Avis would try. "Just tell me all about it." She started kneading the librarian's shoulders, the muscles tense and stiff like a salt-soaked rope set out to dry.

"It's a tragedy," Avis said flatly, instead of pushing her away like Ginny had expected. "You see, I've accidentally started a book club."

"What's so awful about that?"

It was like Avis had been waiting for someone to ask. Ginny knew the type from back on the island: old sea dogs, mostly, who were trapped alone after the first snowfall and could jaw your ear off come spring. She'd always been good at listening to them. Now she nodded along as Avis explained about a nursery school and her brother and the mess she'd gotten herself into.

"Let me guess: this is the same lady who keeps the best books hidden away?"

Avis nodded.

Ginny rolled her eyes. "She's got her hooks into everything, doesn't she?"

"It *is* her building. She has a right to do as she pleases with it."

Well, maybe that was true. Ginny knew she didn't like rich folks on principle, except ones in books, which wasn't exactly fair. "Don't worry, Avis. I bet you'll ace the book club. Why, you wouldn't have gotten this job if you didn't love books, right?"

From the dismayed expression on Avis's face, her encouraging speech had clearly gotten something wrong. "Not exactly."

"Well, at least you like people, then," she amended. But Avis shook her head to that too. "Good golly, Avis, what do you like?"

She gave Ginny a helpless look, like the swooning heroine on the cover of *The Sheik*. "Baking?"

"Well then, do that."

Avis tapped a finger on the desk, looking off into the distance. "I do have an excellent recipe for carrot-cake muffins."

"There, see!" Come to think of it, that sounded pretty good, the musty old library filled up with smells of cinnamon and nutmeg. "In that case, I might even be there myself."

"Please come. And bring a friend. Or two. The whole factory shift, if you like."

She really was desperate. Ginny thought about the other women at the foundry, or the ones she'd met around town.

Martina. That was her best bet. She'd brought a book to read every dinner break, sitting all by herself until Ginny had plopped down next to her and introduced herself.

Ginny riffled through the stack of books next to Avis on the desk to try to find one her friend might like.

She held up one with a spangly explosion of stars on the cover. *Mrs. Miniver*. "Say, is this the Greer Garson movie coming out this summer? All about the Blitz over in London?"

Avis stared at her so long that she figured she must be wrong, until the librarian snatched the book away from her hand and clung to it like an overboard sailor to a life vest. "Ginny, you're brilliant."

"Well, sure." Facts were facts, after all. "But . . . why, exactly?"

"This is perfect for our first book club. Miss Cavendish was the head of the Bundles for Britain committee two years in a row. She'll *have* to like it."

Ginny almost said not to be too sure and that people could surprise you with their tastes. Why, she'd met someone once who didn't like bacon, for goodness' sake. But seeing as that would spoil the hope in the librarian's eyes, she kept her mouth shut.

She left the library with the date and time of the first discussion, a novel for herself called *In the Name of Love*, and the satisfaction of doing a good deed.

Did she have any idea what a book club actually was? Not a clue.

But there would be muffins.

seven

LOUISE
APRIL 13

"Right on my doorstep, I tell you! *L'audace!*"

Oh dear. Louise closed her eyes briefly, not in prayer, but to ward off an impending headache. She had hoped that Hamish, her handyman, was exaggerating when he'd broken his usual stoic silence to pass on a warning that Delphie was in "one of her moods."

But it was clear as Louise marched toward the garden patch torn into her once-lovely lawn that that was too much to hope for.

Delphie gestured with sagging arms at Louise's new gardener, while the object of her wrath protested, "I promise, ma'am, Miss Cavendish told me to expand the garden this way."

"Don't bear tales to me, young man." Delphie's strident voice had slipped into the thick French Canadian accent of her girlhood, the way it always did when she was upset. "I don't know how you talked your way into her good graces, but I know Louise wouldn't stand for this."

Hurrying the last few steps to close the space between them, Louise positioned herself firmly between the two combatants: Mr. Keats, hands in a defensive posture and tools scattered at his feet; Delphie planted firmly on the edge of the ragged expansion.

"Would someone please explain what this is all about?"

Both flinched at her stern tone—how had she grown to sound so much like her father?

Delphie reluctantly tore herself away from the artillery-range glare she was leveling at poor Mr. Keats, her wrinkles bunching. "This young fool said you gave him leave to tear up the ground right next to my kitchen."

"That's right," Mr. Keats's mouth said, while the one eye visible outside of his eyepatch said—begged, rather—"*Save me!*" Poor fellow had likely never seen anything in aerial combat quite like Delphie Morine. If General MacArthur had the sense to enlist her, her scowl alone could drive a panzer line into full retreat.

Directness was the only course of action. "He's telling the truth, Delphie. I did give orders to expand the garden based on the number of vegetables we intend to grow. You can look over the charts if you like."

Delphie turned her scowl on Louise, but her tone descended from outrage to an offended grumble. "Couldn't it push toward the road instead?"

"The trees lining the drive would block the sun," she explained patiently.

Delphie crossed her arms, glancing between them, as if not sure anymore whom she should be angry with. "You could have at least asked."

Ah. So that explained the pique of temper. In some ways, the ways that really mattered, she and Delphie were equals. But when it came down to decisions about the estate, well . . . Louise was the Cavendish. The deed was in her name, the responsibility to govern it well in her hands.

"I'm sorry, but it's what must be done."

To his credit, Mr. Keats simply stood in respectful silence with perfect military posture, not a hint of gloating on his face. Then again, it never paid to upset the cook, who could get her revenge in a hundred subtle ways. Dinner, Louise was sure, would be overdone tonight.

With a huff, Delphie's shoulders slumped. "It's too close to the house, mark my words. You'll see."

Mr. Keats stared after Delphie as she flounced away. "Is she always like that?" he said in a near whisper, as if the older woman might be listening from the kitchen window.

"Since my childhood at least." In fact, either Delphie had mellowed with time, or Louise had just gotten used to her. "Once you've prepared the soil, Hamish will help build the fence and trellises."

He squinted in confusion. "Trellises?"

Perhaps the young man was a bit slow. Then again, an encounter with Delphie could set anyone back a bit. "For the beans and other climbing vegetables."

"Oh, sure. The kind they use for flowers."

"I suppose. But there are to be no flowers." Just in case he hadn't read the note on her chart, though he seemed a thorough type—the army air forces didn't turn out any others. "This is meant to be a functional kitchen garden, nothing more."

"Nothing wrong with a little beauty, Miss Cavendish." He winked with his good eye, and Louise might have been offended, except it seemed almost a reflex. So far, by her watchful count, he'd winked at her, Delphie, Hamish's wife, the postman, and twice at Jeeves, for goodness' sake. If anything, it called attention to the war injury that had removed him from the field of battle and sent him knocking at her front door, searching for work.

"I won't give a cent toward frivolous plants that can't be cooked or canned. You'll have to take your beauty from the sky rather than the land."

Instead of arguing, Mr. Keats merely shrugged. "That's no hardship. There's plenty up there."

She tilted her head toward the sky, where his arm stretched to indicate the peaceful clouds of a spring afternoon.

"Do you miss it?" she found herself asking, knowing he would understand her meaning.

"Every day." His response was immediate, and his expression so wistful it could break your heart. "Not all of it. Not the fighting or the constant giving and taking of orders. But the feeling of being up there . . . free." He touched the eyepatch covering the wound that had sent him home. "It's hard, knowing I'll never pilot a plane again. That others are carrying on the work without me."

I'm sorry. That's what Louise ought to say, and that she, too, knew the pain of a dream dying, feeling tethered to one place when you longed to be part of something meaningful. Her disappointment was from the first world war, not the second, but she could still remember the sting.

But it wouldn't be fitting to say all that, not to the hired help. "We are deeply indebted to you for your sacrifice."

He acknowledged the comment with a tip of his head, then threw himself into digging again. "It'll pass in time, I bet. With a little hard work."

"I look forward to seeing the results of your labor." She turned to go inside but stopped when Frederick's shovel clunked against something in the dirt.

"Biggest stone yet. Might've dented my shovel," he said, kneeling to work the soil around the rock to pry it free—then let out a yelp of surprise.

She jerked her attention to a chunk of familiar white stone peering out at her.

And for a moment, she was a child chasing butterflies, an adolescent suffering through tea-etiquette lessons, a young woman looking over her shoulder to see if anyone was watching as she reached for the statue's base.

All under the cold, distant eyes of the virgin Greek goddess of spring.

It can't be.

But a step closer assured her it was. The face was half the size of human proportions, with dirt-smeared curls and a long, elegant neck, cracked jaggedly at the base.

Persephone, protector of her father's garden.

Mr. Keats's voice pulled her out of the memories. "Scared the daylights out of me. It looked for all the world like a skull."

"It's not possible." Her voice, a whisper, seemed to come from one of the old nightmares from just after Father's death.

"Don't worry, it's not human remains. Only some kind of statue. Part of one, anyway." He looked up and sobered at her expression. "What's wrong?"

"I . . . I ordered it torn down and taken away." She'd watched the workers smash the stone with their sledgehammers twenty-three years ago. Oh, the triumph she'd felt, bringing down a goddess—and the past along with it.

The deed done, she'd walked away, trusting that Delphie and the other servants would see Persephone loaded into wheelbarrows and taken far, far away.

If Mr. Keats found that odd, he let it pass without comment. "Maybe someone didn't feel like hauling, so they buried it under a few feet of dirt and called it a day." He heaved the shovel into the soil nearby, where it clanked again. "There's more of it, I think."

Gather yourself, Louise. Memories aside, the statue was merely a piece of rock.

"Dig it up. The whole body. Then get rid of it."

"Well," Mr. Keats said, leaning against his spade, "that'll be quite the"—his eye glinted again—"*undertaking.*"

Anger flared, hot and sudden. "Do *not* joke about this."

He flinched at the sharpness in her voice, the way Jeeves did when Delphie shouted at him to get out of her kitchen. "I'm sorry."

It wasn't his fault. He couldn't know. Louise brought her voice under control. "Do you promise to dispose of it properly?"

"I promise." After a breath of hesitation, before she could make an excuse to leave, he added, "What's so terrible about it?"

It wasn't spoken out of bald curiosity, the kind she could reprimand with a curt *"It's none of your concern."* His voice was hushed, like he was worried he'd uncovered an ancient curse.

"I don't condone pagan images on my property. It's sacrilege." The half-truth she'd used before was dusty from age but still functional.

Whether Mr. Keats agreed or not, he very wisely kept silent.

She left to the sound of shovel against stone, hurrying inside where no one could see how a simple broken statue had ruined her composure so thoroughly.

She went up to her father's office to bury herself in *Mrs. Miniver*, the book Avis had selected for her first club meeting. Though Louise would hardly call it fine literature, it was oddly comforting, reading about hardy British folk being measured for gas masks in one chapter, then fussing over the right diary to buy from the shops in the next. A factually based, straightforward distraction.

But no matter how many pages she read, she couldn't stop the memories pouring in like the sea at high tide.

JUNE 1913

The moment Louise woke, she threw off the bedclothes to look out the window and couldn't suppress her smile. Over the sea, the sky was a roiling mass of dingy gray, though the pane wasn't yet flecked with raindrops. The perfect gloomy summer day.

On mornings when clouds threatened but had not yet broken into the windy gales that beat against the summer home's cliffs, Father almost always had their driver take him to the library. Which meant Oliver would likely be free from his regular duties.

She finished a hasty breakfast, then offered a hurried explanation that she was going out to the garden, ducking out the back door to escape Delphine's fussing about not spoiling her hair—there would be a caller for tea, as usual. Above her, storm clouds blustered impotently, but Louise only clutched her sketchbook tighter as she approached the cool, impassive guardian of the garden. Her fingers curled under the raised arch of Persephone's foot. As always, when her fingers touched a scrap of folded paper, it sent a spark like the manor's newly installed electricity all through her.

All the note said was 9. She checked the gold heart-shaped locket containing a small timepiece, one of Father's expensive gifts upon her boarding school graduation. Only five minutes from now. She had nearly been late.

And, as always, there was something else with the note, tucked inside the fold: the pressed bloom of a red columbine, native to Maine's woodlands, but likely clipped from Father's wildflower garden. The scarlet petals draped about the dangling stamen like a ragtime singer's evening gown.

She couldn't help frowning. The flowers he left for her were sweet, but if Father ever saw Oliver desecrating his beloved garden without permission, he'd fire his manservant in an instant. The risk wasn't worth it.

What would she do without these stolen moments? At first, their meetings had been full of shirked chores, hushed conversation, and outbursts of laughter, precious stolen minutes in a regimented routine under Aunt Eleanor's hawkish gaze.

Now, two summers and a few stolen kisses later, they'd come to mean so much more.

I'll have to be cautious enough for both of us. Which, by now, came naturally—the second glances at the shadows cast by the garden's trellises and draping bowers, the forced casualness that took her down the path to the storage shed until the ivy-covered arbor hid her from view.

The key tucked under the metal birdbath was gone, the garden shed unlocked. Still, Louise hesitated in the doorway as her eyes adjusted to the dark collection of tools and shelves, watching for movement. Her voice came out in a whisper. "Is everything all right?"

For a moment, there was silence, and in her caught breath, scented with earth and rotting leaves, Louise felt that all her fears had at last come true. Someone had found him. Someone had seen them together, followed him, was on their way to tell Father . . .

But then she heard that deep, familiar, reassuring voice say, "Why wouldn't it be?" and Oliver stepped out from behind the propped-up wheelbarrow. She rushed into his arms, smelling the aftershave he'd likely applied to Father's face after trimming his gray beard hours before. "I'm with the most beautiful woman in the world, after all."

Relief mingled with the blush that Louise could feel rising on her face.

The compliment wasn't true, not remotely. Louise knew she was plain, her greatest charm coming from the dowry promised by Father's fortune, well managed by more business-minded men. And yet, the way Oliver looked at her, she could almost believe she was as lovely as the elegant goddess who guarded their hidden messages.

She'd sketch him someday. Try to capture that look, though she worried it would take a greater artist than she to get at the nobility of that strong nose, the fire in the rust-colored hair, the ambition in those brown eyes. And no picture could really capture Oliver Goodwin, the young man who had made a game of smiling at her when the other servants weren't looking, who had taught himself to read and quoted Shakespeare's sonnets, who was the first to ask what *her* dreams might be—and who somehow managed to take her breath away when the suitors her aunt paraded before her merely made her yawn.

Pulling away, she tried to become her rational self again. "We should be more careful. What if someone finds our notes?"

His laugh came easily, as always. "What, a scribbled number or two? They wouldn't think a thing of it."

"Or finds us here," she insisted.

"You know your father keeps the other key. And he only hires a gardener for the months he's not living here."

It was true, and the one reason she'd agreed to the meeting place weeks ago when Oliver had suggested it. Despite the dirt and labor involved, Luther Cavendish insisted gardening was a gentleman's hobby. Though Louise knew it was more than that. It was his way of honoring his wife's memory, by personally tending a place she had loved so well—and, characteristically, by ordering everyone else away to do so.

When Father was absent from Windward Hall, the threat of his displeasure and the lock on the door kept all others away. For those precious hours, Oliver was hers.

"Don't worry, my sweet flower," Oliver murmured, warming her cold hands with his warm ones. "We're safe here."

Part of her wanted to continue her protest, but another part wanted to believe him. The fact that the schoolgirl who copied her essays two to three times to perfect her penmanship had grown into a young woman who stole away for a rendezvous with a servant had surprised even her. The desire for caution, to avoid being found out, warred with the sheer exhaustion of a life of pressure and perfection.

But as Oliver closed the space between them again, she knew there was a greater danger. No amount of caution could keep her from losing her heart to this man. It was far too late for that.

eight

AVIS
APRIL 18

Every time Avis tried to increase her speed, the china on the tray chattered a warning—and with borrowed cups, no less. She'd remembered only a half hour before the book club meeting that her brilliant idea of serving tea would be ruined by the fact that she had only six teacups.

Given that she'd used her own money for an advertisement in the town paper, in addition to putting up flyers at the post office, town hall, all three churches in town, and the Bristol-Banks Foundry, her meager tea set wouldn't be nearly enough. Avis's neighbor, Mrs. Humphrey, had been willing to lend her second-best set, though she'd coughed uncomfortably when Avis gathered the courage to say she hoped she'd see her at future meetings.

She was only five minutes late. Likely, everyone was enjoying the extended socializing.

With the tray on one hip, Avis threw the library's front door open, pausing to tuck wisps of escaping hair behind her ear and fix on her sunniest hostess smile. She could do this. After all, she was wearing new pumps and a sharp blue suit with gold buttons in honor of the occasion.

She rounded the shelves housing the Dewey 100s to the circle of twenty chairs she'd so carefully set up earlier that morning.

Only three were occupied.

Three.

Avis had made two *dozen* carrot-cake muffins for three people.

Her step faltered, rattling the tray, and Ginny sprang up to steady her. "Finally!" she exclaimed, too loudly for the quiet room. "We can eat the snacks now, can't we, Avis?"

Ignoring her question, Avis set the tray down and turned to the others. *You can do this. Or at least you can pretend.*

What would Anthony do?

"Welcome, everyone, to our little Blackout Book Club," she said, trying to mimic the expression the women's navy auxiliary officer had donned for the cover of the latest issue of *My Day* magazine. Poise, warmth, and eloquence, the three marks of the ideal hostess. "I'm delighted you were able to join us."

No one in the audience seemed to match her delight. Miss Cavendish had, as Avis had predicted, claimed the forest green armchair as her rightful throne, surveying the gathering with marked displeasure. A dark-haired woman Avis had never met looked around nervously, and it was only now that Avis noticed two children on the floor behind her, leaning against the shelves. And Ginny, of course, balanced a plate loaded with muffins, flashing Avis an encouraging grin.

"Why don't we move the chairs to make this cozier?" Avis asked, snatching up the plain black composition notebook she'd set by the muffins. No tea for her—the clatter of china would make it obvious if her hands gave the slightest tremor.

There was an awful clamor of chair legs scraping as the others tightened the circle, and Avis claimed a chair to Miss Cavendish's left.

She'd prepared an agenda for the meeting, written in the first page of the notebook, and grasped at it now. "Perhaps we should all introduce ourselves and share what we like to read."

Though Avis hadn't asked for volunteers, Ginny sauntered

to the middle of the circle like a chorus girl at a casting call. "I'm Ginny Maeve Atkins. Before coming to Bristol-Banks, I was either a barnstormer, a bootlegger, or a Barnum circus acrobat. Your best guess as to which." She licked her fingers, sticky from the sultanas Avis had folded into the muffin batter.

This caused the frown on Miss Cavendish's stern face to furrow deeper. "I don't believe you're taking this seriously, young lady."

Ginny popped a finger out of her mouth and sat back down. "I thought this was a book club, not a funeral."

Avis groaned inside. Why had she thought inviting Ginny was a good idea?

"Anyway, I don't much like reading," she went on, "but when I do, it had better start with either a kiss or an explosion, like a good movie."

That made the shy woman next to her jerk her head up, amusement lighting her dark eyes at the matter-of-fact declaration.

At least she didn't mention the storage closet. Miss Cavendish hadn't yet learned that Anthony couldn't bear to throw away a book, not even one that Miss Cavendish had banned from the library's register.

With a flourish, Ginny stuffed the remaining half of a muffin into her mouth, as if to forestall further questioning, and nodded to the woman next to her.

"My name is Martina Bianchini." Her voice had only the softest of Italian-accented vowels, but Avis didn't miss the way Miss Cavendish's eyes narrowed in response. "I am also working at the foundry while my husband, Patrick, is in the navy."

Miss Cavendish nodded approvingly, and Avis felt some of the tension ease out of her shoulders. Well, that was a relief. A shame that it took military service in the family for the poor woman to prove herself, but tensions were high these days. Although she called him Patrick . . . an Irish name, but an Italian surname. Unusual.

She shrugged the curiosity away. "And tell us more about your favorite books."

"I like to read novels."

"In English or Italian?" Miss Cavendish's question was as pointed as a sharpened pen nib.

Martina shifted in her seat, her voice guarded. "English. I've lived here most of my life."

Suddenly, Avis wished she'd brought aspirin instead of tea. Weren't introductions supposed to help people feel more comfortable with one another?

"I like fairy stories," a small voice piped up. The little girl on the floor behind Martina's chair poked her head out, and Avis couldn't help smiling.

"My daughter, Rosa," Martina said, looking apologetic, "and my son, George."

"Gio," he corrected, thin arms folded across his chest. "I don't like to read anything."

"I see" was all Avis could think to say. "Well, we have a very large selection of books—including many collections of fairy stories—in our children's section upstairs. Ginny, would you lead our young guests there?" Sweet as the little girl was, it would be better to have them out of the way. You could never tell what children would say.

"C'mon." Ginny prodded Gio with her foot. "I'll race you." That set him off, taking the stairs two at a time to the second-floor balcony, Rosa trailing behind them.

This, while gaining a glare of disapproval from Miss Cavendish, at least took Ginny out of range for any snide comments during Miss Cavendish's introduction, which Avis prompted politely.

"I am Louise Cavendish." She folded her gloved hands, ever the lady of the manor. "This association library was started by my father as a project for the betterment of the town where he and my mother spent summers all their lives."

And you're willing to give it up, Avis couldn't keep from thinking, but if Miss Cavendish realized the irony of her proud statement, she didn't show it.

"I have a particular interest in nonfiction, as well as poetry."

Really? Avis tried not to let her surprise show. They'd have to find some poets to read, though she couldn't think of any titles offhand.

The pause stretched too long before Avis realized it was her turn. "And I'm Avis Montgomery." Perhaps she ought to add more for Martina's sake. "My brother was the head librarian here for several years, and I've . . ."

Pretended to fill his role for the past three months.

". . . carried on while he's serving in the army. I enjoy any book with wit, warmth, and characters who feel like friends." That, she'd decided, was a good line, even if it was a bit insincere. With what she hoped was a cheerful smile, she held up her copy of *Mrs. Miniver.* "Speaking of which, shall we discuss the book? I hope everyone had a chance to read it. I know it was short notice."

"I read the interesting bits," Ginny put in, rejoining them without Martina's children in tow, "which, to be honest, wasn't much."

Martina made a faint choking sound, and Avis's smile faltered. "Oh" was all she could manage, staring blankly at her supposed ally. "I'm sorry you felt that way."

"Before we begin, oughtn't we have someone take official minutes?" Miss Cavendish asked, giving a pointed look at Avis's open notebook.

For comments like Ginny's? Those were better off unrecorded. But of course, Avis couldn't say that. "Certainly. I'll be happy to do so."

"As for me," Miss Cavendish went on, "while I felt the prose leaned too far to sentimentality, it gave me a greater respect for what our British cousins endured in the days when America refused to acknowledge the impending conflict." She looked at Avis as if she expected the full comment to be transcribed and attributed immediately.

That prompted a snort from Ginny. "Those Minivers owned a weekend cottage, took holidays in Scotland, and hired servants to prepare meals. If that's what you call enduring suffering, I'm a fried mackerel."

Forget the air raid sirens of the Blitz, Avis could feel alarms going off all around her. Why had she ever thought this would be a good idea?

She pictured Anthony in one of the empty chairs next to her, grinning at the show, delighted that a book could excite such strong emotions. *"This had better be worth it,"* she said to him in her mind, as if he could hear her from wherever he was trooping across the European countryside.

"Never fear, sis, books are meant to spark discussion. Just let it happen."

As if she had any choice. Taking a deep breath, she looked down at her notebook and began to write.

Notes from the Blackout Book Club—April 18, 1942

Taken by Avis Montgomery, Head Librarian and Book Club Secretary

For the record: I was nominated for this secretarial position against my will.

Members in attendance: Louise Cavendish, Ginny Atkins, Martina (can't spell her last name), and Avis Montgomery

Book under discussion: <u>Mrs. Miniver</u> by Jan Struther

From my research, I explained that the book was compiled from a series of newspaper columns published in the <u>Times</u>. ("Like a comic book made from a bunch of Sunday funnies strung together?" Ginny asked. Close enough.)

Debate then began on whether Mrs. Miniver was a realistic character. Miss Cavendish, who I suppose had some authority, coming from a wealthy family, insisted she was. Ginny was the skeptic, insisting "Nobody's got time to wander around thinking about flowers and time passing and all." I—and apparently Martina, because she gave a slight nod—took the middle ground, saying that essays are by nature more reflective than most of us tend to be in real life.

I said I had expected more of the war but hadn't realized when the book was written. Miss Cavendish pointed out some scenes showing the buildup to war, such as Mrs. Miniver volunteering as an ambulance driver and the digging up of Kensington Gardens. This prompted another rant from Ginny, who described the poster from the upcoming movie, which featured bombers and the ruins of buildings, all completely absent from the book.

When I asked Martina, who hadn't spoken, for her thoughts, she raised a question of what was meant by this line: "It's as important to marry the right life as it is the right person."

Miss Cavendish firmly declared that "married women are often defined by their husbands, and therefore their choice of partner is treated as the most important decision of their lives." (Said with disdain for those of us bearing a "Mrs." brand before our names.) Ginny said she figured it meant not tying the knot with "just any looker who can get down on one knee." She referenced several ill-fated engagements in romance novels to substantiate her point. I cut her off before she could bring any out from the storage room for a dramatic reading.

I was too busy taking notes to have an opinion. Or perhaps I simply don't know, having married my high-school sweetheart, our families having practically betrothed us since birth.

At this point, conversation stalled. Given the London setting of this read, Louise felt we ought to read something written by an American woman and suggested Emily Dickinson. And by suggested, I mean stated. So it was decided . . . without my vote. I don't care a whit for poetry. We had to memorize loads of Henry Wadsworth Longfellow in school, on account of his being born in Maine, and I always forgot my lines. I threw the whole text of "Evangeline" in a bonfire at the end-of-the-year party. That's when Russell first took notice of me, actually.

We'll see how Emily fares. I can only hope she's less long-winded than HWL.

nine

LOUISE
APRIL 23

Louise knew it was childish, but she couldn't help slamming the door of her study. "What does it take to find competent workers these days?" she demanded.

Jeeves, the only other occupant of the room in his bed by the fireplace, answered with a sympathetic whine. He leaped up as she stormed over to the bookshelf that once displayed her father's personal library and now held her painting supplies, his tail wagging in delight. The term *man's best friend* displayed the usual male arrogance by assuming women didn't find happiness in the creatures' unconditional affection.

Even giving him a requisite pat on the head made her feel better and helped her put the contractor's warnings out of her mind. "We'll show him, won't we?" she said, satisfied that Jeeves, at least, would always see things her way.

The meeting with the contractor this morning had been a disaster. Before she'd given him the tour of the building, he'd warned her that the work required would be extensive. Afterward, he shook his head with a deep frown, listing off the library's flaws. Plumbing would need to be installed, the balcony blocked off, as stairs would be a safety hazard to the little ones. The library's heating was inadequate for a nursery school, and it would be months before a construction crew would be able to begin. "It's just not suited for a renovation like this."

He's wrong, she insisted, taking the canvas apron from its golden hook and knotting it around her waist. All she wanted were some simple, functional modifications. Even in wartime, it couldn't be too much to ask. The library was the building she had, and so it was what they would use.

Painting would help. The art lessons Aunt Eleanor had insisted on as part of an old-fashioned idea of an accomplished lady had been the one piece of that sham Louise had appreciated.

As she removed her hog-hair brushes one by one, she noticed a book beside her wooden case of oils. Delphie must have set it out, knowing the book club discussion was coming up. *Collected Poems of Emily Dickinson*, the title on the faded green binding declared.

No need to borrow this one from the library or order it from town. It and a few others were old friends. She turned the pages, and the book fell open to one poem in particular.

She quoted it from memory while tying on her paint-smeared canvas apron and opening the north window to let in some fresh air.

> *Heart, we will forget him!*
> *You and I, tonight!*
> *You may forget the warmth he gave,*
> *I will forget the light.*
>
> *When you have done, pray tell me*
> *That I my thoughts may dim;*
> *Haste! lest while you're lagging,*
> *I may remember him!*

"I don't suppose we'll be discussing that one at book club, will we, Jeeves?" She sighed at his responding whine, picturing

Avis's relentlessly cheerful smile. If the young woman had ever known a disappointment, in love or any other area of her life, she certainly didn't show it.

"If the dog ever answers, you be sure and tell me."

The blunt voice from the doorway was easy to identify—no one else took closed doors as an invitation to enter without knocking. Delphie, sharp elbows folded across a sunken bosom, wore her usual half grimace, as well as the latest in her line of colorful aprons, a more important fashion accessory in her estimation than the finest milliner's creation.

"He has not thus far. Nor chewed up the boot scraper in the entryway again." Dogs couldn't really be held accountable for such things, though Delphie certainly tried.

She grunted in response, and Jeeves, as if understanding the scrutiny, lowered himself to his bed and sniffed innocently.

Louise took the drape off her latest work. It was larger than most of her previous projects. The browns and greens of the garden had started to take shape, the horizon line feathered out with grass and the slope of gentle distant hills.

The artist community was abuzz with worry over wartime shortages—vermilion paint, for instance, made with mercury used in shell and mine detonators, was in short supply—so Louise had opted for a pastoral scene without those brighter hues. Soon, she'd begin the detailed work: the scarecrow and carrot tops and mischievous rabbits with noses twitching to steal them.

Delphie took a wide berth around Jeeves to approach the painting, leaning in to get a good look through eyes that had lost the sharpness of youth. "Nice to see you painting again."

"It's for the nursery school, to put up on the wall." Louise frowned. "Do children still read about Peter Rabbit these days?"

Modern writers couldn't be trusted without thorough vetting. At least Beatrix Potter's tales had solid morals at the end about the dangers of greed and gluttony and disobeying wise adults—adult rabbits, that is.

"I say it's charming no matter what they've read." Delphie pointed to the vague pencil outline of a human form in the upper-left corner holding a ghosted-in pitchfork. "Be sure to give the angry farmer an eye patch. Freddy will love that."

The two of them had formed a truce of sorts since the statue's discovery, forged mainly through Frederick's constant second helpings and excessive compliments of Delphie's cooking. Louise couldn't endorse flattery, of course, but it was good to have peace in the house.

"Still, I didn't know a patch of lettuce deserved such a scowl," Delphie added.

"I wasn't—" Louise stopped, catching a glimpse of her face in the gilt mirror that had replaced the awful wall hanging her father had loved. Perhaps her poor mood did show slightly. "I have a headache. That's all."

"Humph." Delphie blew out between her teeth, and Louise could imagine the assumptions and conclusions being made behind her cook's squinted eyes. "'That's all,' she says. I haven't lived to eighty years without being able to spot a fib six feet from my nose."

"You're only seventy-seven."

"Didn't that fancy school of yours teach rounding?" Without waiting for an invitation, Delphie plunked herself down in Father's armchair—new upholstery, of course, to match the rest of the redecorating. Supper preparation, it seemed, would wait. "Go on. Tell me what's wrong."

Given the sheer uselessness of refusing Delphie when she got into one of these moods, Louise related the details of the disappointing meeting with the contractor, receiving sympathetic grunts along the way. "What if all of this is a waste?"

"Now, now. That's no way to talk. 'Hope is the thing with

feathers,'" Delphie said sternly, wagging her finger at the volume of poetry beside the tumbler.

"'That perches in the soul,'" Louise said, unable to keep from smiling as the familiar words crossed her lips.

"'And sings the tune without the words.'"

"'And never stops—at all—'" The words seemed to seep into her, chasing away her worries, all of them borrowing trouble from a tomorrow they hadn't yet reached. "You're right. No sense in giving up yet."

Delphie gave a matter-of-fact nod and stood, her work done.

Suddenly, the idea of painting didn't seem quite so daunting. Louise squeezed a dime of burnt sienna paint, Winsor & Newton, used by the likes of Norman Rockwell, onto her palette. "Thank you, Delphie."

"Puh. Don't thank me. Thank Emily."

But it was Delphie, all those years ago, who'd thrust the book of poems at Louise to read to her father, making those long, tedious days in the sickroom more bearable.

Which, in turn, inspired an idea. "What do I have to say to convince you to come to book club with me this week?"

Delphie scoffed low in her throat. "No one wants a relic like me there."

"I do." It would be nice to have someone thoroughly unsentimental in attendance. A voice of reason.

A friend.

Louise thought of her early opinions of Delphie. A few decades could change people a great deal.

"Fine, then," Delphie said gruffly, as Louise had known she would. "But just this once. For Emily."

Louise touched her brush to the furrows of the garden on the canvas and put thoughts of contractors, failures, and heartbreak aside. "Yes. For Emily."

ten

AVIS
APRIL 27

It was difficult, surrounded by dying bath suds and lukewarm water, to properly take notes on a book, but with effort, Avis kept her pencil steady enough to underline her favorite parts.

How to Read a Book was a masterpiece, and its author, Mortimer Adler, a genius. It made everything so simple: how to scan the pages for key ideas, an outline for taking notes, even four rules to determine the aim of a book. If all went well, she had determined to make it a future book club read, after Emily Dickinson. Who, she had to admit, defied the neat rules Adler set out for interpretation, but that was poetry for you.

Avis inhaled the scent of lavender—the bath salts had been a birthday present from Russell, along with roses and an apology for being a day late—and pictured the next book club meeting: herself, armed with strategies and observations, the others murmuring about how insightful she was, Miss Cavendish looking admiringly at her and saying, *"Why, Avis, I never knew . . ."*

And then the fire siren sounded, distant but shrill, slicing like a letter opener through the peaceful evening.

Avis sloshed to attention, only a quick reaction keeping *How to Read a Book* from tumbling into the drink. "Russ, what is it?" she cried, throwing on her robe, dripping on the hallway rug as she hurried toward the crackling sound of her husband's radio program.

But she knew. They'd spotted an enemy plane. The newspapers said a kitchen table would do in place of a bomb shelter, but they hadn't seen hers, with the narrow, stylish legs that would collapse if a concussion grenade fell within a block.

"We're being bombed, aren't we?" Her voice sounded thin and strained, even to her.

"Only an air raid drill, darling," Russell soothed, standing from the depths of his armchair and snapping off the radio so only the blast of the fire siren remained. "Don't you remember? They announced it in the paper."

A drill. Then . . . this wasn't a real air raid. Avis leaned against the wall, the tips of her hair sending rivulets of water down her back to spot the linoleum as she tried to breathe deeply.

How had she forgotten? She'd been so careful in noting how many Emily Dickinson poems she'd need to read per day that she hadn't even jotted down an air raid drill on the calendar.

Instead of running to close the curtains, Russell's gaze went to her legs—still specked with soap scum and bathwater—and let out a low whistle. "Wowee, you're looking good, missus. Going my way?"

She clutched the lapels of the robe to give herself some semblance of decency. "I'm *going* to prepare this house for an air raid." Maybe a hair more snappish than necessary, but really, who had time for ogling when there was a war on?

She'd memorized the steps of "What to Do in an Air Raid." The first was keep cool.

Well. Easier said than done.

Her fingers, at least, had stopped shaking as she switched off the table lamp, already pointed away from the windows per regulations. The blue signal meant all citizens had ten minutes to make the coast into a swath of darkness, providing no target for enemy planes.

Russell pulled the blackout drapes as she left to do the same in the bathroom and hall. The bedroom lamp was the last to go. Avis shivered, attempting to blot her wet hair with a hand towel beside her vanity. Their home, so cozy and comfortable only seconds ago, now stood darkened in shadow.

"There now." Russell held a candle aloft as he shut the door behind himself, the glow giving his rounded face the wholesome look of a choirboy at a Christmas Eve concert. "All set. Let's get into bed. Too late now to do much but sleep anyway." He set the candle on the nightstand and put an arm around her, but Avis pulled away.

"Shouldn't we shut off the furnace?"

That is what the "What to Do in an Air Raid" article had suggested, in case bombs started falling. They'd also recommended naming one family member the "home air raid warden," in charge of memorizing all procedures. *Mother makes the best*, they'd wisely advised. Avis wasn't that yet—though she hoped to be someday soon—but even the newsmen had the sense to know this was a woman's job.

"I don't think we need to take the drill that far." A series of short blasts from the siren made her startle, and Russell reached for the lamp. "See? There's the all clear."

She gripped his arm. "No! That's the red signal." Didn't he read the instructions? That meant the plane would be almost passing by, and drivers would need to park their cars and take cover.

Even though it was only the town's fire siren—not the ghastly whining moan she'd heard in newsreels about the London Blitz—surrounded by darkness and the flickering shadows cast by the candle, it felt far more ominous. Avis shuddered and dove under their quilt, robe and all.

Collected Poems of Emily Dickinson lay tauntingly on the bedside table. Maybe she should continue reading. After all, she still had twenty more poems left by her schedule to have the book completed by the next meeting.

The siren stopped. The planes, if they had been real, would be passing over now. She shuddered, pulling closer to Russell to feel his warmth, smell the faint traces of cologne still left after a long day, hear the steady beat of his heart. Hers was outpacing his by leagues.

"You're not afraid of the dark, are you?" he asked in a teasing tone.

She ought to say something coy, like *"Not with you here."* But what came out instead was "I'm afraid of many things."

His voice turned serious as well. "So am I."

She pushed back to watch him in the dim light. "You?"

"Sure. Mostly that we coast dwellers will lose the war for the rest of the country. I know why those U-boats keep downing our merchant ships."

Avis frowned. "The papers say we're sinking plenty of them in return."

"Papers don't always tell the truth."

"Russell." An uneasy feeling, one she usually managed to push away by turning down the radio, avoiding the newspapers, and changing the subject, rose within her.

"I'm just telling you what I heard from my buddy Roy in the coast guard." Another organization that refused to let him join because of his health issues. Not that he hadn't tried. "We've spent this whole winter and spring with the coast all lit up, making ships an easy target for the wolf packs. We're what's killing them."

She couldn't help it; she shivered again, tucking herself under the blanket. "That's awful."

"So is hauling in the bloated body of a merchant mariner whose tanker was broken in two by a Nazi torpedo. But Roy says—"

"No, stop!" she exclaimed, her eyes closed shut, trying not to picture it, to think of it. "Please, Russell. I . . . I don't want to—"

"I'm sorry. I shouldn't have told you." And when she opened her eyes again, he had that familiar far-off look on his face.

"No," she wanted to say, *"I'm not fragile. I'm strong."* Like Ginny or Louise or . . . or Mrs. Miniver. Keep calm and carry on and all that.

But it would be a lie.

"It's all right," she forced herself to say. "Just . . . troubling."

Russell's hand found hers under the comforter and squeezed tightly. "We'll get through this, Avis. Remember Anthony's last letter? Sounds like spirits are high after the men heard about our bombing raid on Tokyo. They're predicting we could rout the Axis powers by the new year."

He had said that, hadn't he? That was something, at least.

"I'm sure you're right." Or she hoped he was. "Now, would you read a few poems to me, dear?"

She expected him to complain—Russell rarely read anything other than a newspaper—but he took *Collected Poems of Emily Dickinson* eagerly, as if grateful for a change of subject. A diversion. Something lovely and simple in a world that had gone mad, read in that familiar deep voice.

But that night, even after the wail of the all-clear pattern of the fire siren, Avis dreamed of dark seas and evil men hiding in them, giving a command to kill.

Notes from the Blackout Book Club—May 2, 1942

Taken by Avis Montgomery, Head Librarian and Book Club Secretary

Members in attendance: Louise Cavendish, Delphie Morine, Ginny Atkins, Martina Bianchini, and Avis Montgomery

Book under discussion: <u>Collected Poems of Emily Dickinson</u> by the same

Oh dear, no one new attending except Delphie, Miss Cavendish's cook, even though I talked to three ladies about it at church. If I'd hinted any more strongly, I'd have been on my knees begging. Ginny asked if I'd give her a dime a head for anyone she brought in. She found that hilarious. I didn't.

Delphie doesn't seem shy. She declared her unabashed love for "'Hope' is the thing with feathers" in a way that defied anyone to disagree.

Ginny stood and declaimed the entire "I'm Nobody, who are you?" poem, including a frog imitation that made Martina swallow her tea wrong and start hiccupping. Miss Cavendish, as usual, did not approve. It's going to be quite a time, keeping those two from each other's throats at every turn.

When I asked one of the questions from <u>How to Read a Book</u> about the themes of the works, most of us agreed that Miss Dickinson was uncommonly interested in death, metaphors from nature (more a motif than a theme, but I let it pass), and apparent contradictions.

I expressed my dislike for the fact that the poems didn't have any set form or follow traditional grammatical rules. To which Miss Cavendish said something about how that wasn't the point of poetry. I asked, what if I started capitalizing random words and speaking in fragments with no regard to grammar? Ginny said it might be more interesting (some friend).

So there you have it. Poetry is anarchy, and I still don't like it. Though these were better than Longfellow's. One could never end a recitation of one of his poems with a chorus of frog noises.

When conversation died down, I offered the safest option possible for the next book: Shakespeare. Miss Cavendish banned all the comedies as being "frivolous and full of suggestive material," so <u>Hamlet</u> it is. Martina has apparently always wanted to read it—she doesn't say much, but when she does, it's often surprising.

I do so hate stories where people die. You'd think that during a war, of all times, we'd want to read something more uplifting.

Hand is cramping from writing notes. Which, I should add, no one has requested to read. I asked Miss Cavendish if we could simply list the titles we discussed, but she insisted that every committee she's ever been on has kept minutes. Next week, I'll see if I can recruit another victim to be secretary and spread the burden around.

eleven

GINNY
MAY 3

It wouldn't be so bad, writing letters to a boy on a Sunday afternoon, if only something interesting happened to talk about.

Mack had made good on his promise, sending Ginny three letters already, all stacked up on her bureau. Like her, he'd only gone to school through fifth grade, and even then had apparently dozed off during spelling lessons. Probably penmanship ones, too, but as messy as they were, his letters were full of first-rate stuff: pranks on his chief petty officer, the USO chocolate bars he'd smuggled out, and descriptions of his seasick landlubber comrades when they'd first braved the seas, headed for somewhere in the Pacific.

And all Ginny had to scribble in reply was the same old routine: foundry shifts, tracking down free lunches around town to save a little dough, and walking on the beach, which was where she was now. Poor Mack would die of boredom from her letters before the Japanese could get him.

A beady-eyed seagull scrabbling over the rocks looked far too interested in the remaining half of her baloney sandwich, so Ginny stuffed it in her mouth. "Don't you try it," she mumbled around the crust.

Hamlet lay discarded at the foot of her blanket. Ginny had tried to read it for Martina's sake. It had started out all right, with talk of a ghost and revenge and such. But then some fellow named Horatio went on for pages about "harbingers preceding still the fates" and something called a "moiety competent," which sounded like something a big-city lawyer would say. Better to count the dead bodies, skim the last scene or two, and fumble her way through the discussion with no one the wiser.

That sure wasn't interesting enough to tell Mack about. Ginny sighed at the half-blank letter. She quickly jotted another question to fill up space, then said she missed him, because that's how Mack had closed his last letter. Even that didn't quite feel right.

Do I really miss him . . . or do I just miss the island?

Never mind that. Mack almost *was* the island.

Until he sees the world and backwaters on you, some taunting part of her niggled.

Well, if that happened, she'd change his mind right back . . . or dump him. She sure wasn't leaving Long Island. Once she got enough money to buy back land on the island after the navy was done with it—and maybe her own lobstering boat and traps for good measure—she was staying put.

In the last letter from her family, Ma told her that Pa had settled into his job in Portland so much that she wondered if he really would go back to lobstering at the end of the war like he'd promised. But it couldn't be true, only wishful thinking on Ma's part. Pa would never sell the *Lady Luck* outright. But if they got into debt, if Ma got into the money the government had given them for the house . . . well, anything could happen.

Still holding the letter, Ginny watched the waves come in, beating a sheen over the narrow stretch of beach that ran between the rocky shoals. It wasn't hard to pretend that she was home again while closing her eyes to breathe the salt-tanged air and feeling the spring wind tug wisps of her hair inland. But it wasn't quite the same.

She'd tried wandering down by the landing before coming

here, but seeing the boats and sailors, the sea air filled with familiar hollers and smells, only made her homesickness worse, like taking to a choppy sea with a full stomach.

A bark drew her attention down the beach, where a tallish, broad-shouldered fellow, sleeves rolled to his elbows, was tossing a stick for a German shepherd with brown markings like eyebrows. The dog leaped into the air, all muscle and grace, chomped down on the stick, then headed bullet-straight back to its master.

She gave a whistle of appreciation. "Now, *there's* a handsome one."

The dog, of course.

Ma had grown up on a farm where the dogs herded sheep and the cats ate mice, so she'd never warmed up to the idea of a pet. Ginny had adopted the strays who hung about the harbor, giving them names and slipping them scraps whenever she could.

Ginny stood, careful to tuck Mack's letter under her lunch pail so it wouldn't blow away in the breeze, and waved her arms. "Hey there! Mister!"

The young man turned toward her hailing and jogged over. Closer now, she noticed an eyepatch slung across his face under tousled dark hair, like a pirate. The dog, cheated out of his game of catch, bounded after him.

"Can I pet your dog?" she asked, once he got within hailing distance. That seemed more pressing than how-do-you-dos.

"Sure," the stranger said, smiling amiably. He was a fresh-faced fellow despite the eyepatch giving him a world-weary look, probably not much older than she was. "Though he's not actually mine."

Ginny dropped to her knees, knuckling the German shepherd's neck. Sand flicked onto her legs as the dog wagged his tail, panting and craning his head to get a better look at his new friend. "Dognapping this early in the day?"

His laugh was warm and strong. "Miss Cavendish—she lives

up there on the cliffs—likes me to take him for a walk some afternoons. I'm new to town. Just started working for her."

Sure enough, the tracks on the beach led toward the old manor up on the cliffs that looked down on the rest of town. "Well, I'll be. Didn't seem the type, old Louise."

"To own a dog, or to hire a fellow like me?"

"Both," Ginny quipped, matching his grin. It was a nice surprise. The way he talked, all educated and with a voice like polished wood, she would have thought he'd be too stuck up to make a joke at his own expense.

The pirate-stranger stooped down to pat the dog affectionately, then looked up at her. "I'm Freddy Keats, by the way."

She took his offered hand and shook it firmly, the way she had when her pa's friends chuckled about the "little miss" going out on the boat. "Ginny Atkins."

The German shepherd's low whine told her she'd stopped petting him, a mistake she quickly fixed. "Why don't you tell me this fine boy's name, and we'll all be introduced."

Freddy knelt down on the corner of the blanket. "This is Jeeves."

"Where'd he get a moniker like that?"

"A book, I think Miss Cavendish said."

Ginny snorted. "Figures. Everyone around this town loves books."

"I take it you're part of the Blackout Book Club, then?" He held up *Hamlet*. "One of my favorites. What do you think of it so far?"

For a moment, Ginny wavered, about to say that it was just super, and she couldn't wait to discuss it. The fellow looked almost like Jeeves, so earnest and excited that it felt mean to tell him the truth.

"I've only just started," she admitted, deciding on a compromise. "Shakespeare wasn't much for plain speaking, was he?"

"It was plainer at the time than it is now. Language changes."

She gave him a flat look and opened to a random page, speaking through her nose. "'I have of late—but wherefore I know not—lost all my mirth, forgone all custom of exercises; and indeed it goes so heavily with my disposition that this goodly frame, the earth, seems to me a sterile promontory.' Don't try to tell me anyone *ever* talked like that."

This time when Freddy smiled, she noticed that the skin under the corner of his good eye crinkled like William Holden's in *Golden Boy*. "That's the poetry of it, Ginny. Besides, no one should ever *read* Shakespeare. It only comes alive when it's performed."

"I wouldn't know. I've never been to a stage show." Other than a makeshift Christmas pageant now and then when Pa hustled them into the island church, but that didn't count.

"Well then, we'll have to get you to one someday, won't we?"

"Not a chance," she ought to have said. *"Because I'm dating a nice boy from back home, and anyway, girls like me don't go to city theater shows."*

But the idea was nice, and she found herself saying, "Would you want to join us? For the book club, I mean. We meet every other Saturday morning."

Surprise flickered across his face, then the smile was back. "You know . . . I think I will. As long as I can step away from my work for that long."

Good. Poor Avis needed more bodies in the chairs for her club to please Ye Olde Dragon Cavendish.

"I've got to know," she said. "Miss Cavendish pays you just to walk her dog?"

He laughed. "I've been hired for gardening, mostly, once planting season starts."

"Ah, sure. So what branch of the service were you in?"

Freddy visibly started, looking down as if to check to make sure he wasn't in uniform, then relaxed. "Ah, small town. Word probably gets around, doesn't it?"

"Wasn't that." She ticked off the reasons on her fingers. "You got that injury somewhere, and that patch isn't much faded, so probably new. You stand straighter than a fencepost and walk like you're marching. And there's a dog-tag chain poking out around your neck."

His hand shot straight to it, tucking it away. "You guessed it. I was a pilot in the army air forces. Got shot down on our third crossing, guarding a convoy of merchant ships headed for the English Channel."

Ginny nodded, focusing on Jeeves instead of Freddy and his eyepatch. He probably had enough folks staring at him, and besides, seeing an actual soldier with lifelong scars made the war feel more real—and more dangerous. "And where'd you live before Derby?"

"New Hampshire area," he said vaguely, like a fellow used to naming a small town that no one'd ever heard of. His choice, of course, but even if the only Long Island folks had ever heard of was in New York, Ginny would have gone on for days if he'd asked her where she was from. But he didn't. In fact, he reached for *Hamlet* as if he was going to steer the conversation that way again.

Nothing doing. She'd had enough of dusty old books for the day. "Got any family?"

"Sure. Parents, siblings. They're good people." She was about to ask how many brothers, see if he could beat her three, when he stood, nudging Jeeves, who looked ready to drift into a contented dream of ham bones and squirrels. "Well, I'd better be going. Miss Cavendish told me to be sure to be back by high tide."

Ginny hesitated before pasting on a smile. "Sure, sure. It was nice to meet you, Freddy. And I'll see you at the next meeting."

He nodded, raising a dramatic hand to his chest as he stepped backward. "And remember, Ginny: 'This above all: to thine own

91

self be true, and it must follow, as the night the day, thou canst not then be false to any man.'"

Bold words, she thought, watching him jog away with Jeeves at his heels, *for a man who just lied to my face.* The stretch of hard, wet sand behind her, dotted with limp seaweed and driftwood, was proof enough of that, even if she didn't have the worn calendar from her father's lobstering boat.

There was no way Miss Cavendish told him to make the walk short and hurry back before high tide, because high tide wasn't for another five hours. Clearly, Freddy had just wanted to get away from her, her questions, or both.

It wasn't so bad a lie. Probably, he was just a private fellow who didn't want to tell too much of his past to a stranger. It was none of her business, really.

Still, it bothered her. Why was someone as friendly as Freddy so closed off about himself? Her questions hadn't been all that prying.

Nothing she'd write in a letter to Mack, of course—he might not like the thought of her talking to a handsome pirate-veteran—but interesting, all the same.

twelve

MARTINA
MAY 13

By the time she'd scrubbed the last of Gio's shirts in her bucket swirled with soap flakes, Martina was convinced: Shakespeare was telling her to go back to church.

Reading the play had been difficult, pausing for words even the library's dictionary couldn't help her translate, but she understood enough to know that Ophelia should have taken Hamlet's advice and fled to a nunnery, rather than drown herself over a foolish man.

Still, she couldn't judge the poor woman. Martina herself hadn't been to Mass since Boston. For a while, she'd pretended that her swing-shift schedule made it impossible, or that she had no car to drive to St. Patrick's north of Bristol, with its brick steeple pointing to heaven. But the truth was that she had weekends off and there was a bus station only a short walk from the trailer camp.

No, Martina had stopped attending because the devoted of St. Patrick's were not the familiar faces of the many "aunts" and "uncles" who lined the streets of Mamma's neighborhood. They were strangers, probably mostly Irish Catholics rather than Italians.

Or maybe it was the church's name, the same as her husband's, that kept her away. A silly thing. But then, so many choices in life were based on emotions instead of logic.

Martina hefted the basket of damp clothes and ducked out of the low bathroom door, remembering how it had felt to sit and kneel beside her mother and sister, in Italy and then in America, watching the sun dance patterns on the stained glass.

You could eat bread and wine anywhere and know God was there, but the Eucharist was different. There was something holy and reassuring about joining with others in prayer, spoken in the same reverent tones learned from childhood.

Yes, she would do it. It was Wednesday now. Plenty of time to plan, to tell the children, to iron her best dress.

After hanging the clothes on a line she'd rigged up outside the trailer, Martina made her way to the front office, where a bank of boxes marked with unit numbers served as mailboxes.

She smiled, pulling out a letter in Mamma's distinctive hand. But when she opened it back at the trailer, after setting a pot of sauce to simmer in the narrow kitchen, she frowned. Shorter than normal, just a page. Mamma's letters were always in Italian—she had long ago declared that whoever had created English spellings must have been drunk—and always long, with weeks of news added one paragraph at a time.

This one began not with hovering questions about their health and the children's grades at school but with a single line, set off by itself.

Your husband came by yesterday.

Martina stared at the letter, reading the line a second time. That couldn't be. He was in the navy.

Then again, he might have been granted leave again. And her mother's apartment was the first place he'd look.

But why? His parting tirade had made it clear he wanted nothing to do with them, especially the children. That's why she'd used her maiden name for her new job and encouraged the children to do the same.

She read on. Mamma had demanded to know what he wanted, and Patrick worked his usual charm, saying he only wanted to check on his family.

He wasn't wearing a navy uniform, but his suit was new and his shoes shined. Not that that's a compliment. L'abito non fa il monaco.

Roughly, "the robes don't make the monk," a favorite saying of her mother's, who had taught Martina not to judge a book by its cover.

If only she'd remembered that when it came to handsome suitors.

She read on. Martina could almost hear her mother's stern voice, see the fierce nods that would punctuate each word. Her mother hadn't told Patrick much, vaguely hinting that Martina had found a new job and specifically stating that they didn't want to see him again. To her surprise, he'd apologized for bothering her and left.

Daughter, be careful. There was no trouble in what that man said or in how he acted. But it worries me still. I think he spoke to some of the neighbors before coming to me, and who knows what they might have told him.

In the North End of Boston, the boundaries of family business could be broad, and when Patrick was in one of his hat-tipping and dimpling moods, no Italian mamma with a heart beneath her well-worn apron would think ill of him.

Unless they knew him, of course. *The robes don't make the monk, indeed.* Or as Hamlet said, *"One may smile, and smile, and be a villain."*

She rubbed her temples, feeling them swell with a familiar pressure.

If Patrick knew she was here, he'd look for her at the churches near Bristol. That's how he'd found her before, when she'd moved in with her mother and he'd gotten leave after boot camp. She could almost picture him, slouching in the back of the small Catholic church, where he'd be sure to see her before she could see him.

He hadn't hurt or threatened her. He never did. But that smirking way he spoke to her, the way he begged for money and somehow made her feel it was her fault he was hard up in the first place, the unkept promises he made . . . all of it took a toll.

No, she wouldn't be going to Mass. Not this week.

A bubbling sound alerted her to the red sauce spilling out from under the lid in a violent burst, spattering the stovetop and the wall behind.

She nearly burnt her hand slamming the pot on an unused burner, then futilely tried to scrape what she could into a bowl until she reached the tar-like burnt crust on the bottom. There would be enough for the children, at least. She could eat later.

The dishcloth she applied to wipe away the stains gave her purpose, something to think about and do with her hands. She could repeat this during her shift. She could block out the news. Focus on Rosa's art project, write a grocery list, plan what to say at the book club.

Think of Ophelia, driven to drown herself over the hurtful tirades and actions of a rejected lover.

No, do not think of that.

Martina was still cleaning when the children came home from school. Rosa immediately flopped on the divan, taking out the book with gorgeous painted pictures that the kind librarian had loaned her, escaping into the world of fairies, talking animals, and dancing princesses. A place where evil was easy to identify . . . though often close to home.

Gio nodded at the discarded letter, abandoned in her hurry to salvage dinner. Sauce specked the envelope like drops of blood. "Is that from Da?"

Martina snatched the letter, with its incriminating first line, and tucked it into her pocket, displaying only the envelope. "No, son. It's from your *nonna*."

"Oh." His face, though it was lengthening and losing its childlike chubbiness, still showed the sadness of a boy whose father so often disappointed him. "I bet he's so tired from training he doesn't have time to write."

Martina didn't answer. The last she had told them—the last she'd heard from Patrick—was that their father had gone to a center in Illinois for specialized radio training before deploying. Though he clearly was not there now.

"Did you know that the bullets they use in battleship guns weigh over a ton?"

She bit her lip. "I did not."

You should tell him the truth, part of her admonished. *That his da can't write because you didn't tell him where you were moving.*

No—the separation of his parents was a burden he didn't need to carry.

"I read about it at school." Gio tossed his schoolbooks on the table, making no move to open them. "Last week, everyone with a family member in the service got to wear a red star sticker on their shirt."

Wasn't that what all of them wanted, deep down? To be noticed and praised?

She wouldn't take that from him. Not yet.

"I'm sure your da would be very proud of you." Martina reached out to tousle his curls, then stopped, remembering he'd asked her not to do that anymore. "Better start your homework."

Only fifteen minutes until Ginny came to pick her up.

Another shift of packing sand into molds for hours, too much time to think, to worry, to try to pray and hear nothing but the silence of an offended and long-ignored God.

She forced her mind from the thought. She would focus on *Hamlet*. Think of something to say to impress the other women, something to help her fit in. Maybe she'd even gather up the courage to suggest that the book club read a romance next. The real world had far too many stories that ended in tragedy.

Notes from the Blackout Book Club—May 16, 1942

Taken by Ginny Atkins, Temporary Book Club Secretary (will work on a grander title—apparently Her Majesty is too much)

Members in attendance: Ginny (me!), Louise, Martina, Avis, Delphie, and Freddy

Book under discussion: <u>Hamlet</u> by Shakespeare (Does he have a first name? Or was it just plain Shakespeare? Like how Moses or Cleopatra only have one name?)

Not sure what all to write here, only that Avis said she was tired of never getting to talk because she was writing the whole time. I was the only one who volunteered, or I don't think she'd have given me the job. But I'll show her. These will be the best notes she's ever seen.

Started with a vote on whether Hamlet was crazy from the start, went crazy during the play, or was only pretending to be crazy. Most everyone said talking to a skull was a pretty good sign of madness to them.

Avis used that voice she does when she's trying to sound smart and talked about Important Themes, especially the danger of revenge. That set Louise off on a speech about leaving vengeance to the Almighty. At which point, I asked, "What if the Almighty is too busy, and you have to handle things yourself?" She then switched to a speech on Not Being Irreverent, whatever that means.

Delphie wanted to know what we thought of Ophelia dying, whether it was an accident or suicide. (Sounds like the play got more interesting as it went. Bodies stacked up, anyway.) Forgot I was supposed to keep writing and got up to get more cake during this part—not sure what all was said.

Afterward, Freddy told everyone else his thoughts on Why Shakespeare Ought to be Performed and Not Read. Then he opened to Act III, Scene IV, and took on Hamlet's role, just to prove his point. And you'll never guess who volunteered to read Gertrude: Louise!

They went back and forth for pages. Freddy was better than Louise, but really, I haven't ever heard so much emotion from that crusty old spinster before. Best of all, I got a bit part as Polonius at the end. Mostly I just had to eavesdrop and then get stabbed, but boy, I milked that death scene for all it was worth. Hollywood can come calling any day.

Much applause from the others. We all bowed. Gio even put down his boxing magazine to come over and watch, and we were all convinced of Freddy's point. He was very smug. I told him not to get a big head about it.

Afterward, Avis suggested our next book, something called How to Read a Book. Yes, really. I pointed out that it looked like we'd all pretty well mastered that skill, but everyone else said it was a grand idea. Honestly, who thinks of these things, much less throws money at them?

thirteen

GINNY
MAY 29

The man hanging around the corner of Bristol-Banks looked straight out of a gritty detective flick from late-night double features. Ginny had noticed him while heading to the parking lot to pick up her old beater.

He smoked a cigarette like the other men clustered nearer to the foundry door but didn't move to join them. Wore a nice dun-colored coat and a homburg . . . and stared out from under the brim at Martina, waiting on the sidewalk. His smile wasn't sinister so much as the kind a fellow makes after a mean joke.

Golly, did everyone in this town hate Italians? If you really wanted to stick to that line, you'd end up glowering at a third of Americans based on where they came from, not just the few who, like Martina, still looked and sounded too much like their homeland.

Wasn't fair, and Ginny almost marched over to that bigot and said so.

But whenever someone made an off-color joke or muttered a slur, Martina told her to let things be. She was probably right. Ginny's instinct to pick a fight came from having too many brothers.

Still, by the time she pulled the car up, she was glad to see the homburg man was gone.

Martina closed her eyes almost as soon as she collapsed in the passenger seat, making the dark circles above her cheekbones stand out even more.

"Say, did you see—" Ginny shut her mouth. What was she doing? Didn't Martina have enough to worry about?

Martina's eyes flew open. "What?"

"That they're having another drive next week," she finished, trying to sell it with her tone. "Always pushing us to set aside more of our paycheck for war bonds. As if we earn enough for that."

Actually, Ginny had never had more money to her name than she did after three months at the foundry. Before this, her work on the lobster boat had funneled right back into the family's bills. Now she could save it all up—one of the reasons she'd looked for a job a few hours from home, where Ma couldn't demand any of her paycheck.

Still, not a red cent was going toward checking boxes of the *Bond Goal Sheet* printed in the back of her employee handbook. The government had taken her island, and that was enough.

Behind her, instead of the usual empty streets with dimmed streetlights, another pair of headlights dogged her through town, attached to a dark coupe. Like Ginny, whoever it was hadn't bothered with the government-regulated flaps on his lights, and the sudden brightness made her squint. *He'd better turn off soon.*

But he didn't. Once, at the stoplight on Mayfair Street, Ginny glanced back. There wasn't enough light to be sure, but the driver looked to be the right size for the homburg man she'd seen outside the factory. When she started up again, the coupe didn't turn aside, not even when they left Bristol for the rutted poor-excuse-for-a-road that trailed off to Derby.

Calm down. Might be a local. Ginny had never seen him, though, and she mixed often enough at community events for the free food that she'd shaken hands with half the small town.

Could be everything was on the level. But the way he'd smiled . . .

"Trust your gut, Ginny," her brother Lewis had told her at a dance one time, when she'd motioned him over to steal her away from a stranger getting too handsy. *"You've got a good head on those shoulders."*

When Ginny glanced over, Martina was watching her, and Ginny remembered it had been a while since she'd said anything. "How far've you gotten in that book about reading books?"

It was the right choice of topic. Martina perked up, chattering about reading as discovery and how the author compared readers and authors to baseball players. Ginny strung things along with a "You think so?" and "How about that" every now and then, but mostly kept one eye fixed on those headlights that turned with them down the country roads. Yes, he was following them. She was sure of it now.

Creep. Ginny clenched the steering wheel and thought about her options. Mostly, she wanted to pull over, get out her tire iron, and yell at the guy. His type were always cowards, ready to split at the first sign of trouble. But that was probably illegal, and she was determined to keep her nose as clean as Ivory soap. Hard to save up money while sitting in jail.

We'll just ignore him, then. Show him we aren't afraid.

But she was taking Martina home. To the kids. She thought about little Rosa, who probably still slept with a doll, maybe even believed in those fairies she read about in books.

Across from her, Martina's voice had slowed, her eyes drifted shut. *Not for long.*

"Hang on, Marti."

And with that, Ginny floored it, taking a hard right where she should have gone left.

How fast could this little car go without the rusted bumper falling off? She accelerated even more, feeling the tires pull against the slightly muddy road.

Beside her, Martina shouted something in Italian—Ginny hadn't known Martina could even get her voice that loud—and gripped the side of the car.

Eyes on the road. And sometimes in the rearview mirror. There was still a distant gleam of headlights, but she had put some distance between them. Confused him too, she'd bet.

A few hairpin turns, then she goosed the engine down a straightaway with a stomp to the pedal, squinting in the dark for . . .

Yes, that would work.

With one more glance in the rearview mirror—no headlights—Ginny turned down a dirt path, throwing the old Ford into park beside a decrepit old barn and shutting off the lights.

"That was fun, don't you think?" she asked cheerfully, turning away from the road to see Martina with a hand clutched to her chest.

"No" was all her friend could get out.

Just went to show you couldn't please everybody. She'd thought it was better than a Coney Island ticket. Who'd have thought her little Ford could handle like a real racer?

"What," Martina managed, "were you *doing*?"

Seeing as she didn't want to worry Martina, Ginny had already decided not to mention the tail, but she hadn't thought of an explanation to replace it. "Just read a novel where the hero was a racer in the Monaco Grand Prix. It all sounded so thrilling that I thought I'd try it." Maybe a touch too simple, but it might pass.

Sure enough, Martina rubbed her temples, suddenly looking a decade older. "Next time, test stunts when I am not in your car, please." She shuddered. "And not around Gio either."

Martina didn't even notice that once Ginny started up the car again, she kept glancing in the rearview mirror. No sign of Homburg Man in the dark coupe.

Ginny smiled smugly to herself. Good. And as long as Martina never guessed what had nearly happened tonight, she'd have nothing to worry about.

* * *

The next day, Martina and the kids didn't seem the least bit bothered by anything or anyone. Gio went on about some fellow called the Brown Bomber—a boxer, it turned out, not a plane—while Rosa read quietly beside him in the backseat. By the time Ginny dropped them off and swung around to park against the curb, she was satisfied that the mysterious Homburg Man had left them alone.

She tucked the book about books under her arm, nodding at the people she passed. There was Mr. Hostetler, from the fish fry, and Lucille Dougherty, the grocer's wife who gave away her past-selling produce for free on Sunday afternoons. All of them enjoying a perfect May Saturday.

None of them headed inside the library. Ginny made a note to talk to Avis about recruitment skills. First step: you had to actually talk to folks and ask them to come. She was social enough, but when it came to asking a favor or making a pitch, she blushed and stammered with "If it's no trouble" and "Perhaps you might consider." That weakened the sell.

One person, at least, had arrived as early as Ginny: Louise Cavendish herself, stepping out of her tan roadster in a trim jacket and skirt like a princess to a ball.

Freddy, wearing his military uniform today, was helping Delphie out of the passenger seat and getting a swat and a "*Ça suffit!* I'm not so old I can't step onto a curb" for his trouble. Ginny waved at the lot of them.

Delphie glared—not at her, really, just at the day in general—so Ginny didn't take it personally. Louise nodded regally and without much enthusiasm as she mounted the steps to the library. The two of them deserved each other.

Freddy, though, waved back and waited for her to catch up.

"Hullo there, Ginny! You're bright and early. Trying to cram in some reading before we start?"

"No need. I did an inspectional reading of the whole thing," she felt the need to inform him, proud of her use of the book's own term for plain old skimming. "Nice of Mortimer to put that little loophole in. Probably the most useful part of the book."

Freddy held up his copy, a few torn bits of paper poking out to mark pages. "What'd you think of this one?"

She imitated the woman on the foundry's "Silence Means Security" poster with a finger over her lips. "You won't get a thing out of me until the meeting starts. Can't risk you stealing my brilliant thoughts."

"I suppose that's fair." But instead his eyes wandered over her shoulder to her car, parked just past them.

Ginny found heat creeping up her neck like an itch as she noticed the chipped paint and rust spots of the old beater she'd haggled for to get her to Derby. And what if he noticed the mile-wide dent she'd discovered this morning from a flying rock during her sudden turns?

But he wasn't looking at the damage from last night's chase, just at her headlights. "You're out driving after dark, right?"

"Sure. Swing shift lets out at midnight."

"You really ought to put on some of those dimming blinders. Blackout regulations and all that."

He didn't say it like a member of one of the badge-wearing civilian meddlers writing her a citation, but Ginny couldn't keep from rolling her eyes. "Freddy, if there are any Nazis bobbing around out there, they'll see a fisherman chomping a cigar before my two tiny specks of light a mile inland. Blackout regulations are for the department stores and movie palaces near Portland and Boston."

"Everyone thinks the rules apply to someone else. But you're not the one who's had to go out in a plane to guard ships crossing the ocean from U-boats." He said it kindly but without a trace of his usual joking manner. "The more we help, the safer they'll be."

What could she say to that? "Gosh, I didn't think . . . can you really see so much?"

He nodded. "Two weeks after Pearl Harbor, I flew from Virginia to New York. It was lit up like a Christmas tree. Boats in the harbor silhouetted clear as if we'd lit a signal flare to tell the Nazis 'Aim here.'"

"Well, you've got me there." Made a girl feel like she was signing some GI's death warrant just by motoring around. "I'll stop by the hardware store and try to talk like I know what I'm about."

"Want me to tag along? I put the dimmers on Miss Cavendish's roadster just yesterday." He smiled ruefully. "Not that I'm allowed to drive it. Funny, when you think about it. I have nearly a decade's worth of experience flying planes, and now the fastest I can go by myself is on foot."

Ginny had never been much for math, but even she could figure something was wrong. "Say, that can't be right. That would make you nearly thirty." Not that that was ancient or anything, but still, with that fresh face of his, she'd placed Freddy at least five or six years younger.

But Freddy shook his head. "Guilty as charged, I'm afraid."

She feigned shock. "All right, mister, I'm going to need to see some ID." She held out a flat palm, her other hand on her hip.

He shook his head, taking a step back. "Sorry. Don't carry my driver's license around anymore. You'll just have to take my word for it."

That made sense. Still . . . did Freddy's expression tighten as his hand went to the wallet in his pocket? Just like he'd quickly tucked his dog tags away when she'd mentioned them.

You're imagining things, Ginny.

He shifted, nodding back at her Ford. "Anyway, about that hardware store . . ."

"Sure, I could use the help." Ginny had learned to bring Lew or another brother along for trips like this. Some fellows, if they got a sense a woman didn't know much, tried to take advantage.

"Excellent." The smile was back as they took the steps up to the library, and he held the door open for her. "Maybe we could stop by the lunch counter for a milkshake afterward?"

She stopped on the threshold. There it was. A line in the sand that Ginny was sure, even with her limited know-how about the finer points of real-life romance, she couldn't cross. Too much like a date. Though she and Freddy had joked around after the last book club, she just hadn't found a way to work Mack into the conversation before this.

"I'd like to, Freddy, but I've got a . . ." How to put it? "Well, there's a fellow sweet on me over in the Pacific who might not think much of that."

"Ah. Say no more," he said, waving her awkward explanation away with a smile. "I completely understand. We'll stick to the neutral territory of the hardware store. How could your soldier object?"

She allowed that he couldn't, and they entered the library together.

Freddy was a good sport about it, anyway. Almost too good.

Well, what had she been expecting? That he'd start acting jealous, or at least look disappointed, like he was in one of those novels Avis hid in the storage room? Silly, especially when she had Mack writing "Thinking of you makes the long days better" and "Yours with affection" and all that.

Still, she couldn't help thinking, watching Freddy stand next to Louise and chat as easily with the stuck-up heiress as he had with Ginny outside, a fellow like that, especially with most young men off to war, was going to make some girl pretty happy.

But it wouldn't be her.

From Anthony to Avis

May 8, 1942

Dear Sis,

Jotting you a foxhole postcard. That's not actual army slang—I just made it up because I see so many of my fellows writing whole books to their family and sweethearts, and I feel desperately inadequate. They must be making this rotten sit-about we're stuck in right now into the Iliad, *for all the pages they pen. Or maybe they're relating anecdotes about the way I shake the roof snoring, haha.*

You asked for novel recommendations. A book club, hmm? I should've thought of that ages ago. Probably, I should have a list ready to go—though not the stuffy sort like 100 Classics to Read Before You Die. *(Warning: Chaucer may actually cause you to die.) But other things are on my mind these days.*

Which leads to my main suggestion: no war novels. I stuffed myself with For Whom the Bell Tolls, All Quiet on the Western Front, The Red Badge of Courage, *and all those before we shipped out. Now I wouldn't come close to them. When I get back, I'll probably read nothing but satire and romances and watch nothing with gunfire except comically bad Westerns for at least a decade. We all need an escape. So read something happy for me. And be sure to tell me all about it.*

Not to worry, sis. I leave out some details in letters to Mom and Dad, but things aren't as bad as I'm making them sound. For one, my buddy Alvin Hagen—nicknamed Daisy, don't ask why—went and found a mutt with no home, and our unit's adopted him. I liked him a lot more before he piddled in my boots, but he's a mood-lifter for sure.

Time to sign off before this postcard resembles a real letter. Wouldn't want to set up false expectations.

Anthony

P.S. Came back after mess because I remembered—try anything by P. G. Wodehouse. Miss C got me hooked on him. You'd never guess it, but she loves his books.

Notes from the Blackout Book Club—May 30, 1942

Taken by Avis Montgomery, Head Librarian and Book Club Secretary

Members in attendance: the Regulars (no need to use names anymore)

Book under discussion: How to Read a Book by Mortimer Adler

Decided not to let Ginny take notes again after reading her last attempt. Will have to keep these notes safely away from Miss Cavendish.

    Discussion opened with Adler's four levels of reading, with most time spent on the last one: syntopical reading. (Ginny: "Why can't he just say comparative reading and be done with it? Who's he trying to impress?" Freddy: "Most of his readers, probably." Ginny: "Not me. Once you cut out all the five-dollar words, you've just got a book telling you to read more carefully.")

    Despite that, the consensus was that most of us naturally make connections between the books we read. Though I'm not sure if I ever have. Something to think about. Martina said that sometimes she thinks about which characters from one book might be friends with another. This prompted a sidetrack in which the gathered company speculated on what would have happened if Oliver Twist and Huckleberry Finn had joined forces, how Odysseus would have fared if he'd come home to Jane Eyre instead of Penelope, and whether Sherlock Holmes would have been able to defeat Count Dracula.

    I had no idea who most of those people were. Maybe I

ought to read outside of our selections—they all sounded quite interesting.

We turned then to Adler's thoughts on imaginative works. An all-out war ensued about the author's assertion that they must be read as quickly as possible to understand the unity of the story, rather than lingering. Freddy insisted that's how he always reads novels, and Delphie countered that he also chews with his mouth open, but that doesn't mean everyone else ought to. Martina, blessedly, intervened with her usual common sense, saying the method was less important than the point that we need to step into the story and try to understand the characters and their world.

That was my favorite part of the book, actually. Put in straightforward terms—humans need stories because they appeal to our unconscious needs for love, justice, discovery, etc.—I could finally see what Anthony must have meant all along.

Goodness, I am starting to soften up to this whole reading books business. Best not to let Anthony know, or he'll brag about being right.

Assorted smaller comments filled the rest of the time. (Freddy smug that Adler agreed that plays need to be performed, not read; Miss Cavendish in support of the idea that no one's autobiography could be considered fully true and unbiased; Ginny wanting to know if we thought Adler had read all the books recommended in the appendix.)

Conversation continued after the allotted hour, but I was drawn away by Gio, who wanted to check out several books on gardening. One suspects his admiration for a certain army air force pilot might play into this sudden horticultural interest. It's sweet, really, the way Freddy answers the boy's barrage of questions without hesitation.

Earlier, I had pulled a few Wodehouse books off the shelf for consideration following Anthony's suggestion, but he must've been mistaken about Miss Cavendish's liking them. They're far too funny for a tightwad spinster who has forgotten how to smile. Fairly sure he got the author mixed up with F. C. Woodhouse one shelf down, a historian with riveting titles like <u>Monasticism, Ancient and Modern: Its Principles, Origin, Development, Triumphs, Decadence, and Suppression</u>.

Still, it was worth a try. I didn't see any recognition on Miss Cavendish's face when I brought out <u>The Code of the Woosters</u>, but she didn't object, so Wodehouse it is.

Will have to write Anthony after the next meeting. I'm two chapters in already. He was right. It was good to laugh, for once.

fourteen

AVIS
JUNE 5

Low-slung pumps were not made for digging through sand. Neither was the stiff skirt of Avis's Victory suit appropriate for the job at hand.

For the tenth time this morning, she wished the Office of Civilian Defense would mind its own business. Or at least that Miss Cavendish would get someone else—Freddy, perhaps, or her handyman, Hamish—to do the grunt work. But no, as soon as the office determined homes and businesses should keep buckets of sand in case of bomb-related fires, Louise had added it to Avis's already-long task list.

Even with the breeze off the ocean, sweat trickled down the small of her back, sticking her blouse to her skin. The first of the summer people had started to rent out cottages near the shoreline, but they weren't yet crowding the slope of sand, glinting wet in the sun overhead. The beach was nearly deserted, with the only color and sound coming from fishermen visible down by the piers, and the bold pops of blue of the lupines growing in the tangled greenery among the rocks.

Beside her, Rosa Bianchini tossed pebbles at seagulls that bobbed too close, scattering them in a noisy retreat. Gio, the more likely of her two assistants to provide actual help, carried a shovel slung like a rifle over his shoulder, a serious expression on his face.

Avis had a brief flashback to the only time her stern father talked about the Great War, on Armistice Day. *"Digging,"* he'd said, scoffing at the speaker on the platform speaking of heroic acts and patriotism. *"Digging and dying and mud. That's what the 'noble conflict' was all about."*

Avis shuddered, brushing the memory away. *We're not digging a trench. We're just taking safety precautions we'll likely never need.*

"All right," she said, stopping where the pebbles turned to sand and trying to sound cheerful—children liked cheerful people, didn't they? For all she wanted to be a mother, she knew very little about actual children. "We can stop here. All four of these buckets need to be filled to the brim."

Gio unloaded the milk pails, pressing them into the sand, and began digging without question, good soldier that he was.

"Won't that make the wagon very heavy?" Rosa asked, regarding her with dark, serious eyes.

"Yes, it will. But we're tough," Avis said, making a pose like a circus strongman and getting a giggle out of the girl. "We can do it."

Now that school was out for the summer, Martina's two children hung about the library most afternoons while their mother was at work, so Avis didn't feel guilty enlisting their help.

Gio insisted on using the shovel, so Avis settled for her garden trowel, while Rosa scooped the occasional handful of sand and got distracted by any pretty rocks or shells that shifted loose.

"What's this for, anyway?" Gio asked when they'd filled two of the milk pails.

Avis frowned, weighing how much information to share. "The government requested every home and business keep several pounds of sand on hand. That way, if there's a—" She glanced at Rosa, not wanting to use the words *incendiary bomb.*

Goodness, the child's father was in the navy. She probably heard enough grim talk. "If something starts a fire, the sand can be tossed on it to put it out."

"Because you wouldn't want to spray water on the books," Rosa said, nodding, as if it suddenly made all the sense in the world.

More accurately, because the authorities worried that the water mains might be destroyed in a mass bombing, as had the utilities in Coventry, England, two years before.

Avis patted the girl's shoulder. "That's right, dear. We must keep our friends the books safe."

From the glance Gio sent her, maybe that was a bit too sing-song, but he leveled off the last milk pail with his shovel, clean and flat.

Instead of taking up the handle of the wagon, Rosa dropped to her knees, dirtying the hem of her hand-sewn dress dotted with flowers. "Can we make a castle now?"

Avis paused with a no on her lips, picturing her typewriter and stack of cards, ready to induct new volumes into the Dewey decimal system, sitting on her desk past a locked entrance with a patently false *Out for Lunch* sign. There was so much work to be done.

Then again, the task had gone twice as fast with the children's help as it would have on her own.

"Why not?" she said, and the smile that blossomed on Rosa's face made her sure she'd chosen correctly. She knelt to tug off her pumps. If Miss Cavendish forced her to close the library early and haul sand like a common laborer, she might as well have a little fun.

Pleading the fact that he was "too old for stuff like that," Gio perched on a nearby boulder and reached into his bag for . . . was that a book? She must have been staring because Gio said, "Mr. Freddy said it was his favorite."

The glaring sun made it difficult to read most of the title, save for one unusual name: *Doctor Dolittle*. It seemed he'd lost interest in gardening books already, which wasn't surprising. While practical, they'd all seemed about as exciting as a plate of unsalted turnip mash.

After getting instructions from Rosa about the proper way to build a castle—a mix of wet and dry sand, careful not to make the tower too high, poke the windows in last—Avis was sent on a quest to secure shells to decorate the exterior.

She turned toward the sea, letting the breeze blow her hair back, and breathed deeply. When was the last time she'd felt sand between her toes? Maybe that night on Old Orchard Beach when she and Russell had run out of money for the fancy ballrooms and restaurants and had watched the sunset together, eating hot dogs and drinking a Dr Pepper rammed with two straws. There was something freeing about the feeling, even in the jolt of cold that ran up her spine when the sea spray broke against her ankles.

Avis reached for a discarded mussel shell, then frowned. Something bobbed on the surface of the water, just out of reach. She fished out the burnt-orange rag with a piece of driftwood and examined it more closely. The material felt stiff, like canvas, with a hole in the middle and a thick strap around the back.

This was no discarded tarp. This was a life jacket. Studded with a strange metal insert and rubber tube, but easily recognizable, all the same.

What Avis didn't recognize was the word written in white letters on the device's front: *Tauchretter*.

But she knew it was in German.

The sound of Rosa laughing in the distance, the swooping seagulls, even the thrum of the waves all faded as Avis stared at the sodden flotation device in her hands.

A Nazi soldier had worn this. Whether it was part of the flotsam of a sunken U-boat or had been torn forcibly away from a corpse, she couldn't say. But in the corner was a dark reddish stain.

Blood.

Astonishing how quickly a stomach could lurch, not at all like the tides or the Dewey decimal system or any of the other steady, predictable elements of Avis's life. Clutching her middle, she clenched herself against nausea, still clinging to the life vest like she was the one drowning.

One good toss would send it back into the ocean, like the piece of refuse that it was.

No. Surely someone official would want to know. It was enemy contraband, after all.

She hid the life jacket behind her and hurried back to the wagon. "Gio? Will you and Rosa bring these buckets back to the library? I have . . . an errand to run."

Thank goodness their home was only a few blocks from the library. Avis couldn't tell the time, but the neighborhood was full of cars parked in driveways, indicating it was nearer the dinner hour than she'd like. It would be better if Russell didn't learn about her discovery. He'd been doing so much better these past few weeks, anticipating a promotion at work, showing interest in his usual activities. Time, hard work, and a studious avoidance of anything related to the war had worked wonders, just as she'd hoped.

Still, she'd been unable to think of anything else to do with the dreadful thing. If she could just stash it away until she had time to think, to call someone official who would know better, it would be all right. Maybe, if she was lucky, Russell would still be at work or out with Herb again.

But the moment she opened the front door, careful to let the screen door latch soundlessly behind her—there was Russell in the living room, newspaper in hand, smile on his face. "Now who's the late one?" he teased.

No sense in trying to hide it. Russell wouldn't be so easily thrown off as little Rosa, driven away from her sandcastle by a promise of ribbon candy later. "Hello, Russell."

"What's that you've got . . . ?" His voice trailed off, and the paper dropped to his knees as he saw the strange item in her hand.

"I found it down by the shore. It . . . it's probably nothing."

He was at her side in a moment, examining the life vest, holding it up to the light. "I've seen pictures of these. U-boat crews use them to get to the surface if they have to bail."

"Oh," she said, the word sounding small. She'd guessed that much, but hearing it said out loud, picturing the lurking submarine breaking apart and survivors fleeing . . . well, that was another matter. "What is this?" She pointed to the tube and metal insert poking out from the side of the life vest.

"Hose and mouthpiece." He ran his finger over an empty metal grommet. "Should be connected to an oxygen tank, but this one's been knocked off. Remember, these fellows start underwater—deep, deep underwater—and have to make it to the surface."

"Oh my," she said, feeling the pressure in her own head . . . or, more likely, the start of a terrible headache. *I shouldn't have asked. I should never ask.*

She gave him the details of exactly where she'd found it.

"We'll have to call the coast guard and report it."

How was she supposed to do that? *"Operator, please connect me with the coast guard? I'm holding a bloodied Nazi life jacket, so it's a matter of urgency."*

But Russell had already picked up the handset, spouting off his name and city—did everyone but her know what to do, or was it simply Russell's preoccupation with the military he was unable to join?

His description of the item and where Avis had found it was detailed but concise, his replies to questions from the other side calm.

She'd always admired that about him. No matter what, Russell was never ruffled, never afraid. Like a rock in a harbor, firm and true, even with winter storms swirling all around.

"They're sending someone to pick it up tomorrow," he said, replacing the handset.

"Pick it up?" She'd hoped they'd thank them for the report and tell them to burn it in the backyard. "Do they want to reuse the material?"

"Maybe. I know there's a division that saves anything Axis-made—wallets, watches, even chewing gum—to give to our spies." His hands pressed against the liner as if he were a spy himself, feeling for the outline of a concealed message. "Or maybe they want to study it."

She felt the need to scrub her hands raw, as though the German-made device had passed along some kind of contagion. "You were right. They're out there, Russ. So close to our shores that I can pick up their debris on the beach."

Russell didn't turn to her, just looked toward the ocean, shaking his head in disgust. "They're out there, and I'm in here."

At dinner, which consisted of pork chops far too dry because her mind had drifted during the frying, all the conversation came back to the Battle of the Atlantic and Nazi U-boat patterns and minefields in Casco Bay. Even when Avis tried to change the subject to the work promotion, Russell didn't linger long before steering the conversation back to the battle going on just past their shores.

This was what she'd dreaded. After all her effort to avoid the war, it had come directly into her living room, disturbing their marital peace.

And this time, she was the one who had dragged it there.

fifteen

LOUISE
JUNE 6

Perhaps they were only interested in gossip—the account of what Avis had found by the beach had already circulated around town—but Louise was still pleased with the turnout at the town meeting Mayor Hastings had called. He'd given a formality of an introduction—Louise knew for a fact that only the deputy mayor attended Civilian Defense meetings.

Which was why she now stood on the fourth step of the stairs to the library's balcony, assigned to the actual presentation because of her involvement with the Red Cross and wartime fundraisers. "It should be clear, from the discovery of a Nazi submarine close enough to Derby that its refuse washed up on our shore, that current blackout measures are ineffective. That is to say, they are not being observed."

She delivered a serious look to anyone who would meet her eyes. Reverend and Mrs. Whitson sitting up straight like they were in church. Elvira Buckwold, with a tilt to her chin that said *she* certainly wasn't one of the ones Louise was addressing. The town barber, the hardware store owner, schoolchildren who sometimes visited the library.

They were faces she'd seen many times before—one couldn't spend decades in a small community and not at least recognize most of its residents—but how many did she really know?

I'd know more if they didn't still think of me as one of the summer people.

It was nothing personal, she knew. Delphie was still considered an outsider, and her parents had immigrated to Maine in the 1850s and were buried in the town cemetery.

She blinked as someone in the audience coughed. How long had she paused, distracted? A glance at her notes told her where to pick up again. "Not only that, but last week, north of us, fellow citizens discovered the bodies of two American merchant mariners washed up on the shore. There are brave men dying out there. What's more, they're dying for the fun of it—for our fun, our insistence on flouting national curfews and restrictions so we can attend a bar or movie theater or take a pleasure drive."

Just as she'd planned, this made the listeners shift uncomfortably in their seats, looking down like chastened children. For a moment, Louise wondered if she was being too harsh.

Certainly not. This is a matter of life and death.

"I would urge each of you to attend more carefully to the Office of Civilian Defense regulations, copies of which will be distributed at the door." She indicated Ginny, who waved a fistful of flyers that she had cheerfully volunteered to peddle. "I will now open the floor for any questions or comments."

This unleashed the usual community babble at meetings of this sort:

"What about churches? Will they have to cover up their windows with those awful drapes? That seems like sacrilege."

"Come down to the hardware store for a ten-percent discount on headlight covers for blackout driving! This week only."

"Isn't the coast guard supposed to keep our shores safe from U-boats? Where were they when the tanker was sunk?"

"Won't there be an increase in crime with blackouts on and the streets darkened?"

Louise answered the questions as best she could—no, as

long as churches didn't keep lights on after dark, though she doubted God had much of a preference on window coverings; yes, they're doing the best they can, but there aren't enough patrol crafts; no, other communities had not experienced an increase in crime to her knowledge.

Her composure slipped only slightly when Avis tentatively raised a hand to be acknowledged. "If any of you are looking for activities to occupy yourself with shortened hours and travel restrictions, I'd invite you to join the Blackout Book Club. We meet here at the library every other Saturday to discuss a wide variety of important literature."

Louise frowned. It felt irresponsible, using a serious community meeting to promote a club whose next "important literature" was a work of nonsense British comedy. Not to mention the fact that she hadn't mentioned the temporary nature of the group.

Isn't that why you permitted the club in the first place? To keep people inside, just as you're now reminding them to do?

If she was honest . . . yes.

Then why did she feel so annoyed?

A few moments of reflection, and she had her answer. While people had stared blankly in response to her speech, they watched Avis with interest. She was one of them, a local girl made good, not to mention a model modern woman in loose pin curls and tailored Victory suit, her perfect red lipstick smiling warmly out at them all.

Never mind that. Louise had done her duty, giving this speech, handing out literature, saving lives.

So why did it never feel like enough?

After enduring the exuberant commendation of Mayor Hastings and a quiet handshake from Deputy Mayor Shinn, the Laurel to his Hardy, Louise collapsed into the armchair flanking the biography section. The chair, donated from her father's study, moaned a protest, as if it too had been exhausted by the evening's activities.

She had just closed her eyes for a brief respite when a jab at her temple made them fly open again in time to see a folded paper airplane ricochet to the ground at her feet.

She glanced up sharply. A flicker of movement disappearing behind shelves indicated the culprits were launching their offensive from above, in the children's section.

A brief prayer for patience and someone else to address the situation yielded no results, so Louise mounted the stairs herself. This was, after all, her library, and a meeting she had chaired. The least she could do was protect attendees from aerial assault.

A distinctly panicked "She's coming!" confirmed her instincts, but there was no other way down and very few places to hide.

It is a bit sparse, isn't it? The faded rug on the floor was the only seating, and while the shelves were well stocked, they lined plain beige walls. The gleaming oak balustrades and railing were the only decorative elements. Louise made a note to look into some improvements when the nursery school renovation began. One more thing to spend money on—but it would make the place more welcoming.

"I know you're here," she called. "You might as well come out."

The two Bianchini children, with Gio attempting to stuff two neatly folded models up his shirt, shuffled away from the last shelf and looked guiltily up at her.

"Well, what do you have to say for yourselves?"

"We're sorry," Rosa squeaked.

"We were bored," Gio explained at the same time, which was neither an apology nor a satisfactory explanation, not for a boy of twelve who ought to know better.

"Where is your mother?" she asked, making sure her voice was appropriately stern.

"I don't know."

She circled behind them, guiding them along like Jeeves when he couldn't suppress his herding instinct. "Let's find her then, shall we?"

Martina was more to blame than the children. Mischief and misbehavior were the near-inevitable products of childhood, but an adult ought to know better than to let them roam free and unsupervised, knowing the mischief they were capable of.

After a search of the main floor, they finally found her tucked in a chair in the farthest corner, leaning over *The Code of the Woosters*, eyebrows furrowed in concentration, the rest of the world clearly a distant annoyance.

Even when Louise cleared her throat, Martina didn't look up. It took her name, spoken loudly, to get the woman's attention, and even then, she left her finger on the page as if waiting to get back to it as soon as possible.

That changed after Louise explained the situation. To her credit, Martina immediately prompted an apology from her offspring, along with her own for leaving them to their own devices.

Still, she made no movement to hurry after them when, freed by Louise's acceptance, they scurried away. Instead, Louise caught the backward glance Martina gave to her book, abandoned on the chair, before refocusing. "Again, I'm so sorry—"

"As I said, I'm sure it won't happen again." But was she sure? With their father away and their mother distracted, it seemed unlikely.

A sudden impulse overtook her. "Would you come with me for a moment, Martina? I want to show you something."

Louise wove through the shelves—along the way, plucking a plane that had met its doom in a crash landing on the spines of the biography section—to a cabinet on the east wall, the one

Anthony had installed to be too high for any children to smudge with fingerprints, just as she'd requested. Never checked out, never touched—but, she noted with satisfaction, apparently frequently dusted. Avis had her strong points.

She unlocked the cabinet and stepped aside so Martina could see. "This is my father's collection of first editions. Their value and condition varies, but most are quite rare."

Martina took an uncertain step forward, eyes scanning the spines of the books inside. "I never knew these were here."

"I don't make much of them. Which is for the best, since I plan to auction them off to raise money for the nursery school."

Though she said it casually, this was a new decision, one made when the contractor had presented the final—and outrageous—costs for the construction to begin in September. Wartime supply inflation, he'd called it, rather than her own preferred verbiage: highway robbery. Something had to be done to raise the additional money.

Martina stared longingly at the books, her hands tucked behind her back as if she were afraid of spoiling the yellowed pages by proximity. "Aren't they special to you?"

"Because they belonged to my father?" She shook her head. "Every book in this library is his, in a way. That these are among a few he chose to set aside holds far less weight to me than their financial value."

"But . . . this is an original collection of William Wordsworth poetry. And a first edition *Tom Sawyer*."

There it was again. The same awe and reverence Louise had heard in her father's voice whenever he had spoken of his precious books . . . and never once employed when speaking of his children.

"Martina, I want to tell you something I've never told anyone before. It is quite possible for a parent to become too involved in books. To neglect his family, to defend his solitary hours with such ferocity that all other priorities become secondary at best.

I know this because my father—" she took a deep breath and pressed on—"was one such person."

Martina's eyes widened, clearly not anticipating such a speech. Neither had Louise, really.

"I say this so that you might take it under advisement yourself," she continued, trying to hide her discomfort, "with your own children."

Martina turned then, and Louise followed her gaze to Gio and Rosa. They were clustered around Frederick, who was ostensibly sweeping the floor but really twirling the broom like a parade baton. She had a fleeting thought that he was likely the one who had taught Gio how to fold the paper airplane.

"But still, your father must have loved you."

The gentle words offered an invitation to remember, and Louise tried. She could picture her father complimenting her brother's trumpet playing, his formal questions at the dinner table, the afternoon he'd taught them how to identify different types of flowers.

"Oh, I'm sure he did, in his way. He wasn't cruel or wasteful or lazy. But after Mother died . . . he simply wasn't suited for the task before him." She removed the books from the cabinet to count them for the letter to her New York antique contact. How much had Father originally spent on them? "I soon learned that it's possible to be a good person and a poor parent."

There. That wasn't so hard, once you framed it objectively and told it more as moral advice than your own past.

"That might be what you learned from your father," Martina said quietly, looking again to where her children played with Frederick. "But what I learned from my mother is that giving and receiving love is the greatest risk and the greatest joy. Sometimes at the same time."

"That is a matter of perspective. I do my best to minimize risks, wherever possible." She replaced each book one at a time on the cabinet's narrow shelf.

One of the titles caused Martina to let out a small gasp. "You have a first edition of *Pride and Prejudice*?"

Ah. She'd forgotten about that one. "Unfortunately, no. That's the only one of the lot *not* a first edition. I'd initially thought it was valuable because Father left it to me by name in his will. However, my assessor assured me it was from an early but broad printing, worth perhaps thirty dollars at most."

She shook her head, setting the book aside from the rest and locking the cabinet. "Really, I should donate it to the library's circulation. Either Father was misled about its value or, more likely, he was merely trying to trick me into reading it."

"You've never read Jane Austen?" Martina's expression seemed more fitting for some declaration of treason than a simple statement of preference.

"Certainly not. And I don't plan to. Romance is a foolish delusion," Louise said firmly, ignoring the soft but insistent thought that lingered long after she left the library. *You didn't always feel that way.*

AUGUST 1913

She hadn't asked him to do it. Oliver had volunteered, pressing a kiss to her brow. "Never fear, my sweet flower. We'll work it out, man to man. I'll ask your father for your hand, and with luck on our side, he'll give me his blessing."

For once, Oliver's devil-may-care attitude was more irritating than endearing. As if it could possibly be so simple: Father allowing his only daughter, the one he'd tasked Aunt Eleanor for years now with betrothing to a suitable gentleman, to wed his manservant, the son of a local barkeep. She couldn't imagine it.

Which was why Louise was now stepping carefully over the creaky hallway boards, heeled leather boots clutched in her hands. She should go back to her room, not lurk here outside

Father's study where the maid or, God forbid, Delphine might catch her eavesdropping.

Yet how could she, with her fate being decided just past those thick oak doors?

Even when she pressed her ear to the crack, the voices were mostly inaudible, until she heard Father exclaim, "What!" sharp and angry.

She squeezed her eyes shut until she heard a fragment of Oliver's voice. "Please, sir . . ."

"What do you want? Money?"

When Oliver spoke again, his voice had lost some of its brash confidence. ". . . difficult . . . never intended . . . I promise you . . ."

Then nothing audible for some time, even when Louise edged closer. Whether Oliver or Father was speaking in tones too low to hear, or they had reached a point of decision, Louise couldn't say.

She held her breath, started to pray . . . and remembered that God would surely not listen to her, not anymore.

"Now leave us!" That phrase came through clearly, and Louise sprang away from the door and down the stairs in stocking feet before either could spot her, hearing the study door fling open just behind her.

Oliver strode down the stairs into the main hall seconds later, face impassive, and drew up short when he saw her. After a quick look around, she rushed to his side. "What's wrong? Did he—?"

"Your father was madder than even you thought." Tension kept his jaw tight as he looked over her shoulder to the study upstairs. "Fired me and threatened to report me to the authorities."

No. He couldn't—he wouldn't. She hadn't heard those words through the door, but then, she hadn't heard much.

She sank to the floor, replacing her boots and struggling

to tie the laces, if only to give her hands something to do. "I don't understand. You . . . you said you could persuade him of anything, that he'd be sure to give his blessing to our marriage."

This time, when she met the eyes that had winked at her, stared longingly into her own, she saw an unfamiliar expression there: fear. "I tried. But it wasn't meant to be."

Louise stood, pressing a hand to the buttons of her tightly-fitted jacket, trying to breathe deeply through a wave of dizziness. Then, hearing a door close somewhere in Windward Hall, she glanced to the upstairs hall, the door to the kitchens, the entryway just behind them. There were other questions she wanted to ask Oliver, details about what, exactly, he'd told Father, but not here, where anyone might be listening.

Without thinking, she reached for the locket around her neck, the one with the sketch of Oliver she'd made last month tucked inside. No, she would not give up so easily.

There was only one thing to do now, what she ought to have had the courage to do from the first. "I'll speak to him myself, then."

His voice followed after her. "You'll only make things worse. Louise . . ."

But she was already three steps into her charge toward the stairs, then down the hall and through the doors without knocking—breaking the most sacred rule of the Cavendish household by invading the chamber where Father was not to be disturbed.

He looked up from a paper he was scribbling on, distant blue eyes focusing to a startled expression, then one of resignation. As if he'd expected her arrival—or dreaded it.

"Father," she said, hands clenched in fists, "what is the meaning of this?"

"I believe I made my meaning perfectly clear." He gestured to the door, and she yanked it closed. "Please keep your voice down, Louise. I know you're upset, but I have a terrible headache."

Oh, he was about to have worse than that. For twenty-four years, she had been the model child, the one with perfect marks in school, irreproachable manners, and a church attendance that would rival that of any saint—not that Father had noticed any of it.

But finally, it was time for a tantrum, one that he'd long had coming. Best to be clear from the very start. "Oliver and I *will* be married, Father, with or without your approval."

Of all things, Father sighed. As if this were merely a girlish fancy, soon to be set aside, but troubling his peaceful summer in the meantime. "You won't believe me, I'm sure, but here is the truth of it, Louise. I would be concerned, of course, if you'd determined to marry outside of your social circle. But that is not why I refused to give Mr. Goodwin permission to marry you."

"Then why?" she asked, even while knowing that no answer he could give would be enough.

But the words that came from his mouth were gentler than she'd expected—and harsher—all at once. "He does not truly love you, Louise. Of that, I am quite sure."

"H-how would you know?" If he dared say something about the novels he read, as if that made him an expert on the lives of the real people around him whom he largely ignored . . .

Father began to speak, then closed his mouth. When he continued, his voice was like a man speaking to a startled mare, soothing to avoid being trampled. "You'll simply have to trust me. I will not let you ruin your life, child."

Perhaps he's right. The thought came without warning, voiced by that terrible, irrepressible instinct for practicality. After all, Oliver was practically penniless. Without Father's support, how would they get by?

No, they would manage somehow.

"*Now* you begin caring about my life and choices?" she fired back, crossing her arms protectively around herself. "After all these years? You might not have noticed, but I'm not a child, Father. Not anymore."

He'd lost those years, after her mother had died a decade ago, when he'd sent her and her brother Matthew off to boarding school. Burying his grief in a garden of Mother's favorite flowers, burying his face in his precious books, rarely raising it to look them in the eye, even on visits home.

To his credit, Father had the grace to look ashamed, but only briefly. "The fact remains that, though you are a grown woman, you are my daughter. And as such, I am responsible to protect you."

"From the man who adores me?"

"As I said, I doubt that. At least, he certainly seemed eager enough to take the generous severance package I offered him after refusing him your hand in marriage."

This paused the sharp reply that she had already begun to prepare. "I . . ."

Oliver had accepted money from her father to leave? It wasn't possible. He'd promised.

Even as she thought it, she remembered the defeated look in Oliver's eyes. *"It wasn't meant to be."*

"In fact," Father went on, "I wouldn't be surprised if he's already packed his trunk to depart on the next train."

Only effort and the knowledge the staff might overhear kept Louise's voice down. "You threatened him, then bribed him to abandon me?"

"I gave him compensation for dismissal from my staff," Father corrected. "He'll find another position—without a letter of recommendation from me, mind—and if, once his finances are stable, he still wishes to marry you, perhaps I'll reconsider."

Never had a hesitant *perhaps* sounded so promising, carrying more hope than he'd given her before. Louise clung to it for a moment before seeing a familiar hardness in her father's eyes.

He doesn't believe Oliver will return.

The fleeting thought was confirmed when he added, as calmly as if they were discussing the weather, "And if he does not, I will see to your welfare. As I always have."

She bit back the obvious retort that, after Mother's death, it was his checks that saw after her care, education, and upbringing, not he himself. Money and a few scattered moments around the dinner table, usually a one-sided discussion of a novel she had no desire to read or the latest blooms in a garden that only held her interest because of Oliver.

Oliver, who admired her mind and asked her opinions on current events. Oliver, who stroked her hair and told her she was beautiful. Oliver, whom Father had shouted at and sent away, like he'd been a common thief. All supposedly out of concern for her welfare.

But she could speak none of that to this man who barely knew her. Instead, she took her rage and put it into simpler words, spoken in defiance of the heartlessly calm man before her and to tamp down the flicker of worry that had ignited inside her. "He *will* come for me. You'll see."

But she found, after searching Windward Hall, the carriage house, even the garden shed, that Father was right about at least one thing: Oliver was already gone.

sixteen

MARTINA
JUNE 9

Gio's radio fed the bold, clear sounds of Glenn Miller and his orchestra into the trailer, only the slight scratch of static reminding Martina there was no big band set up in the bedroom. The bursts of brass put a smile on her face as afternoon sunshine poured through freshly washed windows. Alone, she even had the luxury of space to dance a step or two. The broom she held was the ideal partner: tall, quiet, and practical.

She should feel bad for leaving her children at the library, but among a hundred other guilts about her failure as a mother, poking like misplaced safety pins at every turn, what was one more? And it gave her time to clean the trailer and make a dinner for them to eat while she was away into the night.

Besides, it had been Gio's idea. "Rosa likes it there," he'd said casually, but she'd noticed him sneaking a book out of his knapsack a time or two as well.

She was sure it was that kind young man from book club, Mr. Keats, who had inspired it. The moment he'd stepped into the club wearing his military uniform, Gio had peppered him with questions, to her embarrassment, but he'd answered them without a trace of annoyance.

If only you'd married someone like him, a nagging voice

134

whispered, *instead of falling for the first charmer who popped into the bakery and said he loved you.*

Sta' zitto! There was no sense in thoughts like that. *What's done is done.*

She was on her knees, scraping the last caked-on clump of mud from under the table, when a knock, loud and firm, sounded on the door.

Not Ginny coming to pick her up; it was an hour too early. Not a child telling her Gio was fighting; he was at the library. Not a neighbor asking to borrow a cup of sugar; no one did such things at the trailer camp. She had no family nearby, no friends, no one who would come to call.

Unless . . .

Martina snapped off the radio, muttering a prayer that she wasn't sure she'd need. She didn't believe in superstitions—that words or thoughts could prompt bad luck or call an unwanted guest. And yet, she couldn't deny the prickling of dread in her stomach as she opened the door.

Patrick stood there. For a moment that felt like an age, she stared at him, not caring that it was rude: at his square jaw with the tiny scar on the side, at those brown eyes that sparkled when he smiled. Which, unbelievably, he was now. "Afternoon, love. Been a while, hasn't it?"

No need to decide whether she'd invite him in; Patrick stepped inside without waiting to be asked and craned his head around to take in the trailer.

Mamma was right: his dove gray suit was new and perfectly fitted, so probably not won off another man's back in a game of cards. As he passed her, she caught a hint of aftershave and mint, not cigarette smoke and alcohol. And when she looked past him out the door, she saw he'd parked a dark coupe—an older model, but clean and well maintained.

Martina felt a flush of embarrassment. And what a mess she

must look, in a dirty apron and her work clothes, smelling of scrub buckets and the foundry.

It doesn't matter. Hold your head high. Her days of pretending, of sucking in her softening belly and putting on lipstick, hoping for Patrick to toss her a scrap of a compliment, were long gone.

She finally found her voice and tried to make it strong, like Mamma's. "What are you doing here?"

"Can't a fellow come to see his wife?" He reached to knock on the ceiling of the trailer, which he could do without stretching. "Bet it's murder trying to fix a meal in here."

"I manage."

"You always do, don't you?" And as usual, Martina couldn't say if it was a compliment or an insult or something hovering in between.

Never had the trailer felt so small or Patrick so large, looming in her kitchen, though his posture didn't suggest a threat.

Should she call for help? Make an excuse to leave? Drive him out with a broom?

No. He knew where they lived. If she evaded him now, he'd only be back. Better to find out what he wanted and be rid of him, and thank God he'd come while the children were away.

He gave no sign of launching into an explanation, just ran a hand over the storage compartments fitted into the walls. "Cunning design, that."

"Are you on leave?" she asked, even though she knew it didn't fit, not with the timing of when he had visited Mamma. The navy didn't let their seamen wander off for weeks at a time.

Now he turned to her. "The navy . . . didn't pan out." There was a glint in his eyes that told her not to press for details, and she didn't. Whether her husband had deserted, been discharged, or faked a disqualifying injury, none of that mattered. The worst news was already clear: he had found them.

"I've gotten back into fishing. Took out a loan for a trawler, hired a crew of my own. Been doing well, if I do say so myself." He flashed a smile that gleamed as brightly as the cuff links at his wrist, also new. "Most of the younger fishermen left their nets and followed Uncle Sam, so the rest of us are making a killing. Supply and demand. It's the American way."

As if she might not know what was American and what wasn't. "What are you *really* doing here, Patrick?"

"Thought maybe I'd say hello to you. And the kids." He glanced around, as if they might be hiding under the narrow divan.

"If you care so much about them," she wanted to demand, *"then why did you leave them? Why haven't you asked a single question about them?"*

But it wasn't worth stirring up trouble. Not when Patrick didn't seem to be there to pick a fight.

"Maybe it's better they're away. You would have to explain to Gio that you're not a military man anymore."

A frown flitted across Patrick's face. "Ah. Someone else to be disappointed in me." His finger traced a rough pencil drawing of a dog, taped to a rare open space on the wall. "Rosa would be happy to see me, anyway, even without a uniform."

It was true. She never saw the darker side to her father, though she knew he sometimes went away more than other little girls' daddies. Martina had been careful to shield her where she could, and Patrick had never spoken a harsh word to her. Yet.

"They're all right, then?" He spoke in a guarded way, like he didn't want to be seen caring too much.

But still, he had asked, and maybe he deserved to know at least that much.

"Yes. Both are healthy and happy." No thanks to a father who had walked out on them three separate times, always slinking back when he needed something, only to disappear once more.

"And you?" he said, wedging his broad shoulders into the

dinette table bench, undaunted by her sparse answers. "What're you up to these days, Marti?"

Chances are, he already knew where she was working. How else could he have found her? Even so, better to play along. When she stayed on script and he was sober, Patrick didn't turn mean. Usually.

"I'm doing my share for the war effort." She kept it vague in case he didn't have Bristol-Banks's name yet. "It's a good job."

That earned a snort. "Never thought a wife of mine would be working in a factory. They pay you decent, at least?"

"Why? Do you need money?" She had only a modest amount of savings, but if it would get Patrick to leave them be, she'd spare some, even knowing it might send him back to whatever bar or brothel he was wasting it on.

"You think that's what this is?" His voice was part anger, part hurt. "Can't a fellow even visit his wife without getting the third degree?"

"I only meant . . . the questions you asked . . ." She struggled to soften her tone. "You can't blame me for wondering."

It worked enough for him to unclench his fist and reach for her coffee mug. "Guess I can't. But I've got plenty of money this time. Living in rented rooms for now as we go up the coast." He took a sip, then spat the coffee back inside, cold and bitter after an hour of neglect. "We—the fellows on my crew—are looking to settle down somewhere as a base for fall and winter. Could be here, if the fishing's good."

Please let the fishing be bad. The Lord had made his disciples find fish when there should have been none, so surely he could grant quiet seas and empty nets. A reverse miracle, a plague, the ocean outside of Derby turned to blood. Whatever it took to get Patrick to move on.

Patrick sighed, long and loud, jammed his hands into his pockets, and then tilted his head toward her. "Look, Martina, I came to ask if you wanted to get out of this dump."

And that made the heat rise up on her neck, the way his veiled boasts and pompous questions hadn't.

Didn't he see the geraniums out on the stoop, the rug she'd braided, the pillows she'd taken such care to sew and arrange on the divan? The way every surface of the small trailer's kitchen was polished and clean? How could he call it a dump?

"You're still my wife, Martina, whatever we might've said when we were mad. And I want you back."

She chose her words carefully, her tone even. "We had a saying back in Italy. Be careful of *minestra riscaldata*—reheated soup."

"But see, you're not in Italy anymore." He stood and touched her shoulder, not seeming to notice when she flinched away. "That's your problem. That's always been your problem."

"It means," she went on as if he had actually asked, "that once something has grown cold, it's not the same when you try to heat it back up."

The anger was back now, flickering like the silver lighter he always kept in his shirt pocket, close to his heart. "Fine. You want a divorce, then? Isn't that some kind of mortal sin?"

Martina winced at the words. Patrick was just Catholic enough to toss the right words around, most of his religious instruction coming from Father Coughlin, an anti-Semitic priest whose radio program had spewed hate into living rooms around the country until the Roosevelt administration had quietly— blessedly—canceled it.

"In our last conversation"—a generous word for the shouting match they'd had the previous summer—"you said you wanted to be a free man, like you'd never married." He'd said worse too, before slamming the door and leaving them to join the navy.

"Maybe I've changed my mind."

"And maybe you'd change your mind again after a month or two in one place and decide to move on, breaking the children's hearts—again."

He paused, still close enough that she could feel his heavy breath, and for the first time, she saw a crack in his swaggering resolve.

Could it be that he really did care about them?

Her tone was softer now. "We are settled here, Patrick. Can't you see that? The children can't move from place to place with your fishing business. They need a home."

"What about leaving them with your mother for a while?" She was already shaking her head, but he plowed on, ignoring the answer that she meant to be final. "Just long enough for me to save up for a real house. Nice bungalow with a picket fence and all that."

Whatever dream he spun, however beautiful, was as much a fantasy as the land of Oz from the book she'd been reading aloud to Rosa. "I won't leave the children, not for any amount of time. They need their mother."

"But not their father?"

She didn't answer. Couldn't look at him, afraid of what she'd see. Anger or, worse, something genuine, something that would remind her of those early days when he'd been all stolen poetry and shining promises.

So she only heard his sigh, didn't see it. "Think about it, Martina. I know it's sudden. But I'll be in town another few months doing business. Crew likes smaller towns. Safer that way." He scribbled down an address on the back of an envelope he yanked out of the book sitting on the table. "You can find me anytime."

With that, he tipped his hat in a half bow like Errol Flynn and strolled out of the trailer.

She breathed deep and low, her unsteady legs collapsing onto the divan.

He was gone, and he hadn't shown up drunk or shouted at her or threatened the children. He hadn't tried to force a kiss or a decision.

Maybe he's changed.

Don't even think it. How many times had she hoped it would be different? And it never was. The only person Patrick Quinn truly cared about was himself.

Beside her was *The Code of the Woosters*, the book Patrick had tugged the envelope out of. She'd been using it as a bookmark, her ending page now lost among dozens of others. It didn't matter. There was nothing Martina wanted to do less at the moment than to read a comedy.

It all seemed so . . . what was the word? *Frivolous.* That was it. Full of jokes about boarding school and parlor maids that she didn't understand. Bertie and Jeeves and the other characters in the novel all belonged to a different world than she did. For a while, it had been fun, escaping reality while reading about their antics.

But the real world had come pounding on her door once again, reminding her of all her poor choices, all her sins, venial and mortal alike. She should have known there was no way to outrun your past, no matter how far you traveled.

seventeen

AVIS
JUNE 13

A metal fan whirred on the checkout desk, slightly disturbing both the oppressive heat and the cards lined up in the charging tray, each listing a lent-out book. Flies buzzed toward the library windows, pinging against the glass in a useless attempt to escape.

Avis massaged her temple, her hand brushing against a stray curl that had somehow escaped the complex web of hairpins that kept her rolls in an approximation of the Carole Landis style she'd seen in *Screen Guide* last week. For once, she didn't bother to dig out the compact from her purse to fix it. What did it matter?

She stared bleakly at the list of strategies in the open notebook, scribbled among the book club notes, most of them crossed off.

Appeal to the library's trustees. Failed when Mr. Bell at city hall explained that this library—an association library, funded by private donations and membership fees—had Louise Cavendish listed as the sole trustee in its charter.

Convince the city to purchase the building and turn it into a public library. According to Mayor Hastings, even if Miss Cavendish agreed to sell, "We simply haven't got the funds. There's a war on, you know."

142

Find a building code that would make the nursery school untenable. For this, she'd had to turn to Herb Beale, of all people, an amateur electrician, who looked at the plans and said that, as far as he could tell, everything was on the up-and-up. "If ol' Cavendish can find someone to get the work done, it's a solid plan."

Over the past few weeks, she'd researched loopholes and legalities, talked to almost everyone in town with influence, done everything short of throwing on a bandanna and staging a robbery of Russell's bank, targeting Louise's account. Dead ends, all of them.

A knock at the front door caused her to spring up, close the notebook, and straighten the stack of books beside her that threatened to collapse in an avalanche of neglected work.

Probably Louise, coming a few minutes early for the meeting. At least this week's selection would prove relatively uncontroversial. Even Avis had enjoyed *The Code of the Woosters* so much that she'd burned Russell's breakfast bacon two mornings in a row trying to get in a few additional pages.

But when Avis unlocked the door and blinked into the morning sunlight, there were—why, it looked like over a dozen people waiting to be let in, some chatting quietly, a few standing off to the side as if they weren't entirely sure why they were there either.

"About time!" Ginny broke away from the group and strode up the steps. She took the door from Avis and threw it open wider, gesturing for the gathered company to enter.

"What are all these people doing here?" Avis managed in a low tone before the first came within earshot—Mrs. Whitson, the preacher's wife, beaming as usual.

Ginny flashed a brilliant smile Avis's way. "They're here for the book club meeting, of course. Your little speech last week at the community meeting must've helped. Plus my pitch afterward as they left, of course. The personal touch, you know."

Avis trailed after the group, still a bit shell-shocked. Oh dear, she hadn't set up enough chairs. But that could wait until after she'd had a proper explanation. "Are they all . . . friends of yours?"

"In a manner of speaking." Ginny hitched a thumb over at a middle-aged man with a comically long moustache. "Danny Maloney. Pawn shop owner down the street, but the fair sort, don't worry. His late wife—she died six years ago—loved biographies. Can we work in any of those, do you think?"

"I don't know if—"

But Ginny had clearly decided any replies could wait, indicating a woman engrossed in conversation with Mrs. Whitson. "Then there's Carol Ann Hoper. Can't remember if she's from the Baptist potluck or the war-bond benefit ice cream social, but she sews quilts and doesn't like sad endings. Good thing we got *Hamlet* out of our system already."

"But we can't just—"

"And that's Earl Someone-or-other. Likes fishing and books about travel and is thinking of starting up a Victory garden this spring, without any broccoli."

"Why, he's Mr. Bell from city hall," Avis managed to interject. "I invited him last week."

"Well, I invited him too, so we can split that one."

Split?

That's when Avis remembered her dashed-off comment from a previous meeting about paying Ginny a commission for each member she brought into the club. She hadn't realized Ginny took it seriously.

The tour of introductions continued, with Ginny nodding at a woman wearing a bold polka-dot print dress. "That's Arley Lokken, one of Martina's neighbors. Loves Daphne du Maurier, which just goes to show she's got great taste."

Avis had given up trying to guess how Ginny could possibly remember all of this without notes and decided to focus on more pressing matters. "Ginny," she said sternly, "did you lure all of these people here by promising we would read their favorite books?"

Ginny only shrugged. "I hinted, sometimes. But not to everyone. Some of the folks here don't really read much, especially the ones from the foundry."

"Then why," Avis said slowly, trying to contain her rising heat, "are they at a book club?"

"The cookies were a selling point," she admitted. "Or some of them might've gotten the idea this was mandated by their air raid warden. Oh, and Mrs. Norris—Presbyterian Founding Day picnic—thinks you're going to announce you're pregnant and quitting your job, and she wanted to be the first to spread the gossip."

With each new addition, the sinking feeling had intensified, but this last one jolted Avis out of her dread. "Ginny!"

"What? I only said you were making an announcement. Didn't say what." She patted Avis's shoulder, as if that should be a great comfort. "So going Dutch with Mr. Bell, and considering Mrs. Follett brought her two kids, who should each count as halves at least . . . that means you owe me $1.05."

Ginny held out her hand expectantly, as if waiting for Avis to shake pennies from the box of overdue book fines she kept under the counter.

"I was *joking*."

That didn't set Ginny back one bit. "Where I come from, a deal's a deal."

Avis looked over to the periodical section, where someone had scraped over three extra chairs and two benches. The group had grown, and the children, Martina's included, sat on the floor. Even from here, she could see her entire plate of gingersnaps was already gone. "What are we going to do?"

Ginny squinted at her skeptically. "I thought you'd be happier about this. Didn't you say you needed community support?"

Well, yes. She had. But other than Mr. Bell, she doubted if any of these people had ever set foot in the library before. Some she recognized from around town, others—the factory workers from Bristol, probably—were strangers. Somewhere, a baby was squalling, two of the men seemed to be trading fishing stories, and Mrs. Norris was aiming a scrutinizing glance at Avis's middle.

This was not the sort of gathering likely to impress Miss Louise Cavendish, who had taken up her usual chair, fanning herself and observing the chaos with an expression difficult to read.

"I can't say I wanted *this.*" Like Rosa's fairy tales always taught, it paid to be careful what one wished for.

"Well, like it or not, Avis, not everyone's a fancy highbrow like you and Louise. And aren't books for all of them?"

Avis felt a stab of guilt. Of course they were. But all these years, the modest association fee had kept library patrons to only a certain class of people in Derby. Ginny had opened their doors wider than the Cavendishes—or Avis—had ever expected or intended.

But was there anything wrong with that?

She could do this. She *would* do this. Avis leveled her shoulders and marched over to the group.

"Attention, everyone!" All eyes turned to her, a few pausing in their annihilation of her gingersnaps. She hadn't made nearly enough to go around, and they would run out of chairs, and the room was boiling hot and . . . "I'm so sorry. I wasn't expecting . . ."

She trailed off and spotted Ginny trying to get her attention. When their eyes met, she jutted her face toward the ceiling. *"Chin up. You've got this."*

"That is to say"—this time Avis's smile was real—"welcome to the Blackout Book Club."

The applause that followed filled the small library, and the new members began to settle into chairs, waiting expectantly. Mrs. Whitson even gave her a dimpled wave of encouragement.

There. That wasn't so bad. And Ginny was right, this would demonstrate significant community interest in the library, maybe even garner a few new long-term members.

This time, when she looked over at Miss Cavendish, she couldn't help a bit of smugness in her expression. *You see? I told you people cared.*

The older woman merely shut her fan to reveal a raised eyebrow and frown that indicated this wasn't the coup it felt like.

But still, it was something. Perhaps things were finally starting to go right.

Notes from the Blackout Book Club—June 13, 1942

Taken by Martina Bianchini

Members in attendance: Avis always records this, but there are so many of us—twenty-one, including the children.

Book under discussion: <u>The Code of the Woosters</u> by P. G. Wodehouse

Avis gave me this notebook and told me to write down what people say during the meeting. It's difficult to keep up, and my handwriting is not good, but I'll try.

Only two of the new members raised their hands to say they'd finished the whole book for the discussion. Most seemed to be there to listen, so we began.

Louise started with "Wodehouse is the comic writer of this century." Most agreed. Freddy argued for Oscar Wilde, but he admitted Jeeves was a wonderful character. I said I didn't understand many of the jokes, especially the ones with British slang. Then I wished I hadn't said anything because everyone stared at me, and it seemed like I was the only one who felt that way.

Rosa laughed every time Ginny used a phrase from the book like "utter rot," "tut-tut," and "dash it!" Gio asked if Jeeves, Miss Cavendish's dog, was named after the character in the book (he was). They sat quite still during most of the discussion, along with the two new children.

Delphie wanted to know if the idle rich of Britain really were as brainless as Bertie in the novel, and Louise said it was an exaggeration, but that nobility and titles made people lazy because they didn't have to work for their money.

Ginny started to say something like "It's not like you

worked for your fortune either," but I knew where she was going and kicked her. Mamma would say it was my "act of Saint Francis" for the day—a small deed of peacekeeping. Though I think Francis would have found some other way to interrupt. We can't all be saints.

Freddy said the last war, and especially this one, might break down distinctions between nobles and commoners even in Britain, as men of all classes serve together. It was a beautiful thought.

One of the new members, a tall man with a bright red tie, asked what we thought of stealing back something that had been stolen from you first. Many people talked at once, and I couldn't sort them all out, but we ended by deciding that in a comedy, ethics might not be the point.

Then Miss Cavendish talked about the "great danger of premature romantic entanglements." I think she was looking at Freddy the whole time. I hope he isn't in any trouble.

Avis wanted to know what the P. G. in the author's name stood for. Delphie guessed Peregrine Griswold, and Ginny insisted it was Pudgy George. Miss Cavendish added Pelham Grenville to the list. We all agreed that was terrible, until she told us that was his actual name, showing a biography to prove it. Avis declared a formal apology from the Blackout Book Club to P. G. Wodehouse.

That was the end of the discussion. Afterward, a woman I didn't recognize asked Avis if she had any other announcements to make. She blushed and changed the subject to our next book.

And that is where my notes failed. So many people talked at once, regulars and new members both, that I wanted to cover my ears. There must have been a dozen titles suggested and argued over.

Once Avis settled things down, Ginny, the loudest, suggested Evil under the Sun, since the library already had four copies. Louise approved, saying the title is a quote from the Bible, in the book of Ecclesiastes.

I don't think she knows it's an Agatha Christie mystery. Freddy insisted it was a tale of "moral improvement." The rest agreed without too much complaint.

Maybe I should have said something? I'm never sure what to do at times like this. But I didn't, and now the Blackout Book Club will be discussing murder and mayhem.

eighteen

LOUISE
JUNE 17

The mantel clock's quiet chime sounded like a gong, stirring Louise from a world of bluebloods and blackmail, reasonable alibis and resort guests with entirely too many secrets between them to be realistic.

She counted the notes as they fell, then blinked in disbelief. Ten o'clock already? When had the evening disappeared? Piles of paperwork loomed on her father's old rolltop desk, awaiting her attention. She ought to be researching the latest news about daycare facilities, or creating the volunteer sign-up for the Red Cross's Fire Muster booth, or at the very least, working on her Peter Rabbit painting, still half finished, the easel lonely in the corner.

But something about the way Agatha Christie wrote prohibited a person from setting her book down. After all, there was a killer on the loose, and Poirot had just found a box with some sort of powdered drug inside.

Just one more chapter, and she'd retire for the night.

Granted, that was the same resolution she'd made at least an hour ago, but this time she meant it.

A soft knock on the door startled her into setting the book down, and she looked up to see Freddy leaning against the doorway, hands clean but coveralls stained with dirt from a hard day's work planting and weeding, likely ready to retire to his quarters, part of the room-and-board agreement they'd made as part of his salary.

"I was just turning in and saw the light on. Didn't expect to see you still up." Despite her attempt to hide it, his eyes fell on the book on the end table, and he smirked. "So what do you think of it?"

"You mean the 'tale of moral improvement,' as I believe you called it?" She aimed her eyebrows to a stern pitch, but Freddy didn't cower.

"I stand by that description. The modern detective mystery is just a new form of a medieval morality play."

It was uncanny, the way that young man could make almost anything seem perfectly reasonable—if you ignored the playful twinkle in his eye. "You mean that right always prevails, wrong is punished, and the truth wins out in the end."

"Exactly."

Sentimental nonsense, but what could she expect from a young man who sang "Blue Skies" while weeding at seven in the morning? "If only real life mirrored novels more closely."

A few beats of silence, and when she glanced over, Freddy was staring, not at her but the old Philco in the corner, playing softly in the background. "Don't worry, Miss Cavendish. It's always darkest before the dawn."

Ah, of course. She'd been so involved in her reading that she hadn't realized the radio programming had shifted from Bach concertos to the evening's news. From one German man to another, both geniuses in their way, but with very different aims.

". . . in the aftermath of the bombing of Benghazi," the announcer's voice intoned, "a correspondent from Cairo has indicated that the majority of Rommel's armored units are moving toward the Ally-defended border. Reports are still unclear. . . ."

Freddy switched off the program with finality, any further news drifting inaudibly in wave form above them. But Louise could guess what they were saying. The conflict in North Africa would not be ended by one successful bombing of an Axis stronghold. There would be repercussions, retaliations. How many would die on foreign sands far from home?

And where was Anthony stationed now? She felt a tug of guilt, realizing she didn't know. Only a few short months after his deployment, she'd gotten out of the habit of asking Avis about her former employee.

"We'll lick ol' Hitler and his buddies," Freddy said, nodding to give his words emphasis. "It's just a matter of time."

She straightened in the chair. "It is also, I believe, a matter of strategy, economics, global supply chains, control of the Atlantic, and swift access to medical care."

The moment the words left her mouth, she realized it was an arrogant thing to say to a veteran, and cynical. The patch over the unfortunate boy's eye spoke well enough to his willingness to put his life at risk for his beliefs, naïvely optimistic as they seemed.

But instead of becoming affronted, Freddy merely shrugged. "There's all that too, I guess. But the heart of this war is a moral question, just like the novel."

Louise tilted her head, considering. "I don't pretend to be an expert on Adolf Hitler, but he seems to be the agent of an evil so great that even Christie's sleuths would cower."

"Maybe, but there are plenty of us real, ordinary people who won't. That's why I joined up, even before the States officially signed on. I couldn't go on delivering cargo while that small man spewed dangerous lies. And there are others like me." He leaned against the mantel, and for a moment, Louise was sure he was miles away from her cozy office, swooping through the skies in the heat of battle. "I have to believe that'll be enough."

Watching him, Louise felt a touch of pride. Yes, she'd seen something in this young man from the moment he'd knocked on her door, hat in his hand. When others might have turned him away, she'd offered him employment, lodging, and her trust—which he had kept. "You're a good man, Frederick."

For some reason, that, of all things, was the comment that seemed to deflate him, and he looked away. "I'm really not sure I am."

She waved him aside, scoffing to dispel the gloom that seemed to settle around his shoulders. "Nonsense. Jeeves likes you, and he's an excellent judge of character."

Jeeves, snoring slightly from his bed near the fireplace, declined to comment.

Frederick ran a hand through his hair, slicking it back. "Say, Miss Cavendish, I wanted to talk to you about something. . . ."

Oh dear. Louise had never excelled at reading people, but the way Frederick shifted his tone uneasily could mean nothing but bad news.

What could it be? Had he decided to move along earlier than planned? Unlikely, as he'd updated her on the coming harvest just this morning.

An image flashed into her mind, one she'd seen through the curtains of the upper room the day before: young, lively Ginny Atkins perched on the split-rail fence, reading the Christie novel out loud to Freddy and Gio, his new assistant gardener. They had laughed and exchanged glances over Gio's shoulder.

There was, strictly speaking, nothing wrong with young love. Still, she'd not open herself up to the charge of hiring someone who would play with the hearts of local girls, only to leave once winter came. She'd told Freddy as much before hiring him, and if this was what that was about . . . well, there would be no changing her mind.

"Yes?" Her voice had an edge that she didn't try to temper.

"I've been meaning to ask you . . . don't you think you ought to lay off the plans for the library?"

A moment's blinking was all it took to adjust to the unexpected subject. Of course the Blackout Book Club knew about the library's impending closing. She'd made no attempt to hide it. But she hadn't expected Frederick, a temporary resident of Derby, to care. "Why do you say that?"

"I was talking with Mrs. Bianchini, and it sounds like most of the women at the foundry might be too ashamed to use the nursery school. Too much like accepting charity."

What nonsense. "I'm sure she's mistaken. No mother would turn down such a sensible solution."

"But isn't there some other way?" His pleading expression reminded her of Jeeves seeking a treat.

This is all your fault, Louise scolded herself. *That book club is making the whole lot of them sentimental.* Had they forgotten the great need she'd be addressing by starting the daycare facility?

Well then, it was up to her to remind them. "The trouble is, Frederick, no one cares about women raising children alone, not even the government. To everyone else, they're useful tools, expected to work and keep house and mind the children all at once."

"I'm sure, but what about—?"

No, he didn't understand. Couldn't. "Think to yourself what it must be like to be one of these mothers. Their husbands dead, at war, or absent from their families long ago, leaving them to provide and care for children left alone and vulnerable." She took a deep breath, surprised by the passion in her voice. "Can you see how much they need a nursery school?"

Frederick nodded slowly, fiddling with the dog-tag chain around his neck. "To be honest, Miss Cavendish, I haven't heard you speak with such feeling about . . . well, about anything before. It's like you understand what they're going through."

"Of course I don't understand," she said brusquely. "I've never raised a child."

"I only meant that you have a great amount of empathy on this topic."

For the first time that evening, the hour seemed intolerably late, and Louise rose from her chair, folding the blanket she'd draped over her lap. "Since you seem to consider that a compliment, thank you. But I've said all I'd like to on the subject. Good night, Mr. Keats."

He followed her cue, backing toward the door. "Good night, Miss Cavendish." He gave a quick nod at the book, abandoned on the end table. "Best of luck solving the mystery."

She dismissed him with a nod, and soon the creaking floorboards told her that Frederick had made his way to his room in the east wing, the former butler's quarters.

At least it hadn't been about Ginny. That conversation, she was sure, would have gone much worse. Surely a boy like Frederick had a decent enough head on his shoulders to realize a fleeting summer romance would be an error in judgment.

Still, she'd watch both Frederick and Ginny a little more closely. Young people often needed help letting go of silly fancies.

You sound like your father, the old, condemning voice whispered before she could silence it.

No, I'll never be like him.

Still, she didn't deny that some of her protectiveness came from experience. There were some warnings that needed to be passed on, some heartbreaks that could be avoided.

If only they would listen.

With a sigh, Louise picked up *Evil under the Sun*, in case sleep proved difficult and she needed something else to occupy her time.

One thing was sure: she had been wrong. It wasn't unrealistic, the collection of mysterious resort guests populating Christie's novel.

After all, everyone had a past—and most hid at least a few secrets.

MAY 1917

Louise folded the crisp pinafore into a neat square on her dormitory bed, careful to line up the seams. Not a single stain from the graduation ceremony the day before, she noted with pride.

"Oh!" Her roommate, a dreamy girl of twenty who dashed about with a Gibson Girl updo in a constant state of near collapse, swirled her own uniform about. "Isn't it the most exciting, Lou?"

Louise looked up from her packing. "Of course. We've all worked very hard."

Nellie flopped next to the open suitcase in a creak of bedsprings. "Not *that*. I mean all of us parting ways, finding adventure, working with handsome doctors—or sailors." She was determined to volunteer with the nursing branch of the navy, and she regularly remarked that their white dress uniforms looked "masculine and heroic."

"There are strict regulations for nurses' conduct when interacting with men," Louise reminded her, in case she hadn't bothered to read the lengthy guidelines.

"Oh, I know," Nellie said, waving her away. She'd stopped being deterred by such cold-water comments during her first semester rooming with Louise. "But they can't regulate our imaginations, can they?"

"I think you'll find very little fuel for your imagination when it comes to actual battles." Really, Nellie seemed determined to give all nurses a bad name. "Amputations and morphine injections are hardly the stuff of romance."

And yet, even though it meant long hours for little pay, steeped in the sounds of violence and the scent of stinging antiseptic mingling with foul open wounds, Louise would face it with determination, because she would finally be doing something worthwhile.

Her plan was to live with Aunt Eleanor again for a time until the Red Cross accepted her and sent her overseas, hopefully within a few months. They needed more trained nurses. She knew that much from the news bulletins. Even if the Great War was over quickly, as some said it might be now that America had joined, the Red Cross was committed to stitching back together the gaping wounds the battles left behind. Their mission included innocent civilians, especially "the suffering children of Europe."

That was the phrase that had caught Louise's attention and guided her away from applying to a general hospital somewhere safe and familiar.

"You can't ruin my mood, Lou, so don't even try." Nellie peered into the mirror, trying in vain to fix her flattened hair. "Come on, or we'll miss the farewell tea downstairs."

After receiving a promise that she'd be down soon, Nellie flitted off, and Louise turned from where she'd been arranging her stockings by color in her steamer trunk. There was one last personal item to pack.

With another glance at the door, Louise drew her locket out from under her high-buttoned blouse. The latch, unaccustomed to being sprung, clicked open with effort. There, opposite the timepiece, was her miniature sketch of Oliver, staring out in smooth, flowing lines of ink, drawn by a beholder's eye that had found him very handsome indeed.

She took a hairpin from the china dish on her bureau and pried the picture out. The glob of paste she'd applied to the paper resisted, but it was no match for her determination. A dozen carefully aimed stabs later, and Oliver's image was out of her heart and into the rubbish bin—torn into small bits so Nellie wouldn't ask questions.

From her pocket, she took the bit of writing paper that she'd cut carefully down to size and written on in the sharpest quill *Inter Arma Caritas*. "In War, Charity." The motto of the Red Cross, and her motto now too. Didn't Scripture say charity was the greatest virtue? No matter what mistakes she had made in the past, surely volunteering to risk her life in service of others would be enough to atone for them.

Without a pot of scrapbooking paste, she had to settle with folding the paper in two and placing it in the hollow. When she snapped the locket shut and tucked it under her collar again, she felt . . . lighter, somehow. As if the picture of Oliver had turned the necklace into a chain worthy of the Dickens novel Father insisted on reading every holiday season, tying her to her past and its follies.

No longer.

During the first year after their parting, her heart had caught every time she saw the glint of rust-brown hair or the suggestion of a strong Roman nose in profile, at first because she hoped Oliver had somehow come searching for her. Even after she knew that was a foolish fancy, those glimpses were a reminder of all she'd risked—and lost.

No, Oliver had not attempted to contact her in over three years. Whatever he'd felt for her was as fleeting as the waves crashing against Maine's rugged coast. Now that she had a clear, new purpose, it was time to move on at last.

A paper with the bold Western Union logo skittered under the door, the usual way of delivering telegrams when in a hurry, as everyone was today.

Louise stooped to pick it up, noting the sender. From Father. So he *had* remembered her graduation. A day late, as always.

According to his last letter, Father had been feeling ill lately and therefore wasn't able to attend the ceremony. Left unasked was whether she would have wanted him there if he had been able.

At least Father thought enough to send a telegram. Maybe, after all these years, things were starting to get better between them.

Instead of congratulations, however, the first line took a much more dire tone.

```
Sickness worse. Tuberculosis, in advanced
stages. Doctor advises rest, sea air, and a
full-time nurse. Gone to Windward Hall. Please
come.
```

She read the brief message once more, searching for additional information that never appeared. A full-time nurse. He couldn't mean . . . her?

Certainly, retreating to their summer home in Maine to grant his lungs rest from the polluted New York air was a reasonable measure. But Luther Cavendish had the means to hire a nurse from the city to accompany him.

But something in her knew. Her reclusive, bookish father wouldn't trust his care to a stranger, not when his own daughter had just graduated from nursing school.

They'd studied tuberculosis, of course. It was the second leading cause of death in the nation, barely surpassed by influenza. Unlike the flu, however, sufferers from tuberculosis often lingered for months, even years, racked by terrible coughing and pain. But there was no cure.

If Father expected her to tend to him for the duration . . . she'd miss the war, the reconstruction of Europe, everything she'd worked and trained for. But how could she say no if her own father was dying?

She crumpled the note and threw it into the bin with Oliver's photo. *It's not his fault*, part of her—the part that still had her mother's compassion—whispered. *You can't resent a dying man.*

But she found that she could, and did.

Louise slammed the lid of her steamer trunk and, with effort, held in a cry of frustration.

Inter Arma Caritas. They'd had their fair share of war, she and Father. And now duty demanded that she supply charity along with her freedom.

What more could he possibly take from her?

160

Notes from the Blackout Book Club—June 27, 1942

Taken by Lt. Freddy Keats, Pilot (Army Air Forces), Amateur Detective, and Finest Minutes Recorder Ever Seen in This Library

Members in attendance: Ginny, Gio, Louise, Delphie, Avis, Martina, Rosa, Earl Bell, Arley Lokken, Carol Ann Hoper, Diana Follett and kids, and Hamish and Eva Murray. (I invited them. Turns out Eva is mad for mysteries.)

Book under discussion: <u>Evil under the Sun</u> by Agatha Christie

Look out, Blackout Book Club, Freddy's got the secretary role now! And there's no censor looking over my shoulder, making me watch what I say. Who knows what could happen?

Ginny had everyone go around and name who they'd pegged as the culprit at the halfway point of the book. She, Eva, and Delphie insisted they'd known it almost from the start. I called their bluff by asking how, and Ginny tried "women's intuition." Mr. Bell heartily agreed when I said that was the excuse every female used when they retroactively decided they were right all along. That little comment earned us the ire of every woman in the room.

We are outnumbered. Must invite more fellows to the club, or else not say things like that out loud. (Hamish doesn't count; he didn't support me at all. Didn't say a word the entire meeting, although he grunted once, which his wife seemed to take for a whole speech.)

Avis moved along to theories on why murder mysteries are so popular at the moment. Delphie compared it to crossword puzzles and "the way a person feels when they find just the right word to fill in the boxes." This was widely applauded as an excellent answer. Never seen Delphie prouder, not even when I complimented her coq au vin.

I talked about Poirot's methods, especially his claim that the most important step was to learn more about the victim—why they might have been murdered—and move backward, which I thought was brilliant. Avis said it wasn't as convincing to her as Sherlock Holmes's analysis of the details of a crime scene, but when we took a vote, Poirot won 9–4. (Biased because we just read Christie? Probably. But a win's a win, I say.)

When Ginny asked if Miss C was disappointed that Ecclesiastes didn't factor much into it, she responded cryptically, "Of course it did. It was everywhere." Instead of explaining herself, she took a Bible down from the shelf and read (chapter 6, verses 1–2, copied here): "There is an evil which I have seen under the sun, and it is common among men: a man to whom God hath given riches, wealth, and honour, so that he wanteth nothing for his soul of all that he desireth, yet God giveth him not power to eat thereof, but a stranger eateth it: this is vanity."

This gave the club a somber tone. She's a puzzling one, Miss C. Hard to get to know, and, believe me, I've tried.

The subject was soon changed to what to read next. Mr. Bell waxed positively poetic about some play called Pygmalion, which he took his wife to see performed at Park Theatre the year they married. We agreed to read it next, mostly to keep him from summarizing the whole plot along with the full itinerary of the other places they visited on that trip. Nice fellow, but Hamlet had nothing on his soliloquies.

Best news of all: Ginny said she'd come back to read aloud to Gio and me while we garden. Gio pretends he's only interested in the nickels he's getting from weeding, but

I know he's hanging on to every word. Last week, he raked over the same part of the pumpkin patch three times during one of Poirot's interrogations. Can't say as I blame him; Ginny's got a captivating reading voice and really makes the stories come alive.

nineteen

GINNY
JUNE 28

Something about Methodist preaching must attract better cooks, Ginny decided, going back for a second helping of Indian pudding, thick with layers of molasses.

Over the past few months, she'd shown up at a Presbyterian Seventy-Fifth Founding Day Celebration, two Baptist potlucks, and an ice cream social sponsored by the Congregationalist Church, and none of them had a spread like this.

She paused to wave at Mrs. Dougherty, the grocer's wife, who had invited her to the Sunday-school picnic. The older woman beamed from a distance as she poured lemonade for her brood of children, sure she'd done a wayward young woman good by having her sit through a sermon on . . . something or other.

"Well, if it isn't Ginny Atkins," a warm baritone voice said from behind her. "What a surprise."

Careful of her plate's balance, she turned, Sunday-best dress swirling around her legs, to see Freddy and Louise helping themselves to the picnic spread.

"Well, hello to you too," Ginny said cheerfully. Best to pretend this was all normal and neighborly, despite the questioning look ol' Louise was shooting her, having never seen her at church before.

Thankfully, Ginny was saved by a rustle of skirts as two

women—mother and daughter from the looks of their matching upturned noses—swooped in from the other side of the table.

"Why, hello again, Mr. Keats," the matronly one cooed. Her straw hat was so weighted down on one side with artificial sunflowers that Ginny didn't know how she could stand up straight. "I see you've taken quite the serving of my Lillian's blue-ribbon rhubarb pie."

"My Lillian" was a girl about Ginny's age, only freckle-less and prettier, with perfect golden hair that must have taken an hour to pin up around her face. She probably liked embroidery and pressing wildflowers, Ginny decided, and had never gutted a fish in her life.

"Oh, Mama, stop," Lillian said, her voice louder than Ginny would've expected. "It's just a simple old thing. Did *you* bring anything, Mr. Keats?"

Freddy nodded politely. "Just a salad with some of our lettuce and radishes. Plucked a nice batch of each of them just this week from the garden."

"How delightful!" Lillian's mother tittered, searching the dishes to take a hefty spoonful from the indicated bowl. "You really were ahead of the times, Louise. Now that canned goods are slated to be rationed, all the magazines are talking about how more citizens need to sow Victory gardens come spring."

"It's a worthwhile task," Freddy agreed.

"Oh, I'd just love it if you'd tell me all about it," Lillian cooed, and Ginny nearly gagged.

"I'm sure, if there's community interest, Mr. Keats would be happy to make a *public* demonstration of gardening techniques," Louise said coolly, stepping between him and Lillian.

Good for Louise, putting her foot down. Fluttering eyelashes, really. Who did that, outside of *Gone with the Wind*?

"I don't know how interesting—" Freddy protested.

"Oh, *would* you, Mr. Keats?" Lillian's smile spread even

wider. "What about the Fire Muster? Everyone in town goes to that."

"Yes," Ginny said, matching her enthusiasm, "then *everyone* could listen to you go on for hours about the benefits of earthworms and the different types of squash."

He glared at her. She smiled sweetly, imitating Lillian, with maybe a hint of mischief thrown in.

To her surprise, Louise nodded thoughtfully. "I could see that being instructive."

Ginny pushed back a laugh as Freddy squirmed, betrayal written billboard-large on his expression. "But—"

"Then it's settled." The sunflowers jiggled dangerously as Lillian's mother nodded like a judge rendering a verdict. "Oh, this will be such fun! Come along, Lillian. We must spread the word."

Lillian seemed torn between telling others she had convinced Mr. Keats to give a demonstration and actually being in his presence, but a glare from Louise settled the matter, and she scampered after her mother to join a group of women fanning themselves in the shade.

"What was that about?" Freddy protested as soon as they were out of earshot.

"Mrs. Buckwold is an intolerable meddler," Louise said bluntly, "but it *is* a good idea, Frederick. The Department of Agriculture is providing some resources to local communities—pamphlets and starter seeds and the like—but a demonstration would still be of great practical value."

They'd reached the end of the picnic's buffet table, but Freddy's grim expression didn't seem to be because of the lack of ice cream. "I suppose the demonstrator has no say in the matter."

"I didn't know you don't like public speaking," Ginny put in.

"I didn't know *you* were a Methodist," he countered.

Classic change of subject, but Ginny was ready with an answer. "Back home, there was one church. Didn't even have a name, just took in any of us island folk who felt we ought to square things up with the Almighty, regularly or just at weddings and funerals. Not having any labels to choose from, I don't know what I am, except open-minded."

"And by that you mean you'll attend any church that will feed you," Louise said dryly.

So she'd guessed that little pattern. It was pretty straightforward to Ginny's mind. More free meals meant more money for her little tin bank . . . and one step closer to buying land on Long Island once the war was over and the navy gave them their lives back. If she had to sit through a service to get to lunch, then so be it.

"As the Scriptures say," Freddy declaimed, a twinkle in his eye, applying the tone he'd used for the Shakespeare reading, "'For he satisfieth the longing soul, and filleth the hungry soul with goodness.'"

Louise gave Ginny's plate a pointed stare. "I wasn't aware that the 'goodness' promised by the psalmist included deviled eggs and two helpings of fried cod."

"Pretty sure Jesus ate fish." That was one bit she'd picked up at the island church—the men who followed Jesus around were fishermen, almost as good as lobstermen. Made a person think God must have a soft spot for the likes of her family. "Anyway, food's getting cold. Mind if I join you?"

Louise looked like she did mind but was too polite to say so. Freddy led them to a blanket in the shade of the clapboard church, a prime spot. On their way over, Louise got waylaid by Mrs. Dougherty, asking something about a Red Cross blood drive. That left Ginny to try to sink down gracefully to the ground without dumping her plate or showing off her drawers to the families lunching around them. Skirts. Always such a bother. Thankfully, Freddy didn't seem to notice her awkwardness as he kneeled and tucked into his lunch.

"Looks like we're unchaperoned for a bit."

Freddy pressed a hand to his heart in shock. "A genuine scandal. You know, that was one of the three rules Miss C gave me for boarding at Windward Hall." He ticked them off on his fingers. "No drinking. No taking days off without permission. And no romantic entanglements."

"Odd set of rules, that."

"I suppose she didn't want to play chaperone all summer. And American military men have a reputation to work off, you know. The Brits called us 'overpaid, oversexed, and over here.'"

The idea of Freddy romancing a pack of British women was laughable. Why, Ginny felt safer with him than she had with some of the island boys she'd known all her life.

Don't forget about the lying, she reminded herself. Freddy might be a gentleman, but he was a gentleman hiding something. Hercule Poirot sure wouldn't waste an opportunity like this, alone with a potential suspect for . . . something. She'd come over to the house a few times to read to Freddy while he gardened, but Gio was always there too. Nice of Freddy to take the boy under his wing and all, but it was harder than she expected to conduct a proper interrogation with a kid around.

Best to keep things open-ended at first. "So, tell me your story, Freddy Keats."

There it was. That tense, guarded look again, covered up with a shrug. "Not much to tell."

All right, maybe a little more specific, just to help things along. "When'd you join up? Before Pearl Harbor, I'm guessing, from the sound of things."

His shoulders relaxed. So this he was comfortable with. That probably meant she was prodding in the wrong direction, but she couldn't very well throw it into reverse now.

"Right after Dunkirk. After that, I knew we couldn't hide from war forever. And I was *ready*, Ginny. Planned on being the most decorated flying ace in American history. In those early letters back to my family, I bragged myself . . . well, to the skies."

Hadn't Mack said something just about the same? "You were a good pilot, I'll bet."

"I was." He shook his head in disgust, as if landing from whatever soaring memories he'd been replaying in his mind. "But even good pilots can get shot down on their third transport mission with an awful shrapnel wound. And now here I am, my biggest worry whether we'll get enough rain for the green beans."

Ginny swallowed another mouthful and studied Freddy carefully. That expression was a new one, not likely to show up on the "We Can Do It" propaganda posters he always looked to be posing for. "You can't feel guilty about not being able to fight anymore."

He took a bite from his own plate—Lillian's pie, which, Ginny noted with satisfaction, didn't prompt a reaction of awe. "If I stop feeling a little bit of guilt . . . I'll just be angry. And I don't have anyone nearby to get angry at, except maybe God."

"Why not try it?"

He stared at her, and she took another forkful of lunch, calm as a clock, as folks on the island said. "Miss Cavendish was right. You are a perfect heathen."

"That's where you're wrong. I'm not a perfect anything." *Stop grinning.* This was serious, after all. "I only mean that if you keep up a front with other folks, that's your choice. But isn't God supposed to already know how you really feel?"

For a moment, she could see those honest emotions at war on Freddy's face. But then he blinked—and smiled, sunny and warm. "I'd rather keep things cordial between the good Lord and myself. Anyway, given enough time in a hospital, a man starts to wonder who he really is. And I decided to go back to my roots—literally."

Ginny groaned. "Is that terrible line how you got Louise to hire you?"

He glanced over at his employer, now trying to back away

from the chatty Mrs. Dougherty, but still out of earshot. "Pretty much. Oh, I gave her all the Victory garden mumbo jumbo from the Department of Agriculture and told her about my years tending our family's garden. But she was midway through a speech about how some committee could help me locate a factory job when I said . . ."

"What?" She'd often wondered what logic had convinced the old spinster to employ a drifting veteran.

Freddy looked away, picking at a blade of grass. "It's silly."

"Tell me anyway."

"I said, 'I'm a pilot, ma'am, trained to destroy. There's a lot I want to forget, but some things I want to remember. And ever since I put flowers on a friend's grave, all I want to do is make things grow again.'"

That look on his face as he said it—strong but a little sad around the edges—well, if Ginny had been in Louise's shoes, she'd have done the exact same thing.

"Freddy, that's positively poetic. You and Emily D. ought to be friends."

"She's dead, Ginny."

Golly, why were all the writers they read for the book club dead? "So she is. I guess you'll just have to settle for me as a friend, then."

"Settle? The way I see it, I'm lucky to know you, Ginny Atkins."

There was something so honest it hurt in the way their eyes met, and some crazy impulse made Ginny want to reach out and take his hand. Tell him things were going to be all right. That he was doing good work right where he was.

"Dreadfully hot day, isn't it?" Louise's voice caused Ginny to startle, which probably wasn't the best reaction, given the air of suspicion the older woman directed at them. As if Freddy might have up and proposed in the five minutes her back was turned.

While Louise went on about the weather and sat between

them, Ginny popped a piece of pickle in her mouth, making a face at the tart vinegar. Her theory of Freddy Keats running some sort of long con was starting to seem questionable.

After the last book club meeting, she'd hinted around Louise enough to get out of her that no, Freddy hadn't asked for a single thin dime besides his salary, not even to pay Gio. According to Eva, Hamish's wife and Louise's twice-weekly housekeeper, nothing had gone missing recently from the manor, and anyway, Louise had sold all the expensive silverware and antique vases and such when she'd first inherited Windward Hall.

So the only thing she really had going for her theory that Freddy was a con man come to bilk a rich old lady out of her fortune was that he got cagey when you asked after his family and sometimes told small lies.

It would never hold up in court. And it was getting harder for it to hold up in her own mind. How could someone so gosh-darned kind be a criminal?

Freddy was no counterfeit bill or knockoff moonshine. He was the real deal, with resentments and guilt and hurts tucked under that charming smile, just like anyone else. Just like her.

She was lucky to have him for a friend too.

Though for some reason, at this moment, that didn't feel like quite enough.

twenty

AVIS
JULY 3

The pattern book had called her blue-striped dress "the dream summer swing ensemble," and Avis noted with satisfaction that the description was accurate. There were others at the dance wearing showier frocks, but no skirt twirled as dramatically as hers when Russell spun her around, which he did often to cover the fact that he hadn't mastered more complex footwork.

Avis made up for his two left feet where she could, executing the movements she'd memorized in physical-education class back in high school.

When Russell had suggested they take the drive and make a date out of it, she'd agreed almost instantly. It didn't matter that the only decoration was a tattered red-and-blue bunting left over from an another year's Independence Day celebration or that the room, an Elks Lodge by day, was too cramped for the couples who spun to the music. All that mattered was how normal it all felt when the band, a quartet with just enough talent to be better than the record player smaller events used, struck up the familiar strains of "Moonlight Serenade."

A smile tugged at her face involuntarily, and Russell leaned in close enough that she could smell his cologne. "Remember taking a spin to this tune at the Palace Ballroom?"

Of course she did. When she closed her eyes, she could still picture its sign lit golden with electric lights and the dizzy whirl of nearby carnival rides. On the inside, the ballroom boasted vaulted ceilings, elegant décor, and a full big band in shiny brass.

At first she hadn't wanted to go in, seeing the flock of wealthy women with their silks and furs, but Russell had said, "Come on, sweetheart. It's our honeymoon. Let's show those peacocks what we've got."

And they had, dancing the night away, then sleeping in before exploring the piers, the amusement park rides, the shops. By the time they paid for the hotel and food, they'd only had fifty cents between them for a souvenir on their last morning. Avis had bought a postcard for Russell: sensible, cheap, and easy to preserve. He'd spent the rest on a sweetheart lapel pin for her, one side stamped with *Old Orchard Beach*, the other a heart shaped like a lock.

Avis frowned. She hadn't worn it in months. Where had she tucked it away?

"'A love song, my darling, a moonlight serenade,'" the lead singer crooned, and the couples on the floor applauded.

It was only then, in the few beats of quiet between songs, that Avis noticed something odd. Except for a few men in navy uniforms, clearly on shore leave, most of the male dancers were middle-aged or older, enjoying a night away from the children or celebrating an anniversary numbering in the decades.

She turned toward her husband. Even now, after only three dances, she could see Russell struggle to hide a slight wheeze, like he was breathing through a milkshake straw.

I won't mention it. I won't. That would risk giving her the label of *nag*, something *Secrets of Love and Marriage* had told her men abhorred above all else.

"Let's get some fresh air," she said instead, smiling at him and pretending not to notice the cough he hid in his elbow.

Once they were past the cadre of men taking a smoke break,

the sky was clear and the stars bright, like something out of a painting. Across the street from the lodge, the grassy slope of a hill gave them a view a mile across town, toward the cove. There, Avis could see the long granite breakwater pushing out into the ocean, with the lighthouse at its tip.

Don't stare too long. Lovely as the lighthouse was, Avis knew the coast guard was using it as a lookout station. Best not to bring that up either.

"On summer nights," she said idly, "they ought to bring the dancing outside, don't you think?"

But when she took her attention away from the sky and returned it to Russell, he was shifting uncomfortably, as if his necktie were too tight—which she knew it was not, as she'd tied the perfect Windsor knot. "Russell? What's wrong?"

"Nothing. It's just . . . I want to tell you about a job opportunity."

She hesitated. "You mean the promotion at the bank?"

"Not exactly. The bank isn't bad work. But . . ." He shifted his weight on wingtip shoes. "This would help with the war effort, Avis."

Ah. So that's what all this was about. Avis braced herself, tried to maintain an open mind. What he could have found, she had no idea. She'd scoured the want ads ever since the incident with the life jacket, but all the war-related civilian desk jobs, heads of task forces and the like, were in larger cities.

"Roy told me about a new group called the Coastal Picket Patrol that just got established by Congress," he began, clearly expecting her to pepper him with questions.

But *Women's Home Companion* warned wives not to interrupt their husbands during important conversations. "Go on."

"The idea is to use smaller vessels manned with civilians to defend and patrol the coasts."

Now she couldn't resist the tiniest of inquiries, more of a clarification. "Don't we have a coast guard for that?"

"Well, the Coasties are in charge of this new branch," he allowed, "but it's different. The crafts, for one, aren't expensive battleships and destroyers. A bunch of rich fellows donated their yachts and sailing boats for the Coastal Picket Patrol to use—some are joining the crew, like Ernest Hemingway. You know, the writer."

"I know who he is, Russell." What sort of librarian did he think she was?

Russell pushed right on, his words hurried, like he was worried she wouldn't give him a chance to get them out. "Even though it's overseen by the coast guard, crews are independent, run by a skipper, nothing more. No uniforms or roll call or boot camp. And I want to join them."

Of course, that was where this was going. "Russell—"

"Hear me out, Avis." He paused to grasp her hands, which would have been romantic, except his were slick with sweat. "It's great work, keeping our shores safe. But . . . I'd have to be away for a while. The fleet headquarters is in Boston."

Over one hundred fifty miles away. That changed things. If Russell and a few buddies wanted to sail up and down midcoast Maine for a few weeks and radio in reports, who could object? But if he had to leave home, leave her . . .

She hated to bring it up, but there was no way around it. "If it's military-run, won't they have the same concerns about your health?"

"That's the thing." His gestures became more animated, an eagerness on his face she hadn't seen in months. "They're specifically looking for men like me, the undraftables. All they need in recruits is some sailing experience and a willingness to follow orders. I know they'll take me on, Avis. This is my chance."

For the first time, Avis felt a flicker of fear. If this was really a possibility and not another one of Russell's dreams of glory . . .

"What will you do on these civilian yachts, throw darts at German submarines?"

He didn't rise to her jab. "We'll be using a radio, mostly—wiring back with a location if we see or hear anything suspicious. Although I think they'll give us depth charges to use if needed. Maybe a deck gun, if we're lucky."

The mention of weaponry reminded her of the most important question, the one she should have started with. "How dangerous is it?"

He hesitated. One heartbeat. Two. Three.

"Russell Montgomery, don't you dare lie to me."

"It's riskier than staying on land, I guess," he finally admitted, as if she hadn't guessed that already. "If we spot a sub and radio in, the U-boats can pick up on our signals. They'll probably run away to get a lead before the bombers fly in . . . but there's a chance—just a small one—they could do the stupid thing instead."

She tightened her grip on his arm, not letting him look away. "Which is?"

His face took on the stoic bravado of every soldier featured in every other page of her magazines these days. "Surface and fire on us."

The staccato sound of gunfire from the newsreels echoed in her mind, and she shivered.

Like the rest of the nation, she'd known there were U-boats out in the ocean, even before she'd found the life vest. She'd read about their merciless assaults on tankers and merchant vessels, both losses and victories. But picturing Russell out among them, floating on a tiny vessel that could be stoved to flinders as easily as a dime-store balsam model, was a different matter altogether.

She forced her hands into fists behind her back so he wouldn't see them shake. "How long would you be away?"

"They're asking for a three-month commitment. That's all."

That's all? How could he say that? Boston was only a half

day's drive, but with gas rations and her work at the library, it might as well be over in Bataan or Burma for all she'd see him.

She kept her mouth in a tight line, and Russell reached for her face in the near darkness, pulling her close.

Oh no, he wasn't going to kiss away her answer. She pushed against his neatly ironed dress shirt. "Well, now I know why you were so eager to bring me here tonight and got all kitted out without complaining. You don't even like dancing."

"Avis, don't be that way. I only wanted to break it to you gently." It was hard not to believe him, the way he stroked her arm soothingly. "And you've been so busy at the library and then with chores in the evenings, I feel like we haven't seen each other."

So that was it. Hadn't she told Anthony any reasonable man would resent his wife working? Maybe Russell's desire for adventure and escape was really her fault.

"Will we see each other more if you disappear for three months?" she asked pointedly.

"No," he admitted after a pause. "But the world is at war, Avis. We all have to sacrifice something. This could be my chance. . . ."

"There it is again." She bit off the words crisply, crossing her arms so he'd know she wouldn't be cowed. "Your chance. For what? You want excitement and glory and *distance*, far away from me, just like my father did in the last war? And who knows what kind of women you'd find in Boston to take my place."

She froze. Had she really said that? Out loud?

From the hurt and anger on Russell's face, she had. "Now, that's just—"

She wasn't going to listen to excuses. Not anymore. The words, now started, came out quickly, past the lump in her throat that threatened tears. "Don't try to tell me it doesn't happen, Russell, because it does. To soldiers and sailors and bachelors off for some coastal patrol lark. Even to good men like you, like my father, and their women stand by and pretend they don't know. Well, I can't bear that."

For a moment, no one spoke, the grassy knoll quiet as a funeral parlor.

"It's not going to be that way." Russell's voice had softened, begging her to believe him.

But she remembered, with perfect clarity, the day shortly after her engagement when her mother had taken her to a restaurant for tea. She'd perched on the plush chair, still unused to the feeling of a ring on her finger, and listened as Mother warned her to expect wandering eyes and even unfaithfulness in her husband. "It's just how men are," she'd said, stirring cream into her cup, lipstick pressed together in a hard line.

So Avis had bought books, subscribed to magazines, memorized instructions. She'd tailored her clothes to the latest fashion and determined not to hire anyone to clean or cook. She hadn't pushed Russell when he said he wasn't ready for children, even though she ached to cradle a baby in her arms.

And still, after all that, here they were, snapping at each other just like Avis's parents.

"I'm sorry," Avis said, hating the betrayed look Russell was giving her, hating that she couldn't take her words back and mean it. "It's just . . . I don't like being alone." The words sounded so small and frail, and this time, she didn't pull away when Russell wrapped his arms around her.

"I know. But you've got your parents not far away, and the church, and the book club. And it's only for three months. I promise."

Three months. That was something. Concrete. Measurable. *What if this is the only thing that will fix him?* Nothing she'd tried so far had been able to get that old sparkle back in his eyes, the one she was seeing now while he talked about this yachting patrol.

Taking in a shuddering breath, Avis forced herself to ask, "When do you need to decide?"

"Training starts in one week."

So soon.

"I can't just—" She drew in the night air, trying and failing to find the right words. "I need time to think."

He pressed a kiss to the top of her carefully brushed out pin curls. "Of course. Of course, sweetheart. I know it's a long time to say good-bye."

And what if you don't come back?

But it was safer than the military, she reasoned when he led her back inside and held her for a slow dance. More than likely, it was the government's way to keep some wealthy idlers pacified, thinking they were contributing in some way.

As the strains of a ballad drew them closer to midnight, Avis breathed in her husband's scent, clung to his arm, fixed this moment in her memory.

She would think about the picket patrol, eventually. But not tonight. Tonight, she would pretend Russell had simply brought her here because he liked the feeling of holding her in his arms, even if the lie only lasted for a few more dances.

Even on a platform swarming with people—pushing carts piled with luggage, shouting to be heard above the departing train's whistle, weaving through the crowd—Avis felt completely alone.

She watched as Russell stepped into the passenger car, one of the few men not decked out in army drab but more handsome than any of them. Today, his step was jaunty, and the good-bye he'd given her had come off more like he was going off to summer camp than a coast guard auxiliary force.

Dodging the passengers and their farewells, Avis stumbled

in her best heels down the platform, keeping pace with her husband. Just one last look. That would help, surely.

Inside, the passenger car was crammed full, glass panes showing men waving and shouting. One fellow with an army cap over his forehead actually leaned out the window to kiss his sweetheart, standing on tiptoe to meet his lips. Avis blushed just watching the stares and whistles others gave them.

Thankfully, Russell was content to polish the dirty pane and wave at her as the train pulled away. That was all she could manage while keeping the bright smile on her face.

It would be all right. It *would*.

They'd discussed the picket patrol three separate times in the week after the dance. Each time, Avis had brought up a different objection. What if his stable, steady job at the bank wasn't waiting for him when he came home? Would being the coxswain on the rowing team in college and some fishing with Herb really count as sailing experience? How would they get by on the lower salary?

Each time, Russell had a ready and patient answer. Mr. Bloomsbury would recommend him elsewhere if there were no positions open. The picket patrol had already sent him a preliminary acceptance. With their savings, a pay cut would be almost unnoticeable for three months.

Never again had she mentioned her father's indiscretions, but the words she'd spoken in fear were always there, lurking in the background.

When she had no reasons left, she'd finally said, "Russ, you know I wouldn't want to keep you from your duty."

"Are you sure?" he'd asked, looking surprised.

And then she'd told the biggest lie of her life. "Of course. In fact, I-I'm glad you have this opportunity."

She'd given him a chance to say he would stay, that she was more important than anything.

But he hadn't taken it.

Maybe he was so excited that he genuinely didn't notice her moodiness as he packed and planned—or maybe he had and avoided bringing it up, knowing that doing so might ruin his chance at freedom and adventure.

To make matters worse, the morning of Russell's departure, she'd woken to the telltale signs of what her mother had obliquely called the curse and dissolved into tears in the bathroom. After applying her Kotex and washing her face, she'd rallied enough to make Russell a hearty breakfast of bacon and eggs for his journey, not a scrap of Shredded Wheat in sight.

It had been a silly hope, but she hadn't realized how she'd held on to it in the corners of her mind: if she had been pregnant this time, Russell would surely stay home—to care for her, paint the nursery, prepare to welcome their child. Wouldn't he?

But then you'd have to give up the library, she reminded herself. Her mother and others had reluctantly agreed that married women might join the workforce in these unprecedented times, but Avis knew she couldn't bear the gossip she'd face if she kept her job as a young mother.

As she drove home from the station, Avis kept her eyes on the road, refusing to let them blur with tears. *You were the one who gave him permission to go*, she reminded herself.

Maybe, three months from now, he'd realize what a good, selfless wife she'd been, and Russell would return as his old self. Then they could be happy again.

At home, Avis tried to read *Pygmalion*, but she could hear the ticking of the grandfather clock thundering like gunfire in the quiet. And when she turned on the radio to cover it up, it was another report about the war.

No Russell to ask her what was for dinner, to grunt his agreement or disagreement with editorials in the newspaper, to snore lightly into the night. Even looking at his empty chair and the bare place on the hat rack where his fedora usually rested brought a wave of melancholy.

Without pausing to reconsider, she took up her raincoat and tucked the play's thin volume into her satchel. Nine o'clock. Too late to be out and about, but she wouldn't be driving, adding to the lights that made their coast such a target.

All she knew was that she couldn't spend another moment in that too-quiet house, with its reminders of Russell all around.

The library offered a welcome shelter from the pelting drizzle of the street. There, with only a small gooseneck lamp turned on to comply with blackout restrictions, Avis could feel—well, if not peace, then at least the quiet, nonjudgmental watching of a million printed pages.

Surrounded by work and numbers and checklists, she didn't realize how late it was, or how tired she was when she took a short rest in the armchair, her eyes fluttering shut.

All she focused on was forgetting. Just for a little while.

Russell would be back after three months. He'd promised.

But alone in the shadowed silence, it was difficult to believe him.

From Russell to Avis

July 9, 1942

Dear Avis,

Writing you from Boston so you'll have my new address. It's a good thing we'll be at sea for days at a time—this place isn't so much a home as a few pieces of mismatched furniture under a leaky roof. The downside to that is, it'll be hard for me to write regularly (no steady hours like the bank), but I'll do my best.

We'll start our training tomorrow. Some British fellows, retired from their civilian coastal patrol, got roped into the job. Teaching us how to use the radio, what to report or look for, that sort of thing.

I've got to jot down a bit about the crew they've assigned me to. We met yesterday, and I'm telling you, a radio melodrama couldn't assemble such a group of quirky characters. One, Lester, must be about seventy and claims he got sailing know-how from evading the feds while supplying speakeasies up and down the coast in the '20s. Stephen is the son of a millionaire home from college for the summer, with plenty of yachting experience. Then there are others whose names I can't remember yet—fellow with a limp from a football injury, a college man twenty pounds heavier than what the army will allow, a born sailor with a bolt in his wrist from an operation when he was a kid. Even Lt. Rufus Bud Smith, the leader of the whole patrol and the editor of Yachting Magazine, *was turned down by the navy for his poor eyesight.*

Some might think we're a ragtag lot, but as soon as I fell in with them, I knew I was in the right place. They're itching to do something as badly as I am.

They showed us the boat we'll be crewing too. It used to be a ninety-seven-foot schooner called the Gypsy Queen. *Nice name, isn't it? Well, wave farewell to it, because now we're CGR-3028, our glossy wooden hull painted dull gray. Our cargo? A few Great War machine guns, depth charges, a listening device, and eight men ready to sink those wolf packs.*

We'll be shipping off with the paint only barely dry after our training. I can't wait.

One more thing: the night we went dancing, I think we both said some things we regretted, and I'm sorry for that. Please don't be mad for keeps, Avis.

Let me know how all goes in Derby, but remember that

I won't get any mail until my onshore days. Fire Muster's coming up, if I recall. If you go, eat an ice cream cone or two for me, without worrying about nonsense like spoiling your figure. On celebratory days, none of that counts, and that's science.

Yours, ready for action,
Russell

Notes from the Blackout Book Club—July 11, 1942

Taken by Avis Montgomery, Head Librarian and Book Club Secretary

Members in attendance: the Regulars, plus Earl and Madeline Bell, Arley Lokken, Carol Ann Hoper, Danny Maloney, Diana Follett, and Mrs. Whitson (whom I simply can't call Muriel like she asked me to)

Book under discussion: <u>Pygmalion</u> by George Bernard Shaw

Back to taking notes myself this week, as it gives me something to do, and I don't feel much like sharing, since I only read a few pages into the second act. Thankfully, there are so many members now that others can carry the conversation. Hopefully, no one notices that I'm quieter than normal.

 Ginny jumped right in by calling Henry Higgins a "blustering, self-important pig" and seemed about to add something stronger before Miss Cavendish interrupted with a meaningful look at Rosa. Mr. Bell argued that Higgins was just lacking in social graces. Freddy said he tended to agree, at which point Ginny turned on him, reading examples of the worst of Higgins's dialogue at top volume. He quickly backed down. Others chimed in on all sides, some deploring the professor's treatment of poor Eliza, others blaming his insecurity or reading kindness in between the lines.

 Delphie wanted to know if it was actually possible for someone to change their way of speaking so entirely ("not that I would ever want to," she added, heavy on the French accent). It was widely agreed that no one actually knew much about linguistics, but it sounded realistic, and anyway it made for a good story.

Discussion moved to Mr. Doolittle's description of being one of the "undeserving poor" and his views on charity, which Miss Cavendish found appalling. The book club tends to skirt around discussions of finances or politics—but Mrs. Bell admitted that her family had once been so hard up that their only toys had been boats made out of flattened tin cans, so she found Eliza's character especially compelling. I grew up in this town, and I never would have guessed. It's amazing, what you don't know about people you've known all your life.

There was much controversy about the play's ending, which of course, I didn't get to. I still can't tell exactly what happened, but I know what didn't: Higgins and Eliza don't fall in love or marry. Ginny stoutly maintained that was perfect and redeemed the whole play, see aforementioned comment about Higgins being a pig. Mr. Maloney said he never understood why books and movies always show couples who argue constantly and ought to hate each other, then suddenly realize they're madly in love. ("It wasn't that way at all with my Lottie and me," he added, getting a sentimental look in his eyes which I thought was quite sweet.)

Several of the other women, preferring more traditional happy endings, felt disappointed since they'd thought all along the play was a romance. Mr. Bell decreed that you could, if you used your imagination, decide the pair got together after the curtain fell, to which Martina said, with uncharacteristic firmness, that Eliza had too much self-respect for that. Everyone seemed so surprised that she actually contradicted someone that the debate died there.

Ending aside, most members enjoyed the play and its sense of humor. The Bells were quite pleased to have suggested it.

Mrs. Whitson suggested a book set in coastal Maine, The

Country of the Pointed Firs, that she'd read in college and found "full of local color." That sounded fine to me, so it was settled.

Too tired to write more notes in detail today. Didn't sleep well last night—the bed feels so empty without Russell. Only three months. It will get easier, won't it?

twenty-one

GINNY
JULY 11

If you dunked them in tea and got them all sopped up and soggy, Avis's scones weren't so bad, Ginny decided, taking another bite. That and if you bit around the burnt parts.

Eating another was her solemn duty on account of there was a whole heap left after folks realized Avis's baking had failed them for the first time. Wouldn't do to make the poor woman feel bad.

As soon as Ginny had seen the librarian's wrinkled skirt and tousled hair, she'd asked what was wrong outright. It was a raw thing, Mr. Montgomery having to be so far away for the picket patrol, but Ginny thought she knew what he felt. Restless, that was it. What she wouldn't give to be on a boat, breathing in the salt air, letting it blow her braid over her shoulder toward shore. It was peak season now, when the lobstermen would stay out from dawn till dusk, pulling in teeming hauls. . . .

". . . and I hear Hollywood is trying to buy the rights to make it into a musical." Earl Bell's voice—somehow he hadn't used up all his words during the book discussion—cut into her daydream.

Ginny laughed. "Stuffy old Higgins breaking out into song? It would never work." She tried, and failed, to picture his linguistic exercises paired with a tap dance number.

"We won't find out, I'm afraid," Mr. Bell said, absently wiping sweat off his balding head with a handkerchief. "Stout old G. B. Shaw said something along the lines of 'over my dead body,' and that was that. Preserving the integrity of the work and its commentary on class distinctions, etc." He shrugged. "Of course, the fellow is in his eighties, so it's really only a matter of time."

"Oh, and so a person of eighty is halfway into the grave, is that it?" Delphie snapped, her eyes narrowing in on poor Mr. Bell like the bomb that flattened Coventry Cathedral.

Ginny felt sorry for him. Delphie wasn't one to cross lightly. Her bosom had settled at low tide, her figure beamy, as they'd say on the island—like a good ship, wide enough around the hips that you had to give room. If she was all curves below the neck, though, she was all lines and angles above it, her thin gray hair tightly pulled back and wrinkles giving her the look of a perpetual scowl. Or maybe she really was always scowling, and it wasn't the wrinkles' fault.

While they argued, as always, Avis went around to collect their copies, some new, others used, a few shared between members now that the club had grown. The ones the library didn't keep were donated to various drives and charities.

When Avis got to her, Ginny gripped the book tighter. "Can I keep it? Please?" She resisted pointing out that Avis owed her, seeing as she'd eaten three rock-like scones without complaining.

Her perfectly plucked brows tilted up. "You liked it that much?"

"I want to send Mack my copy. Books are better shared, you know?"

That, and she felt guilty that she hadn't sent any packages his way since boot camp. She'd used the excuse that she was trying to save money, but really, people mostly sent cigarettes, chocolate, and socks. Nothing expensive. It was more that it just felt so . . . sweetheart-like to send a gift. Like something you'd do if you were the type to seal letters with a lipstick kiss or sign them *Yours with Love*.

Silly. The play and some chewing gum, she decided. That wasn't so hard, was it? Mack would let out a whoop at mail call, that's for sure. He said he always looked forward to her letters.

She tried to picture him sweating on the deck of a battleship in the Pacific . . . and realized it was getting harder to remember his face, other than that troublemaker grin of his. "Mack's not much of a reader, so I'll mark my favorite bits to make it easier."

"And if your soldier doesn't like it, at least he could use the paper to roll cigarettes," Mr. Maloney added, taking away chairs to put back at the periodical tables.

"That's awful!" She swatted at his shoulder, which he dodged, chuckling. But she'd meant it. Funny, a few months ago, she'd have thought nothing of that idea. Hadn't she used one of her brother's school readers to prop up the crooked table leg back home? But now it seemed plain terrible, like spitting on a cross or something. "Books are meant for reading, and that's all."

He wisely slammed his mouth shut under the moustache. Trimmed better than usual, she noted, and was that a new suit? Good for him, getting out of that pawn shop for an hour or so.

As for the rest, some of the newer members had drifted over to the fiction section to see if Shaw had written any other plays, and Gio was deep in a heated argument with Mrs. Follett's oldest girl, a pretty thing with a stubborn streak hidden under deep dimples, about whether books where the dog dies at the end were even worth reading.

Instead of bustling about her to-do list, wheeling a shelving cart like it was a battering ram, Avis was still standing by the circle of chairs, clutching the stack of books and staring blankly toward the blackout curtain–framed window.

Oh boy. She was in a bad way today. Something had to be

done. Ginny sidled up to her. "You know, I wasn't sure at first, but you've done a good thing here with this club, Avis."

Only a slow blink told Ginny that Avis had heard her, but then Avis tilted her head toward her. "Do you really think so?"

Ginny clapped her on the back like Pa did with his fellow lobstermen during a slow season. "I'm sure of it."

The smile Avis gave her was a hesitant, tired one, but it was there. Ginny felt a burst of irritation at this Russell fellow, the one who had never once come to a book club meeting and now had run off on some grand adventure. If this is what love and marriage did to a person, maybe it wasn't worth it.

As the others drifted away, leaving only the Regulars, as Avis liked to call them, Louise cleared her throat. "I noticed," she said casually, "that the corner theater is showing *Mrs. Miniver*."

It had been for a month, not that Louise probably paid much attention to the marquees. "It's a huge hit," Ginny said. "They say they'll need a wheelbarrow for the Oscars it'll win."

Louise raised an eyebrow at that, then looked down to pull on her rich-person gloves. "I thought it might, perhaps, be beneficial to discuss the translation of a novel to a different medium. . . ."

Ginny gaped. "Louise! Are you really suggesting we go to the *movies*?"

The woman colored delicately. "Well, yes."

Well, would wonders never cease. "Not sure how long it's been since you've been to the theater, but films have sound now. And color too, some of them."

"I am aware, Ginny, thank you." The words came out with an edge, like a spoonful of cod liver oil, but that was just Louise's way, Ginny had learned. She turned to the others. "Is anyone interested?"

"Sounds like fun to me," Freddy said, with his usual easy smile.

"I'm in." Ginny shrugged. "Even if I've seen it twice already since it started showing last month." Movie tickets were the one little luxury she allowed herself.

Avis laughed. "And you still want to see it again?"

"What can I say? Greer Garson is fantastic. Besides, it'll be different with all of you. Better. Assuming you're paying." Ginny was always ready to save a dime, and Martina didn't have money to throw at things like movies, not with Gio outgrowing his shoes about once every two months.

Was that . . . a smile appearing on Louise's face? Hard to say, since it disappeared a second later. "It seems only fitting, since I suggested the idea."

Gio let out a whoop like he'd been told they'd all won a trip to Orchard Beach when he heard the news, and even Rosa tugged excitedly at Martina's hand, pulling her toward the library door.

It was only the original members, plus Freddy and Delphie since they were attached to Louise, who made it over to the corner theater for the matinee, but even so, they took up most of a row by themselves. Ginny claimed a seat near the center, letting her eyes adjust to the darkness.

The booming bass voiceover that cued in the newsreels took the same tone as always: serious but upbeat, like a parade march, as scenes from the week's headlines passed by. Soviet bigwigs' secret meeting in DC, the Grand Coulee Dam, even a bit on nursery schools springing up around the country "so Mother can help win the war." Ginny noticed Louise straighten up at that.

They didn't talk about it much, the fact that in a few months the library would be shut down, but they all knew it was coming. In the beginning, Ginny hadn't been much worried. Even wondered if Avis might let her have the storage-room novels for keeps.

But looking down the row of familiar faces in the dim theater light, she wondered what she'd do without the twice-monthly meetings.

It doesn't matter. You're only here as long as the war lasts anyway, she reminded herself.

As the Metro-Goldwyn-Mayer lion flickered on the screen with its familiar roar, Ginny sat back, pressing the lumpy seat to get comfortable. It did a girl good, sometimes, to step away from the real world and travel across oceans.

Of all the people clapping as the credits started to roll, Ginny was sure she was the loudest. Hard not to cheer with an ending like that, even if she'd seen it before. Right away, Freddy turned to Gio, on his left, to discuss whether the German uniforms were accurate, so there was no asking him what he thought. Instead, Ginny leaned over to Louise, on her other side, who was delivering a verdict with a slow nod.

"She's just like you, you know," Ginny blurted without really thinking about it.

That was enough to pull the older woman's attention to her. "I'm sorry, who?"

"Mrs. Miniver. Smart, calm, collected. Bet you'd grow roses and drink tea and slap a downed German in the middle of the war without breaking a sweat."

"I certainly would not. I wouldn't have any idea what to do."

Now, that was a surprise. "Really?"

Louise blinked, as if she hadn't meant to say quite so much. "Well . . . yes."

"Huh." Ginny considered that a moment. "What about the others?"

"I'm not sure what you mean."

How could she explain it? The way the other women always said the right thing, knew all the manners and how-do-you-dos, never seemed to swear under their breath or worry about money or complain.

"You all seem to know what it means to be a woman, that's all. I could never be Mrs. Miniver, all put together and dignified."

There, now she'd gone and done it. Given Louise the perfect opening for a lecture on proper womanhood and maturity.

But instead, Louise pressed her thin lips together for a moment, then asked, "Could you be Eliza Doolittle, do you think?"

She thought about the fiery flower seller, determined to make something of herself without selling her soul to do it.

"Gosh, I hope so."

"Then do that." Louise nodded crisply, as if it were as simple as that. "There are different kinds of strength. And I, for one, see Eliza's grit in you, Ginny. It's something to be admired."

"You two coming?"

Ginny jerked her head over to see Freddy calling to them, having reached the end of the row.

The credits were over now, and the others were all filing out to where they could talk about the movie without disturbing the folks who just wanted to enjoy the story without tearing it to shreds. Ginny bet Avis had spent half the film making a list of the changes the screenwriters had made from the book.

Ginny waved him away, brushing popcorn off her skirt. "Don't rush us."

He laughed, and she couldn't help smiling. Infectious, that laugh of his.

When she turned back, Louise was giving her an odd sort of look. "He's leaving this fall, you know."

"Sure." He'd said as much before. Back to his family, the one he didn't talk much about, even when Ginny showed a friendly interest. That's what she called it, not *being nosy* like Avis said. "What about it?"

"I simply wanted to make sure he hadn't indicated otherwise to you."

Ah. She remembered Louise's rule about romantic entanglements.

Maybe she'd been watching, when, during the funeral scene at the end, Ginny had sniffled, and Freddy had offered her his handkerchief with a brief squeeze to her hand. "I hate war," she'd whispered to him, after trying to blow her nose quiet-like.

"You should. We all should," he'd said, and Ginny knew there were stories hiding past the haunted look on his face, before he turned back to the screen and the movie rolled on.

But that wasn't flirting, just because a man didn't want her dripping all over the theater and they'd exchanged a few words during a movie.

"Don't you worry, Louise," Ginny said, patting her hand comfortingly before the older woman pulled away. "Remember, I've got a beau in the service."

Even saying it made her feel a twinge of guilt. Better get that package in the mail fast. Mack's letters weren't so long as they once were, warfront life keeping him busy and all, but he still hinted that he wanted to hear from her more often.

Louise didn't look entirely reassured. "Just be sure *you* remember that."

Ginny tried to brush it off. Just a stern old spinster trying to smother romance anywhere she suspected it could spring up. Still, she couldn't help wondering if Louise knew something from Freddy's past, something unsavory, something that might make her want to warn Ginny away.

Stop that. It's your imagination.

She meant well, ol' Louise, probably. And besides, she'd bought them all popcorn too, so that squared things up from Ginny's perspective.

She was just wondering whether she'd have to choke down another scone back at the library when Gio started hollering. And everyone turned to stare at a shadowy figure who ducked out the theater's back exit.

twenty-two

MARTINA
JULY 11

It must have been a mother's instinct that made Martina's pulse race the moment she saw Gio freeze in the theater aisle. She guessed the cause even before he pointed toward the back door, before the awful words fell from his lips.

"It's Da!"

There he was, leaning against the side wall in the flickering shadows cast by the projectors, watching them. Patrick. From the distance, it was impossible to tell for sure, but Martina felt him look right at her before opening the back door, tucked beside the screen, and slamming it behind him.

"Da? Where?" Rosa cried, swiveling toward where Gio pointed. Before Martina could think, her son was running toward the door Patrick had just exited, letting another burst of bright sunlight into the theater.

Faster than she could have imagined possible, Martina chased Gio down the alley, calling his name. But he didn't stop, kept running toward the street. She snatched at his shirt just before he hurtled blindly off the sidewalk and into the street, bustling with traffic. A delivery truck's horn blared at them as she gripped his arms.

"Never run away from me like that again." Her voice shook,

but for once it sounded every bit as commanding as Mamma's. "What if your sister had followed you?"

Whatever shock he'd felt from the near miss in the street faded, and Gio wrenched his shoulder away, looking in all directions. Patrick was nowhere to be seen. "Let me go! Mamma, I saw him."

Anger flared. How dare Patrick stare at them like that? If she hadn't acted quickly, both of the children might have been struck and killed.

The next words fell as easily from her lips as the memorized prayers of her childhood. "That was not your father, Gio." And all the saints could stand in judgment against her, but she didn't feel one bit of guilt looking directly into her son's face and lying.

What was happening to her?

"But I saw him too!" Rosa insisted, joining her. The others were watching from a distance, none of them wanting to interfere, but Martina noticed, gratefully, that Freddy ran over to step between them and the road, in case Gio decided to run again.

"It was only a mistake, *piccolo*." She let go of Gio with one arm to smooth her daughter's hair. "You know he's very far away, training to fight in the war."

Rosa wrinkled her nose. "Oh. I forgot."

"Even sailors get leave sometimes." Gio had stopped fighting her, while still craning his neck across the street, where Patrick had disappeared.

"Don't you think he'd tell us if he were coming to visit?"

They seemed to accept that answer, but Martina's mind was still spinning. Patrick had said he was staying nearby. Was it a coincidence, seeing him like this, or had he been watching them, following them to the theater even?

"Don't be sad, Mamma," Rosa said quietly.

Martina didn't answer. Better not to make more promises she couldn't keep.

"Sure looked like him," Gio said, shoulders slumping again. Freddy gave Gio a friendly cuff to the back. "Come on, sport. Let's talk about the movie over ice cream, hmm?"

That was enough to perk Rosa up. At her age and after over a year on their own, Patrick was a uniformed photograph to her, a happy memory of Irish ballads and crumbly soda bread sopped in milk, the father she must have somewhere because all little girls have fathers.

But while Gio followed their little caravan once again, she noticed him squinting into the afternoon sun as they crossed the street, trying to get another glimpse of his father.

And Martina prayed that he wouldn't get one.

They walked down the street in silence, until the bell on the creamery clattered cheerily and her children led the charge inside, already pointing at the glassed-in wonders beyond.

"I'll wait here." Martina waved them to go on without her. "I'm not hungry, and . . . I need the fresh air."

Only Ginny protested, saying something about hunger not having a thing to do with ice cream, but Freddy took her arm and told her to leave it be and what did she think of hot fudge sundaes?

The others followed after, but Avis paused at the door, then let go of the handle, joining Martina on the sidewalk. "I'm sorry if I'm intruding, but . . . how long has it been since you saw your husband?"

That, she could answer, if indirectly. "Patrick joined the navy over a year ago."

Avis bit her lip, rosy against perfect peaches-and-cream skin. "I would be devastated if Russell— But his term is only three months. He promised. So I just can't understand . . ."

When her voice trailed off, Martina prompted, "Understand what?"

"Why you didn't seem eager to see your husband. Or disappointed that it wasn't him." She reached a hand to adjust her hair, which wasn't as neatly styled as usual. "It's none of my business, of course."

She didn't owe this woman an explanation. And yet, Avis was so young, with so much time to avoid the mistakes Martina had made. "Does your husband treat you well, Avis?"

She hesitated, caught off guard by the personal question. "We have had our differences. Our little arguments, but yes."

"Then be grateful. None of us marry perfect men. But some are capable only of loving themselves, and their wives' worlds narrow. And one day, you realize not only have you lost the broad view of what could be, but you can barely breathe."

It was terrible, maybe even a mortal sin, but Martina forced herself to admit the truth. She had hoped the navy would work out for Patrick. Maybe so that the routine and rules would force him to sober up, but if not . . . there was always the chance that he wouldn't come home at all. So many would not, many of them far better men than Patrick.

If that had happened, she would never have to tell Gio his father had abandoned them.

The younger woman blinked in the bright afternoon sun. "I see." She didn't, of course. But she was trying, and there was a kindness in her eyes that Martina hadn't noticed before. Her next words were spoken quietly enough that no one passing by would overhear. "What will you do when he comes back?"

He already has, she almost admitted in a whisper.

"We'll manage somehow," she said instead.

Avis meant well, and Martina enjoyed talking about books with her. But some stories were too close, too personal, and too dangerous to share.

twenty-three

LOUISE
JULY 18

"Well," Frederick said, frowning at the crowd, "you were right about everyone in town being here."

"I am not prone to exaggeration." Louise looked out at the bustle and tried to see it the way a newcomer would instead of someone who had attended the festival every year for the past few decades. Derby, its population swelled by summer visitors, was out in force for the Fire Muster, looking their best in gingham dresses and boater hats. "Ever since we got that garish ladder truck, it's become a county-wide event."

She pointed, as if he could miss the bright red behemoth blocking half the street in front of city hall. It had been their mayor's campaign platform for years, and he lost no chance to show it off to constituents.

Locals knew it was best to pray nothing caught fire on the day of the Fire Muster. The volunteers that comprised the crew would never be able to get to the scene on time without running over half of the crowd, including many children who mobbed around for a closer look.

"Still," Louise said, trying to inject some enthusiasm into her voice, "it's very festive, isn't it?"

Frederick nodded morosely. He'd dressed in his military uniform despite the heat of the day, but he looked more like he was being dragged to an execution than a mere presentation on gardening techniques. It was almost enough to make her feel sorry that she'd signed him up for this.

Almost. But duty must be done. Anything for the war effort.

Booths lined Main Street, some selling food or streamers on poles, all proceeds to benefit the fire department, others calling out to recruit participants to the various competitions: a bucket brigade, hose rolling, ladder climbing. They always targeted the young, brash men, those sure they could win back the entry fee and cocky enough to risk making a fool of themselves in front of a crowd.

Except, Louise realized, surveying the crowds, there weren't many available this year. Odd how it took occasions like this to really notice how enlistment had affected the population. Even the firemen, sweltering in their uniforms as they waved proudly at the crowd, were of an older set than usual, averaging in their forties and fifties.

"No more dawdling," she said crisply, walking with the sort of authority that made crowds part around her. "Your presentation will begin shortly."

A quick glance backward revealed Frederick's grimace. "How could I forget?"

My, he really was nervous, wasn't he? It didn't seem possible for someone as confident and charming as her young gardener. Louise knew she was rubbish at inspirational speeches, but as this was her fault, perhaps she could try. "You'll do just fine. All you have to do is share what you know."

He managed an admirable attempt at a smile, though not entirely sincere. Still, once the boy got up on stage, the nerves would fade away. After all, his family had tended a garden all his life, back in New Hampshire.

As they approached the platform, Elvira Buckwold was easily made visible by her hat, a sentinel bedecked with fiery red ribbons for the occasion. Rows of benches flanked her on either side, many already filled, and two other women, her daughter and Frances Jefferson, clustered near the platform steps next to her. Louise wondered if she'd have to grip Frederick's arm to keep him from bolting, but he followed obediently behind her, resigned to his fate.

They wove through the gathering audience, and Louise was about to call Elvira's name when she heard Avis's and paused.

". . . haven't seen her anywhere today, have you?" Lillian was saying.

"No," Frances said. "She's probably locked up in that library, and no wonder. Seems to me, she's really let herself go, starting even before her husband left."

Elvira, her back still to Louise, fanned herself with one of the flyers they'd used to promote the event and leaned in to the others. "I've heard—and don't ask me who from—that he might not come back. Or that he's not involved in defense at all. A group of yachters chasing Nazi subs? It's too absurd."

"No!" Lillian's gasp was full of scandal. "She wouldn't make up something like that."

"You don't know the lengths a woman will go to—"

"Say now," Frederick said, stepping up, and the women turned at his irritated voice, faces representing various degrees of guilt.

Louise held up a hand and glared a warning at him, and he scurried off to the podium, notes in hand. Her message had been clear: *Leave this to me.*

Before any of the other women could get a word in, Louise stepped closer. "Good day, ladies. As you can see, we have arrived." She made her voice as frosty as an ocean plunge in December. "I'm sorry that our delay gave you time for idle gossip."

She paused purposefully, prompting nervous laughter from Frances, but Elvira simply fumed.

"Never mind that," Lillian stammered, edging toward the

platform to make her escape. "If I could just have a word with Mr. Keats before he begins. I'm introducing him, you see. . . ."

"One moment, if you please." She pitched the phrase like the genteel threat it was. The women stared at her, held in place, waiting. "I would like to make it clear that I don't approve of gossip of any kind. Criticisms and corrections are sometimes worth speaking, but they accomplish nothing unless said to the person's face. Don't you think?"

To call it a question would be generous, and the Buckwolds clearly knew it, murmuring a halfhearted agreement.

"Oh, but we would never tell Avis—" Frances said, breaking off in a cough.

"Then perhaps," Louise said, "you should consider never speaking slander about a good and capable woman when she is *not* present either."

She left them standing there agape without response, her business done. It wasn't her they needed to apologize to, after all. As soon as she turned her back, they'd probably start whispering about how tirades like that were why Louise had remained single all these years.

Or maybe, just maybe, they'd think twice before gossiping again.

She took a seat in the third row, close enough to hear clearly, far enough away to be polite, and took out her knitting from her bag. No sense in wasting time when one could be productive. Winter was approaching, and the soldiers in Europe would need mittens.

A chuckle beside her made her turn to see Ginny plopping down on the bench uncomfortably close to her, the legs of her tan boating pants set apart in an unladylike fashion. "Golly, Louise, you sure told those old biddies."

It was on Louise's mind to mention that eavesdropping was generally frowned upon in polite society, but she supposed she'd been loud enough that the girl couldn't help overhearing. "Someone needed to."

Louise looked over to where the Buckwolds had intercepted Freddy, the younger of the two leaning flirtatiously toward him. "In any case, we should feel sorry for them if the only thing they have to talk about is other people's lives."

Ginny nodded. "Sure. At the book club, we've got fictional people's lives to talk about instead."

Louise blinked, but it didn't seem like the girl was mocking. Her blue eyes seemed thoughtful. "I . . . never thought about it that way."

But wasn't it true? Certainly, Louise had been kept up late reading the Christie novel to find the answer to the murder, but equally fascinating had been Poirot's observations on human nature and what caused people to love and lie and betray. *Pygmalion*, with the club's discussion on how charity can be offered in a way that takes away a person's dignity, had made her wonder if perhaps she was approaching the daycare center in an unhelpful manner, just as Frederick had suggested.

Father had said something like that several times, to the point where Louise could still remember his words. *"That's what most don't understand,"* he'd said, gesturing at her and her brother. *"Fictional characters are often more real than the flesh and blood people around us—in the ways that matter, that is."*

"What do they know about our Avis, anyway?" Ginny went on, bringing Louise's mind back to the present.

"I'm sure Avis would be more than capable of standing up for herself were she present. But since she's not, it's up to the Blackout Book Club to do so for her."

Ginny gave her a long, squinting look, then grinned. "You know, you're not so bad after all, Louise Cavendish." She tipped a cardboard carton Louise's way. "Peanut?"

Even though she didn't care for the messy treat, Louise took three of the shells, still warm to the touch from the cart by the fire truck.

It was an odd thing. She'd graduated from nursing school with top marks, been named chair of innumerable committees, and received letters of commendation for all manner of charity work, and yet those few words from Ginny felt as if they might be worth more than any of them.

She sat up a little straighter, a faint smile on her face as the program began, and popped a peanut into her mouth. Not so bad, indeed.

twenty-four

GINNY
JULY 18

On the positive side, Freddy looked good up on the bunting-draped platform, his military dress uniform all sharply ironed angles, his dark hair pomaded to a shine.

Trouble was, he sounded downright awful.

Poor fellow. Probably, if you put ol' Freddy in the cockpit of a plane before he lost his eye, he'd be as calm and sure as a sunrise. But here, blithering on about the care and keeping of rutabagas, he stammered like a schoolboy unprepared to be called on in class. It was all Ginny could do to keep a pleasant smile on her face, listening as pauses dangled from every other phrase.

The rest of the lecture guests, mostly housewives, politely listened with the stiff New England posture you learned by being herded into church pews from the time you were red and wrinkly. Ginny settled back on her bench and tried to do the same.

"And broccoli and cauliflower won't mature until . . . round about September."

Interesting. He wasn't glancing around, his eyes looking for a place to land. He was glancing to the side, where Gio sat in the front row.

Probably wanting to see a friendly face. Although that wasn't much good, since it looked like Gio had brought some school-work, running a pencil along a notebook's page, paying poor stuttering Freddy no attention at all.

No, that wasn't right. Watching the boy more closely, Ginny could see that he looked up occasionally, every time Freddy's pause lapsed into seconds.

Was he . . . mouthing something?

She squinted, not caring now that she was staring.

"Treating the garden to prevent insect damage is essential. Pests like aphids can be controlled with a spray of laundry soap mixed with . . ." Right when the pause drifted into awkward, Gio looked up from his paper and his lips moved, sure enough. ". . . nicotine sulfate."

She'd seen—well, participated—in enough cheating in school spelling bees to know what was going on. Either Freddy was so nervous he needed someone to feed him lines or . . .

Or he didn't really know what he was talking about. After all, this ought to be second nature to him, being a gardener.

It was a little thing. Just another tiny doubt. But what if there was something to it? What if she was being tricked by smooth words and a gleaming smile, just like all the dupes that Ma cheated in poker in her younger years?

After another ten minutes or so of tortured speechmaking, Lillian's mother, stuffed into a plaid dress far too small for her, released Freddy from his agony by thanking him and asking people to step up for a copy of a sample gardening calendar.

As soon as the polite applause died down, Ginny bolted over to Freddy, who had collapsed on a bench. Better to head things off while Lillian was still helping her mother distribute leaflets.

"All right, Freddy," she said, going right for the heart of it. "Let's talk about your little secret."

And whatever small part of her had been bluffing to see how he'd react fell away at the guilty look in his eyes. "What secret?"

"That you're as much a gardener as I am. Which is to say, not very much of one."

Freddy let out a laugh, but it was too thin in the middle, like when she tried to roll out a piecrust. "Come on. Did you taste those buckets of spring peas I hauled in?"

"Okay, then. Which crops do you plow under in the winter to ready the soil for the next season?" She didn't know the answer either, but as long as he didn't know that she didn't know . . .

He swallowed hard. "Peas and beans?"

"That was a guess." He didn't deny it. "I'll bet your family never had a garden. And you got a job as a gardener barely knowing the difference between growing a dill pickle and a dandelion."

"You don't grow pickles, Ginny."

"Fine, so you're a *little* more of a gardener than I am." She folded her arms, trying to look like a cop in a movie. "What made you take the job at Miss Cavendish's, huh? Hiding from the law? Dodging the draft? What's under that eyepatch, anyway?"

He swatted away her hand as she reached toward him, which she probably deserved. "Just trying to make a new start. That's all."

That bumped *ex-con* higher up on the list of possibilities. "You know, I always thought it was funny how a flyboy like you claimed to be the salt-of-the-earth farmer sort before the war. Didn't add up."

He motioned at her to keep her voice down, glancing over at the line of women about to swim toward him, Victory-garden calendars in tow. "Ginny, I told you. I came here to get away from my hometown. I needed work. Miss Cavendish needed a gardener. So I embellished my résumé. That's all."

And as much as Ginny hated to admit it, it didn't sound like the load of bilge she'd expected from him. "Is that so? Why'd you drag Gio into it, then?" The kid had hidden the notebook away and was munching contentedly on a sugar-dusted doughnut. His payment, probably.

"Because I was desperate for help. He checked out gardening books for me from the library too, back in the spring. That's how I knew enough to get started."

If he was telling the truth, it wasn't a bad plan. Just like something she would have done. "Golly, I hope you didn't embellish your résumé to plop yourself in a plane cockpit too."

"Thankfully for everyone, you can't fake flying hours or officer training school." Another glance about, worry clear on his face. "Please, Ginny. You can't tell Miss Cavendish."

"Give me one good reason."

Freddy's eyes were pleading. "You're just going to have to trust me. It's what friends do."

That's when Lillian, fresh out of leaflets, rushed over in a flood of giggles and false compliments, and Ginny retreated to a bench a distance away, considering. It could be true. An ex-GI needing work and wanting something as far from combat as possible might make up some experience. It wasn't all that bad.

That's it. That's why. The reason she felt uneasy was because she'd caught him in something small.

And suddenly, Ginny was fourteen years old again, watching as Pa and Lew headed out in the early morning fog, thick as burgoo, on the *Lady Luck*, giving her the chance to ask Ma the question that had nagged at her for a year at least.

Made sense, of course, Pa not wanting to talk about it, pretending his bride was a woman of spotless reputation. But Ginny had heard enough to wonder. On Long Island, children were only hidden from rumors for a little while. And she needed to know. So she'd tiptoed up to Ma, offering to help with breakfast, and asked how, exactly, she'd gotten away with cheating at cards for so many years.

Instead of getting upset, Ma just dusted her hands with flour, pounding down the biscuit dough, and said, "Your pa'll skin me if I show you the tricks." Ginny almost protested, until her mother added, "Setup's what I'm most proud of, anyway."

"What d'ya mean?"

She'd gotten a far-off look, like Mack's gran when she slipped into a tale of island lore and legend. "When I found a mark, I'd settle in, play a bit of the fool. Then I'd be sure early on that I got caught tilting my head to look at the cards of the man next to me."

Ginny frowned. "You wanted to get caught?"

She nodded. "Sometimes the fellow would get spitting mad, and that's when you knew it wasn't safe to go on. But most times, he'd give me a stern look and a chuckle at the same time, telling me to keep my eyes straight ahead. After all, who hasn't snuck a glance like that?"

"Then you'd palm the cards, or pull one from your sleeve, or whatever it was," Ginny finished. Gosh, she never knew her mother was so clever.

"And no one would ever notice or guess." Ma gave the dough a particularly rough knead. "Remember that, Ginny. The ordinary lies, the ones easy to admit to, often hide something worse."

Ginny looked over at Freddy, all smiles now, posing for a snapshot with a spade someone had brought, the younger and older Buckwolds beaming on either side of him.

So what if Freddy was a liar? She was used to playing it cool, staying aloof, not trusting a person until she knew them inside and out. This was nothing new.

Then why, when it came to Freddy, did it hurt so much?

From Russell to Avis

July 20, 1942

Dear Avis,

Well, our first days at sea are under our belt, and it's almost a shame to be back on land after all that salt air. It was good to find the letters from you waiting for me. I read them all twice already.

No derring-do yet, I'm afraid, just testing equipment and running our route. I've got an important role, anyway, because our skipper, Captain Arthur Sherman, said the ones with music training do better sorting out sounds. Fellow without much of an ear might mistake a whale for a U-boat engine, that sort of thing. I talked up my career in brass instruments, so he put me as the sound man on overnights, when the U-boats are most active. Good for me he didn't have a tuba handy, or I would've shown I don't remember much from high school except how to aim a spit valve at the school bully.

We've got a simple underwater listening device—nothing special to look at, just a heavy rubber-coated sausage attached to a cable. When it's light out, a look-out's posted in case we spot a sub. We're also supposed to smell, at night especially, for diesel fuel, the stench when a U-boat surfaces. They have to do that sometimes, for fresh air or pressure sickness, and our craft is small enough that it won't show up on their radar. They'll think they're all alone in the ocean. That's when we're supposed to report them by radio. Or as our training manual said, "Once contact with the enemy has been established, it will not be broken off as long as it is possible to maintain it."

None of this is classified, by the way, from what I've

heard. That's the brilliance of it. We've got the coast guard's backing, but almost none of their rules. No uniforms, no roll call, no censors reading our mail. Just the open sea and a job to do.

If only they'd let us off from coast guard food too. My taste buds are going dull from all the military rations we slug down on days when we don't catch any fish to fry up. I can't tell you what I'd give for just one slice of your meatloaf right now.

Thanks for the update on all that's going on with you. Not surprised your mother had a fit when she heard where I was off to. She always was one for dramatics. Talk up the patriotism to her and tell her I'll be home by October tenth, and she'll come around. I'll even agree to Thanksgiving at her house to smooth things over. Probably won't feel that different from facing down armed U-boats.

*Book club's still going strong, I take it? Glad to hear it. Haven't read much since I was a boy—*Treasure Island *and* Robinson Crusoe *and all that. Guess there's no chance those will be on the list, huh?*

Signing off. These days on land are the only time we get a good bed and decent meals. Got to take advantage.

> *Yours, dreaming of*
> *meatloaf,*
> *Russell*

From Anthony to Avis

July 10, 1942

Dear Sis,
Well, look who got a haul in mail call today! I'm late in responding, but you can blame the army for that.

I'm not surprised Russell finally found some war work, but I'm worried for you. You say you're fine with his leaving, just not the way you let him leave. As I'm currently living the bachelor foxhole life with nary a wife or sweetheart in sight, I can't say I understand exactly what you mean. But as they say, "Fools rush in where angels fear to tread" (Alexander Pope, long poem, you'd hate it for sure), so I thought I'd venture some advice: Tell the man what you're thinking. Chances are, he hasn't got a clue.

Note that I never claimed to be profound. But you, dear sis, have always lived so much in your own head, all worries and wondering. Russell's my best friend, and if you're upset with him or fear you've hurt him or whatever it might be, you've got to talk it out.

But there. Enough of my meddling from an ocean away. Say, thanks for copying down some of the book club notes regarding Wodehouse. Had a good laugh over them.

If I didn't know better, it sounds like you're actually starting to like reading. I should be offended that twenty-five years of being related to me didn't do the trick, but I'll rest content in the knowledge that you've finally agreed to my motto: "He was fond of books, for they are cool and sure friends." (That's Les Misérables. *It's an undertaking—the French like their prose the way they like their baguettes: very long—but you've got to take a crack at it. Maybe during the winter when everything is frozen, and you can stay in with tea and wool socks and voluminous great novels.)*

Speaking of France . . . I can't. Censors, you know. So I'll keep to praising the care package you sent with the compact paperback of Wells's The Invisible Man. *I've passed it around to three fellows so far. We might start a book club of our own at this rate.*

Take care of that library for me, sis. She'll be the first place I visit when I come home (don't tell Mom).

Your brother,
Anthony

Notes from the Blackout Book Club—July 25, 1942

Taken by Ginny Atkins, Owner of a Captivating Reading Voice and Certainly a Better Recorder of Minutes Than Freddy Keats, Thank You Very Much

Members in attendance: Lots. Avis'll write them down later. She's better at things like that.

Book under discussion: The Country of the Pointed Firs by Sarah Orne Jewett (Found out the middle name isn't said like "ornery," which is a shame, I think.)

I started with the rousing question of "How come there weren't any murders?" Lots of secrets and regrets and all (poor Joanna!), but they never went anywhere, really. Freddy said that wasn't the point, but I think he was only picking a fight. Avis protested that it was full of beautiful, peaceful descriptions, and that the author truly understood folks, but Delphie proclaimed it "a real yawner."

Linda Follett, who is maybe about ten with uneven pigtails, said she read the whole thing just to find out the narrator's name and was mad when we never found out. She insisted we all call her Hildegard out of spite.

Freddy said he liked the chapter best where the old sea captain tells of a ghostly town far up north: "There was in the eyes a look of anticipation and joy, a far-off look that sought the horizon; one often sees it in seafaring families, inherited by girls and boys alike," he read, then added, "Reminds me of someone I know." And didn't he look right at me! Whether or not he meant it as a compliment, I'll take it as one.

We talked about the part where "Hildegard" wondered if some castaways on desert islands dread the thought of being rescued. Not even Martina thought she'd feel that way "though the quiet would be nice for a while." (Gio looked offended at that, but I patted him on the back and told him it wasn't his fault he was loud, it's just part of being twelve and a boy. Didn't seem to help much.) "There's peace, and then there's loneliness, and one can turn easily into the other," Mrs. Whitson said, and everyone sort of nodded, because being a minister's wife, she ought to know.

Avis read a few of her favorite parts aloud, and at the end, Mr. Maloney proclaimed, "That's <u>Maine</u>, it is." He's got a point. Not much plot that I could find in this one, but the words were pretty, and the way she described boating out to the islands made me ache to see the sun rise over the seaward horizon. It's been a while since I really felt homesick. Too long, maybe.

Gosh, give a girl a notebook and she goes all sentimental. This is why I should never keep a diary.

Much better review than the book: Avis's banana pudding. She's getting fancier with the treats, probably has more time with her husband away and all. I got over to it in time for seconds.

Avis let Rosa choose the book for next time around. She thought for a moment, in that grown-up way of hers, then picked <u>The Velveteen Rabbit</u>. It's gloriously short, and there are even pictures. What a red-letter day for the Blackout Book Club!

twenty-five

LOUISE
JULY 27

Louise had given speeches at war-bond drives, passed along grim odds to dying patients, and even held her own at the reading of her father's will among contentious family members who resented her inheriting the family's summer home, all without the slightest tremor of nerves.

So why did the thought of stepping inside the Bristol-Banks cafeteria fill her with dread?

It will be fine, she told herself. *They're only women. Just like you.*

Which was a falsehood, of course. They were not like her. It wasn't only the class difference. She'd left her pearls at home and worn her most ordinary day dress to minimize the gap between herself and her audience in that regard. It was the fact that these were wives and mothers, listening to a confirmed spinster telling them how they ought to raise their children.

Nonsense. This was a business matter. A social service. Nothing more.

Frederick exited the cafeteria with a jaunty step, unburdened from the trays of sandwiches and pitchers of lemonade he'd offered to carry in, filling the role of porter instead of gardener today. He gestured to the door with a flourish. "They're all yours, Miss Cavendish."

217

She checked her pocket watch. *3:45*, the time between the day shift and swing shift, the two most commonly worked by women with children. Mr. Hanover had allowed her fifteen minutes to speak to any interested mothers.

She felt Frederick's eyes on her. "You'll do just fine. All you have to do is share what you know." For a moment, she wondered if he was mocking her by repeating her own words from the garden lecture, but his expression was as warm as ever. "Now go knock 'em dead."

"I would prefer that my audience remain alive, actually." And despite her dry tone, he laughed, a deep, welcoming sound that reminded her of . . .

Not now, for goodness' sake.

Some memories were best left in the past.

In a manner she knew would seem abrupt, Louise turned away from Frederick, set her shoulders with one more deep breath, and let her heels click across the bare cafeteria floor with a confidence she didn't feel.

The northeast corner of the room was full of perhaps three dozen women in practical working garb of trousers, headscarves, and sturdy shoes. Many, though, still wore a pop of color or flutter of floral in their bandannas or buttoned blouses, as if determined not to surrender every vestige of femininity. Some used the pamphlets she'd had Frederick distribute to fan themselves, providing some relief from the humid air tinged with the smell of overdone mass-produced meat.

Some of the women looked up as Louise approached. Watching her. Waiting.

She should smile. Yes, that would help. Louise tried her best—and then the glimpse of Ginny and Martina sitting in the front row made it a shade more genuine.

She stood before the group and licked her dry lips as more stares turned her way. "Welcome, everyone." This declaration stopped most of the chatter, though a few women at the fringes still seemed to feel their conversation was too important to be paused and continued it in whispers.

"As a resident of nearby Derby, I have been called upon to address a potential difficulty. I'm sure some of you have comfortable arrangements with relatives for childcare as you work. But for those who do not, we would like to provide a low-cost alternative."

There. It wasn't so bad, especially if she kept her eyes fixed on the back wall and not aimed directly at the women. The few times she did, they seemed . . . well, not eager or excited, but certainly polite.

Her confidence and volume rose as she went through the carefully prepared speech, sharing that by Christmas, they hoped to have an operational facility for children. Ginny paused in ravaging a sandwich long enough to pass out informational cards for the women to fill out to indicate interest, while Louise explained the benefits of professional childcare, then closed the ten-minute talk.

There was no applause at the end—it wasn't the Metropolitan Opera—but she'd ended a full three minutes early, and no one had fallen asleep. That must mean something.

The women pressed the informational cards into her hands as they left, a few thanking her for the food and lemonade, most shyly looking away and hurrying either home or to their stations in the foundry. Some, she noticed, had left their cards on the table nearest the door rather than approach her. It was difficult trying not to be intimidating when you'd spent your whole life trying to become more so.

Soon the cafeteria was all but empty. "How do you think it went?" Ginny asked, swinging up beside her and re-knotting the blue kerchief that bound up her blond hair, Martina by her side.

"Fairly well, I think." Louise straightened the cards with a tap on the table, lining up the corners. "We had ample time for all the information I wanted to communicate, and I trust—"

She paused, noticing something for the first time: the top card was blank.

So was the next, and the next.

Ignoring Ginny's curious stare, she sat and thumbed through the whole stack. Only three women, one of them Martina, had bothered to give their information to be contacted when the center opened.

Maybe she hadn't given them enough time to ask questions, or perhaps the form was too detailed. That was it, probably. She should have asked only for names and home addresses rather than including the names and birthdays of their children. Or perhaps some of them weren't even literate. Who could say?

"Tough sell, huh?" Ginny asked sympathetically, her nose poked over Louise's shoulder.

Heat rose to her cheeks, and she quickly gathered up the unmarked cards. "I don't understand. If they all had alternative means of childcare, why did they bother to attend the meeting?"

"For the lemonade, probably," Ginny offered thoughtfully, then broke off with "Ow!" and a glare at Martina, who shifted her foot off Ginny's a little too late to evade Louise's notice.

"You have to understand," Martina said, dark eyes sympathetic. "It is . . . difficult for some women to accept charity. Even if they need it."

Just as Frederick had told her weeks before.

"It's not charity. They're serving our country with their labor. We're simply making sure their children are cared for. Why, there's even a small cost associated with the nursery school."

"Maybe so. But if you were in their place, wouldn't you wish to be able to care for your own children?"

Louise huffed at the implication. "Certainly not. I would evaluate the situation practically and take the commonsense solution." As she had. As she always did.

Martina shook her head. "I suppose I can't ask you to understand, having never been a mother."

Don't flinch. Martina didn't mean to be hurtful, Louise was sure, so she bit back a harsh response.

A bell resounded, shrill and loud, and Louise startled. "C'mon," Ginny urged, tugging on Martina's arm. "Foreman'll have our heads if we're late."

That left Louise alone with an empty pitcher ringed with a thin sludge of sugar and three dozen blank interest cards.

"It doesn't make sense," she said, shaking her head. The empty cafeteria didn't reply.

She had been so certain that this was an act of Christian charity she was called to do to support the war effort. But what if she closed the library and spent a fortune to renovate it into a childcare center—and no one came?

You could still change your mind. Keep the library open.

But she'd come so far, too far to turn back now. Approved the plans. Signed a contract.

What would Father say?

Not much of a question. To everyone else, even Delphie, she could pretend that Luther Cavendish would be pleased to know his building was being used to care for children and support the war effort.

But she couldn't lie to herself. Her father had loved that library more than anything, even to the end.

JUNE 1917

"Absolutely not." Louise frowned down at her father, leaning weakly against the garden bench, a stack of freshly cut lupines beside him. "Father, Dr. Hoffman is very concerned. You should have visited him months ago. He gave strict instructions that you're not to leave the grounds, and I mean to enforce that."

Wasn't it enough that she encouraged him to be outdoors as often as possible? Old medieval theories about bad air and

221

the danger of drafts had been proven false by modern science, which now extolled the benefits of sunshine, at least on warm afternoons like this one. It had frightened her, seeing how frail and pale Father had become when she first arrived the week before.

Though in moments like these, when the stubborn scowl appeared on her father's face, she realized his diagnosis had changed very little.

"So I'm to be a prisoner in my own home? I never imposed such restrictions on you when you lived under this roof. Though perhaps I should have."

Louise took in a deep breath. He was trying to distract her, and she would not be baited. "This is not just about you, Father. This is about the people you would interact with in a poorly ventilated space while violently coughing. You will not be going to the library today or ever again."

The way Father drooped, like an unwatered plant, made her hesitate. Perhaps she had been too harsh. Perhaps . . .

"But . . . my books."

Oh, for heaven's sake. Father hadn't been ruminating on his mortality at all. "Books are, last I checked, portable. If you compile a list . . ." She held out a hand, and he paused only a moment before pushing past her, leaning on his cane and grumbling, presumably retiring to his study to comply with her request.

That left her alone with Delphine, who had brought out tea for them. She gathered the lupines onto the tray with work-gnarled hands before straightening and looking Louise square on. "Don't be hard on him now, Miss Louise. On today of all days, he's not himself."

"What do you mean?" Despite Dr. Hoffman's dire warnings of a man with one foot in the grave, she'd found that, outside of his pale skin and the occasional fit of coughing, Father was very much his old self.

"Only that it's the day your mother died. Usually, he goes to New York to visit the grave. Now . . . I guess it's hard on him, knowing he might never be back there."

The flowers . . . she picked up a lupine that had dropped to the ground. Purple had been Mother's favorite color, hadn't it? "I see."

"You didn't remember?"

Louise had only been thirteen years old when Mother had died, and in the decade and a half since, the details had faded. "There's a good deal on my mind these days."

The cook grunted. "Can't argue there." She shifted the tray to her hip, cups clattering—then paused. "He didn't think you'd come, you know. After all that happened between the two of you."

How much does she know? Louise wondered. Servants heard more than anyone realized, and Oliver had been one of them, though not especially well liked, given his reputation as a troublemaker.

"Yes, well, here I am." When Delphine remained there, Louise sighed. "Is there something else?"

"Thank you." The words seemed to come with difficulty, like the rusty hinges of an old gate. "For coming. He'd never admit it, but he needs you."

In all her days, Louise couldn't recall the dour cook expressing gratitude, outside of a curt nod of acknowledgment, to anyone. "It was my duty, and I'll stay as long as necessary."

"Good. And you can call me Delphie." With that, she retreated, familiar heavy steps dragging toward the kitchen, muttering to herself about the trouble of bringing a vase up to the study.

Soon, Louise took up the list from Father, accepting her role as both nurse and delivery girl. By the time Father's driver had dropped her off at the library's door, she thought to unfold it . . . and groaned.

A novel with the title writ in gold.

*A book with a character or author who shares your first or
surname.*

One favorite to re-read.

A recommendation from a child.

Difficult man. Sending her on a treasure hunt. Well, she
wouldn't be deterred, wouldn't return home empty-handed
and give him an excuse to push for an outing again. There
was nothing to be done but present herself to Mr. Cliffton, the
librarian, a man at least a decade older than Father, with white
muttonchops and a gold-buttoned waistcoat over a round belly.
"Oh yes, the daughter," he said, smiling wanly and squinting
at the list.

There was no judgment in the words, yet Louise couldn't
help but wonder what Father had shared about her. Did the man
see her as a poor brokenhearted spinster, a determined career
woman proving that she didn't need a family for satisfaction,
a prodigal daughter forced home?

Without giving her time to wonder further, several other
patrons drifted over, bringing their suggestions with them as
soon as they heard about the list.

"For Mr. Cavendish? Oh, he'd love *A Portrait of the Artist
as a Young Man*, I'm sure of it."

"What about *A Christmas Carol*? That's got a gold title."

"It's June, you fool. Why not something by Zane Grey?"

"Or Thomas Hardy."

"No, Keats!"

In moments, the first two items were easily filled. They almost had to settle for a volume of philosophy by Lady Margaret
Cavendish before someone remembered Louisa May Alcott and
decided she would count, despite the additional *a*.

It bothered Louise slightly, the fact that these strangers knew more about her father's likes and dislikes than she did. Maybe that's why he'd made the list the way he had, out of spite, as if it were anyone's fault but his own.

As she balanced the growing stack, Mr. Cliffton quietly slipped her a copy of *Pride and Prejudice*. "He's checked it out a dozen times at least."

Louise frowned at it suspiciously. "Isn't this a romance?"

He nodded. "Probably why he's embarrassed to simply buy a copy and display it on his shelves at home. As for me, I see no reason why a gentleman ought not to learn from the wit and wisdom of Miss Austen."

That was out of her capacity to comment on, so Louise indicated the list. "And the last?"

The muttonchops lifted in a smile. "I have just the fellow for it."

It was a school day, so the only child Louise could see appeared to be four years old. His scabbed knees were drawn up as he sat on the steps, small face pinched in concentration under straw-colored hair poking out from a sailor hat, giving him the overall impression of leaping directly out of a Sears-Roebuck catalogue ad.

He couldn't actually be reading, could he, young as he was? Weren't children of his age supposed to be climbing trees and playing in the mud, enjoying the health benefits of the outdoors?

Mr. Cliffton hailed him, though it was another few seconds before he placed his stubby finger on the page long enough to look up. "Anthony, Mr. Cavendish—you remember him, the man who gave us all of these books—he would like to ask you what book he should read next."

Without the slightest pause, and with the authority of one of Father's business associates, he declared, "One of the bunny books."

"Ah, Beatrix Potter. An excellent choice, Anthony."

"But you can't have this one," he blurted, clutching the small volume to his chest. "I haven't finished it yet." As if realizing he'd been quite rude to a grown-up, he added quickly, "There are others upstairs."

"Thank you, Mr. Anthony," Louise said gravely, nodding to him. "I certainly wouldn't want to deprive you of finding out what happened to"—she eyed the spine—"the Flopsy Bunnies."

He beamed, exposing a missing tooth, and Louise couldn't help but smile too. Well, maybe it wasn't so bad after all, encouraging children to read at a young age.

Mr. Cliffton pointed her to the children's section. "Can't go up there much myself these days. Bad knee."

So she climbed the steps alone. She'd been here once before, when Father first purchased the building. The balcony, rickety and full of missing balusters like broken teeth, had given her a wave of vertigo, and she'd never returned.

The rest of the building had been nearly as rundown, so its renovation had occupied Father's attentions for two full summers. When they had previously, on Mother's insistence, spent long days on the shore and ventured weekly into town to purchase ice creams or watch saltwater taffy be pulled at the confectionery, during those years, Father met Louise's pleas to come out with a curt "There's simply too much work to do on the library."

Soon enough, she stopped asking. Then shortened her summer visits to Maine altogether—until her twenties, when they became an escape from Aunt Eleanor's endless matchmaking in New York.

Upstairs, the children's books were organized by author, and Potter fell on the lowest shelf, forcing Louise to kneel in her long skirt. She selected *The Tale of Peter Rabbit* as the one that looked the least absurd—the other protagonists bearing such names as Benjamin Bunny, Jemima Puddle-Duck, and Timmy Tiptoes—and flipped through the pages.

Simple text, of course. But there was something arresting

about the illustrations, both realistic and fantastical all at once. She paused on a scene of a cunning little rabbit in a blue jacket eating a carrot, his nose so vividly rendered it seemed as if it had only just stopped twitching.

When she returned to Windward Hall, bearing the greetings and wishes for good health of at least six patrons whose names she'd quickly forgotten, Father, reclining in his usual chair, reached for the books eagerly. "Thank you, my dear, thank you."

He held the volumes to his chest, breathing in the scent of them like they were one of his bouquets, and for a moment, Louise felt a tug of longing.

To care that much for books?

No, she realized, in some deep and persistently ignored part of herself, to be held like that by a loving father.

As she watched, a fit of coughing overtook him, and he doubled over, waving her away.

It was, as always, too late.

twenty-six

MARTINA
JULY 28

Martina rolled her shoulders and tried to push the exhaustion back enough to keep pace with the bustle of the core room. The words from her mother's latest letter helped, and she repeated them in her mind with each mold she stacked on the conveyor belt. *Your father was the hardest-working dockworker in all of Trieste*, she'd written. *He'd be proud to know a daughter of his could keep up with the men. You are stronger than you know, Martina.*

And maybe it was true. She, unlike some of the other women, didn't worry about the developing muscle tone that made narrow shirt cuffs hard to fasten. After all, she had no man around the home to impress or to avoid intimidating. She merely did her work, filling and hefting molds, some no larger than a shoebox, some more than fifty pounds, over the long hours until her shoulders and back ached with effort.

What Mamma would have written instead if she'd told her about Patrick's being in town, Martina couldn't say. She hadn't been able to bring herself to make her mother worry, so it remained her little secret.

The ten o'clock bell startled her, indicating a fifteen-minute break. Martina leaned against her station, using her weight to stretch the muscles in her arms crying out for attention.

"Well, look who's descended from on high," Ginny muttered from the other side of their station. She, like many of the others, was staring at Mr. Hanover in his impeccable gray suit and shiny shoes that hadn't seen the sandy scuff of the core room in months. Other than a brief interview, where she'd felt like a head of cattle pushed through with barely any inspection, Martina had only seen Mr. Hanover descend from his office at company war-bond drives.

His face was somber, and workers from other parts of the foundry streamed through the doors, led by their foremen, into the cooler core room.

A litany of fears and questions flooded her, and Martina no longer felt strong. Were they behind on production? Planning to close the foundry? Firing the swing shift?

But no, at the height of the war, every factory worker would be needed to keep production up. Their foreman, Mr. Devons, reminded them of that constantly.

Once Mr. Hanover was sure all had gathered, he said, "I'll make this brief. I'm sure you have all been following the Pastorius trials."

She hadn't. Between work and caring for the children and keeping the trailer clean during a week of hard rains and mud, when would she have time to read newspapers or listen to radio reports?

"What is he talking about?" she whispered to Ginny as others around them muttered and nodded agreement.

"Two teams of Krauts popped up in U-boats off New York and Florida earlier this month on a sabotage mission," Ginny whispered back. "One of them got chicken and turned the others in to the FBI."

That's right. Gio had told her something about it last month, but she'd been too tired to pay attention and hadn't even realized it was a news story rather than one of those radio spy serials.

". . . and in moments like these, our country's fragility is revealed," Mr. Hanover was saying, his voice more droning than the machinery. "The enemy may very well walk among us."

A hush fell over the gathered workers, and Martina took great care to stare straight ahead, her breathing shallow. Were any of them looking at her, wondering? All because her former nation had let a man like Mussolini and his grand promises sway them into disaster.

"We expect all employees to increase their vigilance, on and off the job. Even a seemingly minor act of sabotage could set back production for weeks, destroying the most precious resources we have: time and man-hours."

The speech concluded with the usual upbeat description of what their production meant to the war effort, though from the grim faces around her, Martina knew that no one was fooled into thinking the speech was a positive one.

"Hanover is full of it, I say," Ginny said the moment the man was gone, expertly rebraiding her hair from where it had frizzed out of its plait during the shift. "If the Nazis are trying crazy schemes like that, it just goes to show they're plumb desperate."

She had to ask, as much as she'd rather not know the answer. "Those German saboteurs . . . were any of them American citizens?"

"Two of them, I think. Why?" When she didn't answer, Ginny frowned. "No, Marti, don't even think it. People here know better. They know you."

But did they? Other than Ginny, who had practically forced her to be friends, she'd said no more than a polite good-night to most of her fellow workers. Between their short breaks and the core room's pace and noise, there wasn't time for conversation. How many of them considered her the enemy?

On their break, Martina usually went to the cafeteria to eat or catch a few minutes of shut-eye in the corner, but not today. Today, she needed to be alone. Just to think, to clear her head.

She hurried out the back door quickly enough that the usual group of smokers hadn't yet congregated. Good. Better not to hear what they would almost certainly be discussing. *"You think anyone here's rotten?" "Not sure, but we ought to keep an eye out."*

Stop. Think of something else. The Blackout Book Club's latest pick, yes, that would do. Rosa was so excited that they'd chosen her favorite storybook. She wanted to show everyone her favorite illustration, the one of the Velveteen Rabbit and the Skin Horse—

A whistle in the narrow alleyway startled away her dreams of clover fields and playthings in the attic. There was nothing threatening about the sound itself, just the rousing marching tune "Praise the Lord and Pass the Ammunition."

It was the person attached to the keening whistle that made her tense.

Patrick.

His lips unpursed, and he rumbled a line of the song, an ironic smile on his face. "'Praise the Lord, we're all between perdition and the deep blue sea.'" Planting his feet, he stood between her and the stretch of alley leading to the foundry door. "Isn't that right, Martina?"

It chilled her, that voice, where it had once warmed her like a shot of Irish whiskey.

"Hello again, Patrick." A silly thing to say, but what else was she to do?

He lit a cigarette in a smooth motion, the song cutting off as he drew it to his mouth. Even when they hadn't had money for Gio's school materials or Rosa's birthday present, he always found a way to keep packs of Chesterfields around.

Had he found where she lived first or where she worked? How long, how often, had he been following her—or the children?

"You haven't visited the address I gave you."

"No, I don't plan to. What's this about, Patrick?"

He sighed out a puff of smoke, and she waved it away with a cough. "Listen, I need a loan. Just a hundred dollars."

She studied him for a moment as he took another drag on the cigarette. A striped tie poked out from the collar of his light-brown trench coat, spotless and new, and his face was still cleanly shaven. Not his usual look when he fell on hard times and came scraping back to her.

"I thought you said fishing was good." Maybe her reverse miracle had been granted after all, and this slump would move Patrick along, out of Derby.

"It is. This is for a legitimate business expense. I'm expanding my scope, you might say."

She'd heard that explanation before, the other times he'd slunk back to them after claiming his time as a family man was over. Once, it had been for tuition to welding school, then money for a used car so he could take on work as a traveling salesman. Neither had lasted more than a few months, and who could say where her money had actually gone? Given Patrick's habits, though, she had some less-than-reputable guesses.

But his "legitimate business" was no longer her business—or her responsibility. From somewhere deep inside her, she could feel a new resolve. No, she wouldn't let her fear of her husband steal from her children and their future. Not this time, not ever again.

Her voice was steady, almost confident. "I can't give you the money. I don't have it." Not entirely true—she'd saved a good amount from her foundry work—but she certainly didn't have any to spare. "But I can help you in another way."

"Yeah?" He perked up, waiting for her reply.

"Danny Maloney, Bond Street," she said, naming one of her fellow book club members. "He's a pawn dealer and an acquaintance of mine. He'll give you a fair price for anything you need to sell to raise the money."

Patrick's mouth twitched in disgust. "Do you know how

much a fuel tank costs? I can't pay for that by hawking a few odds and ends."

"You already have a fuel tank." Her knowledge of fishing trawlers was limited, and Patrick knew it, but she wasn't so naïve as to think he and his crew would row into the Atlantic.

He ignored that, as if she hadn't just caught him in a bold-faced lie. "Besides, the circles I run in now . . . I need to keep an image up. These threads are part of it." As he spoke, a cinder fell off his cigarette, landing on his left coat sleeve. Cursing, he batted it away, but not before it left a singed speck on the pristine cuff.

"Stupid woman," he muttered, "look what you've done."

Martina drew in a sharp breath. She had to remember that later when Patrick was in control of his emotions enough to be charming. He hadn't changed; he'd only changed what he wanted from her.

"Didn't tell the kids about me, either, I take it? Is that why you chased after Gio when he saw me at the theater?"

Good, he'd accepted her explanation that she didn't have money to give. Still, this wasn't the topic she wanted to move to. "Why would you care? You wanted me to send them away to live with my mother."

Frustration briefly cracked the suave mask he'd put up. "I just want to talk to them."

"No."

"You can't stop me. Not legally. I'm their father. We're still married."

Only because she had felt there was no way to get an annulment and was too ashamed to start the legal proceedings of a divorce. While Patrick made demands and belittled her, he'd stopped shy of ever striking her or, God forbid, the children. What would the church be able to say or do, even if she could gather the courage to ask?

"Please, Patrick. Leave us in peace. That's all I want."

He took a step forward, and despite the careful grooming, the new coat, the smiles, her heart beat faster in alarm, muscles tightening to run. "Maybe that's not all *I* want."

He'd never hurt her before, but something had changed, and there was a desperation in those eyes as he reached for her.

"Hey!"

They both turned to see Mr. Devons striding their way from the group of smokers, scowling under thick eyebrows. "What's this? Everything all right out here?"

"Yes, sir," Martina managed, gratitude for his timely arrival mixing with humiliation. "I was just—"

She gestured to her husband, but Patrick had disappeared into the shadows, leaving only the scent of smoke behind.

"That man asked if I had a cigarette," she finished.

If anything, that seemed to increase Mr. Devons's suspicion. "Does he work here?"

That at least was an easier question to answer. "I don't think so."

The foreman gave her a long, hard look from deep-set eyes, as if he could detect lies by sight alone, like Christie's Poirot. "You'd better get inside. Break's almost over."

He didn't warn her not to speak to strange men or to be careful when going off on her own at night. Of course not. It wasn't her safety he was concerned about.

Here, she was the threat.

The rest of the night, Mr. Devons hovered around her station, so much that Ginny muttered, "What's with the buzzard?" when he turned his back.

Martina had shrugged and continued her work, packing sand in the molds with deadly efficiency, never pausing, no matter how tired she got. Once again, Patrick had put her in danger.

Please, she prayed, wishing she still had her rosary, *let him leave. For good this time.*

But as seemed to happen so often these days, heaven was silent.

We might need to be the ones to leave. The thought had occurred to her before, but even if she could find another job before her savings ran out, even if housing was as affordable as it was here in Derby, it didn't feel right to uproot the children again. Rosa had made friends at school. Gio thought he might join a baseball team in the spring, and he and Mr. Keats seemed to be genuinely connecting. Besides, there was the book club. How could they leave all that behind?

With a grunt, Martina hefted the filled mold onto the conveyor, setting it down harder than necessary.

The song was right. She was stuck between perdition and the deep blue sea, unsure of where to turn. And soon she'd have to decide between them.

twenty-seven

GINNY
AUGUST 8

Ginny tried to drown out the cheering around her and focus on the syrup-soaked bit of pancake on the end of her fork.

Then again, given that it was her seventh pancake, maybe that was a bad plan.

Stop whining and open that cargo hold. She did and chewed. Warm, soggy, like a sponge filled with dishwater—hadn't these been good at one point?

With a flourish, she let her fork clatter to her plate and waved over the volunteer with the *Support the Red Cross* sash draped across her neatly tucked-in blouse. "Bring us another!"

The burly man sitting across the table from her grinned. Harry, according to the taunts from his buddies, last name unknown. "Oho! Slowing down, are you, little lady?"

"Not on your life," she fired back, trying not to breathe too deeply. Wasn't room in her belly for that anymore.

The bystanders who had crowded around them to watch took up the chant started by a freckle-faced youth hovering at Harry's shoulder: "Number eight." It was like being stuck in those boxing rings Gio talked so much about—and she was about to be down for the count.

A full two dollars were at stake, when entrance to the Red Cross Benefit Pancake Breakfast had only been a quarter.

236

Spend twenty-five cents. Make two hundred cents. That was . . .

She frowned, but the cash register buttons of her brain that usually tallied up profit seemed to be stuck. By syrup, probably. Well, anyway, it was a good percentage. Something to weigh down her coin bank, and a free meal—or three—besides.

"I'm just getting started," she bragged, and it must have been convincing, because she saw a flicker of worry on Harry's face.

She'd weighed her chances carefully from the start. From the dishes beside him, Harry had drunk two full cups of coffee before their bet, while she'd had none. He also, she assumed, hadn't skipped supper the night before, working until midnight on an empty stomach in preparation for today's breakfast. White collar job, based on the cuff links and shiny shoes. Middle-aged, not some college man who'd swallow a whole stack at once.

They were fair odds. Still, he had a good ten inches and hundred pounds on her, at least.

To trick her stomach, she folded up the last quarter of pancake number eight and rammed it past her gag reflex. So did Harry.

"Come on, Harry! Don't let the girl best you," one of the spectators jeered, slapping him on the back while the Red Cross–sash lady slapped pancakes onto their plates.

The others laughed and clapped. One even whistled. A good crowd, this one. Stood to reason. They were comfortably full on a sunny Saturday morning, supporting a good cause. They weren't the ones with pancake nine flopped in front of them like a beached whale in shallows of syrup.

She twirled the fork in her fingers before spearing another bite.

Across from her, Harry groaned. He raised the napkin beside him, but instead of pressing it to his face, he waved it before dropping it over the half-eaten ninth pancake. "That's all for me, folks. I know when I'm beat."

Boos, laughter, and applause mingled as Ginny offered Harry a sticky handshake. "Well done, miss," he said, the good-natured smile never faltering.

And that was the last factor in her calculations: she'd sized up Harry before agreeing. The way he laughed with his friends—real friends, like Pa's fishing buddies—told her he didn't take himself too seriously. The kind who would be so sore on being bested that they'd accuse you of cheating, glower, and generally make things hard on you, that's the kind you never made deals with.

Maybe there was a little of her mother's betting savvy in her after all.

But I won't let it get out of hand. Selling off scrap to pawn shops or taking all-you-can-eat challenges was one thing. Honest money. Well . . . honest-ish. But gambling was a different thing. Win it all, or lose it all. That could be a trap, sure enough.

Harry rummaged in his pocket for the two dollars, setting them on the table. "You earned this, little lady." A few of his friends even flipped in a few extra coins, which she gathered up with a bow, clutching her stomach with a moan that was only a little hammed up for effect.

Not a bad haul. Plus, she wouldn't need a scrap of lunch—or supper.

She'd write to the family, tell them about today. Might give them a smile. How long had it been since her last letter to them?

Silly. No reason to feel guilty, not when she stuffed those two dollars in the tin bank as soon as she got home, tapping the monkey on the head. They'd understand in time.

A half hour till book club, enough time to at least start. She pulled out the last letter, this one from Pa, and read it again. Turns out, construction work was steady these days, and while he missed the *Lady Luck* and the island, friends from back home told him the place wasn't the same after being swarmed with navy officers and their families. The boys were growing like weeds. They had regular back-stoop begging from one of Portland's stray cats—she wasn't to tell Ma—and would she be visiting soon?

It painted a more cheerful picture than her mother's letters . . . but maybe not as trustworthy. He always was an optimist, her father, boasting of get-ahead days on the lobster boat even when the seas were empty, telling embellished stories of the triumphs of his boyhood, always believing his pretty wife would stay away from the gambling tables this time.

Sometimes he was right. Sometimes he wasn't. That was just the way of things.

She'd just sat down with a clean sheet of paper to start her reply when a knock at the door interrupted her.

It was the Western Union delivery man—or boy, actually, swimming in his uniform. Must be a high schooler too young to enlist. He mumbled her name with a just-changed voice, and when she nodded, he thrust the paper at her before beating it down the apartment stairs.

Why would anyone pay to send her a telegram?

Slowly, Ginny unfolded the telegram and forced herself to read the words in block type. First, the sender. Mack's ma.

Army reports Mack died from infection. Wounded at Midway.

No—*it can't be.* The Battle of Midway was a success, a turning point.

The eight pancakes in her stomach turned over, and she ran for the toilet before her stomach emptied right on the welcome mat.

During wartime, no one wanted a telegram. And now Ginny knew why.

From Russell to Avis

August 5, 1942

Dear Avis,

Not much to report so far. Calm seas, good visibility. Not that we've seen anything of importance, though Stephen, the city boy, yelled that he'd spotted a periscope. Thankfully, I checked it out before anyone grabbed the ship-to-shore radio. It was the fin of a porpoise. An American one.

Besides that drama, we've shot at some floating rubber targets with a machine gun for practice, and they even let us try out a depth charge. To be honest, it looks a lot like a plain metal paint can with a detonator, only heavier. You're supposed to chuck it overboard as close to your target as you can, then let it sink down deep as you row away. From the coast guard's safety drills, we thought it'd cause a geyser you could see miles around. Sure, you could hear a boom, but the spray barely went up three feet. I don't mind saying we were a little let down.

We've heard some have taken to calling us the Hooligan Navy. (I don't mind the name, but Lester went on for fifteen minutes straight about disrespect when he caught wind of it.) Just because the coast guard has more rules and regulations doesn't mean we're not real sailors. In fact, we're more so than they are, if you ask me. We follow our instincts, our sea sense, not rules out of a book.

How narrowly I missed all of that! You know, I'm not even mad anymore about the recruiters turning me down because of my asthma. It all worked out for the best, didn't it?

We do some fishing. Lester, the old rumrunner, taught me to use a harpoon to strike at swordfish, though I'm no *good yet. Biggest danger so far is from sunburn and heat stroke. We've all had to get used to drinking more water.*

If Hemingway ever writes a novel based on the Hooligan Navy, mark my words, it'll be more about long days fishing and staring at the ocean than dangerous exploits.

Boy, do I miss you. A lot of the other fellows are true bachelors, young pups who haven't settled down, or widowers like Lester. They tease me sometimes for writing these letters, but I think they're just jealous they don't have someone out there waiting for them.

Yours, sunburnt and with
regrets,
Russell

Notes from the Blackout Book Club—August 8, 1942

Taken by Avis Montgomery, Head Librarian and Book Club Secretary

Book under discussion: <u>The Velveteen Rabbit</u> by Margery Williams, illustrated by William Nicholson

Members Present: the Regulars, minus Ginny and plus Danny Maloney, Muriel Whitson, Earl Bell, Arley Lokken, Carol Ann Hoper, Diana Follett and kids (Linda, age ten, and a toddler they call "Duckie"), Hamish and Eva Murray, and Tom and Hazel Joyce and Susanna (age nine, heard about the club from Linda).

Odd thing: Martina and the kids were nearly a half hour late, since they'd had to take a bus into town. Apparently Ginny never showed to pick them up. Probably sleeping in or just forgot. Rosa was quite upset, but we assured her we hadn't started the club without her.

Once settled, I said the story was a charming childhood tale, though a bit unrealistic. Mrs. Whitson claimed it was more than that—it was a parable about the risk of loving and being loved. Delphie disagreed, saying she thought it was more about why you oughtn't to judge or snub someone for how they looked. Martina asked why they couldn't both be right, and that settled things, more or less.

When prompted, Rosa declared that she liked the rabbits, especially the way they danced and their fuzzy tails, and the fairy saving things in the end. This was celebrated as the literary criticism of the evening, and my plate of sugar-cookie bunnies with frosted features was passed around in celebration. Rosa was very pleased with the attention.

Somehow, hearing what others loved about the story made me want to read it again.

We also talked at length about what it meant to be Real, especially the Skin Horse's idea that "when you're Real you don't mind being hurt." Quite touching.

In any case, The Velveteen Rabbit was another success. Miss Cavendish grumbled about how it might give children the idea that their toys were real, thus creating unnecessary attachment, but we all told her there was very little chance of that.

If I'm a mother someday—when I'm a mother, I mean—I want a picture from this book hanging in the nursery.

All in all, a good discussion. Miss Cavendish was so pleased that she didn't even make another of her pointedly arch comments about our time here drawing to a close.

Of course, given that Rosa had her turn, we let Gio select the next book, which saved us from another quarrel. He chose Treasure Island. Didn't Russ pick that as one of his favorites? I should write him back and tell him.

twenty-eight

GINNY
AUGUST 16
LONG ISLAND, MAINE

There would be seafood chowder at the funeral dinner, Ginny knew. Maybe even lobster, and plenty for all. The Conways didn't have the money for that, but the whole island pitched in when there was a death of one of their own.

Even the promise of a good meal couldn't tempt her away from the graveyard, now that everyone else was gone after the short memorial service. Somehow, it felt easier to pay her last respects in front of the simple headstone alone, rather than squirming under the preacher's droning in the tiny island church. It felt like one of the only unchanged structures on the island—she'd cringed to see the waterfront dominated by a concrete block of a boiler plant, then Wharf Street studded with low, ugly navy buildings.

At least here, in the churchyard, there wasn't an eyesore of a bunker or artillery piece in sight.

Ginny shifted in the uncomfortable borrowed shoes above a plot of dirt without a body buried underneath it. "You were loved, Mack. An awful lot." Maybe she'd never have been able to love him the way he wanted, but he was a good friend who'd died a hero.

It didn't feel like a real good-bye. Ought to at least go with the dropping of a flower or the saying of a prayer, but she didn't have either at hand. So it would have to do.

When a hand rested on her shoulder, Ginny near about jumped out of her skin, whirling around. It was her brother, next oldest in the family after her, clomping along in a dark gray suit that slid on his shoulders—borrowed from Pa, it looked like.

"Lew!" She glared at him. "You can't just go sneaking up on a lady in a graveyard like that."

He shrugged. "Thought you'd want to see me."

"I do, of course." Had he gotten taller? There was no sign he'd been crying.

He was studying her too. "Fancy dress."

In a flash, Ginny was conscious of the pearl buttons, the plaited belt at the waist, the perfectly shined leather shoes, all loans from Avis, along with more pity than she'd wanted. "Borrowed from a friend of mine." He couldn't think she would waste her money on something like that. "I didn't see you in the service."

"Came in late. Sat in the back." Lew wandered out of the churchyard, and she followed, but instead of taking the road toward the Conway place, he meandered down the path that wound around the coast.

"Did anyone else in the family come?"

"Nah. They didn't know Mack so much."

What did you say to someone just after a funeral? It was hard enough to drag words out of Lew on an ordinary day. Before she could come up with something, Lew sent her a sideways glance. "You don't write much anymore."

It wasn't like she didn't try. "These days, I'm just . . . busier."

He grunted. "That book club of yours?"

Why had she even told them about that? "Some. And work and other things. It's no crime to have a social life, you know."

"Ma's mad you haven't sent money."

Ginny knew that much. It had been hinted between the lines of nearly every short letter she'd gotten from her mother. "Didn't figure I should."

The look that passed between them was enough to confirm what Ginny had feared. Away from home and flush with cash from the sale of their land, Bluffing Betty Atkins was back in business. How much of their family's money had she gambled away this time?

No sense in scolding Lew for not keeping her under control. He likely tried. Of all of them, only Ginny, the lone daughter, ever had much luck in that department.

And I left them.

Sure, it had seemed the smart thing at the time. Pa had given her a chunk of the cash from the sale of the house to get started, and she'd saved every last cent she could since then. The government had promised them they'd be able to buy their land back, but Ginny wasn't counting on it. Still, with the money she'd stored up, she was their hope for getting back on the island somewhere, at least.

She just had to stay out of Ma's reach.

"What's Pa up to?" she asked, to change the subject.

"The same. He gets construction jobs here and there. Travels to worksites. It's not steady work, but he doesn't want to get too tied down. Figures the war's gonna end any day."

Ginny knew from conversations with Freddy that that wasn't likely, but she didn't say it. Better to let him hope.

They'd walked all the way down to the coast, on John "Patsy" Patterson's land. And there, moored to a dock, was the *Lady Luck*, bobbing in wind-tossed waters.

"Want to see her?" Lew asked, sounding casual, but she knew he'd brought her here on purpose.

"Of course."

They picked their way across the rocks toward where the *Lady Luck* was moored. No sand here, because the island coast wasn't made for sunbathers and picnickers but for hard folks willing to scratch out a living on the shoals of overlapping granite that sloped down to the water's edge.

She was small but beautiful, with a high, slanted bow in front of the windshield and a broad, flat stern. Clean enough, but stark and bare without all the ropes, crates, and traps they'd used every day.

"Looks like he's taking care of her, anyway," she managed through the sudden squeezing around her heart.

Lew grunted. "Pa threatened Patsy within an inch of his life if he didn't."

"He's coming back, yeah?"

"Says he is." For a moment, the only sound was the waves striking the shore. "I asked him, you know."

She tilted a questioning look his way. "What did you ask who?"

"Why Pa didn't find us a place to stay near the coast, where he could keep his route, just travel an extra hour instead of moving inland."

She'd wondered that herself but had been so worked up over starting the foundry job that she hadn't bothered to ask.

"He started out talking about how he didn't want to keep up with the new government rules. Can't take a radio out, have to let the coast guard do random checks to sound your fuel tanks, that sort of thing."

"Why's that?"

Lew shrugged. "With gas rationing on, they're worried about racketeering. Folks stockpiling fuel, selling at jacked-up prices to other ships. Maybe even Nazi U-boats."

Figured. Usual government meddling, complicating things for the little guy. Still, that wasn't so big a deal, to Ginny's mind, not with a war on. "That's all?"

"Not just. Pa went on to say he doesn't trust the buyer in Portland, and the price of lobster is bound to go down with the war on, and he's getting too old for this anyhow."

From the look on Lew's face, they both knew it was a pack of lies, or more generously, a pack of half-truths.

She loved her pa, but if he wanted to make it work, he could have. The spirit was just plumb knocked out of him, losing the family home. He didn't do well with change. He'd stared out the window a full week while the rest of them packed and cleaned, muttering to himself about how *"it weren't fair."*

And it wasn't. But the way Ginny saw it, you could let the storm dash you on the rocks, or you could roll with the tide.

It was a little windy, but not a storm cloud hung in the sky, and there were still several hours of daylight left. "Wanna take her out? She could use a little attention."

He didn't say yes so much as give a jerk of his head, which for Lew might as well have been an enthusiastic cheer. "Can't go to the west side. Submarine nets."

Ginny grimaced. Sure, it was to keep folks safe, but the thought of those huge, ugly things spread out in her ocean along her father's old route . . . it was a worse change than the ferry she'd taken into the island, painted from white to gunmetal gray for camouflage.

Soon, the low putter of the *Lady Luck*'s motor sang in harmony with the high-pitched squawks of seagulls as Lew steered the boat along the shore. That had always been his job on his days going out with Pa. Ginny liked to watch for buoys and ease the warps onto the hoister when they got close enough. The moment when the rope pulled taut, lifting the wooden trap full of wet and writhing cargo, never got old.

Today, she just watched the ocean, standing beside her brother. The tide chart was still pinned near the compass, with notes in Pa's scribbled handwriting, and it warmed Ginny clear through the chill from the water spraying across her bare arms. "He'll be back," she whispered to it, flipping the calendar pages to the right month. So much time wasted. "Don't you worry. We all will be."

For a while, they stood in silence. The *Lady Luck* had always been a two-person boat, the two of them trading off days after they turned twelve and Ma let them drop out of school.

Normally, they'd be scanning the fog for buoys with Pa's number, marked carefully on a map. Deep down on the ocean shelves, the traps waited to be hauled up, full of keepers lured by the smell of bait into the outer compartment, the parlor. Then they'd crawled into the kitchen, where they got what they wanted . . . but lost their freedom. Couldn't get out the way they came, through the funnel-like opening. Their fate was to be bunged into a bushel basket, wet with just enough water to keep them alive. One last taste of the ocean till they went ashore to the receiving station to be unloaded and weighed.

"I felt sorry for them once," Ginny said idly.

"Lobsters don't have feelings, sis," Lew said—just like he'd said years ago, when Ginny had come back crying from her first trip out with Pa.

"But girls like me sure do," she'd shot back then—and now. Was that a smile that tugged onto his face? Must be the salt air. It healed people, filled in the broken cracks from loneliness and grief, gave them a purpose.

It smelled like home.

"Are you doing all right?" Maybe looking out at the choppy water through the windshield, he'd be more likely to talk. "Bet it was hard to get the news about Mack."

"He was only two years older'n me. I joshed with him, before he left, how as soon as I turned eighteen in December, I'd be over and joining him. Outshooting him too."

"Now?"

"I dunno."

Funerals had a way of dampening a person's rah-rah for the USA. Ginny didn't try to tell him what to do. He wouldn't listen, and anyhow, who was she to give advice? One drowning person couldn't do much good for another.

"You?" Lew asked, surprising her. "Guess it's a different thing, losing your sweetheart."

"Probably not much different. It'll heal in time, like a broken bone."

Here, with only Lew around, there was no use pretending. They'd both lost a friend, nothing more. But nothing less either—and a friend was a mighty thing, out here on a lonely island.

"There it is," Lew said at last, pointing. As if Ginny wouldn't recognize this stretch of coastline, its curves more familiar than the lone photograph of a loved one. Though, to be fair, she'd been avoiding looking at it, turning instead to the open sea.

Now she forced herself to angle toward the shore—and her grip on the railing tightened.

They'd turned her home into a navy fueling depot. Long, ugly piers jutted into the water, fronted by unfamiliar vessels.

Coastal defenses are important, she tried to remind herself. *To give us a base and protect the shores in case the Krauts attack.*

But it sounded more and more like the fluff that people like Louise Cavendish passed along from the government to get folks to buy war bonds and wait in line to use ration coupons with smiles on their faces.

Even thinking about Louise was funny, out here in what felt like the real world. The book club and its tea sandwiches and literary themes seemed not to matter at all, in the face of submarine nets and oil storage tanks.

Ginny shook her head and shivered as the promontory that used to be their home faded from view. The wind had kicked up a nasty chop at their bow. "We really ought to head back."

He nodded, steering them around. Not another word passed between them until they docked at Patsy's wharf.

But when he lent her a steadying hand to step out on shore, Lew actually volunteered conversation for the first time. "Don't get too familiar, Gin." His voice was quiet but with an edge of urgency she rarely heard.

She tried to laugh it off. "What's that supposed to mean?"

"With those town folks you're chumming with."

Was that all? "Don't you worry. They're nice, and they'll pass the time all right until the war's over. But they're not island people."

"Still, got to be careful, going into someone's parlor. They always want something out of you. And if you wander into the kitchen . . . wham! They get you." For once, Lew met her eyes, dark and serious. "And then you won't be coming back."

twenty-nine

AVIS
AUGUST 17

Avis huffed in frustration as she wrote yet another check for seventy-five cents. Three quarters. What was the point?

Her earlier investigations had taught her that an association library was funded partly by member dues rather than public funds, an annual fee for anyone who wanted the privilege of checking out books. And now that Miss Cavendish had decreed the library's doors would close once and for all on the last day of September, that meant each of the library's ninety-three dues-paying members were owed a refund for one-fourth of their membership. "It's only fair, after all," Miss Cavendish had said.

Avis shook her hand from where it had cramped around the fountain pen. Easy for her to say. All she had to do was sign the checks, not write or deliver them.

"Well, it's quitting time," she announced. She'd developed a habit of speaking aloud when the library was empty, knowing she'd go back to an empty home as well. "Time to rest, until the tyrant cracks the whip tomorrow."

She heard the deep, hearty chuckle before she could see the person attached to it. "Aw, come on, now. It can't be as bad as all that."

Her blush was immediate and furious as one of the book

club members stepped out from where he'd been shielded by the shelves. "Mr. Maloney, I didn't realize you were there." How could she be so careless? "If you wouldn't mind, could I ask that you . . . ?"

"Keep quiet about all that?" His moustache twitched as he smiled. "I run a pawn shop, Mrs. Montgomery. I know who's hard up but trying not to look like it, what engagement got broken off, who's always hated their grandmother no matter what she left them in her will. And I never breathe a word of it. Come into my shop sometime. You can practically smell the secrets."

That was a thought. What would secrets smell like? Chardonnay? Cigar smoke? Dried blood and salt on a German life jacket washed onto shore?

Avis shuddered. Better to leave thoughts like that to poets like Emily Dickinson, who could do something productive with them.

"Can I help you find anything, then?" she asked, using one of her brother's classic lines.

"No, I should be getting home." But he didn't move for the door. "It's been nice, having a reason to come back. I feel closer to my Charlotte here."

For a moment, Avis was confused, until she remembered during a book club meeting he had mentioned a wife who had died.

He traced the spines with a finger. "Wish I knew which ones she read. Never paid much attention at the time. I can't remember the titles, but she was always reading about missionaries to China and Africa."

"That would be in the 270s," Avis said automatically, leading him down several shelves.

He pulled out a volume to look at the cover, then shook his head and replaced it. "It was her way of traveling the world, but it being about religion and all, she said it didn't feel selfish. She was like that, my Lottie."

It was a charming story . . . and one that Louise would certainly approve of, with her love of charity. "Do you mind if I write that down?" she asked impulsively. "Share it with . . . others, perhaps?"

"You mean Miss Cavendish? Do you really think you can change her mind?" Mr. Maloney asked dubiously.

So much for subtlety.

"I don't know." With her previous schemes scuttled, Avis seemed to be out of ideas—and almost out of time. "But I have to try."

"Then go ahead." Mr. Maloney scratched at his chin thoughtfully. "You know, there are plenty of people in this town who'd stick up for this place. Maybe they all have stories like me and Lottie."

Avis stopped from where she was inspecting the shelves of the Christian History section for places where she'd failed to dust. That was a thought. Dozens of members had passed books over the desk during her short time here, and outside of recording the checkout and return dates and reminding them of any overdue volumes, she'd never wondered much about who they were as people. Maybe Louise hadn't either.

I bet Anthony did.

She could tell from the descriptions he'd given of his work, the way people still asked after news of him when they came in, and the fond regard that even Miss Cavendish seemed to have for him, that Anthony had loved the readers as much as the books they'd read.

It's too late for you to start that now.

Or was it?

Avis found herself digging out another plain black notebook from the supply stash behind the checkout desk. Only this time, she wasn't being forced into taking notes against her will. This would be different.

On the clean first page, she wrote *The Importance of a Li-*

brary. It sounded like the start of a grammar-school composition, but Avis hadn't done any writing since then, so it would have to do.

She looked over at Mr. Maloney, pen poised. "Tell me more about Charlotte."

A broad smile spread across the man's face. "Gladly."

Four days later, Avis had delivered all the refund checks, many of them in person to members eager to express their condolences over the closing of the library, like they would for a friend who had died. The perfect chance to ask them what they'd loved about it. To take notes, collect stories.

Not everyone felt they had enough of significance to share, but Avis's notebook was soon brimming with memories: Marilyn Carlson met her husband in the natural science section and bonded over their mutual love of seashells. Mr. Bloomsbury, Russell's former boss at the bank, had used the library to study for his college entrance exam, away from family members who told him he would fail. Mr. Bell, it turned out, read the funnies page of the *Times* first every week, though he tried to angle the paper so no one else would notice.

Somewhere along the way, Avis had realized this wasn't just about her reputation in the community, about the loss she'd feel without anything purposeful to do in Russell's absence. It wasn't even about Anthony and the way he'd loved this place.

Others cared about the library too. And now, so did she.

That, more than anything, was what gave her the grit she needed to speak up when Miss Cavendish bustled in for her weekly check-in. "Miss Cavendish, I'm glad to see you."

"Yes, good morning, Avis. I have excellent news." She brandished a typewritten letter with an official seal at the top. "I've heard back from the Maine State Library after inquiring about what to do with our surplus books once the library closes. It turns out they're coordinating a book drive this winter for the Victory Book Campaign, to donate books to our soldiers."

"The soldiers?" Avis repeated, clutching her leather satchel. This wasn't the argument she'd prepared for.

"Yes indeed. They've found that our boys overseas, lacking constructive activities, have become avid readers, devouring anything sent to them." Miss Cavendish ran a hand over some of the spines, smiling faintly, as if already picturing them in the hands of GIs. "I was worried at first about finding a good home for the books upon the closure this September. It was positively providential that I heard about this campaign."

Avis nearly groaned out loud. Why was it that Providence always seemed to be on Miss Cavendish's side?

Probably because of heretical thoughts like that.

"Here is a list of categories most in demand by the program. As you have time around your other duties, I'd like you to go through this list, then withdraw and pack anything suitable, preferably within the next month."

Avis took the paper, scanning the list.

> For military libraries, up-to-date textbooks or reference materials are requested. For the troops' recreational reading, we are seeking adventure novels, humor books, sports books, mysteries, Westerns, etc.

There would go Wodehouse and Stevenson and Christie into boxes to be sent overseas.

> Please, no children's books, romances, or books primarily pertaining to women's issues.

The Velveteen Rabbit was safe, anyway, as well as Ginny's entire storage closet.

But most important, books must not be dog-eared or tattered; they are not junk donated to a scrap drive. Only books in first-class physical condition can be used in this battle for improved morale.

This wasn't a simple withdrawal of a few dozen books. Why, hundreds of items in the library's collection might fit this description.

Avis remembered Anthony's letter about passing around the paperback novel she'd sent him among his brothers-in-arms, pictured his foxhole book club discussing the now-tattered copy in animated voices. Did they get into good-natured arguments like her little group? Were they finding that a good book had the power to take them away, if only for a moment, from the brutal realities of war?

"It does sound like a good cause," she had to admit, "but we need books here in Derby too—and we need them in a space where we can gather together. Can't you see? All those new club members, they don't keep coming back only because reading gives them something to do. They come back because they're tired of being alone. We all are."

By the time Avis paused to take a breath, she noticed that Louise had lowered her clipboard, just slightly. And the look in her eyes . . .

Maybe she understood. Maybe she too had found the club to be a refuge.

Louise cleared her throat. "I've given that a great deal of thought. The book club is welcome to continue meeting on a reduced schedule—perhaps monthly, or even quarterly—at Windward Hall. I can provide funds for the chosen books, as long as they're appropriate."

That wasn't the answer Avis had expected to hear, and she let out the breath she'd been holding. It might not be so bad if they could keep gathering, even if it was less frequent. The chairs at Windward Hall had to be more comfortable than the stiff wooden ones supplied to the library.

And yet . . . *"She's got her hooks into everything, doesn't she?"* Ginny's comment from months before flickered back through Avis's mind, and this time she didn't try to defend against it.

Do you know, she wondered, looking at Louise's clear-eyed expression, finger tapping the inventory list as if she could advance the conversation to a faster pace, *how controlling you've become?*

Likely not. Offering her home to the book club was another good deed to add to her résumé.

"While that's a generous offer," Avis said, attempting diplomacy, "it's not the same. The library and its books allow people to browse, discuss, explore."

"And now its books will do the same for hundreds of soldiers, and the building itself will become a welcoming place for needy children."

Avis felt an old frustration rising, and now she could finally name it: the feeling of being pulled between two good things, as if by wanting to keep the library open, she was insisting that soldiers ought never to receive care packages and the children of war workers should be abandoned.

But each day she spent dusting the antique oak shelves, improving at giving recommendations to patrons who stopped in with obscure questions, losing herself in stories during the slow hours, Avis realized how deeply she would miss this place. "Why?" she blurted out. "Why are you so set on closing the library?"

Instead of the expected speech, Miss Cavendish paused thoughtfully. "'In War, Charity.'"

"Excuse me?"

"The motto of the Red Cross. In times of great hardship, we all have to make sacrifices, Avis. And I don't mean only reduced sugar rations or the inability to buy a new washing machine. Sacrifices must cost something."

After so many book club meetings, Avis knew Miss Cavendish didn't mean to sound condescending. It was just the tone she drifted into when making speeches. Still, Avis couldn't keep irritation from building within her. "I think I understand sacrifice, Miss Cavendish, after waving good-bye to my brother on a troop train and watching my husband leave to search the Atlantic for U-boats." She gripped the Victory Book Campaign list tighter, watching it crinkle in her hands. "It's all well and good to donate money and serve on committees, but how many loved ones have you sacrificed, Louise?"

Avis had meant the words to hit hard, but even she wasn't prepared for the hurt in Miss Cavendish's eyes.

The truth crashed into her, seconds too late to have stopped her angry reply: *She doesn't have any loved ones. Not really.*

Her parents were both gone. There was a brother and his family, she'd heard, but they were estranged. She'd never married, had no children, and had few friends, certainly none of drafting age.

It was, as Gio would say, a below-the-belt strike, but once the words had slipped out, Avis couldn't take them back.

"I suppose I have no reply to that." Louise turned away, her shoulders bowed from their usual confident posture, pumps beating a more subdued pattern on the library floor. "Good day, Avis. Let me know if you have any questions about the Victory Book Campaign."

This was not how this meeting was supposed to go. "Wait! I have something I want you to see." Avis gripped her satchel, fumbling through it, hurrying while there was still time and nerve. Her hands found the notebook's binding, and she thrust it at Miss Cavendish, who frowned.

"What is this?"

"I thought you might like to know what your father's library has meant to so many in this town."

It was only a slight motion, more a twitch than anything, but Avis caught Louise's reaction to the mention of her father. Perhaps that had been the wrong tactic.

"I see." Louise held the precious notebook of stories between two fingers as if she meant to toss it in the nearest bin.

"Will you promise to read it?"

"If I must." Her retreat toward the library entrance was more hurried now, as if afraid Avis would attempt to say something more. "I will see you on Saturday."

Avis stared after her. *That could have gone better.* Yet Miss Cavendish was a stickler for keeping her word. She would read the stories Avis had collected, and maybe somehow it would make a difference.

Reluctantly, Avis spent the next couple of hours before the library closed gathering books for donation. As she readied to leave, she reached into her satchel to tuck Miss Cavendish's list from the Victory Book Campaign inside the front pocket and brushed her hand against a notebook. Removing it, she frowned at the opening line: *The Importance of a Library.*

Then what . . . ?

No. She couldn't have.

But as seconds passed and Avis searched in her satchel, just to be sure, certainty and dread struck at the same instant. There had been two very similar composition notebooks in her satchel, both taken from the library's supplies.

And she'd accidentally given Louise Cavendish the notes from the Blackout Book Club.

All of the snide comments she and others had made about Louise—her pretentious opinions, lack of humor, moral stuffiness—came flooding back to her. And that wasn't even mentioning the personal details about Russell or the existence of the storage closet filled with contraband romances.

"Oh, Anthony," she whispered. "I've lost your library for good. And this time, it's all my fault."

From Russell to Avis

August 17, 1942

Dear Avis,

Finally, some action!

Probably shouldn't start off a letter to my wife that way, but I figured you'll know the Jerries didn't blast us to bits since I'm here to write this. So I've spoiled the ending.

Just at dawn, I heard a strange new sound: a mechanical whirring from the listening device above the noises of the ocean that nearly lull me to sleep. I knew it was them, Avis, sure as I knew my own name. When I ran to the deck, the fellow on watch was pointing. Water was dark as tar, but we could still see it only forty yards away: the top of a German U-boat pushing through the water.

Captain Sherman got on the radio—knowing the fellows in the sub were listening too—and reported the U-boat, giving our exact location.

For a moment, all of us held our breath.

Then the sub dove under the surface. Ran away, tail between their legs, just like I told you they would. Not fast enough, though.

Two bombers came and salted the water with depth charges, sprouting up plumes of water to the sky, then confirmed a hit and told us to get out of there while they dealt with things. Wasn't much of a thanks, but we celebrated on deck and again once we came back to shore.

We did it, Avis! Finally. Oh sure, we've been useful

before now. A preventive measure, Cap always says. What he means is, the wolves can't come up for air anymore, not with the picket boats swarming everywhere. Too easy to be spotted.

But it felt good—better than good—to actually spot one and get rid of it.

Only Stephen kept looking back where we'd come from, searching for the telltale oil slick on the waves. "Guess the crew all died."

That sobered us up. It's all kill-or-be-killed in war, isn't it? Reminded me of that life jacket you found. Whoever it belonged to was following orders just like us. But his orders were from a crazy man across the ocean who decided all of Europe was his to take over. And we can't let that happen. We won't.

I couldn't wait to write to you, to say you can hold your head a little higher. Your husband has finally done his part in the war. And remember, my term's up in eight weeks. Chin up, Avis. I'll be back soon, with lots of stories to tell. (I promise I won't exaggerate them much.)

> *Yours, a hero at last,*
> *Russell*

P.S. Almost forgot to say glad you enjoyed Treasure Island. *That kid has good taste. I'd like to meet him someday. Keep a copy around, will you? I want to give it another read when I get home.*

Notes from the Blackout Book Club—August 22, 1942

Taken by Lt. Freddy Keats

Members in attendance: The usual crowd, except Ginny's still not here. Martina said it's been hard for her since the funeral. The rest of us haven't seen her in a while. There's just something missing when she's gone.

Book under discussion: <u>Treasure Island</u> by Robert Louis Stevenson

Avis handed a new notebook to me, this one larger and with wider lines. Wonder what was wrong with the last one—it was only a fourth full.

Jokes were made about my eyepatch being on theme for this book, and should we all dress up for future clubs? I didn't mind the attention. When you get to where folks will rib you, you know you've found real friends. Although I said I'd draw the line at a tunic and tights if we ever got around to Robin Hood like Danny Maloney is lobbying for.

Even Miss C admitted that "the narrative was certainly compelling," though she gave Gio and Rosa a stern lecture on how real pirates are not so romantic and tragically heroic as their portrayal in the story.

The other fellows in the group and I tried to reassure her that no one really thinks brigands are role models: they only like the adventure they stand for. You'd never think it to look at him, but Earl Bell apparently went through a stage where he tried to persuade his parents that piracy was a legitimate career option. I carved wooden swords and made friends walk the plank as a boy. Hamish claimed he'd always wanted a pet parrot. The women of the group looked at us like we were crazy.

We let Gio pick questions to ask. He started off with a great one: What did we all think of Long John Silver? Opinions varied; no surprise there. "Gentleman scoundrel" was the term I used, and while Danny Maloney thought his kindness to Jim was faked the whole time, Mrs. Lokken maintained that there was some good in him after all.

Only Martina didn't seem to find him compelling. "I didn't trust him from the start," she said quietly to me. "You can always tell with some men, no matter how polished they sound." I told her that was really smart of her, making predictions like that. But then I thought about the man at the movie theater, the one Gio ran after. Makes a fellow wonder. Anytime I ask Gio, though, he says everything is fine at home and talks all about his da training for radio work, so maybe it's nothing.

The corrupting power of greed was the next topic, and we all answered Gio's question about what we'd do with our share of a vast treasure. Avis tried to tell us she'd donate it all to charity, and when we booed her for the trite answer, she added that she'd get a new hat too. Delphie wanted to visit Paris, "or whatever's left of it after that awful man finishes tearing it apart." As for me, I said there wasn't much I wanted that gold could buy. After me, Rosa said she'd buy all the ribbon candy in the world, and everyone laughed.

A good time was had by all. Even Louise said so, and Gio practically beamed. Good boy, that one, and a hard worker. I'll miss long days in the garden with him once the harvest is in, talking about everything and nothing.

Delphie piped right up when it was time to take suggestions for the next reading, offering up Edgar Allan Poe as another great American author. The work she suggested, "The Tell-Tale Heart," sounds suspiciously like a romance, but Miss C didn't say a word. And no wonder. It takes a lot to cross Delphie. I haven't tried it again, that's for sure.

P.S. Looked up Edgar Allan Poe afterward. Two revelations: First, "The Tell-Tale Heart" is a short story, not a novel. Second, it is most definitely not a romance.

This is going to be fun.

thirty

LOUISE
AUGUST 25

Louise could feel the shift in temperature as she stepped from the dining room into Delphie's domain. Despite all the windows being wide open, the kitchen resembled an inferno, steam rising from enormous pots on the stove, the counter a mess of bruised tomatoes leaking pulpy juice and seeds.

Her cook, brilliantly red-faced, was midway through pouring water from a kettle into a soup pot with glass jars bobbing inside and didn't turn when Louise cleared her throat. Perhaps it wasn't loud enough to be heard over the bubbling water. "Delphie, I need to speak to you."

Not so much as a glance over. "Can't. It's canning day. Now shoo."

No one, not even Delphie, told Louise to "shoo." She planted her practical pumps right there on the mat, immovable. It might actually be better to speak to Delphie when she was distracted and off her guard. "Why did you have us read this ghastly story?"

That got Delphie's attention, and she turned, metal tongs in hand. "What's that?"

Louise held it up like an exhibit at a trial. "The Poe story. About the buried heart." The one where a man, trying to hide his misdeeds, was exposed and found out in the end by the dismembered body that brought the truth to life.

266

There was too long of a pause before Delphie answered. "I thought the young people might like it. Is that a crime?"

No, but it also wasn't the truth. Louise was sure of it by the way Delphie's voice rose in defense. This time, when Delphie lifted a deep-frying basket of whole tomatoes from the second pot of boiling water, her veined hands shook, spilling water down her arm. A stream of half swears in French followed, and Louise felt a flicker of guilt, rushing over with a dishtowel to help.

"I'm fine," Delphie muttered, pushing her away and bringing the tomatoes over to the sink.

"But that's not all, is it?" Louise pressed. "Why else did you choose it?"

The only sound in the kitchen was the spray of cold water splashing over the tomatoes to loosen the skins.

"Maybe I thought you'd learn something from it," Delphie finally admitted.

And that was all Louise needed to confirm her theory. The thought had occurred to her days ago, but she'd pushed it aside, certain it was her mind playing tricks on her. Now she had to say it.

"That's why you protested Freddy expanding the garden. You knew he'd find that awful statue. Because you buried her there."

Without missing a beat, Delphie drew out a knife. "I did." Not a trace of shame on the wrinkled old face as she calmly peeled the skins off the tomatoes, revealing the shiny flesh below.

Even though she'd suspected, it hurt to hear such a calm admission. "Why? When I expressly ordered—"

"Your orders don't apply to me. They never have." Another smooth motion, and the cored tomato was cut in half. "Anyway, I didn't think there'd be any harm, burying her. Your father loved her so."

So that was it. Delphie had always been loyal to her father.

"You did too once," she pressed when Louise didn't respond. "Before."

Before what, she didn't say, but Louise knew.

Had Delphie seen Louise slipping out to meet with Oliver those hot summer nights after checking for a message under the statue's heel? She had never outright admitted to it, but Louise knew very little escaped the old cook's sharp instincts.

"I thought there might come a day you wanted her back. For the good memories you had, mixed with the bad. Your father loved you, you know."

No, she didn't know. Not really. He'd never said as much, not even in those last days.

A timer chimed, and Delphie ran to the stove, lifting a lid to inspect the boiling pot with full jars of tomatoes inside, their lids now sealed tightly shut from the pressure.

Once, when Louise was a girl, she'd crept to the pantry, hoping to steal a treat before dinner, only to meet the terrifying sight of tomatoes exploded against the pantry wall, a simulation of gore that could have inspired one of Edgar Allan Poe's macabre tales. When she'd asked what had happened, Delphie explained that the seal hadn't set properly in the hot pack, causing fermentation and, eventually, an explosion.

Now, Louise could feel the same thing happening inside her: a slow, growing bitterness reaching dangerous levels. "Regardless, you had no right to hide this from me."

"Does it matter? That gardener of yours wouldn't let me have her this time, not even her face, when I ran out to beg him for it. Said he'd made a promise and he meant to keep it. The statue is gone."

Bless Frederick. He'd kept his word. That small comfort evaporated in a moment, like water in the uncovered pot between them. Because that wasn't the heart of it, not really. "If, after all these years, you thought I had made the wrong choice, you should have simply said so. Rather than hiding behind a story."

Delphie didn't answer at first, her towel-wrapped hands setting out each sealed jar on the counter. "Stories help sometimes. I only wanted you to think about it, that's all."

"Think about what?"

"For one thing, why you're still so dead set on shutting down your father's library." She paused her work and raised a hand before Louise could protest. "I know, you've told me it's about the children. But I have to wonder, is it really?"

"Of course." Why would no one believe her? "Besides, I've signed the contract, already committed part of the cost."

First Avis, now Delphie. Couldn't any of them see that there was nothing to be done at this point?

Delphie wiped her hands dry on her apron, seemingly for the sole purpose of planting them on her hips, and turned to Louise with an accusatory look. "Admit it: you love that book club as much as any of us."

Ah. So that was it. "It's enjoyable, but it's become a simple social club. Half the people there would prefer I wasn't around anyway."

"That's an exaggeration, and you know it. Tell me the truth, Louise. Would you miss this group if it was gone?"

She thought of the laughter over clinking teacups, the lingering conversations after the last discussion had ended, the people who now had stories and opinions attached to them instead of being merely names. "Yes, I suppose so."

The satisfied nod Delphie gave was sharper than the tomato-spattered paring knife lying on the board. "Then you should think long and hard about what you'll lose in destroying another place your father loved. And whether it's worth it."

How, after all these years, could Delphie still be bitter about the garden? "It doesn't do any good to be sentimental. We all have to move on at some point."

"Maybe that's so." Delphie rolled a tomato in her hands before facing Louise squarely. "But the older I get, the more I know that story is spot on. The past won't stay buried. That's the plain, awful truth of it, Louise. It's only a matter of who's going to do the digging."

NOVEMBER 1918

The doctor had departed from his monthly visit, having driven from one of the larger cities up the coast. As he left, he merely nodded to her from under his gauze mask, a common sight on medical providers since early fall, his expression giving no indication of how the meeting had gone.

Louise didn't need to hear a medical report from him. It was apparent enough to anyone who looked at her father that his health was failing, as most patients did after enduring nearly two years of tuberculosis.

Louise's concern was with another disease entirely: influenza.

In the U.S., it had started in Fort Devens outside of Boston, where in September, over a fifth of the returning soldiers from the Great War had contracted a new, deadly strain of the flu, brought back from their time abroad. Some claimed the Germans had sent the plague as a final war offensive, though the Red Cross nurses who tended the sick and dying knew better.

In Maine, it was expected that the epidemic would spread to Portland . . . but it also found its way to Bath, only a short distance away, and then to the small coastal towns like Derby. By October, county fairs and war-bond drives were canceled, schools, theaters, and finally churches closed—except for a few, like nearby St. Patrick's, which refused to do so, claiming that "Praise of God upon a Sunday is more essential than any other work in all the world." They and a few other Catholic churches held Mass in the open air of the bitter autumn cold, praying for divine relief that seemed slow in coming.

In Derby, two of the churches remained open as well—as

hospitals. And it was there that Louise had begged her father for weeks to serve.

Not because she, a grown adult, needed his permission. Even though she'd agreed to act as his nurse, such a promise could certainly be broken for emergencies like this.

No, it was the fact that her decision would greatly impact his life as well that made her agree to wait for Dr. Hoffman's professional opinion. Because if she brought back the disease from the makeshift sick wards to her tuberculosis-weakened father, he would almost certainly die.

Her knock at the sickroom door was more timid than usual, and when Father rasped out permission to enter, she waited.

"Ring for Benson" was all he said, in a voice made strong with effort. "I'd like to visit Pemaquid Point one last time before winter sets in."

It was already too cold for a stroll to Father's favorite nearby lookout, but he had that set of his eyebrows that told her he would brook no argument. She'd long since given up restricting him to Windward Hall, as long as he avoided close contact with others. If he wanted to take his time to share his decision, she would play along.

Benson, who served as both driver and butler, helped wheel Father's chair to the overlook once they reached Bristol. Though Father was buried under layers of blankets and scarves and the temperature hadn't yet fallen below freezing, Louise knew she ought to insist they keep the visit brief.

There was something striking about the lighthouse, a tall white beacon against the blue sky, dwarfing the keeper's lodging tucked beside it. It supervised an embankment of striped rock, broken up here and there with yellowed grass, bent over and dying, like so many other growing things as winter moved irrevocably forward.

For a moment, Father simply watched the ocean crash against the rocks. "The doctor tells me," he finally said, "you want to establish and serve in a ward specifically for local children."

"Yes, they ought to be separated as much as possible, given whatever resources we can spare, since they're at higher risk." Though even the young and strong were at risk, as demonstrated by the soldiers dying in droves. Even worse off were pregnant women.

The elderly.

Those suffering from tuberculosis.

A fit of coughing interrupted them, muffled with a blood-spotted handkerchief, and when Father spoke again, his voice was weak. "You won't be able to save them all."

"I can save some."

"A good answer. A brave one." His words surprised her enough that she looked down and noted his thin, pale hand clutching the chair's wooden armrest. "But, Louise . . . it's not your child you'll be treating."

Louise pinched her eyes shut, trying to ward off the headache sure to come. She knew what Father always thought when the subject of children arose. Her campaigns for stricter underage labor laws. Her desire to rehabilitate the starving children of Europe after the war. Now the juvenile ward for influenza patients.

As if, in each child she helped, she was trying to atone for the one she'd given away.

Only he'd never said it outright until today, always remaining distant and averse to conflict. *He must really be dying.*

She managed to keep her voice dispassionate, as a good nurse needed to be. "I am aware, Father."

Though if things had been different, perhaps she would be worried about protecting her own child. If she'd never agreed to live with Aunt Eleanor and deliver in secret, if she hadn't asked for another family to raise the baby . . .

Foolishness. There was no going back, not after so many years.

"I'm sure he's safe from the flu, wherever he is," Father ventured.

"She," Louise corrected, goaded into speaking after all. She hadn't held the baby after the long hours of labor, had never asked for anything but medication to take the pain away before they whisked the child away, so she didn't know the gender of her baby with certainty. Still, she'd been convinced it was a girl. Had prayed for that over and over while feeling the nudges and kicks of the baby inside her.

A boy might grow up to be like his father, inconstant and greedy, while a girl would, God willing, inherit her mother's practical nature. It was all Louise could leave her, along with a letter and a hefty check from Father to cover her education someday.

The wind cut deeper, and Louise shuddered. It was in the past, and none of it, however painful, could decide the question in front of them now. "Please, Father, I'm not one of your fictional characters whose motivations you can endlessly debate. I'm a trained nurse waiting to hear if I'm to be allowed to assist in a global medical crisis."

His features drooped in resignation. "So you are. Though I had hoped you were more than that."

Don't let it show. It was easier, four years removed, to hold back visible signs of emotion, but still painful. "I'm sorry to disappoint you." *Again.*

"Dr. Hoffman was deeply opposed to my permitting you to work in a local ward. He felt that any contagion you might bring back to our home would be too much for me."

It was not a surprise. Dr. Hoffman had looked nearly as haggard as Father on this visit, likely as overworked as any of the medical professionals in the nation. His first thought would be for his wealthy patient, not the poor of Derby.

"His recommendation," Father continued, "was that we allow other nurses to travel to Derby."

She'd thought of that, had used it as an excuse out of fear when the epidemic first began to spread. "No one will come, not to a town this small." Not when cities like Boston and New York were seeing cases in the tens of thousands. "Certainly not until spring."

"I told him the same."

She let out the breath she'd taken in to continue the argument. "What changed your mind?"

"Charles Cliffton came by the other day to drop off books. He told me Anthony, one of our youngest patrons, has taken ill."

It wasn't about her persuasive arguments or badly needed skills at all.

Still, did it matter? She remembered the towheaded boy bent over his children's book, sounding out each simple syllable, and pictured him shivering on a cot in the makeshift hospital, burning with fever.

Whatever the reason for her father's change of heart, she would finally be useful.

"I can't keep you to myself any longer. Not when the need is this dire in the community I've come to love."

"I will do good work, Father. I promise."

"Take care of the children, Louise." His eyes wandered across the rocks. "As for me, my fate is in the hands of Providence."

Overly dramatic, as usual. Still, she couldn't help but ask, "Are you afraid of dying, Father?"

He looked up in surprise. "Well, I don't exactly like the idea. Too many good books left unread."

It was his attempt to lighten the mood, but Louise felt herself stiffen all the same. That was his greatest regret?

They stood in silence again, her mind already thinking through the supplies she would need to order, the hours she could reasonably work without collapsing, the hygiene she must practice before returning home each day.

"Lighthouses are tragic, you know."

The comment, so far removed from nausea and nursing wards, caused her to pause. "Whatever do you mean, Father?"

He gestured toward the structure on the promontory, untouched by news of the Great War or the Spanish flu or the troubled conversation between father and daughter. "They are strong, courageous even. A beacon of light in the midst of a storm. Everyone admires them . . . but from a distance."

She wondered if she ought to wave Benson over to wheel Father back. When he got in one of his fanciful moods, it meant he'd overtaxed himself. "Of course they do. That's their entire purpose—to serve as a warning of danger."

"And so no one ever gets close to them." When he looked at her, she realized they'd stopped talking about lighthouses.

Sentimental nonsense, of course. What greater calling could a woman aspire to than being useful? Here at last was her chance to make things right, to serve those in great need.

And every night, she prayed that somewhere another mother was caring for and protecting her child since she could not.

thirty-one

GINNY
AUGUST 26

Most days now, Ginny slept past noon, rising only to get ready for the swing shift. Harder to get to sleep at nights, thinking about Mack and all. Besides, what was there to do when she woke up? She hadn't felt much like reading lately.

Today, though, she scooped the newspaper from the apartment door as soon as it was delivered. Instead of slapping it open to scan for pancake breakfasts or charity luncheons, she ran a finger over the Help Wanted section.

It had taken some thinking, but Ginny decided Lew was right. Maybe it was time to move on from Derby. After all, the book club was shutting down soon thanks to Louise, and the hotter it got in the foundry, the more she remembered those mornings out on the *Lady Luck* with Pa, free from shift bells and midnight schedules and mindless work.

A change of pace, a change of scene. That's what she needed to help her forget and start over.

Pitch in and help! one ad proclaimed in bold letters.

Farm labor shortage means our crops won't be harvested—not without you! Women welcome. Must be

*physically fit and ready for vigorous labor, September to
November. Good pay, housing provided.*

Sounded promising enough. She circled it, along with the
number to call. It wasn't lobstering, but it'd be better than being
cooped indoors all days. She could spin her time spent weeding
with Freddy and Gio into experience if she didn't mention she'd
been reading a book to them most of the time.

She'd just started reading an ad for a stenographer when a
knock stopped her pencil midway through circling.

Another telegram?

Maybe this one would tell her they'd gotten the dog tags
mixed up and Mack was really alive, recovering in a field hospital somewhere and charming all the nurses with his tales of
derring-do.

Or maybe it was news that her mother had slipped back
into her old ways and needed bail money, or Pa had gotten in
an accident at a construction site, or one of the boys ran into
the street without her to look after them . . .

Stop it. She stood, the old floor creaking under her, and took
a hesitant step toward the door. Probably just the landlady,
come to collect the week's rent.

But instead, she opened the door to see Freddy Keats, a
paper bag in one hand, cleaned up from garden dirt. The part
of her that wanted to grin and welcome him inside clashed
against the part that wanted to slam the door in his face and
lock it, so instead, she stood there dumbly, trying to sort things
out.

"I come with greetings from the Blackout Book Club," he
said, bowing. "And condolences too, but I didn't think you'd
want to spend much time on those."

At least he was smart enough to know that much. "Thanks,
I guess."

"People have been worried about you, you know." His voice

was kind, as always, which took away the option of telling him she didn't want to talk to anyone, so please get lost.

Instead, she tucked her arms around her middle and tried not to worry about her unkempt hair and the pile of dirty dishes visible behind her. If she'd known she was going to have company, she'd have straightened up at least a little. "Did you get drafted to come here?"

"Nope, I'm a proud volunteer." He held up the bag, stained in the corner with a spot of grease. "Though I didn't make these shortbread cookies. Avis did, if it helps."

That did help, but when she reached for the bag, Freddy pulled it away, like he might tease Jeeves with a bone. "Want to take a walk down by the cliffs?"

That sounded suspicious. "Are you bribing me?"

"Almost certainly."

She considered for a moment. This would have been easier if Freddy had dropped off the cookies and split. Then again, if she didn't give the book club proof she was doing fine, they'd just send someone else.

Anyway, wasn't she the one always telling Avis to get outside before winter came? Everybody native to Maine worth their sea salt knew that much. "Fine," she grumbled, tugging her favorite bandanna off the heap by the door to keep her hair from blowing in the wind. "But I don't have long."

They walked clear out of town, down quiet streets now that the summer people had left for the season, leaving behind faded signs advertising photo development and five-cent ice cream cones.

Strangely, Freddy didn't ask Ginny how she was doing or promise her Mack was in a better place or anything like that. That's what Ginny had braced herself for, not a long walk into the wind, until they reached the two-story plunge to the ocean below.

Locals, she'd learned, called it the Cliff Walk, like there was only one worth mentioning. The gables of Windward Hall poked into the sky fifty feet away, partially hidden by scruffy stands of white cedars and fir.

Freddy stopped and strolled to the edge, sitting and dangling his legs toward the sheer layers of wind-scoured stone in mottled gray.

Fine. She wouldn't be bested by a one-eyed vet, not that easily. Ginny sat beside him, ignoring the slight wave of dizziness when she looked at the rocks below, struck with seafoam. Back on the island, they had plenty of trees, three sandy beaches, even promontories for whale watching—but all of them were flat and level, like God intended. "That's a fair piece down."

He nodded, pointing at the beach. "It was just about there that we met for the first time, when I was out walking Jeeves."

"Should have brought him with you." At least that would have given them something to talk about. "I hear dogs are supposed to be able to help with grief, so you could check me off your list and leave me in peace."

"Hey now." He frowned. "You're no charity case, Ginny. We only wanted to make sure you were all right."

Here it came. He'd been waiting for the right moment, when they were too far away from her apartment to retreat. "I'm fine."

"That's what Delphie said you would say. She also told me not to believe it."

Wise old crone, that one. Maybe Ginny wasn't fine exactly, but there was nothing Freddy could do about it. "Sometimes, a body just needs time alone after . . . after they've lost someone."

"I'll grant you that. I've done the same myself."

For the first time, despite the lingering suspicion about his past, Ginny was glad Freddy was the one they'd sent. He, more than the others, knew the unfairness of funerals without bodies and grief without someone to blame.

279

"But it's been a while, and it feels like you're pushing us away, Ginny. All of us."

It wasn't like she'd planned on dropping out of the book club. When last Saturday had come, it had just felt like too much. "Why does it matter? I told you from the start, I'm not staying here long."

He shrugged. "What does that have to do with it? I plan to go back to my family after the harvest, but you don't see me pulling away, pretending not to care so it'll be easier to leave."

Now he was just being difficult. "That's not what I'm doing. I just . . . This isn't home."

"It doesn't have to be. What matters is, it's *here*." He leaned back, palms flat against the rock, and watched the waves come in below them. "When you think about it, we're all passing through, in and out of this world quick as a passenger boarding a train, on the way to something that lasts. Until then, you might as well make friends with your fellow travelers. Because, like it or not, you need us, Ginny. And we need you."

Ginny stared at the young pilot, who in turn stared out at the ocean.

He made it sound so easy. Like good-byes were only see-you-laters, like you could give away bits of your heart like penny candy offered to someone in the seat next to you. Like it wouldn't hurt when you left them or they left you, when they lied to you or turned a cold shoulder or up and died in the Pacific Ocean.

As if reading her mind, he added, "'When you're Real, you don't mind being hurt.'"

She'd heard that before. . . .

Rosa's book, the one with the toy rabbit. The first Blackout Book Club meeting she'd missed, right after the telegram about Mack.

She sighed. "We don't live in a storybook, Freddy. Here, there aren't magic fairies to make everything right."

He pulled an offended face. "What do you think *I* am?"

A laugh burst out of her without permission at the image. "Annoying, mostly." She tossed a pebble and watched it skitter down the slanted cliff. "Why do you care, anyway?"

He paused, giving her just enough time to feel bad about how that might have sounded. "I probably shouldn't care so much. But I do."

The words themselves were ordinary enough, but the way he turned to look at her . . .

She backed away from the edge, tucking her legs underneath her, almost feeling Lew's scowling brotherly presence behind her, though she knew he was miles away. "Soon as harvest is over and you move on, you'll forget all about me."

"Oh, I doubt that." When she didn't reply or return his smile, he coughed and opened the paper bag set beside him. "Time for the cookies, I guess. They're leftovers from club. Supposed to look like gold coins from *Treasure Island*. Avis is getting fancy."

Ginny accepted the cookie, though not the compliment. It felt wrong, in a way, listening to him flirt with her, with Mack dead only a few weeks.

Worse, what if Lew was right, and Freddy or the others tried to convince her to stay . . . or she started to want to?

She had to make it back to the island. Folks there had lost enough already.

Freddy waited until she'd taken a bite of buttery goodness to speak again, raising his hand to the scruff of his neck and taking in a gulp of air. "There is another reason I wanted to be the one to check on you today. See, what I told you at the Fire Muster was true but not the whole truth."

"Ha!" she burst out, spewing crumbs. "I knew it." Her mind raced ahead, going through all her theories, the ones she'd pushed aside to grieve. "So are you a spy for the fifth column or the Communists?"

"You're not making this easier." His sigh was long and drawn out. "I came to Windward Hall specifically. Because I wanted to meet Louise—I mean, Miss Cavendish."

"Because she's rich?" Was he really admitting to some kind of con job?

But his next words tipped her so far off-balance that a stiff breeze could have sent her tumbling off the cliffs: "Because she's my mother."

No matter how long she stared, it didn't look like Freddy was going to break out in laughter and admit it was a joke. "Your . . ."

All of it made sense now. Not just the bits about Freddy, but Louise, the way she hated romances and was always doing good deeds, like she was making up for something.

For some reason, the first thing out of her mouth was "Is Freddy your real name?"

"Middle name, but it's what everyone calls me. Samuel Frederick Powell. I changed the last name to that of a favorite poet, in case Louise had ever found out my parents' names—the ones who raised me."

Ginny leaned forward eagerly. "What did she say when you told her?" Louise didn't seem the swooning type, but if anything would cause the ol' spinster to faint, it would be this news.

"I haven't . . . exactly . . . told her yet."

"What?" Ginny turned her outrage on Freddy, who was studying his cuticles.

"I meant to tell her straight out that first night when I knocked on her door." He shrugged helplessly. "But . . . you've met her. She greeted me all formally and turned the conversation into a job interview from the start. I had the feeling that if I told her the truth, she'd . . . well . . ."

"Stuff you in cement shoes and heave you into the ocean?"

He let out a laugh. "Not exactly, but at least deny everything and tell me to go away. I couldn't let that happen, after how

282

long I'd wondered about her, about my father. I thought maybe it would be better to get to know her first."

That made a strange kind of sense, though Ginny knew she'd have burst out with the truth in the first five seconds if she'd been him. "Are you going to tell her now?"

"Well . . ."

"Freddy," she said sternly. "You've got to. Your own mother!"

"I don't know if she'll be angry or turn me out on my ear. She doesn't approve of lying, or sinning in general, you know."

To Ginny's way of thinking, someone who'd had a child while unmarried probably wouldn't make too much of a fuss about that, but then with Louise, you never could tell.

"Don't be a ninny. Anyone would be proud to have a son like you."

"My father wasn't, I guess. His name wasn't even on the birth certificate."

Wasn't that just a bombshell? Louise Cavendish, partner to a doomed romance. This was better than a Hollywood drama. "Still, she's got to know. And soon."

"I know." The familiar smirk appeared on his face, the one she'd been so suspicious of. "If I promise to tell Louise the truth, will you promise to come back to the book club?"

Oh, he was a clever one, that Freddy. She snatched another cookie and considered. "That depends. What're you reading this time?"

"We're starting 'The Tell-Tale Heart' by Edgar Allan Poe. I'm pretty sure he wasn't all right upstairs, if you know what I mean. You'd like it." She snorted, not sure if that was meant as a compliment or an insult until Freddy grinned. "It's short."

Short was good. Shakespeare ought to learn a lesson.

And really, what harm could it do, going back to the book club? It wouldn't bring Mack to life, fix things with her ma and pa, or fill up her bank to buy her home back. But maybe it was better than being alone.

"Well, in that case, I might as well try to catch up."

She asked him more questions on the way back—yes, the false name was why he hadn't wanted to show her any ID; no, the eyepatch wasn't part of a disguise.

"And how about your parents? Do they know why you're here?"

"Shh," Freddy cut her off as they climbed the stairs to the apartment. "Let's talk about that later."

"Why?"

But when he opened the door, she understood.

There were people in her apartment. Just making themselves right at home, like they owned the place.

Avis, looking up guiltily from where she was rising with a full dustpan, spoke first. "Just cleaning up a bit." Mrs. Whitson didn't even try to contain her smile and kept right along folding a rumpled basket of sweaters.

"So," Ginny said, swiveling to confront Freddy, who didn't look one bit apologetic, "this was all a trap."

"Only slightly," he protested. "I did want to talk to you."

"This is breaking and entering, you know," she accused.

"The door was unlocked," Delphie's voice countered from the kitchen. "So it was just plain entering."

Ginny marched over to find the old woman, a gingham apron wrapped around her sagging figure like a machine gun belt, stirring a pot of something warm and inviting with a wooden spoon.

"It's a good thing we thought to bring food with us. Goodness, child, the shantytown in the hollow has better-stocked pantries than yours." Delphie gestured at the open cabinet. "*C'est pas vrai!* Is that . . . canned ham?"

"It's none of your business what I eat." Good golly, weren't old ladies supposed to be covered in cat hair and offer hugs and peppermint tea?

If they were, Delphie had clearly decided to take a hard left while everyone else went right. "We'll see about that," she said primly. "Now sit down, keep your elbows off the table, and eat."

Avis shot her an apologetic glance, but Freddy pulled out a chair for her, and Ginny plopped down into it. When Delphie dished the chowder into the bowl, swimming with cream and vegetables and shrimp, she couldn't keep her mouth from watering. And as Mrs. Whitson said grace over the impromptu feast, it felt like God was listening after all.

She still wasn't sure anyone here needed her, like Freddy had said. But, well . . . maybe she did need them. At least a little.

From Russell to Avis

August 27, 1942

Dear Avis,

Today, I keep thinking about what our British friend said during training: "That's the trouble with you Americans. We learned back in '39 that self-reliance isn't a virtue. Not at sea."

He scowled then, and we all cringed, thinking we'd done something wrong, but it turns out his ire was aimed elsewhere. "That's what I've been trying to tell your navy, but they seem determined to let your entire merchant marine fleet get blown to bits before listening. Escorts, convoys, power in numbers—those are the strategies that work. We must stick together. War is no time to isolate yourself."

He was a bit raw, I think, because Admiral Ernest King wasn't much for accepting British advice. But we heard him, we ragtag fellows with our commandeered yachts, and we've stuck together ever since. I've never felt so much like I've belonged before. Not with my family, not at college or at the bank. Here, I'm one of the team. My crewmates—Stephen, Lester, even Captain Sherman—are like brothers now.

Maybe you're asking why I'm telling you all this. Well, they announced yesterday that we have an option to renew our term for six months, until April. And I want to do it. I'd come home for Christmas still, but Hitler won't let his men retreat when the weather gets cold. Someone's got to stop them.

Listen, Avis, it was probably awful of me to leave when I could tell you were upset, but I thought you might grow into the idea of me joining up. That's why I told you about everything I was doing here, so you could see that it matters.

But I haven't committed to anything, and this time, we need to talk about this like a husband and wife should.

Once I explained, the captain gave permission for leave. That means I'll be back home for ten days, starting September 1, arriving on the 5 o'clock train. I know this is sudden and a lot to think about. But we can think about it together.

> *Yours hopefully,*
> *Russell*

From Anthony to Avis

August 9, 1942

Dear Sis,

I just got your letter from a few weeks ago today— guess we shouldn't expect a country that took two full years to join the war to prioritize speed. I wish you'd have told me earlier, sis, about the library closing down. That's a hard thing.

Listen, it might seem bad, but don't give up. I know you—you're that beautiful mix of practical, clever, hard-working, and stubborn, to boot. That's what caught ol' Russ's eye, all those years ago. I've never told you this, but as all big brothers should, I had a good talking with him after he took you to the movies for the first time. He said the usual sappy things about your pretty eyes and the way you smile, then, "I've never known another girl like her." It's the only reason I didn't grumble during the "speak now or forever hold your peace" bit of your wedding.

All I'm saying is the two of us know a quality woman with a good head on her shoulders. What you need is a little more grit. So that's what I'm here for, to remind you not to let something you love slip away without a fight.

But if you try your best, and it all falls apart anyway, it's okay. Really. People will find the stories they need right when they need them. They always do—you included.

The point is, I'm proud of you, sis. And I always will be.

> *Cheering you on from this*
> *side of the Atlantic,*
> *Anthony*

Notice on the door of the Cavendish Association Library, September 1, 1942

The library is closed until further notice, due to a family emergency. We apologize for the inconvenience.

thirty-two

AVIS
SEPTEMBER 1

Avis was only halfway done with her frantic vacuuming of the hallway when she heard the front door slam shut.

Russell was home.

She caught her breath and rubbed the Old Orchard Beach lapel pin at her shoulder. "Hello, darling," she called, setting down the vacuum. "Be there in a moment." She threw on her floral-print housecoat, belting it at the waist, before hurrying out to the sitting room.

There he was, his skin several shades darker than she remembered, wearing a brown mackinaw coat dirty around the cuffs, a small suitcase at his feet. Worn down by a long trip and time at sea, but just as handsome as ever.

She smiled tentatively. "Well, you certainly didn't pack much."

"After two months away, I'm used to traveling light."

A beat of awkwardness followed, and Avis blushed as Russell seemed to study her, glad she'd thought to put on lipstick before vacuuming. "How was the train?"

"Crowded with troops, as usual." This time, though, there wasn't the slightest hint of bitterness in his voice when he mentioned his drafted brethren. "I hoped you might be there to pick me up, though."

"I haven't driven the car in months, dear. Saving gas rations and all." Besides, there was dinner to fix, the house to clean, and on such short notice, she hadn't finished half of her to-do list. . . .

But despite the undusted surfaces and the streaks on the windows she hadn't had time to wipe with a rag, Russell was looking around appreciatively. "Good to be back here again. The quarters they have us staying in when we're on land are a bachelor's slum."

They stood there for a moment, staring at each other, and Avis thought she knew what Russell must be thinking. So much they hadn't said. So many hard questions they would have to face now. No running this time.

"Welcome home, dear," she said, stepping into his arms for a brief embrace. "It's so good to see you . . . even if it's not for long."

That made him shift uncomfortably, rocking back on his heels. "You got my letter, then? About the extension."

"I did."

"And I suppose you've already made up your mind?" He said it with such resignation that her next words caught in her throat.

This had been a terrible idea. He would think she was a fool. This would only start the old argument again. It had been too long, and they'd been too far apart for any of this to matter.

But above the din of fear and loneliness were the words from Anthony's letter, so clear that she could almost hear him say them in older-brother exasperation. *"Tell the man what you're thinking. Chances are, he hasn't got a clue."*

"I wanted to say I'm sorry." The surprise on Russell's face threatened to stop her right there, but she let the words pour out without bothering to make sure they followed the tips in some useless advice column. "For not being honest with you. For avoiding everything important and burying myself in magazines and work and . . . and meatloaf while pretending you were fine when I could see you weren't. For comparing you to my father and for . . . well, for being selfish."

Russell stared at her, as if unsure where the flood of words had come from and completely unable to match them.

That was what they didn't tell you in the novels about heroines and their fine speeches: that the most difficult moment of all was still to come, full of the fears that collected in the silence after a declaration of true honesty.

When her husband finally did open his mouth, his words were thoughtful. "I never—well, thank you, Avis. For all of that. Let me wash up and have a second to think. Then we'll talk."

He turned toward the bathroom, and she stiffened, lurching toward him. She hadn't had time to tell him . . .

"Don't go in there!" She closed her eyes, wishing she could somehow disappear.

His hand froze on the doorknob, as if he suspected some sort of minefield. "Why not?"

"Because there's sand in the bathtub." Borrowed from the four milk cans stationed at the library's front doors, which, thank the Almighty, had languished free from incendiary bombs since Gio and Rosa had put them there.

"There's . . . what?"

"And a lobster in the sink." The stare continued, and she added meekly, feeling miserable, "His name is Long John Silver."

The shocked expression could only hold him for so long, and he pulled open the door. Right on cue, the rope Avis had attached to the doorknob dropped the needle on the record player and the first strains of "Moonlight Serenade" echoed smoothly off the grouted tile.

Peering around his shoulder, Avis could see the whole pathetic scheme as it must seem to him. A thin layer of sand, patchy enough that the brown tarp showed through in places, with a seashell placed artificially in the center. The record player on the floor, occasionally spattered with a drop of water from the sink, where the lobster she'd christened Long John Silver scrabbled inside. And her wedding veil hanging over the window, the pale pink roses sewn to the headpiece clashing with the green of the walls.

"I don't understand."

She undid the belt of her housecoat and let it slip away, revealing the cherry red bathing suit she'd purchased for their honeymoon—and never worn since. Even after only two years, it fell more snugly across her middle, and the daringly short flared skirt revealed wider thighs. Though with everything else, maybe Russell wouldn't notice.

"I'm not trying to manipulate you or convince you to give up the Hooligan Navy, Russ. I promise. It's just been so long since we've been happy that I thought we might . . . recreate a happy moment this way."

The idea that had seemed so romantic after getting Russell's letter only seemed ridiculous now, more Abbott and Costello than Rita Hayworth and Fred Astaire.

For his part, Russell was still staring, his head turning from the small-but-energetic lobster flicking water onto the tile, back to her.

"I'm sorry. I've missed you, and . . . you've been gone for so long. . . ."

But before she could finish, Russell stepped toward her, smelling of sweat and damp wool and the ocean, and lifted her chin gently. "I believe you, Avis."

He did?

"And I'm the one who was selfish, leaving the way I did when I knew deep down you didn't want me to."

She couldn't stop now, not before she'd said everything she'd planned. "I want you to be happy. And I know you love your work on the picket patrol. But I also need to know that, when all this is over, you'll come home to stay—and that will be enough. That I'll be enough."

She'd tried to imagine all possible scenarios of what Russell might say in response. In none of them had she anticipated the way he stepped back and bowed.

"May I have this dance?"

Numbly, she took his hand, melting into the familiar pattern of steps, waiting for him to say something, anything, else. He didn't.

Developing sea legs certainly hadn't translated into dance skills, but Russell led her in a slow waltz as the record spun out its last verse.

Even then, Russell didn't make a dramatic declaration of love or burst into another argument or even ask more questions. He only knelt by the bathtub, picking up a handful of her jury-rigged beach and letting it fall. "Sand?"

"It really was silly."

This time, when he looked up at her, all confusion was gone, replaced by the boyish smile that had once won her heart. "Should I turn the shower on, do you think? To remind us of the time we got caught in that awful storm?"

A laugh bubbled out of her. "I'd forgotten all about that. All my careful makeup smeared. I was a mess."

"You were still beautiful."

The unexpected compliment made Avis look away. My, Russell had been gone a long time if this was all it took to send her back to the days of her stammering teenage crush. "All we need now is that postcard I gave to you."

"You mean this one?" He fished his wallet out of his trouser pocket, thumbing past a few bills, and drew out a silver dollar-sized paper heart. Flipped over, the source became obvious: the corner of a Ferris wheel overlapped with the white text from the postcard's motto: *Where lovers meet.*

The sight of it made her take in a little breath. "You kept a piece of it all this time?"

He placed his hands around the smooth bathing-suit material on her waist and pulled her in for a kiss. "A man's got to remember his honeymoon, doesn't he?"

A splash of water spoiled the moment, and they both turned to the lobster in the sink, putting up a fuss at being forced to remain as a witness, and Russell laughed. How she'd missed that comforting sound! "I still can't believe you did all of this."

"I had help."

More, in fact, than she'd expected or wanted at the time. As soon as they'd seen the note on the library door, the book club members had started calling and visiting, concerned for her. With only a day to put her plan into action and months of neglected housework to make up for, Avis was forced to call in favors.

Ginny had picked up the lobster, proudly bringing it in a bucket instead of properly dead like Avis had expected, and insisted it would be better boiled alive. Mrs. Whitson had lent her record player, Freddy had helped mow the lawn, and even Hamish had quietly volunteered to drive to the train station in Miss Cavendish's car to pick Russell up. All of them claimed to be happy to do it—except Delphie, of course, who had merely shoved an unrequested basket of fresh bread at her without comment.

Despite the fact that none of Avis's books on homemaking included a section on asking friends for help, it hadn't been so painful after all.

"I thought we might want to continue this conversation over dinner." That is if she had the heart to boil poor Long John. Naming him really had been a mistake.

"By candlelight?" Russell grinned roguishly.

"Of course. Blackout regulations, you know," she said seriously.

"Sure thing." Russell wrapped his arms around her again, and this time, she rested her head on his chest, listening to his heartbeat. "I'm glad to be home. With you."

And when they let go, for the first time in months, Avis felt as though the war were thousands of miles away.

thirty-three

MARTINA
SEPTEMBER 4

Martina watched as Gio slid the library key into his pocket, trying to look businesslike, though a hint of his bucktoothed grin slipped through.

"Don't lose it," Avis warned sternly, guiding him to the checkout desk, where he'd just learned how to sort the cards in the charging tray.

"I won't. I promise."

"Good." Avis nodded, her smart navy hat perfectly pinned in place. "Now see if you can find the Dewey decimal numbers for the nonfiction categories requested for the Victory Book Campaign."

Gio bent over the work with more eagerness, Martina noted, than he'd ever given to schoolwork. She'd come with the children to the library this morning to make sure Avis's offer of a job at the library was genuine and not just charity. To her surprise, Gio had demonstrated that he already knew many of the library tasks, from shelving books to using the Royal typewriter stationed behind the desk. Those young eyes took in more than she realized.

"He'll do a fine job as a page," Avis reassured her. "At twelve, he's the youngest we've had but not by much."

The title of page made Martina smile every time, as if Gio

was a court attendant out of one of Rosa's fairy books. "I'm surprised Miss Cavendish agreed to this."

"Oh, she didn't. Gio's wages are coming out of my paycheck." A protest sprang to Martina's lips, but Avis shook her head firmly. "Don't say a word about it. It might be short-lived, with the library closing, but with Miss Cavendish's astonishing list of tasks, I need the help more than ever. Gio's worth twice the pay I'm giving him."

She hummed a cheerful tune, her plaid skirt swinging widely as she danced more than walked to a cart of books, taking a stack that nearly reached her chin. When Martina had complimented her on her new shade of lipstick, she'd admitted that she'd taken extra care today because her husband was home on leave for the week.

"And now," she said, tottering toward Martina with books in tow, only her face visible above them, "I'd love it if you'd help me with an errand."

Martina surveyed the library, a few browsers wandering among the shelves, including Rosa tucked into the children's section, as usual. "Are you sure we should leave him alone?"

"It's just down the street. Won't take but a moment. And Gio can handle it, can't you?"

He actually saluted—in imitation of his father or Freddy, she couldn't say—before returning to parade rest. "Yes, ma'am."

"He certainly can," Martina agreed, and the boy's chest puffed out with pride at her words. Maybe, despite her flaws and failings as a mother, he would grow to be the right sort of man after all.

Avis loaded her arms with half of the stack of books. "We have a special delivery to make to Danny Maloney."

She glanced at the spines of the volumes Avis carried. *The Life of William Carey. Lottie Moon. Christianity and the Nations.* This for the man who routinely had to check his colorful language at the club with children present and could hold his own in a debate with Gio about the British and Empire light heavyweight match in London.

"Are you sure? These don't seem to be . . . well . . ." But her objection faded there. How many times had she been surprised by the preferences and opinions of other book club members? Miss Cavendish loved British comedy, Freddy performed Shakespeare like someone in Boston's theater district, and sweet Mrs. Whitson had confided that she was going to lobby for *The Strange Case of Dr. Jekyll and Mr. Hyde* as their next read.

Avis waved off her concern, an excited smile teasing her face. "You'll see."

Outside, the overcast sky paired with a cool breeze reminded Martina that summer was almost at an end. The children would begin school on Tuesday. A few trees had begun to be tinged with reds and yellows, but most stubbornly clung to green, unwilling to surrender so easily. Even Maloney Pawn Dealership had changed for the season, with a handsome fur coat out in the window to snag the attention of passersby.

Inside, though his shoulders slumped slightly when he realized they weren't paying customers, Mr. Maloney covered it admirably. "Good afternoon, neighbors! What can I do for you?"

"Actually, we hope we can do something for you." Avis set the books on the counter and gestured for Martina to do the same.

But Mr. Maloney had already backed away, hands up. "Sorry, ma'am. I don't buy books, except an encyclopedia set every now and again. No money in it."

"Never fear. We're not selling. Just lending a few that might be of interest to you." With that, Avis opened the first book, then pointed with a neat, manicured finger to a line midway down the card tucked in the back: *Charlotte Maloney.*

Mr. Maloney turned the book toward him, his expression unchanging for so long that Martina began to worry he wasn't well. Then his Adam's apple bobbed as he swallowed. "You found them."

Avis nodded. "All patrons sign the checkout cards, and there are only a few dozen books in the section you pointed out. From there, it was a simple matter of opening them to check the records."

"Charlotte read all these books, did she?" A gleam of tears had come into his eyes, one breaking free and plummeting toward his moustache. "Always was a clever one, my Lottie."

Martina fumbled in her pocket to offer him a handkerchief—thankfully, one not stained with foundry oil—which he accepted, blowing his nose with gale-wind force. "Thank you," he said, beaming at both of them and clutching the books to his chest like no greater treasure had ever come through his shop's doors.

"You're very welcome." Avis was practically glowing.

"I'll read them all." He traced his wife's signature again, then raised the handkerchief to his eyes. Martina looked away to give him a moment of privacy, browsing the wares set out in displays with neatly labeled tags dangling from them. A set of golf clubs hung beside two fine tennis rackets. Used musical instruments in open cases, from a violin to a dented bugle, had been arranged with a kind of weary pride. Avis seemed to be taken with a bassinet dripping white lace.

Martina stopped at the china cabinet, looking through the fragile objects arranged inside, including a tan rabbit with ears thrown back, pink nose alert. How Rosa would love that!

From behind her, she could feel someone standing close, too close, though she hadn't heard any footsteps. She flinched, turning . . . and laughed out loud in relief. Only a mannequin, though the calf-length men's coat draped over it had given it human proportions.

Wait. She'd seen this coat before.

"Sorry to dash off so quickly," Avis was saying to Mr. Maloney as he returned from the back room to gather the second armful of books, "but library business calls." She nodded at Martina, clearly expecting her to follow.

"You go on. I'll join you soon."

Even in a small town like Derby, there were likely dozens of coats of this description. Trying not to draw attention, Martina leaned over and sniffed the collar. Was that really Patrick's cologne or only her imagination?

She picked up the left sleeve. There, almost unnoticeable, was an oval-shaped burn from the Chesterfield Patrick had smoked in the alley outside the Bristol-Banks Foundry.

So he really had been here. The thought settled oddly in Martina's mind. For Patrick to be desperate enough to sell part of his carefully crafted image . . . what could he be up to?

"Looking for something for the man in your life?"

Though she knew the booming voice was only Mr. Maloney, Martina couldn't help startling, dropping the coat sleeve. She forced a smile as he stepped around the counter, traces of concern weighing down his eyebrows. "No, I most certainly am not."

"Are you all right, Mrs. Bianchini?"

This was her chance. Maybe, if Patrick had sold some of his possessions, he'd given up making money here in Derby and had moved on. If she could know for sure . . . "The man who sold you this . . . what can you tell me about him?"

He hesitated, tugging nervously at his collar. "No offense, ma'am, but I don't make a habit of talking about customers." He said it like the people who skulked into his shop were as worthy of dignity as the ones who patronized perfume counters in high-end department stores.

She'd have to give him some reason, mixed with as much truth as possible. "Please, I . . . think I might know him from Boston, and I would not like to meet him again, if he's in town."

Her words and the genuine anxiety in her voice seemed to settle the matter. Mr. Maloney indicated a height a few inches above his own. "Tall fellow, dressed nicer than most I get in here, but that's nothing too unusual. Brown hair, scar by his chin, slightly crooked nose." He shrugged. "Does that help?"

Any doubt she had went away instantly. Though she would choose different phrases—Mr. Maloney, it seemed, hadn't picked up on the Errol Flynn swagger and good looks that a woman would notice immediately—it sounded like Patrick, but a physical description alone wouldn't give her the information she was looking for. "It might be."

Mr. Maloney leaned back against the display case, his frown deepening. "To tell the truth, I didn't like the cut of his jib." Noticing Martina's confusion, he added, "Forgot you were from away. In Maine-speak, I didn't like the look of him.

"Understand," he went on, "in here I mostly see folks at their worst. Desperate, lonely, in some kind of trouble. You've got to look a little harder to see the good in them when they're beaten down like that." His eyes wandered to the stack of biographies behind them on the counter. "Charlotte taught me that."

Before he could tear up again, Martina quickly asked, "What do you mean by the look of him?"

"His sort, I check any bills a little closer, if you know what I mean. He kept trying to get me to pay top dollar for his things, too. Real smooth talker."

That was Patrick, all right. "Did he sell anything else?"

"A suitcase and a gold watch chain. And . . ." He rounded the display case, pulling open the glass door to remove a tray with jewelry arranged in a neat row. But it was the simple gold necklace he pointed to that made her heart nearly stop beating.

"This one. Told me it was inset with real turquoise."

Martina reached for the crucifix, the body of Jesus vague from generations of wear, four small blue stones at each point to indicate his wounds, the clasp that took several minutes to fix properly. Her crucifix.

She'd given it to Patrick when he'd confronted her in the

church back in Boston, all she had with her of value. She hadn't even told Mamma, she'd felt so much like Judas, betraying her Lord, not for silver but for the momentary promise that Patrick would leave her alone.

Had he kept it this long out of superstition? Sentimentality? Had he used it for prayers of his own?

"I've got a jeweler's loupe and enough training to know real gems from glass," Mr. Maloney went on, his chin still tilted down at the velvet tray, missing her reaction entirely, "but that foreign turquoise, well . . . I don't do much dealing in that. So when this fellow countered my price, I told him I'd bring it to an appraiser, and to come back in three days when I knew what it was worth."

She had a feeling she knew the ending to this story. "He took the lower price, didn't he?"

Mr. Maloney nodded. "Either it was a fake and he didn't want to be caught out, or he needed cash right away. Maybe both."

"When was this?"

"Just yesterday." Mr. Maloney shook his head. "Tried to get me to set the coat aside in the back room, saying next week he'd be able to buy it back. Got angry when I said I couldn't do that. Bad business model, you know. I'm used to folks insisting they'll strike it rich and return for their goods. They rarely come through."

Martina frowned. "He said he'd be rich in a week?"

"Sure. Don't they all?"

Strange. That didn't fit with her theory that Patrick needed money for wharf-side drinking, or that he'd hit hard times and needed to move on.

Still, except for the crucifix, there was nothing wrong with Patrick selling some of his things—hadn't she been the one to recommend it? Even his comment about coming into money could be his usual empty bragging.

"Think it's the fellow you used to know?"

The question pulled her from her thoughts. Yes, it was the same Patrick . . . and also not the same. He had always been a bully, but whoever he'd connected with after leaving the navy had taken him into something darker. What, she couldn't say, but it gave her an uneasy feeling all the same. "It's possible. But please don't worry about me. Just . . . tell me if he comes back, if you would."

From his expression, Mr. Maloney wasn't fully convinced. "Are you sure you're all right, Mrs. Bianchini? If you need someone to walk you back to the library . . ."

"It's nothing, really." Her hand went to her purse, with its few bills and coins. "But I'd like to buy that crucifix."

For once, Martina was glad the core room required only endless repetition.

Fit the two halves of the mold. Dust it with powder. Scoop in sand. Press down. Pack in a few reinforcing steel bars. More sand. Repeat until overflowing the edge, and apply pressure to pack the sand in. Scrape the extra off. Poke a hole for release of gases during the metal-pouring.

By now, every movement was efficient and practiced, which certainly didn't mirror the state of her thoughts. Her crucifix, heavy under her blouse after all this time, was a constant reminder of Patrick's strange interaction with Mr. Maloney. Her instincts all shouted that something was wrong.

By the time she sat in the cafeteria beside Ginny, picking at the supper she'd brought from home, she'd given up trying to silence the worries. She closed her eyes, trying to remember conversations Patrick had had with friends in Boston. None of them were the sort she'd invite over for dinner, but had any of them hinted at crime or mob connections? She didn't think so.

"Marti?" She opened her eyes to see Ginny squinting at her

in concern. "That's the third time you've nodded off. You all right?"

"I wasn't sleeping. Just . . . worried."

Her nose wrinkled in curiosity. "About what?"

There it was, the invitation. No one here knew that her story about a noble husband toiling in the navy was as much fiction as the books they read for book club. She'd come close to telling Mr. Maloney the truth but hadn't needed to.

In the North End, neighbors were called *paesani*, roughly "our people." That created a kind of bond, especially between the women, one you could rely on in hard times for favors or loans, and in ordinary times, for sound advice, last-minute child-minding, or a listening ear.

Ever since coming back from her beau's funeral, Ginny hadn't been so ready to joke and laugh. But she was still trustworthy, a true friend.

"My husband might be in trouble," she blurted before she could change her mind. "Or may be causing trouble."

Instead of looking surprised, Ginny just took a thoughtful bite of her sandwich. "Really? Your husband? I'd have banked on ex by now."

"You . . . already knew?"

"'Course not. But it's easy to tell there's no love lost between you and the fellow." Before Martina could protest, she held up a hand. "I know, I know, don't tell the kids. I get it. So you got news from him?"

"More than news." And with that, Martina told her everything: his appearance in town, the request for money, the suspicious way he'd talked when pawning off his coat.

"What'd he need the money for?" was Ginny's first question when she'd stopped.

"He claimed he needed it for a fuel tank"—Ginny leaned forward at that—"but I don't know what he really spent it on."

Ginny snapped her fingers, a glint in her eyes that Martina

hadn't seen since before the funeral. "Smuggling. That's got to be it. That's why he needs a second fuel tank."

"Shh!" Martina looked around at the other workers, but all of them seemed absorbed in their own troubles and thoughts. The last thing she needed was for someone to inform Mr. Devons that the Italian woman had been talking about smugglers.

In fact, all Martina knew about smuggling was from Daphne du Maurier's *Jamaica Inn*, none of which seemed to apply here. "But what could he possibly smuggle in the fuel tank of a fishing trawler?"

Ginny stared at her as if she was dense as the metal the workers in the next room poured into their molds. "Fuel, of course."

Now Ginny shared what she knew about the black market from her brother. One part stood out to Martina: "I heard they can get two or three times the price of the fuel."

That *would* explain how Patrick planned to quickly get his money back.

The shrill whistle calling them back to their stations from supper interrupted the conversation, but Ginny tugged on her arm as she stood, clearing uneaten scraps into her paper sack to be disposed of. "You've got to report this, Martina. Now."

"I . . . I can't. Not until after our shift, at least."

The other workers were already streaming into the core room like tin soldiers, trained on principles of productivity. Any delay would hurt the war effort.

"Listen, Martina, this is serious." Ginny lowered her voice to a whisper, tugging Martina closer. "Some of these profiteers, they're selling to German subs."

That couldn't be. "How could they possibly . . . ?"

Ginny shrugged. "Beats me. Guess that's why the coast guard says you can't have a radio on boats these days, except one set to their approved channel. Must be a way to contact U-boats. Bet they pay even steeper prices to make up for it being treason and all."

Treason. Martina had tried not to pay attention to the headlines about the eight German spies who had landed on American soil, but once she knew what to look for, it was difficult to miss. Two, the ones who informed the FBI, were thrown in prison. The other six were executed. Electric chair.

She shuddered, as if the current had reached her through Ginny's words. Though she didn't like Patrick and certainly didn't trust him, if she turned him in, he might face the same penalty. Did he really deserve that? And of course, with their father featured as the headline in all the newspapers, the children would know.

Did Gio deserve to have his father taken from him so brutally?

"Maybe he's only cheating the ration system. Taking extra fuel." That, while illegal, wasn't serious.

"That wouldn't make a profit worth bragging about," Ginny pointed out, "just let him travel farther for his fishing. Not worth the risk."

"We don't have any proof. Only suspicions." The authorities might search the trawler and find nothing, leaving Patrick angry and suspicious of who might have turned him in.

"Who cares? Lew told me the coast guard is doing random searches already, at least down near Portland. Maybe not so much up here."

What had Patrick said, the first time he'd stopped in unannounced at the trailer? *"Crew likes smaller towns. Safer that way."* How long had he been involved in black marketeering?

Long enough to pay for the suit, cuff links, and car, that much was sure. And she'd simply accepted his story that fishing prices had risen, like he'd known she would.

But would Patrick really sell fuel to Nazi submariners?

Yes, if the price is right.

Still, it wasn't that easy. "The police would never listen to me."

Ginny considered that for a moment. They'd reached their station again, back to the hustle of the core room. "Russell Montgomery's home on leave, and he's part of that coast guard patrol. He'll know who to talk to, and his word'll hold weight."

Something like hope fluttered inside of Martina. Yes. Avis would vouch for her. That wouldn't be so hard.

She nodded, taking a shaky breath. "Good. As soon as our shift is over, I'll find a telephone and call Avis."

"But it'll be midnight by then. What if she's asleep and doesn't hear? Or doesn't get out of bed to answer?"

Martina hadn't considered that. Not everyone's home was the size of her trailer, where a loud noise from any corner could be heard in all the rest.

She had no watch, and no clocks were visible in the core room, but supper break ended at seven thirty. Avis would still be awake and likely at home. And yet, she couldn't just step away from her station. They were making gears the size of dinner plates today, for use in a new defense industrial plant. Important work that couldn't be slowed for . . .

For matters of national security? Surely that was a good enough reason.

"You've got to do this *now*," Ginny said firmly, putting her hands on Martina's shoulders, like images of boxing coaches with their contenders in Gio's magazines. "Listen, you just march up to Mr. Devons and demand to use one of the telephones in the foundry offices."

This, finally, was something she could do. Like the heroines on the propaganda posters in the cafeteria who stopped rumors and reported suspicious activity and kept on the lookout for saboteurs.

But when Martina actually walked across the room to Mr. Devons, going over production schedules with the men who hauled in molds, her resolve seemed to drain away with one curt "What do *you* want?"

She took a deep breath, and when she released it, she pushed out, "I need to use the telephone."

Mr. Devons's face seemed to glow red, though she knew it was just the temperatures of the foundry. "You what?"

"It's an emergency." He waited, as if expecting her to give more details, but what could she say that wouldn't sound absurd? "A . . . family emergency."

"An emergency would be falling behind our quota while every mother who wanted to check on their children jawed on the phone."

She winced. There were posters about that too. *Don't Be a Production Slacker*, they warned.

"Please, sir. I promise I'll never ask about anything like this ever again."

He looked at her, and Martina could almost see what he was thinking. *Lazy Italian. Probably trying to slow down the war effort.* He shook his head ponderously before turning away. "No, ma'am, I can't allow it. Back to work, now."

She could explain that she needed to report potential black marketeering.

No, that would just look like the babbling excuse of a desperate woman. It was too late to change her story now.

So Martina obeyed, slinking back to her station. She was no heroine. She couldn't even do this one simple thing.

It didn't help that Ginny offered her no sympathy. Instead, she smacked her forehead with a sand-stained hand. "Marti, Marti, what am I going to do with you?"

This time, Martina didn't try to hide her annoyance. "He's the boss, Ginny. He makes the rules. We follow them."

"Rules are for people who don't have good reasons to break them." Ginny's hands expertly cupped sand into her mold, and Martina had a foolish hope that she'd given up, until she turned back, face animated. "Listen, here's what you've gotta do. There's a pay phone down Mayfair Street by the bus stop. You've seen it?"

Martina nodded, and Ginny dug deep into the pocket of her overalls and pressed some coins into her hand. "Wait a while, then pretend you're going to the privy. Instead, sprint down there for all you're worth and make that call as fast as you can."

"W-what? I can't."

"Sure you can," Ginny said soothingly, as if that would calm Martina's suddenly racing heartbeat. "I'll cover for you. Spin some story about how you stumbled off sick to your stomach if someone notices you've been gone awhile. No one wants vomit in the core room."

She never meant for anyone to have to lie for her. "No, I can't do it. I'll wait until midnight and call Avis. Or the police. Or—"

Ginny looked at her sternly, gesturing with the steel rod she should have been packing into the sand. "Martina, this is your moment. If you wait, who knows what could happen?"

It was that question and its answer that found Martina out on the street in the charcoal gray sky. Almost dark enough that Patrick and his crew could slip out early for their secret mission, and all of this would be for nothing.

No, don't think of that.

To fill her mind as she ran, she hummed the melancholy song her mother had sung to her before they came to America, when the streets were filled with rioters and they both knew Papa might not come home. Named after the same moon that gave her just enough light to see the sidewalk in front of her.

"*O crescent of a waning moon, you that shine on the deserted waters.*"

The soles of her shoes were thin enough that she could feel each rock that she kicked aside, but she didn't stop. How far down the street was the phone booth? How much time had passed?

"*O waning crescent, what harvest of dreams wavers in your pale glow down here!*"

There. The narrow wooden shack stood at the intersection,

and she tugged the door open, leaning against the side for a moment, trying to catch her breath.

"No song, no cry, no sound goes through the vast silence."

Not tonight. Tonight she would break the silence.

Once she clicked in the coins from Ginny, the operator cheerily inquired and connected, and soon she was telling Avis about the potential smuggling in quick, exhausted bursts.

The pause at the end was so long that Martina feared the call had dropped, until Avis spoke. "You mean that some fisherman has gathered extra fuel to sell to the Nazis?"

Martina judged her tone. Shocked but not skeptical. Avis, unlike Mr. Devons, believed her.

"Yes. Russell works for the coast guard, doesn't he?"

"In a way, but . . ."

"He must get someone to inspect Derby's landing, early this morning, before the boats go out." Already, it had taken far too long to answer Avis's confused questions. "I have to go. Only please, make sure they do something. Soon."

"Did you hear the fellow's name? This captain?"

Martina stared blankly out at the night. She hadn't admitted that the man was her husband, just that she'd overhead a fisherman hinting at a second fuel tank and a coming profit. She could still claim she didn't know his name.

But if it helped them find him . . .

"Patrick Quinn." She flinched, her eyes shut. "Write it down."

"I've been writing all of this down." Saints be praised for Avis and her ever-present notebook. "And his ship?"

Why had she never thought to find that out? "I don't know. Only that it's a fishing trawler moored just outside of town. That's all I know, Avis, I swear it. And I have to go."

"Wait. Russell will want to speak to you directly—"

But she hung up, trusting Avis to pass on the information to her husband. She slammed the door of the phone booth, her worn shoes slapping the uneven sidewalk back to the factory, creating a rhythm for the comforting strains of her mother's song.

"Oppressed by love, by pleasure, the whole world is fast asleep."

At least no one walked by on the sidewalk this late. Everyone was inside working, or at home with blackout curtains drawn. She reached the cold steel of the door handle and pulled.

"O waning crescent, what harvest of dreams . . ."

It had been ten minutes, maybe more. Surely it would be all right. Surely . . .

But when Martina slipped into the core room, it seemed like every worker's eyes lifted from their monotonous work to stare at her, and it soon became clear why.

Mr. Devons was standing at her station next to a worried-looking Ginny, his expression cold.

Notes from the Blackout Book Club—September 5, 1942

Taken by Avis Montgomery, Head Librarian and Book Club Secretary

Members in attendance: Russell, plus nearly everyone who has ever attended a book club, except Louise Cavendish.

Story under discussion: "The Tell-Tale Heart" by Edgar Allan Poe

When I asked Delphie where Louise was, all I got was a cryptic "Some people just don't like to face things." Russell muttered that she was probably afraid to show her face since we all knew she planned to shut the place down. He shouldn't have said it, but I appreciated the support.

Even Ginny was back. We all agreed discussion was much livelier with her around, and I could tell she was pleased to be missed. (Also, she ate seven raspberry jam cookies. Seven!)

Maybe because Louise wasn't there, bedlam ensued about five minutes earlier than normal. That is to say, immediately.

The book discussion was soon replaced with a trial of Delphie. Accusation: What made you choose this terrible story? Prosecution: myself, Martina, most of the other women present. Defense: Ginny, Mr. Maloney, Freddy, and Mrs. Whitson, of all people. Neutral: Gio and Rosa because they weren't allowed to read it.

Martina stopped as soon as she realized the point of the story and hid it from Gio. I made sure to note the nightmares I'd had two nights in a row after finishing, and how I'd had to move the clock to the closet to keep from hearing the ticking. Mrs. Follett felt that the whole thing was wholly inappropriate. ("There's a difference between Gothic and the macabre.")

At this point, Delphie said something odd about how "we could all learn something about the cost of secrets," then clammed up. Mrs. Whitson tried to argue that there was spiritual value to a horrific depiction of guilt, and Freddy said there was a rhythm to the lines of the story, like poetry. But that couldn't outweigh the thought of a body cut up and stuffed under the floorboards. (Gio listened particularly well when we got to that part. Ginny was perhaps <u>too</u> detailed in her description.)

The others attempted to carry on a coherent discussion of unreliable narrators. We came around to the fact that most of the group does not properly appreciate horror. Russell just sat back and watched the whole thing. ("Better than a radio drama," he said.)

Delphie was unrepentant. Ginny has checked out <u>Selected Works of Edgar Allan Poe</u>. Freddy thought we'd love <u>Dracula</u>. The motion was not seconded and died in committee.

Instead, we settled on a new title, <u>The Robe</u> by Lloyd C. Douglas. From what I understand, it's an account of a Roman centurion investigating the death of Jesus Christ. That ought to exorcise the madman-murderer streak from our club.

I felt I had to mention that the next Saturday might be our last book club at the library, as renovations are set to begin shortly afterward. This dampened spirits somewhat, including my own. I've been to Windward Hall only once, for a Red Cross event, but it reminds me of a badly decorated English country home, straight out of a Wodehouse novel.

I have to believe Anthony that it's not my fault. But still, looking out at all those grim faces, seeing the crates of books to be donated filling up one by one, more and more shelves stripped bare, I can't help feeling like a failure.

P.S. Afterward, Martina asked about the tip-off she'd given me and was disappointed to find I'd heard no news either.

The coast guard tends to keep things like that hush-hush. They'd probably deny that U-boats existed if people couldn't see the tanker fires from the beaches.

Then she admitted she'd lost her job over her report. Can you imagine? I was so upset that I offered for her and the children to live with me while she looks for a new position. Russell is leaving in only a few days—we've agreed that he'll renew his term for three months, and we'll reevaluate at Christmas—so we have room. It will be nice not to be living alone, even if it's only temporary.

thirty-four

LOUISE
SEPTEMBER 7

By the time Freddy and Hamish set down the twelfth box of books, Louise began to suspect it had been a mistake to tear down so many of her father's shelves to make more room for her painting supplies, all those years ago. Well, she'd fill what space she had, then deal with the rest later.

"Where's this one going?" Hamish asked, and she indicated a scrap of unoccupied real estate by the rug. Atlases, from the looks of the label, though it was barely legible. Not Avis's neat handwriting, unless it had gone downhill sharply from the last Louise had seen of it. *I wonder if she's gotten some lackey to do her work for her?*

Well, there was no harm in that. Louise hadn't specified how the work should get done, just that it must.

She picked her way through the maze of crates, careful not to catch her skirt on the rough wooden edges. Yes, the full dozen had arrived.

Hamish, as always, slipped soundlessly out, but Freddy lingered in the doorway. "Do you need help shelving the books, Miss Cavendish? There are an awful lot here."

"I rather doubt you'd understand my system." It didn't mimic the library's. Heavy volumes on the bottom, most used at eye level, collector items on the top, all of them vaguely grouped by subject.

"It's no trouble," he insisted, twisting his gardening cap in his hands. "Actually, I wanted to speak to you, if it's a good time."

She turned away and lifted one of the crate's lids. "I'm sorry, Frederick, but it will have to wait until later. Besides, Delphie is planning another day of food storage with the pressure canner, and she's demanding a steady supply of nonacidic vegetables."

He offered a small smile. "Well, I wouldn't dare get between Delphie and her string beans."

"Pity the fool who would."

Alone once again, Louise eyed the boxes warily. With something to set her hands to, she'd hoped she'd be filled with a burst of industry.

Everything was going more or less to plan. She'd been to the library the day before, seen the stacks of boxes labeled for the Victory Book Campaign, the shelves half bare, a *Closed* sign in the window. Avis insisted she needed to devote all her time to sorting, and besides, who would want to weave through the maze to find a title that might not still be there?

All of it was said with the resignation of someone who, after a series of devastating battles, was seeing that the end of the war might be surrender, not victory. She'd even reluctantly agreed that the club should start meeting at Windward Hall.

It would be crowded, perhaps, having all the regulars in her small drawing room. Windward Hall was designed as a summer getaway, not a mansion equipped for entertaining large groups. But if she moved out the piano and brought in another settee . . .

It won't be the same.

There was something comforting about being surrounded by shelves, the way the tall windows let in morning light, the smell of the old tomes mingling with whatever baked good Avis had set out for them to enjoy.

But it was too late to turn back now.

It's never too late.

Ah yes, the old sentimental optimism she'd inherited from Mother asserting itself. Louise attempted to push it back by attacking the first box of books when she saw the Beatrix Potter books placed on top, the ones she'd specially requested.

Had she ever recommended them to Rosa? The little girl would love them.

With a sigh, she stood. What could it hurt to make a simple inquiry? It would never do to make an uninformed decision, after all.

In the hallway, she cradled the handset to her ear and requested that the operator connect her to Milton Hanover.

He seemed surprised to get her call, a week earlier than her usual monthly update on the nursery school project. "Yes, well, I thought I should let you know. There have been . . . complications."

"Perhaps you'd like to elaborate?"

She most certainly would not, but of course she needed to. Starting with the most straightforward: the contractor's concerns about completing the work by the first snow. From there, she moved to the women's hesitance to accept charity.

For once, Mr. Hanover barely interrupted, inserting only the occasional question. "Is that all?" he asked when she paused once again.

This time, she chose her words carefully. "There has been . . . increased community involvement in the library lately that I would be hesitant to lose. People seem to have found it to be a helpful location for civic engagement. Including myself."

"I see," Mr. Hanover said dully, though she guessed he did not. "I wonder, Miss Cavendish, why you didn't mention any of this earlier?"

Gracious, this was painful. Louise barreled on past that question rather than give the obvious answer: pride. "To be clear,

Mr. Hanover, I do not intend to abandon my duty. Nothing has been decided yet. My call is simply to inquire if there are any other options." Another group, perhaps, that she could donate to, a promising charity closer to Bristol, anything at all.

A hum on the other end. "As it turns out, the city council announced to a group of local businessmen that a federal grant, newly passed by Congress, might be available to our community to fund a nursery school. We won't know for certain until the new year, but it is a possibility."

It was in that moment that Louise realized why characters in silly Hollywood movies were forever dropping telephones as an indication of surprise. It wasn't so much a clumsy fumble as the fact that one's mind was so occupied it couldn't spare the effort for gripping things.

In the next moment, she'd recovered both her hold and her voice. "I thought you said it might be years before the government intervened."

"It still might be. With Uncle Sam's busy schedule, I'm inclined to be skeptical. In the end, it is your choice. Move forward with the library renovations to ensure a timely center, or wait to see if another is founded with the grant money and without your help."

Without your help. The phrase landed bitterly, implying that she wasn't needed after all.

She thanked Mr. Hanover distantly as she replaced the handset, her thoughts in tangled knots.

What would she do now?

Later that night, Louise pulled her shawl tighter against the chill of dusk. Half of the garden stretched out before her was empty. The harvest had begun in earnest, a reaping of what had been sown.

Even after pondering the matter all day, she hadn't arrived

at a conclusion. If she proceeded with the project as planned, she risked duplicating a federal nursery school. If she halted it, she'd have to trust the government would keep their word, not to mention accept the loss of her deposit money—and a fair bit of pride.

Her father would insist there was a book, somewhere, that she could escape into to find the answer, to give her insight into what to do.

But she'd spent too long escaping, hiding, lying. Even avoiding the last book club meeting because she worried that someone would start talking about guilt, then see her and guess her long-buried secret.

The rest of them could learn more about one another, but she would always be forced to stay a distance removed. Safe. Where no one would know that she'd given her heart to a man who abandoned her, then given up the child they'd had together.

"The past won't stay buried. That's the plain, awful truth of it, Louise. It's only a matter of who's going to do the digging."

She stood, leaning against the fence, breathing in the cool scent of turned-over earth . . . and thinking of another night, just after Windward Hall had become her legal possession. The night she'd burned her father's garden.

MARCH 1919

Rosebushes crackled as they burned.

Louise watched, entranced, as the flames spread, smoke billowing into the cuttingly cold winter air. The heat that flared off the dried branches twined around the collapsing wooden arbors promised a dramatic, if brief, spectacle.

She'd stationed Father's servants around the perimeter with buckets of water to douse any sparks that leaped the trench they'd dug, though if she wasn't mistaken, they watched her with more fear than they did the fire blazing through the dead patches of gladiolas.

Fine with her. Soon the servants who were not local would leave to work for her brother, who had inherited the Cavendish mansion in New York, freed by her father's death from their indenture to this lonely Maine coast. Until then, she could bear a wary look or two.

The garden's trees had been cut down, the hedgerows uprooted, the paving stones dug out of the barely thawed ground one by one. But if she'd had the servants merely pluck out the perennials, they—stubborn things—would simply appear the next year. Besides, it would take far too long. She'd touched the first flame to a rosebush herself, watching the bare, thorny canes curl to black. An appropriate color, one of mourning, for the man who had loved them so well.

Towering above it all from her waist-high pedestal, the statue of Persephone mocked her, beautiful, pure, untouched. Soon, she would be crumbled to gravel, as Louise had ordered Benson to do, despite his protests about the expense. Without a garden, there was no need for a statue, a protector of secret messages containing lovers' secrets. Not anymore.

Once Oliver had whispered lies of love to her within those tangled bowers. Her father had disappeared into this garden nearly every day, ignoring the young girl who desperately wanted him to take notice of her. Now both had left her alone, and the flames consumed the garden like the wrath of the Almighty.

"Your father had his faults, I'll admit, but he's gone."

The voice at her elbow made her startle, and she relaxed only slightly when she realized it was Delphie, her face in a tight scowl like she'd downed a tumbler of vinegar, waggling a finger at her like she was still a child, scolded for drawing sketches in the margins of her father's precious books. "You can't anger him anymore by throwing a hissy fit against his garden. It won't help."

"I don't want it to help," Louise murmured, watching the pattern of dancing flames before her. "I want it to hurt."

And though she'd never said it in so many words, she was surprised to find just how true it was.

When Delphie didn't reply, the words kept coming. "I thought, maybe, it would make me feel something."

Five months of treating the critically ill, exhausted from the long days with no rest, had numbed her to any emotion. It was all she could do to wake up in the morning, don her bleach-white nursing uniform, and stagger to the hospital-church full of moaning patients separated from one another by the rude curtains she'd hung up. Many citizens of Derby, treated as best she could with limited supplies, recovered after a week of battling the disease. A few—feverish, weakened, and susceptible to pneumonia after the ravages of the Spanish flu—did not.

By Christmas, new cases slowed, but she hadn't relaxed her precautions, wearing a mask and scrubbing her skin raw each night before returning to Windward Hall, interacting with Father only when absolutely necessary, his care given over to Delphie and others.

And still, he died quietly in the night only a month into 1919. Dr. Hoffman reported symptoms of influenza as a contributing cause, stony eyes regarding her with open hostility.

He would have succumbed to tuberculosis soon regardless. It was a heartless thought, but true, and all that had kept her functioning the past month, through the funeral and the censorious stares from relatives, even her own brother. As if they believed that in saving others, she had killed her own father.

"I didn't kill him. Or at least I didn't mean to. He wanted me to serve," she wanted to shout at all of them.

In the end, Luther Cavendish had looked up from his books and his blooms and done one great unselfish thing. And she had kept her promise. Not one child under her care had died, not even Anthony, her first patient, brought to her in a state of coughing, feverish fatigue, like Tiny Tim from the novel her father had loved so much. It had taken two weeks before she'd declared him safe to return to his family, particularly since he had a sister who was just a toddler, but the healthy flush in his cheeks had increased her determination to see her work through.

Delphie didn't utter another word of protest. Perhaps she couldn't. Maybe the older woman also felt a rawness in her throat that wasn't from the smoke, full of grief and loss and the difficult choices they all had to make.

That night, Louise breathed in the scent of smoke that had seeped into her clothing and hair, waiting for a sense of triumph, relief, or even sorrow. It never came, even as she opened her window to look down on the black gouge in the lawn from above, the cold breeze carrying the acrid scent to her.

It might not be right. But it was done.

Louise sighed, picturing the garden that had been overlayed on the garden that was. At the time, she'd fashioned the destruction as burning away memories of her old life, with its expectations and heartbreak and failures.

Now, sitting among vines and neat furrows, she could finally admit that it wasn't about creating a new start. It was an empty attempt at revenge. Against Oliver, her father, and even herself.

The scorched earth had long since healed. For a while, she had left it barren and scarred, like pictures she'd seen of the Battle of the Somme. But in the early '30s, when she'd hired Hamish as her handyman, he'd suggested raking in grass seed to cover the unsightly patches, and she'd allowed it. A pristine lawn soon replaced the ruins, and now there was something growing again. Something purposeful and practical, not delicate and decorative like Father had always demanded of his gardens—and his daughter.

It was a quiet night, with only the slightest of breezes, so she heard the footsteps behind her, and when she turned, Freddy approached.

She held up her hands to prove they were empty. "Never fear. I wasn't going to burn it this time. Not after all the work you've put in."

He looked stricken. "I didn't think—"

"But you knew I had once."

"Yes," he admitted. "I'd heard."

Of course he had. Derby didn't keep secrets well, and certainly not about the offense that had first led to her isolation, no matter how hard she tried to invest in the community afterward. She'd allowed them to whisper all these years, hoping to be dismissed as a wealthy eccentric, hoping no one would ask further questions.

To her neighbors, rich summer people merely lounged on beaches, made extravagant demands of locals, and occasionally did unbalanced things like burn down gardens.

How old she must have looked just then, how weary, because Freddy took a cautious step closer, concern on his face. "Are you all right?"

"No."

It was an answer she'd never uttered in all her years to that particular question. But tonight, there was no way to scrape together enough composure to answer otherwise, especially not to this disarming young man who knew the meaning of loss.

"Delphie told me the two of you quarreled last week about the garden."

The sympathy in his voice was almost too much to bear. There was nothing keeping her here, not even social expectation. She could—should—make her excuses to the boy and turn in for the night.

Something, though, kept her leaning against the rough wooden fence, maybe only the sheer weariness of thinking of the effort it would take to walk into that drafty hall and climb the steps one by one.

"It's been known to happen before. The two of us are quite set in our ways. Perhaps you've noticed. But it's fine between us, really."

"Maybe." Frederick leaned against the fence next to her, just close enough to share the space while far enough away not to feel intrusive. "People will hurt us. The ones we love most often and deepest of all, because we've let them in."

"Then perhaps we shouldn't be foolish enough to do that."

"It's not foolishness. It's courage."

She couldn't help snorting at that, and Freddy turned, frowning.

"Haven't you ever hurt anyone, Louise? Disappointed someone?"

Somehow, in her exhaustion, after all those memories, it slipped out: "My daughter."

Had she said that out loud? Or had she merely pictured the tiny, squalling infant, seen only for a blurred, drug-hazed moment before they whisked her away?

No, she'd spoken the words, but no shock appeared on Freddy's face.

"Or son," he said quietly.

"No. Even though I never was told, I've always been sure—"

Every nerve in her body tensed. Even if Freddy had heard a rumor somehow, there was no reason for him to make a comment like that.

Unless . . .

Instead of staring out into the garden, he was looking right at her, steadily. Waiting.

"My . . . son?" All the shock she felt went into those two words. It couldn't be, not after all these years.

He pulled in a breath. "Samuel. My given name is Samuel,

same as my adopted father, which is why I sometimes answer to my middle name, Frederick."

"I-I left instructions," she stammered out. "A letter. Asking for a biblical name for my child." Every time she met a child of the right age, a Hannah or Esther or Mary, a flicker of a question would rise: Could it be her? She'd prayed for a little girl, someone who shared no traits with Oliver—certainly not for this tall, charming young man before her.

Frederick nodded, and his hand disappeared into his coat pocket, taking out a yellowed paper and passing it to her. "You signed it too."

She recognized the words written in her own hand to the man and woman who would raise her child. They blurred as she blinked back tears, remembering instructions about the use of the money, wishes for the child's health, a request not to be contacted again. So cold and businesslike. She'd agonized over what to say, crumpled up a dozen drafts, and had finally decided it would be wrong to pour out a teary good-bye to a child she was leaving to another.

"My adoptive parents were strict about never revealing anything about you—at your orders, I'm told. I never even saw this letter until recently."

She nodded dully. It had seemed like the best plan at the time. A clean break. A chance to start over.

"When I was in the hospital over in Britain, I wrote them and asked about you. It might have been wrong, playing the 'I have to know before I die on the battlefield' card, but I'd always wanted to meet you."

He had? For long stretches, she'd tried never to think of him—to crowd out the memory that she'd ever given birth with more projects and causes and committees. As the years passed, she'd thought of her baby less and less, pushing away fruitless wonderings about where the child might be now.

She cleared her throat, suddenly dry, and handed back the letter. "And they told you?"

He nodded. "Your name, and the name of the town where you lived. That was all they had. Thankfully, Derby is small enough that it wasn't hard to ask after you once I arrived."

That explained why he'd looked so nervous that first day, knocking on her door. She'd assumed he was ashamed to ask for a job as a wounded veteran, had thrown herself into a practical need without wondering if something else might have brought Frederick—Samuel—to her home.

And then the guilt, so long pushed aside, seemed to rise, an unspoken specter, from the tilled earth of the garden. "I only wanted to give you the best life possible."

"I know. And you did. As I'm sure you can tell from my impressive zucchini crop, I turned into quite an accomplished young man." He smiled, but there was a hesitation, as if he still half believed she might chase him away.

She had dozens of questions, and he certainly must have too, but the one that came out first was "Why didn't you tell me sooner?"

"I almost did, a few times. But . . . maybe I was afraid of being hurt too."

He stood, hands clasped together, as if holding his breath. Vulnerable in a different way than he'd been when she said good-bye to him all those years ago but fragile all the same.

Steeling herself, she stepped forward and put her arms around him. "Thank you for coming."

Holding him wasn't as painful as she had imagined. In fact, some part of her seemed to finally fall into place, the happiness she'd been chasing for so long finally arriving when she stopped striving for it.

When she stepped away, she stared at his face for any hint of her own. His brown hair perhaps, or the shape of his chin.

But his wink and smile were Oliver's. She knew now why he'd occasionally reminded her of her long-lost love.

That added fear to the mix of emotions inside of her. He'd want to know about his father, surely, and his grandfather. All the stories she'd tried to forget would need to be told. And it would hurt.

What had Martina learned from her mother? *"Giving and receiving love is the greatest risk and the greatest joy."*

Whether she was right or not suddenly didn't matter. This was her *son*, finally home.

"Come inside," she found herself saying. "We have a great deal to talk about."

thirty-five

MARTINA
SEPTEMBER 8

It felt bittersweet, unpacking boxes again less than a year after she promised the children they wouldn't need to move again for a long time. Martina had hesitated when Avis offered her home to them, but it was closer to the school, and it wouldn't be for long.

Most importantly, Patrick wouldn't know where to find them. Even without her foundry paycheck, her savings could have paid the low rent of the trailer camp until well into the winter. But knowing that the children would be someplace safe while she searched for a job . . . that was something money could never buy.

There's a chance he's in jail already, she reminded herself. Avis promised that Russell had relayed her information to the coast guard, including Patrick's name. Surely they'd acted on it, the way everyone was so paranoid about espionage and sabotage these days.

Each day since Saturday morning, she'd tuned Gio's radio to the news, hoping to hear something, but that was foolish. Even the ring of German spies had taken a week to leak to the press. Local black marketeers wouldn't be announced on a radio program the next morning.

Think of happier things, she scolded. School had begun that day, but when Avis had told Gio he was released from his part-time job at the library, he had shaken his head with passion. "I haven't finished finding books for the soldiers." That was a project he'd latched on to immediately. Likely, he still didn't fully realize the library was closing as he boxed up the best of its collection. He only knew that men like his father would be reading everything he chose, and that was enough to send him back to the library after school. He was there now, past closing, determined to finish sorting the fiction collection.

Beside her, Rosa took out the dresses Martina had sewn for her doll, each made of an outgrown item of clothing, humming an army marching tune she'd learned from Freddy.

It would be all right. They wouldn't have much space, with Gio sleeping on the couch in the sitting room, but that was nothing new after living in a trailer for months.

A knock on the door revealed Avis, apron donned to prepare dinner. "Who's ready to help me crush crackers for meatloaf?"

Rosa shot up from the bed, one of the doll dresses sliding to the floor. "Me!"

Clever, that Avis. She'd make a good mother someday.

"Unpacking going well?" Avis asked once Rosa had charged past.

Martina nodded. "We won't stay long. I'm sure I'll find work again soon. Even if it's not in a factory, I have experience sewing and baking, and—"

Avis shook her head. "None of that, now. You're welcome to stay as long as you like."

"But your husband . . ."

"Agreed to this too."

At first, Martina had thought Avis's marriage was just like every other part of her life: neat and tidy and perfect. But even in just a day of living in their home, she'd seen moments of tension, the small irritations of daily life, the flashes of longing whenever Avis remembered Russell would be leaving again soon.

They were young, but they were trying. That was more than Patrick had ever done, choosing instead to run away whenever times got hard.

"Speaking of Russell," Avis added, "he wants to talk to you. Without Rosa."

Martina dropped the book she'd been placing on the shelf by the window. That could only mean one thing: they'd finally gotten news from the coast guard.

She hurried to the porch, where Russell was leaning against the railing, beaming. "It sounds to me like you're a certifiable war hero, Mrs. Bianchini."

Did she dare hope? "What do you mean?"

"The trawler you reported—I rang up my coast guard buddy this morning for news. Turns out, they sounded its fuel tanks and found double the allotted amount of gas one craft is allowed to hold, plus an illegal radio."

Not knowing her personal connection, he wouldn't understand the relief she felt, causing her to sag against the side of the house. "Good," she managed. "I'm glad to hear it."

"I didn't know what to think when Avis told me your hunch, but they found a paper with German phrases on board too." He shook his head in disgust. "They were planning a rendezvous with the very fellows who would shoot down my Hooligan Navy buddies, so I have a personal reason to thank you."

"You're welcome." It was a decision that had cost her, but, thank God, it had paid off. Patrick was locked away. One link in the black market was broken. She might even have saved lives, causing a U-boat to return to Germany to refuel instead of gaining an extra month to prowl the Atlantic Ocean.

"My buddy in the coast guard couldn't tell me until today because customs agents got involved and detained the crew. The arrests will be in tomorrow's paper."

She'd have to tell the children tonight, then. "What will happen to those men?" *Please, not the electric chair.*

Russell's shoulders lifted in a careless shrug. "They didn't catch them in the act, so intent to commit treason is as high as the charge would go. I'm guessing they'll only be convicted for gas profiteering. That's a prison term for sure. Maybe ten, fifteen years? Enough to put them out of commission for the rest of the war, though that's better than they deserve."

Martina counted the years. After a decade in prison, even if Patrick returned, Gio would be twenty-two, Rosa eighteen. A man and a woman. Still vulnerable, but at least their childhoods would be free from fear.

The breath she let out was a prayer of thankfulness, until Russell eased back on the railing, a frown on his face. "Only one fly in the ointment. They didn't get the captain."

All the fears that had just been banished came back with double the force. "They didn't?"

"Raid had to be done while the ship was still in port, so they moved in, but he wasn't aboard. Must've gotten close enough to see the Coasties swarming the place and split."

Of course he did. Always looking out for his own skin.

After all she'd sacrificed, after all she'd prayed, Patrick was still a free man.

"Don't worry, Mrs. Bianchini," Russell soothed, clearly noticing her alarm. "They impounded the ship and everything on it, so he won't be able to operate. Besides, once criminals like this get into the black market, they don't get out. He'll be caught eventually."

Eventually was not soon enough. Not for the children.

She couldn't bring herself to tell Russell that the captain was her husband, that she might have brought danger into their home. Surely it would be fine, and all her worries were merely that.

Still, a passing fear made her hurry into the kitchen, where Avis was helping Rosa measure salt into a teaspoon. "It's late. I'd better make sure Gio is all right by himself."

"Are you sure?" Avis asked, dusting her hands on her apron. "He should be back in a half hour, and it won't be dark yet."

"He loses track of time easily." Also true, but this was no instinct of a hovering mother. Patrick was out there. And if he'd followed them to the movie theater, he'd likely seen them coming out of the library. If he was looking for them and he'd tried the trailer camp, the foundry, and the local Catholic church, he might go to the library next.

It was the blackout curtains, Martina decided, that made the library ominous after closing. Without them, the shelves would tower in the silence, but they wouldn't have a funereal look, one that felt oppressive from the moment she entered the front doors.

She stepped hesitantly through the entryway, and the voices she heard turned her stomach.

In the main hall of the library, Gio stood in the halo of dim light cast by the checkout desk's lamp with Patrick beside him, clapping him on the shoulder and chuckling. The perfect scene of father and son, one that might be sketched for a magazine cover.

The floorboards creaked under her steps, and both looked up. "Martina," Patrick said evenly, a gleam of victory in his eyes. He was enjoying this, wasn't he?

She ignored him, focusing on her son, hurrying to stand between them. "Give me your key, Gio. I'll lock up."

That stubborn set came back to his face, the one she saw more and more often these days. "I want to stay."

What he wanted didn't matter because it was dangerous. But she couldn't say that, couldn't explain now. "Gio, go home. Your father and I need to talk—alone."

This time, the challenge in his raised chin was different, his words hitting her like a knockout blow. "Only if you promise to tell me why you lied."

She rallied, taking in a deep breath, not denying his accusation, however unfair. "I promise." At least he would give her that chance, an opportunity to counter whatever lies Patrick might have already passed on.

The moment he was gone—*Please, let him get home safely*—she turned on Patrick. "What did you tell him?"

He crossed his arms. "Not much. Said I'd wanted to visit for a while. Asked him how school was going, what he thought of Joe Louis and so many other champs joining the army. He told me you don't like him to listen to boxing anymore."

That wasn't true, not fully, but she didn't try to defend herself. If it was a fight Patrick wanted, he would have to begin it himself.

"Better be careful, or he'll wind up a sissy." He gestured to the shelves surrounding them. "Son of mine shouldn't be working here. Ought to be getting his hands dirty."

She was almost baited into small talk, almost said that all summer Gio had worked long hours weeding and tilling the soil. Told him that there was nothing wrong with a son who loved hard labor under open skies and the satisfaction of shelving books under high ceilings. But that was a level of fatherhood Patrick didn't need to be guided to, not after all he'd done.

She tried to think of what to say. Nothing about the pawn shop, the black marketeering, the arrests. Maybe he would assume it was a random search.

But his next words crushed that hope. "I heard those Coasties. Watched from a ways away, knowing something wasn't right. They were asking around for Patrick Quinn." His eyes narrowed dangerously. "Only I don't go by that name here. Couldn't get a fishing license under it because of my dishonorable discharge. You're looking at Rick Sullivan."

"Oh?" She fought the ironclad grip of panic that pushed the word out of her throat in a squeak. She had to stay calm, to think.

"Which means the only person in this rotten town who knows my real name is you." He took a menacing step toward her, disgust in his voice, like he'd expected no better of her. "What did you tell them?"

Nothing but the truth would do. He already knew the worst. "That you and your crew planned to betray your country for your own gain."

"And what's my country ever done for me, huh? Or for you?" There was a slight slurring to his words, though he didn't seem drunk. Patrick had always been able to hold his liquor well.

"We break our backs for her, punch the clock over and over, say our pledges and our prayers. And what do we get? A kick in the rear out the door, taxes, and rules that don't look out for people like us. They tell us 'Uncle Sam Wants You.' Wants you to line up to die, that's what. Not me. No, sir, not me."

She'd never heard him talk like this before, certainly not in the days when the navy had been his ticket to freedom. Like all his schemes, that one hadn't lasted long either.

"Why did you come here?" she asked.

Could he possibly have come to say good-bye?

The part of her that knew not to hope too soon anticipated his next words. "I needed that last haul. Bad. You don't get a fake ID and a hidden fuel tank for free. And the people I owe aren't patient."

"Then you'll have to find work elsewhere." Legal work, she wanted to say but didn't dare.

He shook his head, the dangerous glint, the one that had been covered up with expensive suits and flattering words, now back. "I need money fast. And you're going to help me get it."

Her mind turned over possible reactions and discarded them just as quickly. Maybe she could take Miss Cavendish's thirty-dollar *Pride and Prejudice* from the shelves and convince him it was a valuable first edition. No, he'd never believe her. There was no cash in the library, outside of change for overdue fines.

She had the crucifix around her neck—maybe he would accept it as payment again—and most of her savings in her purse, tucked away there for the move.

But that was grocery money, fees for schoolbooks, all they had to live on until she found another position. It wasn't Patrick's, not for all he blustered.

"No," she said simply, and the word felt good and right, like the fulfilling of a thousand broken promises. "I won't give you anything."

The anger sparking in Patrick's eyes corresponded with his hand shifting toward his side, where a tattered coat concealed his body from view. She might have missed it if she hadn't had every sense trained on him, ready to shout for help, back away, flee.

Patrick had a gun. Of course he did. Going on a dangerous mission on the open seas, delivering fuel to the enemy, carrying an incredible amount of cash back to port with an untrustworthy crew. He would have to be armed.

But he relaxed, didn't reach for the gun. Why would he? This was his mousy immigrant wife, trying for once to assert a shallow independence. Even now, he thought he had the upper hand.

"Then you'd better get some from those rich friends of yours. Because once this blows over, I'll be back. And don't think I won't know if you try to turn me in."

Her throat constricted. It was happening all over again. That threat: do what I say, or I can find you—and the children—at any time. Leave if you want, try to hide. It will never be enough.

He tipped his homburg at her, all smirks once more. "Until we meet again, Martina."

"We will *never* meet again." She clutched at the cross beneath her blouse and prayed it was true, but Patrick only laughed cruelly.

"Oh? Who says?"

"She did." A new voice booming into the high ceilings caused both of them to turn and see Freddy, standing in the entryway. "But we'll back her up on it, if needed."

Patrick recovered quickly, as he always did, taking a step behind her for protection if he needed it. "Who're you? Her lover?"

Martina felt a blush rising. What would Freddy think of her, that her husband would suggest such a thing?

But Freddy didn't hesitate, taking a firm step forward. "Something even more dangerous for you. We're her friends."

We?

Louise Cavendish stepped out beside him, her head held at an imperious angle, like the queen from *Hamlet*. "Friends who, you might like to know, have already called the police."

It was likely a bluff. The telephone was at the checkout desk, between Martina and Patrick and the two newcomers. But Miss Cavendish's voice held such unwavering authority that she could see Patrick hesitate.

"Listen, whoever you are," Freddy said, walking forward, menace in his step, "you will never, ever, contact this woman again. Or we'll know."

Martina turned back to Patrick. The way his eyes slid around to her, the cocksure expression gone, she knew he understood the message they were sending.

She was not alone and defenseless anymore. And she never would be again.

"Understand?" Freddy pressed. He was at the checkout desk now, a threat in his words, his tone, his stance.

Don't make him angry. Don't scare him. He has a gun.

But she couldn't say it, couldn't warn Freddy to stop advancing, the military training in his taut muscles making clear what he would try when he got close enough. And Patrick, knowing it too, brandished his pistol in a flash of metal, his arm moving to aim.

It was too late to think, too late to do anything but let

her heart direct her before her mind could catch up. Martina slammed into her husband's side, knocking him into a shelf with a clatter. A shot went wild, the gun dropping to the floor among a tumble of books, but Martina watched it and kicked it toward the checkout desk with all her strength.

Out of the corner of her eye, she saw Freddy diving for it, but in front of her, Patrick, scrambling up, stared at her, wearing neither a smirk nor a condescending sneer.

He was afraid.

Of her. Of the new strength in her arms and the long-burning fury he must see in her eyes.

And with one last glance behind him, he ran past the boxes of books Gio had painstakingly collected for the Victory Book Campaign, out the door, and into the night.

Even if they called now, the police would be too late, just like the coast guard had been. That should bother her, she knew. Maybe she should have fired the gun, or blocked the exit to let Freddy pin Patrick down. But she'd acted on instinct, and the only energy she had left went toward collapsing on the floor and leaning against a shelf. It was over. For now, at least, Patrick was gone.

Freddy knelt beside her. "Are you all right, Martina?"

"I'm fine," she said, for once meaning it. Deep breaths drew in a bit of stability, and she let him help her up and lead her to a chair.

"Well," Miss Cavendish said, calmly surveying the darkened library, "we'll have to get someone to repair that bullet hole, or people will talk."

Patrick's shot had created a dent in the plaster between the windows. How much worse it could have been if . . .

Stop. Do not think of it. It didn't happen.

Freddy seemed to be waiting for an explanation, though Miss Cavendish was scribbling on her clipboard, back to business as if Patrick were a mere interruption.

Martina swallowed, licking dry lips. "He was—is—my husband. But I promise, I didn't mean to lead him here." Where to start, what to say to cover the past eighteen years of decaying trust and hurtful words and difficult choices? "I . . . I don't know how to explain."

Miss Cavendish looked up from her paper. "You don't need to. Not to me, at least. I'm sure the police will want a report of some kind."

Martina saw something unexpected in the older woman's face. Not horror or even pity.

Understanding.

"It is, unfortunately, not difficult for me to know what it's like to be driven to desperation because of the folly of an unreliable man."

How it was possible, Martina couldn't say, but it seemed she and Louise Cavendish shared something in common.

"Why did you come here?" Martina asked. "Besides being an answer to my prayer."

"The Almighty works in mysterious ways," Miss Cavendish said dryly. "I knew Avis and your son were working late nights, packing books to prepare for a closing that, I recently decided, will no longer happen. And I felt I should tell them myself."

"But that's a story for another day," Freddy interjected. "Is Gio all right?"

She nodded, suddenly overcome. Gio. Rosa. She had to get home to them. Had to explain to Gio . . .

"Your thoughts?" Miss Cavendish stepped closer, holding up the paper from her clipboard, and Martina gasped. It was Patrick, the lines forming his features rough but clear. More than that, Miss Cavendish had captured something behind the strong jaw and powerful eyes. She showed the slight sneer that always seemed to twist those handsome features, just the slightest bit off, like spoiled milk. Martina shuddered.

"That good, hmm? I want the police to be able to recognize him."

Martina had a blurry photograph of Patrick in his navy uniform to give, but this image captured him in a way a camera never had.

It was more than she thought she could handle, but Freddy insisted they call the police immediately. Once they arrived, Martina had the additional shame of explaining the details to the officers. Patrick's name and his alias, the various titles he'd worn over the past few years. Navy dropout. Black marketeer. Her husband. They listened with the interest of small-town authorities eager to have something more to investigate than jaywalkers and the town drunk, and Martina knew her story would soon be public knowledge.

As for Patrick, Derby would no longer be safe for him. He'd fade into a big city—New York, or maybe Boston.

Mamma. She'd send a telegram, ask her to move, just in case Patrick was foolish enough to come back. It ached, knowing she'd need to leave her *paesani*, the neighbors who had become like family. But she would love Derby, the quiet beauty of it all. She'd be able to sleep without fitful awakenings to the sound of traffic. She and Delphie could trade recipes. . . .

But there was no time for that now. Her children were waiting for her. Waiting for the truth.

Freddy walked her home, and she heard him talking to Russell and Avis in low tones in the sitting room. Good. At least one explanation she wouldn't have to give herself.

Instead of joining them, she tiptoed to the guest bedroom. Rosa was already tucked in the small bed they would share, reading, as usual. But Gio, who turned to glare at her as soon as he heard the door open, paced the floor by the window. "I told her I saw Da. That you lied to us."

And she had. Painting them a picture of their father as a heroic soldier, considering even telling them that he'd died in battle like so many other husbands and fathers. Letting him fade out of their lives nobly instead of slinking into infamy. But that was the path he had chosen, the way he would be remembered.

"I want to know why," Gio went on, filling the silence. "You promised."

"I know, son. I know." She sat on the bed and held Rosa tightly, rocking her like she was still a baby who could be soothed with a lullaby.

Maybe confronting Patrick was the easy part, and this, the truth telling, would cost her more. But it was time.

"I need to tell you both something," she began, not sure what she would say next.

"A story?" Rosa asked sleepily. "I like stories."

But this wasn't one of her fairy tales, full of magic spells and hungry trolls, of curses and dragons and victorious knights.

Or maybe it was.

Wasn't that one purpose of stories? The best ones might be about good and evil in fictional lands, but they were meant to help people recognize them in the real world. And maybe even teach them how to respond with wisdom and courage.

In the quiet, Martina thought of the best stories she had read—of Henry Higgins using his power to belittle and bully Eliza, Hercule Poirot uncovering the inevitable end of greed and deception, Jane Eyre saying to Mr. Rochester, *"I am no bird; and no net ensnares me; I am a free human being with an independent will, which I now exert to leave you."*

And then she found it, something that might make sense to them, a fragment of something true that could help them understand the father who had hurt them all.

"Do you remember," she began, "in *Treasure Island*, how Long John Silver was always kind to Jim? But that didn't make him a good or safe person. . . ."

thirty-six

AVIS
SEPTEMBER 8

Avis's homemaking books contained extensive notes on hospitality, but none had given advice on how to outfit one's home for four additional overnight guests, particularly with a violent man on the loose looking for them.

She'd had to improvise—serving an after-dinner snack of graham crackers and cocoa when most around the table had picked at their dinners, trying to keep conversation light, checking the locks each time she passed the front or back door, making sure everyone was comfortable for the night.

Martina and the children had already taken the guest bedroom, and Freddy refused to leave them alone with Martina's husband unaccounted for. He and Russell would take turns on the sofa, the other staying awake in case of any trouble.

Now Avis turned over in the dark, lying flat on the mattress, anything but tired. Just thinking about the night's events was enough to make her shiver. A gun going off in her library! And poor Martina keeping her secret for so long. Worse than that ghastly Poe story.

A cry, muffled and sudden, pierced the quiet. For a moment, Avis wondered if she'd conjured it in her own mind with thoughts of hearts beating under floorboards, but then she recognized Martina's voice. She snatched her robe from the closet and threw open the door.

In the hallway, little Rosa stood with stuffed bear in hand, blinking at the switched-on lights that broke every blackout rule in the book. Martina knelt beside her. "Rosa, tell us where your brother is."

Avis felt her heartbeat speed up involuntarily. Gio was gone? How? She'd locked the back door.

Silly. Doors were only locked from the outside.

"He made me promise not to say," Rosa whispered, ducking into her mother's side, as shy as she'd been at that very first book club meeting.

Her mother turned her out by the shoulders, meeting her eyes. "That is not a fair promise. We want to make sure Gio is safe. Don't you?"

She nodded miserably.

"Then tell us where he went."

Avis held her breath and Rosa's bottom lip trembled. "He wanted to find Da. He said he didn't believe Da was a rotten pirate like in the book."

Somehow, Martina's voice was still level, calm. "And where did he go to look for your da?"

"Back to the library."

Relief washed over Avis in waves. Not wandering the street or the bars by the ocean. "He's safe, then."

"Unless," Martina said, looking as if she were about to be sick, "Patrick came back."

No. He wouldn't, would he? But if there was even a chance . . .

"Sit down in the living room. We'll make a plan." She guided Martina, her whole body shaking, down the hallway, Rosa staying so close she practically hung like a tassel from her mother's skirt.

They woke the men—even Russell, sitting in a chair by the door, had nodded off—and explained the situation.

Russell caught her worried look and nodded. "Come on, Freddy. We'll find him and bring him back."

Martina, wrapped in a blanket-like shawl, stood too. "I'm coming with you."

"Not a chance," Freddy said, and at the same time Russell said, more gently, "It might be better for you to stay."

Avis could see the indecision on Martina's face. It would be safer for her to stay here, and Rosa would want her mother. But her son was out there.

"Maybe we should—" she began, but she was cut off by the shrill, distant sound of sirens.

Reflexively, Avis reached for the lamps. The air raid wardens would be passing by soon, and if they saw any light . . .

Wait. She looked at the grandfather clock keeping vigil in the corner. Nearly midnight.

Something was wrong. Very wrong.

Rosa had started crying again, louder this time, sensing the adults were upset. "An air raid drill?" Russell asked hopefully, looking to Avis for confirmation.

Which she couldn't give. Ever since missing the first, she'd recorded the schedule from the newspaper with the vigilance of an army stenographer transcribing battle plans. "Not a scheduled one."

"Dear God," Martina whispered, as if trying not to let Rosa hear, "you don't mean it might be real?"

It was what newsreels and posters had warned them of all along: The enemy might advance on them at any time. And the Germans might have chosen this night, of all nights, to drop their bombs on American soil.

Each one of them, faces set in different degrees of fear, turned to her.

And the precautions, carefully memorized, from "What to Do in an Air Raid" rushed back to her, numbered in precise order. "Russell, turn off the lights. I'll shut off the gas. Everyone else, stay away from the windows. We'll take shelter under the dining table if needed."

An odd calm settled over her despite the sirens.

"No!" Martina cried, as Russell reached for the table lamp. "We have to get Gio. If he's out there—if there are bombs—"

Avis paused, wasting valuable seconds when dropped explosives might come crashing through the ceiling at any moment. It must have been her frayed nerves, but it sounded like the sirens were getting louder, closer, wailing their midnight warning. "The men will find him, Martina. We have to stay inside where it's safe."

The men . . .

Russell.

Everyone knew being out on the streets, open and exposed, was the worst place to be in a bombing.

If she insisted they wait to search until after the danger had passed, Russell would stay safe.

A moment later, her senses returned. Of course not. A child might be out there, alone, unprotected.

Russell had already thrown on his coat. "We're on our way."

"Wait." Freddy turned toward them, hand still on the blackout curtain. "It's not an air raid."

Avis blinked. Had she heard him incorrectly? "But the sirens . . ."

"Are actual fire sirens. That's all."

He spoke with such conviction that she could hardly doubt. "How can you be sure?"

"I just saw the fire brigade pass by."

Of course. That's why the sound of the sirens had changed. Strange, so strange, to be thankful for someone else's misfortune, but a blocked chimney or a brush fire that had caught a storage shed was a disaster so much smaller than the buckled sidewalks and destroyed buildings she had pictured. Avis nearly collapsed on the couch in relief, until Freddy added, "Avis, they're headed toward the library."

MARTINA
SEPTEMBER 9

At the Fire Muster—had it only been two months, and not a lifetime ago?—Gio had watched with a fascination usually saved for heavyweight matches as the men competed to roll out thick fire hoses and connect them to the nearest hydrant.

Now the same volunteers, called out in the middle of the night, were hurried along not by a competition but by real smoke billowing from the library's roof. Martina was sure if Gio had been wandering anywhere within a mile, he'd have heard the sirens and come running to watch.

Unless he was inside the library.

The thought wouldn't leave her, even as she agonized from the sidewalk. Her son was in there. A mother's instinct was never wrong, and she knew her boy, proud of his new job and its responsibility, wouldn't stand aside while it burned.

So while Russell shouted over the sirens, organizing a search and telling everyone to stay out of the way of the firemen, she slipped away, down the alley, to the back door. The door where Patrick had disappeared.

It was unlocked.

Martina had watched Louise secure all the doors before they left, checking them carefully, but Gio had a key too.

"Gio!" she shouted, stepping inside. "Where are you?"

That was a sound, wasn't it? Maybe a reply, though it was difficult to tell over the awful crackle of flames on paper. She drew in a breath to call again, but only got a lungful of smoke and bent over in coughs, her body screaming at her to get away, stay away.

Not without my boy.

Most of the fire clustered near the south wall, where a broken window sprayed shards of glass glinting in the smoke, but it had spread to the reference section, shelves broken and charred, onionskin dictionary pages catching like the tinder they were.

"Gio!" She couldn't see movement, couldn't hear him.

The words of the old prayers tumbled together in a blur of scattered sacredness, Latin and Italian and English, all mixed together. *Ave, o Maria, piena di grazia, your kingdom come, your will be done.*

Kyrie eleison.

Lord, have mercy.

"Here!"

That was Gio for sure, his thin cry coming from the far corner of the library, where smoke hung a curtain over her view.

Martina stumbled through the murk toward where she thought Gio's voice had come from, past a row of smoldering books.

She hadn't imagined his voice, had she?

There. The boy was looking all around, taking in the shelves licked with flames and a floor blocked by debris. As if he didn't know which way to go.

Thank God. She closed the distance between them, gripping his arm.

Now he was close enough that she could make out his babbling. "There used to be sand. Right by the door."

Sand? Smoke had already addled him. "Come, son. We must leave now."

But Gio twisted his arm out of her grip and bolted toward the stairs to the children's section before she caught him again. "But—" he broke off, coughing, and she wanted to shout at him to stop breathing in the smoke—"we can't leave the books."

Right then, Martina knew that Louise should not have worried, warning her not to put a love of reading before family. Nothing, nothing was more important than making sure Gio was safe. She'd torch a hundred books, a thousand, before risking her son.

All the fierceness of an Italian mother went into her firm "You *will* come with me. Now."

But it met the stubbornness her son had inherited from a father used to getting his own way, and in one smooth motion, he'd broken her grip on his wrist and lunged toward the nearest box, struggling to heft it into his arms. "I'm not leaving without them."

It was one of the crates he'd packed for the soldiers, she realized. Labeled *Adventure books.*

Dizziness spun at her. Too much smoke. She reached for the box, trying to pull it from Gio's arms, but couldn't find the strength, her vision blurring around the edges. *Have mercy.*

"Gio!"

A new voice. Freddy. Easy to identify from the eyepatch, even with a bandanna wrapped around his mouth. A second miracle. Without a word, he seemed to take in the situation and pulled the box from Gio.

"Follow me." The forceful way he said it seemed to break Gio out of his haze. The path to the front door seemed to be relatively clear. None of the flames had spread past the checkout desk.

Cinders fell on them, and she swatted them away, where they fell on the wood floors, the wood shelves, all those books. . . .

It was a fire that ended *Jane Eyre* too. Only in that case, Thornfield's burning and Mr. Rochester's blinding had somehow been a good thing, the start of a happy ending.

Martina shoved out the sound of crackling flames and the burn of hot air, and focused on holding Gio's hand, pulling them toward the front door, still clear. She could hear the sirens. Finally, her hand was on the door's handle, letting in a whoosh of night air, clean and breathable. She took it in in gasps, tugging Gio farther along, toward the fire engine, the dew-soaked grass, the sidewalk.

Then she collapsed, exhausted, wanting to tuck her head onto her knees and close her eyes. Instead, she watched others move around her. Freddy set the box down on the grass and joined the other volunteers. The firefighters had connected the hose, baptizing the flames. Avis sat with Rosa in her lap, sound asleep, unaware of their near escape.

The books were burning. But Gio was safe.

He leaned against her, shivering from the sudden chill.

"Never run away from me again."

"I won't. I promise." Then the two of them sat on the sidewalk, watching smoke streak the charcoal gray of the early morning sky, interrupted only when Miss Cavendish herself bustled over.

Of course someone would call her immediately. The library belonged to her family.

Without so much as a greeting, she knelt beside Martina, a bracing arm on her shoulder. "Breathe deeply, please." At her questioning look, Miss Cavendish added, "I'm a trained nurse. Freddy told me what happened."

"But don't you need to—?"

She dismissed the question with a wave of her hand. "This is more important." She leaned in closer, her ear pressed nearly to Martina's chest. "Now, breathe in."

Martina did as instructed, and Miss Cavendish moved on to Gio.

She had them open their mouths wide, inspecting their throats, and then had Avis shine a flashlight to examine their eyes and the color of their skin.

One by one, Louise went through a battery of businesslike questions: Did they feel dizziness when they stood? Any shortness of breath? How deep did the coughs feel when they'd first exited the burning building? Had they sustained any burns?

Finally, her curbside examination complete, Louise rose. "You will both be fine, thank the Almighty." The relief on her face was genuine, though replaced quickly with a stern frown. "Do not exert yourself, and for goodness' sake, as soon as this madness has calmed down"—she waved at the firemen showering the roof with their hoses—"find someone to take you home to get some sleep."

"Thank you," Martina whispered.

But even when Russell offered to drive them back to their warm bed, she couldn't seem to look away from the scene. Time passed slowly as dawn began to color the sky. Each moment dragged on, her tired eyes drooping closed in between, ignoring the buzz of activity. Near sunrise, Gio told her what he had seen.

"I fell asleep waiting for him to come back. And he did."

Do not panic. He is safe now, she reminded herself. "Did he see you?"

Gio shook his head. "I was about to shout for him when I saw him throw a brick through the library window. Then I was too scared to move. He . . ."

And the story might have stopped there, if not for Martina's stern "Did your da set the fire, Gio?"

Instead of saying it, Gio only nodded, though Martina had guessed as much already. The lighter Patrick always carried, his threats, that murderous look in his eyes as he was forced to run away for the first time in his life.

And her heart broke. Why was Gio allowed to see the man he loved most destroying the place he loved most?

The answer came a heartbeat later. *Because he wouldn't have believed it otherwise.*

"Why did he do it, Mamma?"

There were a dozen answers she could give. Because he'd probably drunk too much. Because he wanted revenge and had nothing to lose. Because that's what men like Patrick did—they took beautiful things and destroyed them.

But all she said was "He was angry. And this is what happens when anger rules a man."

Gio paused, then nodded. "Like Jack Dempsey beating up boxers bigger than him. *The Ring* article said his greatest strength and his greatest weakness was his rage."

She gestured to the chaos around them. "Does this look like strength to you?"

His voice was small and quiet as he picked at a blade of grass. "No."

Good. He would become a better man than his father. She had to believe that.

"I'm sorry for running away," he said, moving closer to her in the chilly evening air.

She wrapped her arm around him. "I'm sorry too. I should have told you the truth long ago."

"I know why you didn't. It hurts."

"Yes, it does."

So many things she wanted to tell him: he didn't intend to hurt you like this; you don't have to be like him; we'll find a new place to be safe; everything will be all right.

"I love you," she said instead.

It was enough for now.

They would face whatever was left in the morning.

GINNY
SEPTEMBER 9

Pa had told her about the Fire of 1914 that ravaged Long Island before Ginny was born. "Awful blaze. Took down the Granite Springs Hotel and Casino first, then spread to the wharf and the business district. No one died, but the island never did recover. Hardly anyone rebuilt, and the summer people just stopped coming."

"How could it burn down so easy with water all around?" Ginny had asked.

Pa had only shaken his head. "Bucket brigade wasn't enough. And it took the city too long to bring a fireboat from the main."

That's when she'd first learned a harsh lesson: Portland, impressive though it was with all its shopping and food and shiny automobiles, didn't care about them. Islanders had to look out for each other. They were family.

Which is why she stormed up the morning after the library fire, boiling mad. Wasn't she family? How come she'd found out about the fire practically ages later, when her landlady mentioned the commotion in the night on the other side of town?

The lawn was full of people, some staring at the gaping hole in the roof, others clustered in groups, trading stories of what they'd seen the night before. Only she didn't have any stories because she'd been sound asleep the whole time.

She finally spotted one of the targets who deserved a good raking down. Freddy, for once looking scruffy, the creases on his face dull with dirt, took a step back as she marched up to him. "Ginny, you—"

Oh no, she wasn't going to let him get out a single excuse. "Why didn't you tell me?" Sure, she didn't have a telephone, but he knew where her apartment was, could have knocked on the door, and she'd have been up in a flash.

"It was late. I knew you'd be asleep and—"

"Don't you think I would have wanted someone to wake me up?"

"I was helping the fire crew," he protested, as if she couldn't tell from the layers of sweat and grime that clung to him.

"The whole time? Ever since midnight?"

He ducked his head like a man avoiding gunfire. "Okay, okay. I'm sorry we let the library burn down without your supervision." She glared until he added, "And I'm glad you're here now."

The way he smiled like he really meant it took some of the aggravation clean out of her. "Just don't let it happen again."

"That seems like a safe promise." They both looked out at the library. It wasn't in heaps, at least, though you could see part of the stoved-in roof from the street, the rest soggy from the fire hoses. Inside, judging from the state of the firemen, it was probably worse.

Still, maybe the books in the storage closet got off all right.

She tilted her head at Freddy, like she was trying to get a crick out of her neck instead of studying him a little closer. "You all right, then? I heard you were quite the hero."

Avis, who was spared Ginny's angry speech because she looked plumb tired out, had filled her in on some of what had happened the night before, the bits her landlady didn't know, about saving Gio and all.

"I only wish we'd have gotten here before the fire spread." Freddy wasn't watching her anymore, and she followed his gaze to where Louise was talking to one of the firemen. As she surveyed the landscape, Louise looked over, nodded at them, and—wonder of all wonders—actually smiled.

Either she was happy the library had gone and burned or . . .

"You told her, didn't you?" she demanded.

He nodded. "We've got a lot of lost time to make up. A lot of questions to answer. But you were right—it felt good to tell the truth."

She scoffed at that. "Of course I was right. I'm always right."

"I don't know yet if she'll want others to know who I am. So if you wouldn't mind . . ."

Story as scandalous as that would rock a town like Derby, sure enough. Between that and the fire, they'd have enough to jaw about for years. Still, it was up to Louise. "Don't worry about me. I can be as silent as the dead when I mean to." At Freddy's expression, she tacked on, "Which isn't often, but this is serious." No one ever accused Ginny Atkins of being a busybody.

At the moment, Louise looked too involved in conversation with the animated fire chief to do much deep thinking about her long-lost son.

"We should help," Freddy said, which Ginny allowed was probably right. "That is, if you're done lecturing me."

And Ginny found that she was done, all her anger worn out in one burst. "Sorry for biting your head off. It just makes a person mad, someone destroying their home like this and all."

Freddy raised his eyebrows. "I thought Long Island was home."

Well, what was she supposed to say to that? "It was. Always will be."

"But . . ." he prompted, his good eye gleaming far too much for her comfort.

"Maybe this can be home too. For a while."

The nod he gave her felt like a promise. This conversation wasn't done—but it was started. And that was something.

She shivered, wishing she'd brought a sweater. That was Maine for you. One day, it was all sunbathers and shell collectors, the next you were layering like it was twice as cold as zero. Another reminder that winter was coming, and soon Freddy would be gone.

Hamish intercepted them on their way over to Louise, handing them a tarp with only a few curt words and a gesture to tell them what it was for.

She took one corner while Freddy took the opposite, rolling it out. "Bet it'll take months to rebuild this place."

"At least," he agreed. Didn't add anything more.

So he was going to make her do all the work. Figured. "Thinking about staying?"

They pulled the tarp out flat on the lawn, ready for use. "Why would you care?" he asked with that annoying twinkle in his eye.

"No reason. They could use your help is all."

"And . . ."

His trailed-off prompts were getting annoying. "Fine," she huffed. "It's good to have you around, Freddy. I'd miss you if you went. Are you happy now?"

"You know," he said, a broad smile on his face, "I really am."

And smoke and fire and all, Ginny found she was too.

LOUISE
SEPTEMBER 9

In the bright morning light, the damage looked much worse than Frederick's initial dawn report had indicated, but Louise supposed that's the way fires always were. With permission from the fire chief, she'd circled the building for her inspection, though he'd warned against stepping inside until they had fully assessed the roof.

By the time she returned to the front lawn, the crowd gathered there had grown. Not to Fire Muster level, certainly, but numbering in the dozens.

The usual spectators flocking to the site of a disaster, she supposed.

Then she looked more carefully. There were a few bystanders lurking around the edges, but most seemed to know exactly what they were doing there.

There was Hamish, lending his precious tools to book club members to clear the rubble. Avis, barking orders to anyone who would listen—goodness, how had she ever considered the librarian fragile? Delphie, handing out sandwiches to the exhausted firemen. Martina, her children beside her, sorting people into groups. Muriel Whitson, holding a broom and ready to charge. Frederick and Ginny, working together to unfold a tarp on the lawn.

They were all here, and more—longtime members of the

association library, newcomers to the book club, fellow church members, even strangers. Ready to do all they could.

Some of the volunteers, cleared by the fire chief, were beginning a brigade to pass books out of the building to the lawn. Louise had pinned her hair in a bandanna for the occasion, like one of Milton Hanover's foundry workers. Today they were up against a different sort of war work, and she was prepared to do her part.

Until Delphie marched over, planting herself in Louise's path. She had been quite pleased when Louise announced her decision privately the day before—along with an apology. As usual, they'd stumbled back into their old familiarity, their quarrel set aside.

"Just so you know," Delphie said, jerking her head toward the building, "everyone hates those old chairs you put in there. Fine to look at, but they make your backside ache if you sit in them for longer than fifteen minutes."

Louise had noticed but thought perhaps it was only a consequence of aging. "Then it's a good thing we'll likely be forced to order new ones now."

With a satisfied nod, Delphie thrust a familiar book at her: *Pride and Prejudice*. The copy her father had left her. "Martina found this. She thought you'd want to keep it apart from the rest."

"Ah. So it survived." Naturally romantic nonsense like her father's favorite book would remain while more worthwhile books turned to ashes.

But Delphie didn't hurry back to her place at the tarp. "Ever look inside?"

"No." Why would she?

"Muriel told us to fan through the pages of the books to knock out any dirt or soot" was all Delphie offered in answer. "We saw something that might interest you."

With that, she hobbled off to supervise another station of

workers by telling them exactly what they were doing wrong, leaving Louise alone with the old novel.

What had the antiques expert said? Something like *"The printing was too late for it to be worth much, not to mention the condition and the interior markings."* One line in a detailed letter that could have referred to stray underlines or blots on the pages. It hadn't even occurred to her to check.

Sitting on the stoop of the library while volunteers swirled around her, Louise opened to the title page to read a note in spindly, shaky handwriting.

December 10, 1918

Dearest Louise,

    Now that my time has come to leave this world, I realize there is much I have not told you. Far too much to fit on this flyleaf, so I'll begin with the most important:

    I love you, child. I'm afraid that I, like Mr. Bennet, did not always show it like I ought. (You'll understand once you read the novel. Which you should. It's excellent.) And I'm proud of you, especially for the way you've cared for me and for this town in a time of sickness and need. It could not have been easy.

    I hope that now you are able to live the life you want, away from this old invalid and his dusty books, whatever path you choose to pursue. I hope you find happiness, companionship, and purpose, and that your child finds the same. I wish more than anything that I had been a part of that all along.

    Instead, all I can leave you is the summer home you used to love, before it became a prison, and a library you never quite loved. That, I believe, might be my fault as well.

    There are others, though, in this town who do love it.

I hope you meet them, and that you let them into your life. For I have found that books make fine friends—but fellow readers even better.

With all my love,
Father

Louise stared at the book in her hands, rereading the words that had been left unsaid for so long. The only one of her father's collection not a first edition, yet now the most valuable of all.

I didn't do this, Father, she felt like assuring him, knowing how he'd ache to see this scene. Yes, she'd burned the garden but not the library. That had happened on its own.

But something about the letter and the determination of the volunteers bustling around gave her hope that perhaps it wasn't destroyed after all, not for good.

After tucking the book away in her car, where it wouldn't be accidentally packed away, she scanned the crowd for one face in particular. In the chaos of the night before, she hadn't been able to pass along some important news.

Whatever amount of sleep Avis had managed to get, it hadn't been nearly sufficient, but Louise knew better than to order her home to bed. It would be like trying to reverse the tide. Instead, she only asked if she'd step outside, away from the group of women who had begun to sweep ash and small bits of rubble into wheelbarrows to be carted away.

"Is there something else you'd rather I do, Miss Cavendish?" Avis asked anxiously. Always so eager to please.

"Not exactly." She cleared her throat. "I only wanted to say that I look forward to future meetings of the Blackout Book Club. We can use Windward Hall until the rebuilding—unless, of course, you're worried about me making some of my 'pointedly arch comments,' as our eminent book club secretary once put it."

Avis became the timid mouse she'd once been, swallowing hard. "You . . . you read them."

Louise tried to keep the amusement from her face. "I did. In their entirety. Yesterday, actually, trying to decide what to do next."

"That was *not* what I meant to give you."

Louise had gathered that much. "I found them refreshingly honest. Even entertaining, in parts. I hadn't expected that from you. It reminded me of your brother." She'd always thought of Anthony as Avis's opposite, but perhaps they had more in common than she'd realized. "Do you know what he told me twenty years ago when I first thought of closing the library?"

"I couldn't guess."

She'd have been too young at the time to remember. Louise, though, could picture him, skinny and determined. "He said, 'Miss Cavendish, people say you're going back to New York. I bet it's a real nice place. But if you go, can you leave the books? We need them more than we need you.' I tried to keep a straight face, because he was so earnest, but I don't recall ever laughing so hard in my life."

Avis raised a hand to her cheek, blushing on her brother's behalf. "I'm sure he didn't mean it."

"He did mean it, and he was right, in a way. No one in this town would miss me if I were to fade away, only what I've given them." The present efforts on the library lawn were proof of that.

Instead of offering an empty, overly cheerful assurance, Avis studied her for a moment. "There's still time."

And Louise found herself nodding. "There is, isn't there?"

"If you want, I'll give you the other notebook," Avis added. "The one with the stories. People love this place."

Louise looked around at the workers shaking ash from bindings, opening crates to check for water damage, spreading children's books open to dry in the bright autumn sunlight. "That's fairly apparent."

She'd read the testimonials eventually, if only to know why each of these people had taken a weekday morning to volunteer in the rubble.

This town did need books. Oh, so did soldiers overseas and children at a nursery school. But she'd find other ways to get them reading material.

"I'm not closing the library."

Avis blinked as if she'd just stepped from a dark room into sudden sunlight. "Pardon?"

Louise explained about Mr. Hanover's call and the federal grant, but it didn't seem like Avis was registering the details, as though her comprehension had stopped at that first phrase. "Do you really mean it?" she interrupted partway through.

"I'm not in the habit of saying things I don't." But despite herself, Louise couldn't keep from smiling at the young woman's widening eyes. "I'll leave you to your work. Simply wanted you to know it matters more than you might have guessed."

"Thank you," Avis managed.

Louise nodded. "And do tell Anthony for me, would you?" They'd have to make sure the rebuilding was done by the time the young man came home.

On the other side of the library, Frederick waved Louise over to the back door, where the original book club members were evacuating the fiction section, a grubby Gio passing books to his mother, then to Ginny, who set them on a tarp to be packed.

"Will I be of any use?" she asked doubtfully. Some of the stacks looked heavier than she could handle.

Delphie, stationed at the end of the brigade, snorted. "They let me join in, so clearly they're desperate."

Louise had to chuckle at that. "Thank you, Delphie. And all of you."

Her cook squinted suspiciously. "For what?"

"For being here when I needed you."

Fortunately, they acknowledged her thanks with smiles and

kept at the work of passing books, so she didn't have to reveal the catch in her throat.

Silly. She'd assumed she'd cried all her tears the day before, processing what it meant to meet the son she'd thought she'd lost so many years before. But apparently there were at least a few tiresome drops left. Louise dashed them away before anyone could notice.

She took up a place next to Frederick—Samuel—as he passed along an armful of books, carrying with them the scent of smoke.

"Be on the lookout for our next club selections, now," he said. "We might find some obscure gems in this lot."

"So long as the last few pages aren't burned to a crisp."

"Might be fun for a change. Everyone can argue about how the story *ought* to have ended."

This time when he winked, Louise smiled back at her son instead of shaking her head.

Rebuilding from ashes, especially with a war on, would be a daunting task. But she'd faced more than a few of those in her life. This library had too many people who loved it to let it die.

Louise had wasted enough time already. Best to get started.

Notes from the Blackout Book Club and Grand Library Reopening—March 12, 1943

Taken by Avis Montgomery, Head Librarian and Book Club Secretary

Members in Attendance: All, plus half of the town, at least.

Tonight's grand reopening of the library was a smashing success. Everyone did their part, distributing flyers and arriving midafternoon to set up, so that by the time we opened the doors at six o'clock—blackout curtains drawn, of course—there was a line down the block.

Martina's mother, who still lapses into Italian when excited, put herself in charge of the children's gallery on the floor near our makeshift stage, a short platform constructed by Hamish from scrap wood. She stationed herself on a stool, ready to shush the little ones or keep them from toddling off.

This, thank God, was the only security precaution we needed, since Martina's husband was caught robbing an OPA office of ration stamps several weeks ago. When I asked her if she was relieved, she said it was more complicated than that. But it's good to see her smiling and laughing again.

We pooled our sugar rations to serve gingerbread for all, sweetened with maple syrup to make up the difference, a trick Delphie taught me. Since coffee was added to the ration list, it was a sparse offering, but no one seemed to mind, filling their plates before the official start of the performance.

After a welcome from the mayor, where he thanked the firemen and subtly took credit for the rebuilding, I read my latest letter from Anthony. In it, he thanked us for donating proceeds from the night's performance to care packages of books for his unit, and passed along a comment from a buddy that "books are more popular than pin-up girls over here."

Next up, Freddy and Gio gave a joint performance of the poem "Casey at the Bat," with Gio delivering the narration perfectly from memory while Freddy pantomimed it to great applause. Everyone agreed that the spontaneous kiss Ginny planted on him after the famous strikeout made the ending much less depressing.

Mr. and Mrs. Bell delivered a selection from "Rip Van Winkle," complete with a lengthy beard made of wool, and Mr. Maloney surprised us all by bringing us to tears with a stanza of "Evangeline." Almost enough to make me reevaluate my opinion of Henry Wadsworth Longfellow.

The final performance of the night was a joint effort of the original book club members—a dramatic reading excerpted from the opening of Little Women, with Louise as Meg, Ginny as Jo, Martina as Beth, and myself as Amy. We offered the role of Marmee to Delphie, but she turned us down flat ("I don't know that there's anyone in the world less suited to it"), so Mrs. Whitson did the small part admirably.

Overall, it was a hit, despite Ginny slipping in off-script comments. Martina was frightened to death to be in front of everyone and never spoke a line above a murmur, but that was in character for Beth, so it was all right. And I got a good laugh from the crowd over the running gag of mispronouncing words, which was quite satisfying.

Best of all, halfway through, Russell slipped in the back. I stared so long that Louise had to prompt me to find my place again. He didn't think he'd be able to get leave so close to the end of his term, but there he was, directly off the train from Boston. I hurried to his side as soon as the applause ended.

This was followed by the unveiling of Louise's painting, reminiscent of Beatrix Potter's style, although the farmer and his wife were decidedly more friendly looking than the McGregors of the books. Afterward, examining it closer, I noticed that they resembled a certain one-eyed veteran and his sweetheart.

Hamish hung it in the restored children's section, now with comfortable seating to encourage the younger set to visit. Come September, I'll be spending more time there myself . . . Russell and I are expecting. He was a little startled by the long list of literary names I've picked out for us to choose from. (Hercule and Hester, it seems, are already out, but Arthur and Elinor are still in the running.)

I ended the evening by inviting one and all to the Blackout Book Club, now meeting again in our usual location. I think everyone's glad about that. Windward Hall did perfectly well for a few months, but we had to split into two, and then three, groups to fit everyone in the compact rooms. Besides that, Mr. Bell is allergic to poor Jeeves and sneezed his way through our discussion of Their Eyes Were Watching God, and Gio managed to take down a decorative sword from the hall to act out a scene from The Count of Monte Cristo. Louise appreciated his zeal, but not his near decapitation of Mrs. Whitson, and has banned family heirlooms as props at future club meetings.

Must set these notes down. Most of the members have gathered downstairs to discuss next month's book, and I want to join in.

It's good to be home again.

Author's Note

I hope you enjoyed stepping into Derby, Maine, a fictional place (though you might recognize real locations like Bristol, Pemaquid Point, Old Orchard Beach, and St. Patrick's Church referenced throughout). However, the home-front challenges faced by residents of the New England coast portrayed in the novel were very real. Blackout regulations proved difficult for authorities to enforce, and unlike Londoners, who regularly experienced the effects of the Blitz, coastal Americans rarely felt the impact of their laxness during 1942, but it was the main cause of a series of naval disasters.

The German Navy began planning U-boat attacks as soon as Germany declared war on the United States—Operation *Paukenschlag* (Drumbeat). They knew that American forces were woefully unprepared to fight surprise attacks on the ocean—and they were right. Over the first seven months of 1942, the Nazis sank 233 ships in the Atlantic Ocean and the Gulf of Mexico, killing five thousand people.

Most New Englanders knew very little about these tragedies. The government suppressed reports of the attacks whenever possible, even though the closest coastal residents could hear the depth charges exploding in the ocean and sometimes even encountered survivors and the debris of attacks.

Eventually, the US Navy figured out how to fight back: mining harbors and escorting freighters with warships and bombers. Civilians were forced to comply with blackout drills and dim-out restrictions once Americans finally realized that they were providing the U-boats a shoreline blazing with light to assist in the attacks. With those widespread changes, the casualties in the Atlantic went down. By 1944, with far better tactics in place, more U-boats were sunk than merchant ships, but those early months were times of great frustration and peril for American ships.

Russell's involvement in the Coastal Picket Patrol, also known as the Hooligan Navy, was a fun and often-forgotten chapter in American history, a brief window of time when civilian yachters helped the coast guard as a preventive measure against U-boat attacks. All of the experiences he relates in his letters really happened to various crews up and down the coast.

Another stolen-from-the-history-books issue is Louise Cavendish's quest to provide a childcare solution for war workers. It was a serious problem on many social reformers' minds. By the end of the war, one out of eight mothers of children under age six was employed. As in the novel, when private solutions couldn't address the shortage, in late 1942, grants from a defense bill known as the Lanham Act led to government-sponsored childcare centers springing up around the country. But because of the stigma of childcare as a charity handout, only a small percentage of working mothers felt comfortable allowing their children to attend, and centers were sometimes underfunded, unsafe, or inadequately supervised. With time, however, many became places where young children thrived, though most of these centers were closed at the end of the war.

WWII also did much to inspire a love of both reading and gardening in the American people. While the Blackout Book

Club and its members are fictional, the government did encourage reading as a war-appropriate activity, and libraries often became community centers for wartime fundraisers and announcements. Victory gardens like Louise's were popular as a way anyone could support American troops, and nutrition experts credit the movement with causing Americans to eat a greater variety of fruits and vegetables.

To find out more about the real-life history that inspired this story, such as the eminent-domain takeover of Ginny's beloved Long Island or the success of the Victory Book Campaign for troops, visit the "History" tab of amygreenbooks.com.

Besides the historical figures who inspired the events of the novel, there are, of course, many real-life people I'd love to thank.

As always, my parents and sister have been enthusiastic supporters throughout the writing of this book, along with my extended family. My friend and writing buddy Ruthie gave feedback that encouraged me through the stage where I wanted to give up on the whole mess. My husband, Jake, spent many hours helping me talk out the issues of fictional people and was a consistent encouragement during the many times I felt frustrated. And a special mention goes to my baby girl, who was present in her preborn state for most of the writing of this novel. While she may have made publishing deadlines slightly harder to meet, I would never trade all the joy she's already brought to this little family.

Even though I stepped away from full-time publishing work this year, it's a delight to know what goes on behind the scenes to get a book to readers (spoiler: it's a *lot*). I'm so thankful for the editorial team at Bethany House, especially Dave Long, Rochelle Gloege, Kate Deppe, and those who gave early feedback, for helping me craft my most ambitious novel to date. On the marketing side, Jenny Parker gave the novel a lovely cover that you are welcome to judge this book by, and I'm thankful to work with Raela Schoenherr, Anne Van Solkema, Rachael Wing, Brooke Vikla, and so many others in promoting this book.

I'm also indebted to the community of historical fiction authors and readers who have cheered me on in various ways throughout this process. Particular thanks goes to Amanda Dykes (author of a lovely, lyrical Maine-set book, *Whose Waves These Are*, which you should certainly read) for sending along some of her Maine research books for me to use.

If you enjoyed *The Blackout Book Club*, I'd love to hear from you via the "Contact" page of my website, amygreenbooks .com. Fictional characters are wonderful to spend time with, but the real, thoughtful, openhearted members of the reading community do truly make the best friends of all.

Books Read by the Blackout Book Club

In the process of writing this novel, I tried to choose a wide variety of titles, both classics and 1940s bestsellers, for my characters to read—and I read them at the same time. If you'd like to do the same, here they are for easy reference. Want to find out what I really thought of them, instead of just my characters' opinions? Drop me a line via the "Contact" page on amygreen books.com. I love discussing books with readers!

Mrs. Miniver by Jan Struther
Collected Poems of Emily Dickinson by Emily Dickinson
Hamlet by William Shakespeare
How to Read a Book by Mortimer J. Adler
The Code of the Woosters by P. G. Wodehouse
Evil under the Sun by Agatha Christie
Pygmalion by George Bernard Shaw
The Country of the Pointed Firs by Sarah Orne Jewett
The Velveteen Rabbit by Margery Williams, illustrated by
     William Nicholson

Treasure Island by Robert Louis Stevenson
"The Tell-Tale Heart" by Edgar Allan Poe

Other books mentioned:
    The Robe by Lloyd C. Douglas
    Their Eyes Were Watching God by Zora Neale Hurston
    The Count of Monte Cristo by Alexandre Dumas

Books recommended by characters:
    Les Misérables by Victor Hugo
    The Invisible Man by H. G. Wells
    The Story of Doctor Dolittle by Hugh Lofting
    The Tale of Peter Rabbit by Beatrix Potter
    A Christmas Carol by Charles Dickens
    Pride and Prejudice by Jane Austen
    Little Women by Louisa May Alcott
    Robinson Crusoe by Daniel Defoe
    Jane Eyre by Charlotte Brontë
    Anything by Georgette Heyer or Daphne du Maurier

Discussion Questions

1. The four women narrating the novel have very different personalities and backgrounds. Is there one you enjoyed reading more than the others? One that you grew to like more as the novel went on?

2. Throughout the novel, Martina faces discrimination because of her Italian background, including suspicion of espionage, which was a real threat for first-generation immigrants. Given the extremely low number of actual incidents of spying or sabotage, why do you think Americans were so quick to suspect their fellow citizens?

3. What did you think of the author's choice of using notes to portray the discussions between book club members?

4. How many of the books discussed by the club have you personally read? Did you have strong opinions about any of them?

5. Putting yourself in the place of New Englanders of the time, what do you think would be the most challenging aspect of home-front living? Gas and food rations? Blackout regulations and air raids? Fear for loved ones deployed overseas? Something else?

6. At one point, Avis muses that the difficulty with fighting to keep the library open is that it would mean saying no to other good things—a childcare center and book donations to soldiers overseas. Did you feel that same tension? What would you have done in her position?

7. Several characters grow to appreciate fiction more throughout the novel. Did you identify with any of their attitudes toward books?

8. How much did you know about U-boats along the Atlantic coast before reading the novel? What was the most interesting historical detail you learned in the course of reading?

9. Do you agree with Louise that it's possible to love a good thing, like books, too much?

10. Freddy tells Ginny, "We're all passing through, in and out of this world quick as a passenger boarding a train, on the way to something that lasts. Until then, you might as well make friends with your fellow travelers." Have you also experienced a time when you've been in a place temporarily that didn't quite feel like home? How did you handle it? What do you think will happen to Ginny and Freddy in the future?

11. Through glimpses into Louise's past, we get to learn more about her relationship with her father. How did you feel about him as a character? Do you think she has an accurate view of who he was and why he acted the way he did?

12. Avis and Russell appear to be in a place where they are working through the issues in their marriage, something that wasn't possible for Martina and Patrick. What would you name as the key differences between those two couples' relationships?

13. When you learned the reason behind Freddy's deception, how did you feel about it? If you had been in Ginny's place, what advice would you have given him?

14. All four of the narrating women start the story exhibiting a strong independence but each for different reasons. Why do you think Avis, Ginny, Louise, and Martina felt they had to handle their problems on their own? What helped them change over the course of the book?

Amy Lynn Green has always loved history and reading, and she enjoys speaking with book clubs, writing groups, and libraries all around the country. Her debut novel, *Things We Didn't Say*, was nominated for a 2021 Minnesota Book Award, won two Carol Awards, and received a starred review from both *Booklist* and *Library Journal*. Amy and her family make their home in Minneapolis, Minnesota. Visit amygreenbooks.com to learn more.

Sign Up for Amy's Newsletter

Keep up to date with Amy's latest news on book releases and events by signing up for her email list at amygreenbooks.com.

More from Amy Lynn Green

After Pearl Harbor, sweethearts Gordon Hooper and Dorie Armitage were broken up by their convictions. As a conscientious objector, he went west to fight fires as a smokejumper, while she joined the Army Corps. When a tragic accident raises suspicions, they're forced to work together, but the truth they uncover may lead to an impossible—and dangerous—choice.

The Lines Between Us

You May Also Like . . .

In this epistolary novel from the WWII home front, Johanna Berglund is forced to return to her small Midwestern town to become a translator at a German prisoner-of-war camp. There, amid old secrets and prejudice, she finds that the POWs have hidden depths. When the lines between compassion and treason are blurred, she must decide where her heart truly lies.

Things We Didn't Say by Amy Lynn Green
amygreenbooks.com

When their father's death leaves them impoverished, the Summers sisters open their home to guests to provide for their ailing mother. But instead of the elderly invalids they expect, they find themselves hosting eligible gentleman. Sarah must confront her growing attraction to a mysterious widower, and Viola learns to heal her deep-hidden scars.

The Sisters of Sea View by Julie Klassen
On Devonshire Shores #1
julieklassen.com

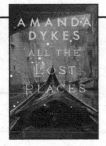

Discovered floating in a basket along the canals of Venice, Sebastien Trovato wrestles with questions of his origins. Decades later, on an assignment to translate a rare book, Daniel Goodman finds himself embroiled in a web of secrets carefully kept within the ancient city and in the mystery of the man whose story the book does not finish: Sebastien.

All the Lost Places by Amanda Dykes
amandadykes.com

BETHANYHOUSE

More from Bethany House

In 1910, rural healer Perliett Van Hilton is targeted by a superstitious killer and must rely on the local doctor and an intriguing newcomer for help. Over a century later, Molly Wasziak is pulled into a web of deception surrounding an old farmhouse. Will these women's voices be heard, or will time silence their truths forever?

The Premonition at Withers Farm by Jaime Jo Wright
jaimewrightbooks.com

After an accident brings businessman Eric Larson and eccentric Eunice Parker together, the unlikely pair spend more time with each other than they would like while facing challenges beyond what they imagined. As Eunice comes to accept her terminal illness, they both wrestle with an important question: What matters most when the end is near?

Where the Blue Sky Begins by Katie Powner
katiepowner.com

Fashion aficionado Iris Blakely dreams of using her talent to start a business to help citizens in impoverished areas. But when she discovers that Ekon Diallo will be her business consultant, the battle between her desires and reality begins. Can she keep her heart—and business—intact despite the challenges she faces?

To Win a Prince by Toni Shiloh
tonishiloh.com

BETHANYHOUSE